THE WALWORTH BEAUTY

MICHÈLE ROBERTS

B L O O M S B U R Y

LONDON · OXFORD · NEW YORK · NEW DELHI · SYDNEY

Bloomsbury Publishing
An imprint of Bloomsbury Publishing Plc

50 Bedford Square   1385 Broadway
London   New York
WC1B 3DP   NY 10018
UK   USA

www.bloomsbury.com

BLOOMSBURY and the Diana logo are trademarks of Bloomsbury Publishing Plc

First published in Great Britain 2017

© Michèle Roberts, 2017

British Library Cataloguing-in-Publication Data
A catalogue record for this book is available from the British Library.

ISBN:	HB:	978-1-4088-8339-6
	TPB:	978-1-4088-8340-2
	EPUB:	978-1-4088-8341-9

2 4 6 8 10 9 7 5 3 1

Typeset by Integra Software Services Pvt. Ltd
Printed and bound in Great Britain by CPI Group (UK) Ltd, Croydon CR0 4YY

To find out more about our authors and books visit www.bloomsbury.com. Here you
will find extracts, author interviews, details of forthcoming events and the option to
sign up for our newsletters.

THE WALWORTH BEAUTY

ALSO BY MICHÈLE ROBERTS

Novels
A Piece of the Night
The Visitation
The Wild Girl
The Book of Mrs Noah
In the Red Kitchen
Daughters of the House
Flesh and Blood
Impossible Saints
Fair Exchange
The Looking Glass
The Mistressclass
Reader, I Married Him
Ignorance

Plays
The Journeywoman
Child Lover

Poetry
The Mirror of the Mother
Psyche and the Hurricane
All the Selves I Was
The Heretic's Feast
The Hunter's House

Short Stories
During Mother's Absence
Playing Sardines
Mud: Stories of Sex and Love

Non-fiction
*Food, Sex & God: on
    Inspiration and Writing*
Paper Houses
The Lille Diaries
    (with Sarah LeFanu and
    Jenny Newman)
Silly Lady Novelists?

Artist's Books
Poems (with Caroline Isgar)
Fifteen Beads
    (with Caroline Isgar)
Dark City Light City
    (with Carol Robertson)
The Secret Staircase
    (with Caroline Isgar)
The Dark and Marvellous Room
    (with Caroline Isgar)

for my friends

Joseph

T HE TERRACED CUL-DE-SAC DREW its name
from the former orchard on the site. Those fruit trees
had been felled, their roots torn up. Now Apricot Place
had planes newly planted along it, and a brick coach-house
forming its end.

To the right of this building opened a narrow passageway. It ran between the side of the last house in the row
and a low stone wall crossed halfway along by a stile.
Beyond lay a patch of scrubland; a dip of swamp in the
middle, edged by ditches flowering with yellow irises
in May and blue water mint in August; rows of green
vegetable plots beyond. Gypsies sometimes camped
here, putting up their canvas shacks amidst pink sprays
of rose bay willow herb. Smoke from their fires of
scavenged wood drifted towards Orchard Street, and
beyond, to the main road, and their lean dogs prowled
about, guarding the territory; snapping. Sometimes the
women, wearing gold earrings and red-embroidered
black shawls, came knocking at the area doors, offering
cooks and maidservants whittled pegs in exchange for a
screw of tea. Tell your fortune, missis? You gave them a
halfpenny, to avoid being sworn at, or cursed, and sent
them packing.

Young people courting came here too, under pretext of picking blackberries, or rose hips, or garlic leaves, depending on the season. You could lie in the long grass and pull it around you and be private for as long as you chose. You could make the grass rustle and ripple and sway. You could hide in a nest woven of green stalks, fringed seed heads, your own whisperings.

Here, town finished, and countryside began. You crossed over, from pavements and shops, towards copses and streams, and meadows full of grazing cows. The streets and the fields seemed to push at each other, the city trying to sprawl further out and the fields resisting. The planners and architects and merchants would obviously win. What force had buttercups and earthworms and cabbages against the need of human beings for dwelling places, against developers' chances to make money? Alive as a strange creature in an aquarium, the city stretched out its tentacles, grew and swelled, gobbling the pastures and hedgerows that lay in its path. Fields were bought, and new rows of houses built, and then the process repeated. Teams of workmen dug up hedges, filled in ponds and streams, put up neat streets of flat-fronted brick dwellings with steps and railings.

Soon, to see any green fields at all, you'd have to travel further out, down towards Camberwell and Brixton. Walworth was hardly a village at all any more. Nowadays it bristled with shops and pubs, churches and meeting-halls. It even had a zoo on its common, with a great glass viewing structure built round it from which to admire its five dromedaries and their Arab keeper. Here, you could stroll under the palm trees, eat ice cream, and watch a monkey swing past on one paw.

Some of Walworth's pleasure gardens still remained, and local people patronised them on Sundays. Around the ornamental lake they'd wander, back and forth along the sandy paths between the pleached hazels, the beds of artichokes, the plantations of medlars and quinces. They admired the wide borders of pink and yellow dahlias, set with lozenges of red geraniums in front. They sat on benches, read the paper and smoked, shouted at their children not to run too far away. Watch out or the gypsies will get you!

Sooner or later the gypsies would be driven off, and the land they squatted reclaimed for building. No sign of them on this misty morning in late October, apart from their dying fire. They'd probably decamped, to get away from trouble, or else they'd shifted quarters only temporarily and were biding their time behind the plantation of ash and oak in the distance.

The patch of scrub over the wall at the end of Apricot Place seemed empty. When Joseph climbed down from the stile, he saw at first just a wide, flat heap of grey ashes, a wisp of smoke threading up from it, and a muddy bundle of white-ish rags the gypsies had left behind, dropped near a mound of brambles and nettles, half in and half out of a tangle of thorns, bearded weeds.

Joseph's mother had looked like a bundle of rags as she lay dying, muffled in her nightgown, her cap pushed awry over her grey hair. He'd stroked her work-hardened fingers, then taken her hand in his. Don't go. Don't go. Death tore people from you as a dentist tore teeth. Dangling and loose then ripped out; a bloody gap left, for your tongue to explore. Gap in his mind, filling with dreams, night after night, of his mother struggling up from her box, calling to him not to abandon her.

Joseph stepped away from the stile and plunged forwards into the field. Rooks and magpies flew up and cawed as though warning him. Don't come any nearer. Don't.

Look away. Look away now.

The bundle of muddied white rags was a nightgown. A baby flung face down in the mud. Tiny limbs sprawled.

The child was limp because it was dead.

He wanted to cry and to be sick. He threw up first, then sank down onto the cold ground, put his hands over his face, and wept.

People despised grown men if they cried. Even worse: he was weeping not just for the child but for himself too. He'd visited Apricot Place for the first time only a week ago, and since then he'd lost everything. He was lost. He might never get home again.

ONE

Joseph

W HEN DID IT BEGIN, his progress towards that cold field? Looking back, he thought that the first chapter of his slow fall had been announced by that foolish song, Milly's current favourite for her parents' after-tea entertainment.

I know where I'm going/ and I know who's going with me./ I know who I love,/ but the Lord knows who I'll marry.

Milly pounded the piano keys. On and on she warbled, until at last Joseph and Cara put their hands over their ears in playful protest, begging her to stop. Milly slammed down the piano lid, came to sit on the arm of Joseph's chair: Pa, don't be mean to me! He said: you should practise more, that's all. She retorted: but there's never any time!

Cara wagged a forefinger – his cosy armful of wife, in a brown cotton gown sprigged with pink rosebuds. She said: you could make time easily, dearie, if you wanted to.

Milly scowled. Joseph lifted his hand and stroked her wrist. So much for your passion for music. So much for nagging me for months to buy you a piano!

He had got the piano cheap, second-hand, at an auction, for Milly's eighteenth birthday. What his darling wanted she must have. Glaring with varnish, rigged out with a gilt music-rack, yellow brass candle-holders, the instrument dominated the tiny parlour. Cara had thrown a fringed orange chenille rug across it, and a bouquet of artificial red poppies on top of that, a large china dog, complete with chocolate spots, nestling alongside. She had shoved their two wooden armchairs almost on top of the grate to accommodate the brown cuckoo, which warbled out of tune. He hadn't paid for the piano yet. The bill hid in his little portable writing-desk on top of the bookcase wedged into the alcove. Also the bill for the new sideboard. Most of the time he could forget they were there.

He rose, stooped over Cara, kissed her forehead. I've got to go out again, sweetheart. I shan't be back late.

I know where I'm going,/ and I know who's going with me.

Milly's ditty seemed remarkably inappropriate on this foggy evening. He had hardly a clue where he was going, and no one journeyed with him except for the cab driver, who grunted through the muffler pulled up over his mouth and nose. Perhaps the song's words made sense to a south London cabbie. This one negotiated the rapidly darkening streets beyond the river with seemingly careless confidence, jolting along over the uneven surfaces, swerving and shouting at other drivers. The flaring gas lamps of Blackfriars Road left behind, in the grey-blue shadows of dusk the looming clutters of brick façades melted together. Houses, and what must be manufactories and warehouses. A reek of sewage, and soot, and tanning leather. The cabbie's muffler began to make sense.

They skirted the dark mass of the Borough on their left. Once past it they left behind the worst clatter of traffic. They emerged into wider, open space, some sort of common; a gleam of water in a bush-edged fold. They drove under massing trees, then entered a street lined with terraced houses standing back from long narrow gardens.

Dusk dissolved into night. The cab turned right, drew up by an anonymous pavement, dropped him in darkness at the opening of what seemed merely an alley. Joseph protested. Sure this is Apricot Place? Certainly, guv'nor.

Wind gusted. He struggled forwards. Under an archway he blundered, into further darkness. Houses façades reared up. Some lowish building blocked the way ahead. He had entered a narrow cul-de-sac, containing the dankness of the nearby river between its brick sides. And yet, at the same time, somehow holding sweetness under the stink, the air breathed a hint of countryside: earth and wood-smoke and manure.

His boot soles slipped on soft filth that could be anything: wet straw, dead rats. He inched forwards, counting. The sixth house on the right, at the end of the row, her note had said. His breath puffed out in the chill air. He advanced between railings, mounted stone steps. To his left, another flight fell away into the area. A pale gold light showed at a first-floor window: a fire burning, or candles. So she was indeed at home. He felt for the knocker, gripped the curve of metal in his gloved fingers, and banged it three times, as instructed.

Absurd, this prearranged signal. Over-dramatic. Perhaps she lived in dread of a visit from the police. Like magpies robbing nests, these women. Swaggerers scared off by shows of strength. Any hint of trouble, a constable asking questions, the landlord due to turn up, chasing rent arrears, and they did a night flit, decamping with all their possessions.

The chance-met man in the Waterloo pub had explained this in exchange for a drink. Pursing his beard-fringed lips. Odd old fellow, playing with his handkerchief, red and blue paisley, rolling it into a ball, tossing it between his hands. It's the system they all live by, d'you see? The landlords have to demand a large down payment, when they take on new tenants, because there's every chance said tenants will clear off at the drop of a hat, taking with them whatever items they fancy. Unscrew the very door-knobs, some of them will. Dismantle the grates and flog 'em for scrap.

Joseph waited, wrapping his arms around himself, stamping his feet. After some moments the door opened a crack; then wider. A girl, wrapped in a brown linen apron, a blue woollen shawl, peered out. Eyes glittering like gravel chips, set wide apart in a broad face tapering to a pointed chin. No cap: just a frizz of brown hair.

I'm Joseph Benson, he said: I'm expected.

Stepping inside, stripping off his gloves, he left the cold scents of the street for warmer ones: floor polish, vegetable soup. The servant, shrinking back against the wall, was wrinkling her nose, pushing out her bottom lip. A child still, who hadn't yet learned to school her face. New to service, perhaps. The chit didn't bother offering to take his hat and topcoat, his stick, merely hovered, hands tucked into her shawl, watching him lay down his things on the chest placed against the wall. A candle in a tin holder burned there, its flame wavering in the draught. Some current of dust caught his nose, his throat. He felt an urge to sneeze, and pulled out his handkerchief.

The maid yawned, showing even white teeth, a pink tongue. She jerked her head, moved her bow lips: you're to come straight up. To her he must be just another punter sliding in on his own discreet business. One of hundreds she had seen on to the premises and then off again.

He said: thank you.

She unloosed her shawl, bent and picked up the light. Sharp wrists. Blue sleeves rolled back to her elbows. Her skirts scooped over one arm, bunched clear of the steep rise of the stairs, she climbed ahead of him, up the narrow wainscoted shaft into the blackness above. She clutched the wooden banister with her right hand, and in her left the candlestick bearing its lit stub. Tilting, it spilled wax: a slop of grease, translucent, ran across her thumb; hardened to opaque pearls. The candlelight's golden haze surrounded her brown curls. One ear outlined in gold. The sway of her waist. Her thin, lifting ankles. Her stockinged feet, thrust into backless felt slippers, shifted hush-hush from tread to tread. A darn emphasised each heel.

Their ascent seemed slow, dreamlike. As though encumbered by the darkness. Muffled by it. The girl smelled of soap, warm animal.

At the top of the stairs she turned right, pressed into further shadows. Along a short passage she led him, the flame in her upraised hand flickering, a will-o'-the-wisp dancing along just ahead. The wooden boards shifted and creaked under his boots. She paused beside a tall black oblong outlined in gold. A door, light springing out all round it from the room beyond.

He lost his balance, knocked against the maid. She swerved, avoided his clutching fingers, shot him a fierce look. He wanted to protest, you misunderstand, I meant no harm, but choked on a cough, his throat clenching. Her fist made a brisk rat-a-tat-tat. She clicked the latch, thrust him inside, and departed.

He fell into a cave of gold: candlelight, firelight; suspended within darkness. The radiance confused him: he tripped on the matting and let go of the handkerchief he held. It floated to the floor.

He ducked his head, stared at his feet. He made a mock half-bow, bending to pick up his handkerchief, stuffing it into his trouser pocket. His fingers met the soft bulk of his purse, and his breathing slowed. The banknotes were hidden where no pickpocket could ever find them, deep inside the stitched-up inside pocket of the topcoat he'd left downstairs, but the pouch of coins he liked to have always at hand. To weigh, to jangle.

Mrs Dulcimer?

Her back turned, her head bent, she stood facing the glowing red fire. Over at the window, a half-moon mahogany table bore a brass candelabra stuck with glimmering tapers. Caught between fire and candles, she gleamed, the thick folds of her orange shot-silk dress bright as the flames. A crimson stole, threaded with silver tinsel, looped her shoulders, hid her neck. Tongues of light licked towards the clasp of a gilt chain, her black hair falling in oiled curls from a high silvery comb, a red ribbon, tied round her head, finished with a flourishing bow. Was she really so shy that she had to present her back to him? Impossible, in her line of business. A pose, merely. A game she played. Very well. Humour her.

I am Mrs Dulcimer.

Her contralto voice sounded over-genteel. She was in disguise, trying to pass herself off as refined; but her accent gave the game away. She'd clearly had a bit of education. Her note confirming their appointment had been decorously expressed. Well written enough. A neat copperplate hand, with tidy flourishes. Some kind of dame school, perhaps, before she took her first false step. Away from her shop-keeping family, her milliner mother. Many women of her sort came from that kind of background, he felt sure. Too much access to the world of the street. Brought up decent, then their heads turned by customers' flattery. You expected a woman presiding over a shop counter to be neatly turned out, even a trifle gaudy. A woman letting rooms to prostitutes to be even more so. Mrs Dulcimer fitted the part exactly. With her glittering threads, her red velvet ribbon, her elaborate ringlets, she'd have graced a fairground. The cramped little room smelled right, too: the over-sweet perfume of lilies. Cheap scent bought in some low nearby shop then ladled on. Part of her tawdry scenario.

No. These lilies were real: small, flaring trumpets of white, bruised around the edges, spilling orange pollen, tall stems stuck into an ebony jar placed on top of a low cupboard. Who bought her flowers? Or did she buy them herself?

Mrs Dulcimer half-turned. A frilled black mask hid most of her profile. The firelight leaping behind, her face stayed in shadow, dark and inscrutable. Glisten of full, plump lips, painted crimson. Such absurd theatrics! He put up a hand to hide his smile.

Deep frills of lace covered her fingers. She held a sheaf of papers, which she set down on a side table, next to a small stack of books. Patting them into place, aligning them exactly.

With a swish of her silk skirts, she turned fully in his direction. Blank black face-cover. Unnerving not to see her expression. She said: my eyes tire easily. And then the light hurts them. But I must have light for my visitors. Now that you are here, I shall dispense with my eye-shade.

She shook back her lace cuffs, reached up her hands and untied the red ribbon, wound it around her fingers, swung the eye-shade back and forth in a curiously childlike way. As though she were considering what to say next, while he surveyed her: arched black eyebrows above shining black-brown eyes; smooth brown skin over curved cheekbones; that fat mouth enamelled red as sealing-wax.

A black woman. How on earth had she landed up in Southwark? Black folks lived in Africa, in mud huts thatched with grass. They pierced their noses with rings of bone. They wore grass skirts and little else. Savages who threw missionaries in pots and boiled them alive.

The question flew out of him. Where are you from?

No spring chicken, forty at least, but in good shape, with plenty of juice still in her. Plump bosom outlined by her orange bodice. She'd hidden the flesh at her throat, surely webbed with lines, with a black choker strung with golden beads, clasped at each side by bunches of gilt chains. The ornament drew attention to her delicate collarbones, their little hollows filled with shadows. Salt cellars. You dipped your finger in then tasted it.

She said: from Deptford, Mr Benson. My family roots in London go back generations. Further than yours, perhaps.

He jumped. Sudden flash of his mother's face, half hidden among pillows. Yet again she whispered her tale of her long-ago journey up from Kent in that drover's cart. You slept most of the way, Joseph. You only woke up when we stopped to rest the horse. You were hungry, and you wouldn't hush. She broke off, coughed. Your stepfather was a good man, Joseph, when all's said and done. Not everyone would take on a widow with no money, another man's child.

Mrs Dulcimer stretched out a neat foot towards the fender. Black velvet slipper, a slim ankle in a thin grey stocking. She was pretending not to notice his scrutiny, lifting her chin and turning to stare at the turquoise pot on the mantelpiece, a Chinese-looking thing painted with red dragons, sprays of pink blossom. She was displaying herself; goods in a shop window. Satin at so much the yard.

He breathed in the sticky lily scent. Don't let her see how she disturbs you. Study the contrast between pools of golden light and pools of gloom. Two flimsy gilded armchairs padded with gold satin cushions, a red and blue Turkey rug before the fire. Coloured prints in varnished frames on the pink-plastered walls. An ornate ormolu clock under a glass dome, gilt pendulum swinging, on a pedestal stand.

Mrs Dulcimer waved him forwards: let us sit down.

He said: I didn't explain in my note my reason for wanting to call on you, because I preferred to tell you in person. I'm here on a very particular mission. To start with, I require a girl. One of your best.

She frowned. Twiddled one of her gold earrings; heavily chased and frilled half-hoops. Delicate ears she had, their long lobes weighed down by the lumps of gold. She opened her mouth, shut it again. In no hurry to speak. He had to admire that. Taking her time while she decided what to say. Where had she learned such self-confidence?

He waited. Mrs Dulcimer merely surveyed him, her brown hands beginning absent-mindedly to stroke the black pleats of lace edging her black mask.

After some moments her face changed, as though she'd taken a decision. Her mouth quivered, as if she were trying not to laugh. She said: as a rule, I find, gentlemen don't make appointments. They just turn up.

She reached across to the side table, deposited the mask, lifted the stack of papers to her lap. She riffled through them. Making him wait. Just for the pleasure of it. Well, he would show no impatience. Let her feel she was in control. Then in the end she would do what he wanted.

The paper crackled and scraped, leaf by leaf, as she searched. Yes, she said, pulling out a creased sheet: your letter. Yes, I have it here.

He patted his jacket pocket: and I have yours.

She stretched her brown hand to the fire. Long fingers with oval nails. She smiled at him with closed lips. More of a grimace, almost a shrug, that conveyed boredom. Surely an act. She must be as alert to the smell of money as he was to the sparks and flames of new ideas. She said: plenty of girls on your side of the river, surely. The Haymarket's heaving with them every night. And then, if you're determined to come south, so's Waterloo Road. So's much of Lambeth!

He banged his fist on his knee: well, of course! And yet here you are, ma'am. Doing your bit for the Surrey side!

Before setting out, he'd looked up Apricot Place on the map. Her establishment was just within striking distance of the railway terminus at London Bridge, the London end of the Kent Road; the busy thoroughfares lined with pubs, lodging-houses, shops. And of course brothels, tucked away in the side streets, sucking in plenty of customers. Not just the young swells driving out from the City to breathe cleanish air, watch cricket, visit the Zoo, stroll past fancy flowerbeds under green trees, but the waves of incomers too. Up from the country they journeyed, the labourers, would-be costermongers, the hawkers and fortune-seekers, all of them in need of cheap shelter, cheap food and drink, cheap women. Joseph did not need some flashy black madam to tell him that. The handkerchief-tossing man in the pub had been a great explainer.

Anything you wanted you could buy in London, if you could afford it. Depending on how much you'd put aside from the week's wages, you could buy a girl in a brothel or in her own lodging. As a young man, before his marriage, Joseph had learned from his male acquaintances exactly where to go. Saturday nights, a gang of lads fingering their collars, smoothing down their hair, elbowing each other as they surveyed the jay-bright little birds hopping about, flourishing their plumage at passers-by. Go on! Say hello to her! She won't bite! Joseph learned about rooms that could be rented by the hour, about discreet, respectable-seeming landladies who looked the other way when necessary, took their cut, and topped it all off by calling you sir when you came in.

Mrs Dulcimer twirled her eye-shade, threw it down. She said: so why come to Southwark?

Now she was twiddling her thumbs. Mocking him. Despite his best efforts, he felt a frown break across his face as he stared at her, leaning back on her gold cushions. He glanced away, at the turquoise pot on the mantelpiece. Back to her reddish-purple lips.

He said: precisely because Walworth is a neighbourhood I do not yet know. Your name and address were given to me by someone previously acquainted with you. In a similar line of business. The suggestion being that this might be a good place, one that might suit my purposes.

She said: and those purposes are?

Joseph said: I'd prefer to make that clear to the girl herself. I want a young one. One who'll tell me the truth when I question her.

Lots of chaps say that, she remarked: pretend they just want to talk. Others come straight out with it: they want virgins. Not many about, unfortunately.

She changed role: now she beamed like a benevolent aunt. She was trying out a new register of voice on him, full of trills and runs. Well, Mr Benson, you can choose. Pick any flower from my bouquet! Only, of course, they're not back yet, any of them, the dears. They're all out, my busy little bees, gathering nectar!

How far afield did they go, her girls, touting for business, before bringing back their clients? Did they stick to their own particular stamping ground? Presumably you avoided straying into someone else's patch. Rattling through Walworth in the gathering darkness he'd gained little sense of the district. Still semi-rural, presumably. Quiet, apparently. Yet it must seethe with building labourers separated from their families, bored at night after work, kicking their heels, in need of diversion. Consolation for their grim existences in work gangs on low pay, digging up clay for making bricks, throwing up houses, levelling paths into streets. Mrs Dulcimer's mob of little starlings would spot them fast enough, flap down, settle on them, peck out their eyes if need be.

He hesitated. It's getting late, and I've a cab waiting. I mistimed my visit, obviously. I should have come earlier.

Mrs Dulcimer said: they'll be back soon, I daresay. Sit here with me for the moment, why don't you? We could take a drink together, if you like.

Her lips gleamed, satiny as plums. What did black women drink? Rum? Gin, perhaps, same as other female wrongdoers, white or brown or yellow.

Mrs Dulcimer nodded towards the cupboard: I've everything there. Wouldn't do to leave it downstairs, where Doll might get at it. Will you join me?

Why not stay and keep her company? That would induce her to talk more, he could see, and after a glass or two she would put aside all reserve and spill information he might find useful. On the other hand he hadn't journeyed across the river to listen to her ramblings. He knew her story already, he felt sure. She probably rehearsed it in front of her mirror, while she pinned on her front of false curls, to serve up to those romantic clients who liked a bit of a chat to get them going.

Hers would be a worn-out tale, such as he'd heard from the girls at Mother Busk's in Waterloo, tweaked to garner sympathy from do-gooders: initial respectability, seduction by some nice-seeming gentleman, thus the fall. More likely she had set out from the start as a businesswoman with an eye to the main chance. Her mother would have been not a milliner, no indeed, but some black seaman's doxy. Cherishing her daughter over any son, wanting to set her early on her mother's own track, make money from her. The girl moving away from her squalid beginnings in the docks into a more genteel part of town. First of all, perhaps, keeping a baby farm for the working mothers of the neighbourhood, then discovering that farming the mothers themselves brought in better money.

But the chit downstairs, now. Those indifferent eyes, grey as stones on the river shore. That slender waist. The way she dodged above him, swaying from step to step. He said: what about the one who let me in? Is she the one you call Doll?

Mrs Dulcimer hesitated. She tapped the bunch of papers against her chin and looked thoughtful. It was all pretence. He just needed to give her a few minutes, to let her go on feeling in control. He glanced at the red fire jumping in the polished grate. She made plenty if she could afford such a heap of coals. The candles too: wax not tallow. And what had that dress cost, its yards of silk? Flashy it might be, but effective too, wrapping her in flame-tints. The colour of oranges. Their pungent scent. Stinging sweet taste. Every time she moved, her skirts rustled.

He laid a bet with himself: after a count of five she'll come round.

She said: well, Doll's a bit special. A cut above some of the others. Because she's so very young. Time with her will cost you a fair bit. But I'm sure that for you, Mr Benson, money's no object. Aren't I right?

He said: she was a good girl, once, was she?

The woman nodded, and sighed. They all were once, poor dears. All children are good to begin with, Mr Benson.

He persisted. So she's not simply the maid? Normally she goes out, too, like the others? If she doesn't, she's no use to me.

Mrs Dulcimer propped her chin on her hand. She's been going out since she was ten years old, that little one.

He pushed his chair back from the fire's suddenly oppressive heat. From his increased distance, he could look at her and wonder. Presumably, once a woman got a taste for sensual sin, and its rewards, she couldn't abandon it. Poor creature. Like opium, or alcohol, it seized and controlled and eventually killed you.

He sat back, shivering. First too hot, suddenly too cold. Was this how cholera began, with a sick chill, a touch of fever? And yet the air outside had smelled cleaner than that in the Borough this morning. Those cloying, creeping miasmas, sidling in from the sewage-filled Thames, becoming trapped in the narrow streets, surely infected any passer-by careless enough to linger there. He did want a glass of something now. A measure of good brandy mixed with hot water. A ham sandwich, with mustard. He hadn't had time to eat earlier, too busy, hovering in that squalid wine-shop in the Mint with that haggard woman, waiting for her to consume enough spirits that she'd become willing to give out. She hadn't been sober even when she picked him up in the street and then she kept wheedling for more. Maisie needs another little tot! That was prostitutes' problem, surely: their dependence on drink, their willingness to do anything to get it.

Mrs Dulcimer said: we can settle up afterwards. And then I'll write you a receipt.

For services rendered. Around them the house seemed to sigh. The window sash gave a faint rattle. The wind getting up again, bowling city-stink across the Thames. Those winds that scraped your face raw, if you stayed outside any longer than you had to. Those flint-faced women, big gilt earrings jangling, patrolling Borough High Street, decked out in flimsy finery, shivering. Presumably the drink hardened them somewhat against the freezing air.

A board creaked outside. Mrs Dulcimer said: there's a nice little room come free this week, just off the kitchen. You can use that.

He hesitated. It did all seem so pat. Was that it? He wanted to make this moment last. Why? He didn't want to be disappointed. That was it. He wanted Doll to be different from other prostitutes. But why would she be? These women were essentially cold. Manipulating lonely men, exploiting their human need for company, in order to get money out of them. Tantalising respectable fathers of families by offering forbidden excitements. Don't be shy, sir. Shall I show you?

He put out a hand to the sinking flames. A sudden draught whistled in and lifted the edge of the matting, roused the fire, which jumped up like a dog to his fingers.

Mrs Dulcimer said: she'll be sitting in the kitchen, ready to open up for the others when they come home, the dears. I'll take you down myself. And then when you're done you'll be very welcome to that drink.

She picked up the candelabra, went through the door, which he held open for her.

He followed her down the stairs, into whistling cold air.

The front door of the house stood open. The hall was empty. His coat, with its freight of banknotes, was gone, along with the girl. Vanished into the darkness hiding the street, and the river behind.

Black branches crashed together in the wind. Water gurgled down roofs, shot from gutter spouts. Joseph swore. Mrs Dulcimer ran past him, onto the doorstep. She peered out at the rainy night, biting her lip. She shouted the girl's name, turned back to Joseph. She can't have gone far. Such weather! She'll catch her death.

More worried about the girl than about his coat, damn her. She couldn't know about the money, of course. At the far end of Apricot Place, a horse stamped and whinnied. The cab's lights showed under the archway. The cabbie shouted: you coming or not? I'm off! Joseph seized his hat and stick. At least the little wretch hadn't stolen those.

Wait! Mrs Dulcimer swerved back inside, fumbled in the dark entry. She pressed on him a tweed cloak, threw it up over his shoulders. I'll find out what happened. I'll get your coat back very soon, Mr Benson, never fear.

She might be more effective than the police. Worth trying in any case. Joseph descended the steps. Over his shoulder he said: I'll give you twenty-four hours. That girl of yours should be clapped in jail.

Mrs Dulcimer went on jabbering. Joseph strode into the gusting wet. He plunged inside the vehicle, pulled the door shut, shouted at the driver. Just go!

Madeleine

I SPOTTED A WOMAN shoplifting today, Madeleine tells Toby: in the supermarket. Two packets of lamb chops. She just dropped them inside her coat. Then she walked out, cool as can be, and nobody noticed a thing. I suppose because she looked so ordinary.

In the cartoon strips of Madeleine's childhood, robbers were easily distinguished. They wore black eye-masks, striped jerseys and black tights, and carried sacks marked Swag. They leaped, catlike, across roofs, by moonlight, by starlight. They were male. They were youthful.

Madeleine often wears black tights, like a lifter of jewels in the *Beano*. Tonight, black fishnet holdups. When she put them on they seemed glamorous and sexy. Now, seeing Toby glance at them, twitch an eyebrow, she's less sure.

Mutton dressed as lamb, Madeleine's grandmother Nelly would have said. Any woman over fifty using too much makeup, flaunting too much décolleté, too short a skirt. A cook attempting to pass off a dish of old sheep as something less tough. These days you wouldn't speak of dressing a dish. You wouldn't call a woman a dish any more either.

Madeleine picks up her glass of house white. The over-oaked wine tastes oily, makes her cough.

Toby's pale, broad face has taken on an inward look. Blue eyes lowered. He plays with his empty crisp packet, folding it, flattening it. They're drinking near St Paul's, in the Broker, formerly a pub called the Bow Bells, recently sharpened into a bar shiny with beech flooring, chrome fittings, black leather seats. Crowded with chattering people in suits. No one else in fishnets. The young women pulling pints wear black T-shirts and black minis. No stockings or tights at all.

Toby wakes up from his meditation and eyes Madeleine's hair. Looks different, he says: blonder than before.

Madeleine says: I had it done two weeks ago. You've only just noticed!

Toby says: sorry. Lots on my mind.

They have to shovel their words at each other under the hullabaloo of the drinkers, the music. Madeleine won't bother coming here again: a place for young City workers in thrusting groups, bellowing, letting off steam after their long day cooped up inside.

Living in the City, Madeleine sees few people of her own age. From Lombard Street to Ludgate Hill, from Stew Lane to Paternoster Row, she can roam without spotting anyone whose eyes crease up in deep wrinkles when they smile. Few people smile in the City, anyway. When she flings on her old coat and dashes out for her morning paper she bumps into commuters banging down from Cheapside with clenched faces, briefcase in one hand, little brown carrier bag of café takeaway in the other. Bunched up at the lights, jostling like horses at the gate. Racing to get to work on time.

Toby's shaved head shows a faint downiness. Is he letting his hair grow back? His wide-set blue eyes, his unlined face and full lips, make him look younger than he is. Fiftyish. A man in his prime. Madeleine turned sixty last birthday, but her prime still feels some way ahead. To do with wisdom; finally getting the hang of things. How will she recognise that blessed state when it arrives? If only it would come like a burglar: in a significant costume.

Toby says: it's how people feel inside that matters. Not their age or their hair colour!

Madeleine crosses her fishnetted legs and regards her foot in its black suede ballerina pump. Petals of pink blossom clot the shoe's rain-darkened toe; grains of grit.

She says: yes and no. Depends on whether you're looking for a job or not, doesn't it?

Inside herself she feels only thirty-odd. She still dances at parties, runs for the bus, flirts, would welcome another lover if one turned up. However, she has certainly reached the age of being ignored in City pubs: that besuited youth over there tried to muscle ahead of her at the bar just now, had to be nudged aside.

Sharp and smart, with gelled locks, he resembles the official from Human Resources with whom she negotiated her compulsory redundancy. Forcibly retired, at the end of last term, by the college, when they cut most of the humanities courses, including the literature she taught, Madeleine no longer gets up early twice a week, as she's done for twenty years, to walk towards Liverpool Street, and so she misses the cry of the newspaper-seller, that man with tight grey curls, as she rounds the corner at London Wall: hello, darling! Plucking up folded papers from the tall stack and slinging them right and left, fielding coins, he sings out quick snatches of jokes. One morning when she dawdles, and business is slack, he tells her about growing up in Bethnal Green. No bathroom. Coal-shed and lav out in the back yard. You know Bethnal Green? Full of yuppies now. Council gave us the right to buy, then we sold it. Should have hung on to it and made my fortune.

Indeed she knows Bethnal Green. To visit Toby in his new-build canalside flat in Mile End she takes the number 8 bus eastwards from Threadneedle Street, sits eavesdropping as it chugs towards Whitechapel and the sights prod older passengers' memories and get them chatting. Their past springs out from every Victorian-Byzantine building, stucco-decorated pub with acanthus-laden capitals, every scrap of blue tessellated pavement under the porches of former dress-shops; it endures in the arched entrances to warehouses, workshop courtyards. The newspaper-seller at London Wall looks sixty-odd. Perhaps, when he retires, no one will take over his stall. Only old people read newspapers. What does 'old' mean? Anyone born fifteen years earlier than Madeleine.

Toby says: you're not listening! He picks up his empty beer glass: my round. You want the same again?

Madeleine says: drinking's made me hungry. I need to eat.

Cold air outside the pub needles her face. Blue-grey evening thickens in the doorways opposite. Arm in arm they descend Bow Lane, halt at the crossroads at the approach to Southwark Bridge, where traffic seethes along the concrete pipe of Upper Thames Street. The gathering darkness can't soften these bleak angles and soulless forecourts, this lack of greenery, this impersonality. The ugliest street in London, surely.

Toby recites: O City City, I can sometimes hear/ Beside a public bar in Upper Thames Street,/ The pleasant whining of a mandoline/ And a clatter and a chatter from within.

He looks at her. Did I get that right? Madeleine hesitates. She says: no, sorry, I'm sure Eliot said Lower Thames Street.

Oh, Mrs Teacher, he says, pinching her fingers. She pinches him back: come off it. Literature's my life's job.

Was. Was. The pedestrian light turns red. They pause on the pavement. Four lanes choke solid with halted, snorting cars. The wind whistles between the high blocks, blowing petrol fumes and sour dust in their faces.

On the far side of the street, facing them, Southwark Bridge arches up, close-pressed between concrete and stone buildings. It leaps away towards south London, into grey sky. They turn westwards, pass the Vintners' Hall, enter a bleak lay-by.

Gold lettering on a black plaque distinguishes Queen's Wharf, a red-brick apartment building. To its right, Stew Lane cuts south between lofty warehouses, lets you catch sight, at its end, of a deep slice of sky, and, below it, a patch of rippling waves held between the tall façades to left and right.

The Thames laps against the parapet dividing water from cobbled stone. As night falls, the river sinks back, merges into greyness, melts from view. Only if you walk to the far end of Stew Lane do you find it again. You lean your elbows on top of the wall, stare into mist, the reflections of opal-coloured lights.

Once, alone here at dusk, almost dissolved into the water, the gull-filled air, Madeleine heard a hiss of laughter, the rattle of wheels over cobbles, felt a damp finger on the back of her neck. When she whipped round, the alley was empty.

Toby scoffed at her tale, recounted to him over the phone next day. You wanted to experience something, and so you imagined it. What's so special about Stew Lane? Stew means brothel, I know that much.

Madeleine said: it's where men used to embark from in Shakespeare's time, to go and visit the stews in Southwark.

Brothels were banned in the City in those days, so men wanting to buy sex had to cross the river. It's mentioned in the history of the City I've been reading.

Toby said: there you are, then.

Madeleine said: a man I got talking to on the bus the other day told me that the lives of people in the past may coexist with ours, invisibly, behind a kind of looking-glass. Sometimes we can see through it, glimpse each other. He thought as well that perhaps we're avatars, sent forth by those people.

Toby hmmed. Let's meet up soon, catch a film.

A plate-glass wall, in shadow, makes a dark mirror that reflects their approach to Queen's Wharf. So who would she and Toby have been, say, a hundred and fifty years back? Two porters meeting a barge, unloading crates of tea, hauling their load on a handcart up the muddy lane from the river? The tea warehouse still stands nearby, turned into offices and flats. Or perhaps Toby would have worked as a porter and Madeleine as a prostitute, chancing her luck, importuning him. What was the punishment in those days for soliciting? She doesn't know.

A surveillance camera dangles above the heavy, metal-framed glass door that opens into the foyer of Queen's Wharf. Inside, a second surveillance camera swivels towards the lifts. They share the ride up with a couple of burly men in banker's uniform of striped shirt and navy suit, who tread across the foyer just as the lift door begins to close. They stride in, bark hello, then take up position well back, clasp their gilt-cornered briefcases, study their toecaps. Toby gives them a quizzical glance, touches Madeleine's arm. Shall we eat on the roof? It's not too cold, is it?

The two bankers frown. Madeleine says: oh, no, we're not allowed up there. It's out of bounds. We've no right as tenants to use it.

Toby shrugs. They reach the third floor, halt. The bankers exit the lift. Madeleine and Toby whoosh on upwards.

Sorry about that, Madeleine says: it's just that I don't want anyone to know I sneak up there. I should have told you before. I'd be in big trouble if I got found out.

The broad, flat roof space, edged by low iron railings, looks out over the water. The Globe Theatre and Tate Modern rear opposite. The brown-grey-green river thrashes along below. Madeleine comes here at dusk, to watch police boats dart by, tourist-laden pleasure boats plough past, occasional ferries ply up and down. On the left trains grind, slither and squeak into Cannon Street. On the right, the Millennium Bridge sways out like gossamer.

She considers. It wasn't too cold last Saturday. I was up there with some friends, we had a bit of a party.

Toby says: why didn't you invite me?

She says: you've forgotten. You were busy. Dinner with Sid's parents you said.

The lift jolts and rattles, opening and shutting its doors on empty landings. Toby grimaces. They got out all their photograph albums, showed me every picture they'd ever taken of Sid as a boy. They insisted on giving me some to take home. I tried to explain to them, I'm not interested in turning my flat into a shrine.

What did you do with the pictures? Madeleine asks.

Toby says: I put them in a drawer. I look at them sometimes.

On the sixth floor they push through heavy swing doors, emerge into a corridor wallpapered in pale blue. Madeleine's studio flat, with its close-up view of a red-brick wall, is adjacent to the utility room, the lift foyer, and she enjoys hearing the long hush-rush of the lift coming up the shaft, the soft whump as it lands, the clunk of the metal door sliding open then closing again. During her sleepless nights after her divorce, and again after the enforced redundancy, the lifts have kept her company, rising and falling like musical notes.

They edge into her narrow entrance hall. Off it open a tiny windowless bathroom, a galley kitchen, a single cramped room for living, working, partying, sleeping. When she moved in, ten years previously, after parting from William, she painted it green. The peapod; and she the newly single pea. She grows herbs and anemones in pots on her desk, and roses and clematis in troughs ranked on the little stepladder in front of the window. Already, in only April, the climbers reach to the ceiling and twine to the light fitting and she has to cut them back.

Toby perches on the wooden chair near the wall of bookshelves, starts to turn over the heap of cloth-bound hardbacks lying nearby on the carpet. Frayed silk ribbon bookmarks. Bruised spines stamped with gold letters. Madeleine goes into the kitchen, opens a bottle of Medoc, pours them each a glass, carries Toby's through to him.

She stirs the pile of books with the toe of her shoe. I got them in the charity shop in Leather Lane the other day. A job lot. I wanted to give them a good home. I couldn't bear the thought of their being pulped if they remained unsold. Which one's that?

Toby holds up a blue volume: Mayhew.

He reads aloud from the title page: *London Labour and the London Poor*, by Henry Mayhew. *Volume Four: Those That Will Not Work*.

He looks up at her. Victorian sociology? Bit off your usual track, isn't it? I thought you mainly read fiction and poetry.

She says: I haven't read Mayhew since I was a student. It's interesting finding out what I think of him now. I like re-discovering writers.

Arriving home with her sack of books, she'd opened Mayhew and found she had bought an odd volume of a mid-twentieth-century edition of his work, complete with introduction and explanatory footnotes. She'd plunged into Mayhew's categorisation of the London poor. Two strictly divided groups. On the one hand: the respectable hordes who sold fish and cabbages and flowers, drove buses, emptied cesspits, made glass eyes for dolls, groomed horses, and so on. On the other: the denizens of the London underworld, criminal characters carefully sorted according to types of villainy practised: house thieves, pickpockets, swindlers, prostitutes, cardsharps, kidnappers.

She says to Toby: I'd forgotten how he classifies everybody! Prostitutes, for example.

She holds up her fingers and ticks them off in a parody of herself at a blackboard: three classes. One: women who are privately kept by individual men of independent means. Two: women who live in their own lodgings and work the streets. Three: women who live and work in brothels.

Toby tastes his wine. I don't suppose he even mentioned male prostitutes, did he?

Madeleine wanders back to the kitchen. She shreds grey-green sage, washes silky lettuce leaves, pats them dry on a cloth. She mixes vinaigrette and spoons it into the bottom of the big bowl, crosses the salad servers and puts them in, loosely piles the leaves on top. Her mother's trick, to keep the salad from getting soggy. You toss it at the last minute. Would Mayhew have classified types of female salad-tossers? Probably. Take that other fervent Victorian classifier, Dewey, who devised the Dewey Decimal System for public libraries. Dewey put women in section seven, sociology, alongside lunatics and gypsies. The bureaucrat in Human Resources treated her as though she were a lunatic: pitying glances; measured, modulated tones. Now he's put her out of a job. To wander, like a gypsy. A tosser.

The smoky stink of garlic about to burn catches her back. Pay attention! She fishes the tiny dark-gold chips out of the pan, throws in the sage, swigs her red wine. Concentrate: you're making supper for Toby, that excellent cook. Chop walnuts and dry-fry them. Cube Gorgonzola. Boil water. Measure out fusilli.

Toby leans in the doorway. He strokes a hand over his skull. You noticed I've started growing my hair again? What d'you reckon? Madeleine says: good idea. Sid liked your curls, didn't he? She loads a tray with food, crockery, cutlery, fills a basket with bottles of wine, candles in jars, matches, a copy of *The Waste Land*. Toby puts the basket over one arm, picks up the tray: let's go.

She follows him out, carrying cushions and blankets, a couple of folding canvas chairs, a folding card table.

At the southern end of the corridor on the floor above they confront a large hatch. Toby stands in front of the surveillance camera set to one side of it while Madeleine produces a credit card, slips the lock. They climb through. They step from a brightly lit indoors into blowy blackness. They go slowly into this darkness pierced by diamond lights. Madeleine feels herself shrink: a tiny person in the City's whirligig. The enormous indigo sky wheels overhead and the wind whips them. They settle themselves close to the railings, with a view down over the water.

The glitter of the City springs up all around. Shadows cast by people walking over Southwark Bridge, to the left, stretch and flap, distorted and lengthened, on the surface of the river; wavery black silhouettes. Insubstantial; intangible as the dead.

Madeleine lifts her glass: to Sid.

Toby lifts his: to Sid's memory.

He lifts it again: and to you. *Chapeau*, chef!

Madeleine says: you haven't tried it yet.

Shawled in blankets, they watch the racing clouds, the glimmer of stars and moon, the points of red and green lights on late river-boats, the curls of blue neon on the buildings bulking opposite. They talk and eat. They read T. S. Eliot's poem aloud, taking it in turns. Their voices intertwine in the dark, composing a body of sound. A body of meaning, floating high and light.

Toby lights a roll-up, stretches, leans back. He says: Sid and I used to read poetry to each other all the time. It's good to be doing it again.

They finish the wine. St Paul's tolls out eleven o'clock. Back downstairs, they hug goodbye.

In the morning Madeleine blinks awake to pale green light, a steady splashing of rain. Her quilt, light as a cloud, folds her round in the semi-darkness. Dry and warm while the rain swishes down next to her just beyond the glass. Why get up? No job to go to. She could stay in bed all day. No one would care. No one needs her to introduce them to novelists they've never heard of, argue passionately with them about literary values, aesthetic values. The man from Human Resources talked only of financial values. Short sentences staccato as gunfire, picking off the troublemakers, the union members. The humanities did not deliver adequate economic value. Did not deliver outcomes that could be properly measured. The union would have to accept that. The union won the war over redundancy packages but lost the overall battle. Madeleine and her colleagues were kicked out.

Three months on, the wound still smarts. So why not hide in bed? Eventually she could stop washing, stop changing her clothes, stop cleaning, never open the window, let the flat stink sour and stale. So get up this minute.

She drinks coffee, tidies, returns the futon bed to its daytime folded position. She stands under the shower in the bathroom. She looks at herself in the mirror. Grey eyes, piled-up curly hair, flushed face. Lips tight shut. A mouth that wants to fly open, shout. It's not fair!

A week after their supper on the roof Toby rings to tell her he's off to Paris to research a round-up on experimental theatre. He'll stay with journalist friends, to save on expenses, see two shows a day, catch up on new directors.

Come and see me off at St Pancras, he proposes: if we meet early, we can try one of the bars.

On the day of his departure it rains. Madeleine puts on a black chiffon dress, a tight-waisted chestnut silk jacket fastened with twists of black braid. After a second's thought, she dons the black fishnets. She darts to Bank tube under her umbrella through mists of wet, the smell of petrol and flowers. Outside the ruins of the Temple of Mithras, surrounded by office blocks, tourists in pale plastic rain-capes take photographs. A line of broken wall. The gods hide far below with their golden helmets, their spears, their hoards of gold coins. She plunges into the airless underground. The lift door clunks shut. Down they drop. Grey metal surrounds her, like the sides of a submarine.

The escalator up to St Pancras International flashes with ads. They twinkle like the silver stars streaming from a fairy godmother's wand. Follow the stars, into the shopping mall. Gallery of luxury goods displayed behind plate glass: toys to distract nervous travellers.

People wheel elephantine plastic suitcases towards the coiling queues for the electronic ticket gates. Officials in crisp grey uniforms marshal passengers between lines of tape. Toby emerges from the throng; grey raincoat slung over his shoulder, bag in hand. He seizes her elbow, steers her away from the crowds, back into the main hall, up another escalator.

In the glass-sided bar, slung above the platforms, they sit on a chocolate-brown leather sofa. A waiter with flopping blond hair, eyes like flakes of turquoise, brings them a bottle of champagne in a silver bucket clinking with ice. He pours streams of foam into flutes, clicks his heels and departs.

The clammy leather seat sticks to Madeleine's thighs. It smells of industrial cleaning agent. Chemical lemon. She says: I wish I could come with you. I wish I could run away. I wish I still had a job.

Toby says: I wasn't going to tell you yet, but things are very bad at the paper. This Paris piece looks like being my swansong. So I thought we should celebrate! Another wake!

Madeleine gapes at him. You as well? Oh, I'm so sorry.

He says: I suppose if I'm going to chuck myself under a train, I've come to the right place to do it.

Madeleine cries: Toby, don't.

He throws an arm round her shoulders, hugs her. I must be off. Stay here and finish the champagne. I'll ring you on Sunday night when I get back and we'll make a date.

Next morning, Saturday, she goes out for a walk. She strolls south over Southwark Bridge. White clouds scud across blue sky. The river shines and ripples like bales of tossed-out silk ribboning blue, indigo, olive green. The wooden window-boxes slung outside the pub on the quay under the bridge brim with pink hyacinths glittering with raindrops. The cobbles glisten, and the tarmac, and the edges of the metal chairs outside the cafés.

Mayhew, or one of his researchers, came this way once, surely. Pursued vagrants and ne'er-do-wells into their dens, tried to interview them. Excuse me, madam, are you a thief? A prostitute? Both?

She strides along the edge of Borough Market. Green-painted iron struts rise above French delis on one side, newly restored pubs on the other. Gap of grey-blue sky roofs the cobbled street. The railway soars and clatters overhead. Groups of tourists photograph heaps of wild mushrooms. She turns along Borough High Street, wanders in and out of its side alleys: Mermaid Court, Kentish Buildings, Queen's Head Yard. She zigzags towards Newington, through squares and streets named after Dickens and his characters. The vast Elephant and Castle roundabout stumps her: a shiny metal fortress circled by hurtling traffic.

She swerves away, taps down a side street, back towards Borough. Neo-Venetian industrial façades beckon. She plunges into Marshalsea Road reaches Waterloo.

A black arch of the railway bridge frames the entrance to Redcross Way. She halts, studying the artwork of huge coloured dots hung to one side of it, then enters the narrow street. A pub to one side, the Boot and Flogger, overlooks a wire fence opposite, a tall screen smothered in dead flowers, lengths of faded ribbon, as though the wind has collected all the local rubbish and hurled it against the metal mesh.

Seen closer up, the barrier reveals itself as a weave of beads, necklaces, dried bouquets, medallions, bows of gauze. A tapestry-collage displaying corn dollies, tiny toy dogs, handwritten cards and labels, strings of buttons and sequins. The soft fence rustles in the breeze.

A notice covered in protective plastic names the sealed-off wilderness as a former burial ground for prostitutes and vagrants. Nameless women in nameless tombs covered by rose bay willow herb and ragwort. A battered stone statue of the Madonna stands on a stone plinth wound about with ivy. Her hands stretch out towards her daughters' graves.

So this place is a shrine. Madeleine fingers a green silk belt, a strip of lace: part of a veil protecting the hidden bones beyond. The decorated fence invites you to get involved with the messages and poems and stories hung on it. At the same time it tells you to keep a distance. Grasp this padlocked gate and shake it all you want: you won't get in to the graveyard. The shut gate sends you away again, towards the main road, the hurtle of traffic, the cries and roars of the living.

Three days later Toby rings her. You want to hear my news?

As he expected, he's been made redundant, along with ten other journalists on the arts pages. The union has secured them decent severance packages but that's it.

He adds: I shan't see you for a bit. I'm off back to Paris, to spend some of my redundancy pay. I'm going to comfort my soul with a Cordon Bleu course. And as soon as I'm back I'll cook for you.

Early May gives Madeleine the fidgets. She paces to and fro in her studio, banging into the chair, the desk. Rain-drenched white petals stick to the window. The flat burgeons with plants. Green leaves veil the light. Pots of frothing green stand three deep next to the door. Green writing spells out: give us a home! Or we'll crowd you out.

Why not experiment, change her life? Why not move to a flat with a garden? Find somewhere to live that's a proper neighbourhood. The City isn't that and can't be. It is ancient and eccentric and thrives on mystifying traditions and spectacles. The police wear special helmets. The Mayor, clad in fur and velvet draped with gold chains, rolls past in a horse-drawn gilded coach. The Christ's Hospital scholars, dressed in black doublets and hose, process by, banging drums. The master-boatman families of the river row annual regattas and keep their ancient fame enshrined in Watermen's Hall with its insignia of crossed oars over the entrance.

On a morning of glancing light and brisk winds, pollen blowing in gusts, she turns out of Queen's Wharf and walks down Stew Lane, leans on the parapet at its far end. Sour river smell. The grey water bobs with driftwood, empty plastic bottles. Pale yellow sky and sharp breeze and the incoming tide slapping up onto mud and black stones. A foreign country, over there, which she hardly knows.

Southwark. It beckons her. Come back, come and explore again.

No chilliness on the nape of her neck this time. Just this kindly voice. A character out of Mayhew, perhaps. Brisk tones. Giving her instructions. Tie on your bonnet. Pull on your cloak. Hoist your skirts over your arm to keep them from trailing in the mud. Descend the slimy green steps, hail a boat, ask the boatman to row you across the choppy grey waves, land you bang opposite, on Southwark's shore. Start searching from there.

Marcia, the young Italian estate agent, confirms the sense of this. South of the river can be cheaper, still quite rough in places, you see, those are the areas to look at. Madeleine says: I'm quite rough in places too, south of the river will suit me fine.

Selling one flat and buying another mainly involves chivvying solicitors and filling in complicated forms. Patience, she tells herself at every fresh setback: patience. Marcia offers counsel: but at least, selling a studio flat in the City, you're making a profit, you've paid off your mortgage, you can pay for the new flat outright, can't you? Madeleine blinks: I know, I'm very fortunate. Marcia says: sorry, I probably should not have said that, I'm always in trouble with my boss for the way I talk to clients. Madeleine says: no, it's OK, I like it. It's the truth, anyway.

Eventually the deal is done, a date in late July named for completion. On moving day the three removals men labour for two hours, carrying out her futon mattress, chairs, desk, boxes of kitchen stuff, boxes of books, trays of plants. The driver claps shut the back of the van. We're not insured to cover you as a passenger. Best come under your own steam. We'll see you at the other end, after we've had our break.

Laden with bags, she decides against the bus. So blow some money.

Sturdy black cab, shining like a beetle. She collapses onto the seat, bags spilling on the floor. The taxi slithers through streets gleaming with wet. Goodbye Cheapside goodbye Queen Victoria Street goodbye Upper Thames Street goodbye Stew Lane.

Over Blackfriars Bridge they trundle. Past the Borough. She finds herself humming. I know where I'm going,/ and I know who's going with me./ I know who I love,/ but the Lord knows who I'll marry. Picked up from a favourite Kathleen Ferrier CD. Not really apt. No one travels with her except for the taxi-driver. He does, however, certainly know his way through these south London streets.

Stop at the estate agency, to collect the new keys from Marcia. On through Newington to the Elephant, swerve into the hurly-burly of Walworth Road. The railway bridge runs along overhead. Turn right into Orchard Street. Then under an arch, into Apricot Place.

Traffic noise dropped away. Short cul-de-sac of shabby, flat-fronted terraced houses, shaded by massive, speckled-trunk plane trees flourishing fans of green leaves. At the far end a warehouse, and behind that the tower blocks of a high-rise council estate.

Her flat's a semi-basement, down in the area. She opens the finial-topped gate set into the black iron railings, picks up her haul of bags, descends steps braced on one side by a wall of yellow-grey brick and on the other by more railings. A neat little boot-scraper, set low down, separates two of the iron struts. Tradesmen coming to the kitchen door of the house would have been able to knock the mud off their soles. What cooks, what kitchen maids, worked down here? Mind my clean floor, mister!

She stands under the porch formed by the steps overhead. She unlocks the front door. She steps across the threshold into the narrow hall, silted with dust and bits of fallen plaster, walls stuck with dead insects. On first viewing the flat, she winced at its grubbiness, then shrugged: I'm not brilliant at housework myself, am I? Marcia gave her a coaxing red-lipstick smile: sure, the whole place needs re-decorating, doing up, but that's why it's cheap. I know it will be the right flat for you because it's so old. Full of history! You're the kind of person who likes that, I am sure.

Marks on the hallway's paint, faint diagonal lines, show where an inside staircase would once have led up to the ground floor. What must have formerly been a cubbyhole under those stairs remains, now a plasterboard casing holding the fridge and hot-water tank. Beyond it, alongside the small bedroom and bathroom, a galley kitchen has been squeezed in, no more than a passage leading to the back garden.

Two whole rooms to herself; not just one. Riches. Madeleine edges through a doorless opening, into the sitting-room. Bare boards. Alcoves opposite the doorway suggest the existence of a chimneybreast and fireplace, now covered over by white plasterboard. Light floods in from the big, almost floor-length window, pearled glass at the bottom and plain at the top, facing the street. So quiet after the din of the City. Just the buzzing of an invisible fly.

Entering, she feels she has disturbed the air. Like parting a curtain, its folds slipping over her hands. That odd sense of something brushing the back of her neck that she felt before in Stew Lane. Skin tingling, she stands in the middle of an empty space which yet feels full, currents of pulsing, unseen life, echoes of phrases she can't catch tickling her ears, pushing her back.

Marcia confided, on that first viewing, that she had New Age beliefs. Each time she took a client to check out a place she would utter a prayer to the resident spirits: may we come in? Have we your permission? She did this in silence, she explained, lest the clients decided she was crazy and the sale fell through.

So how would Marcia acknowledge the force of this atmosphere? Say something? Should Madeleine clap her hands and call out hello?

Superstition. Placating the gods of the hearth. Ridiculous. Nonetheless, just thinking of Marcia's silent invocation works. The air subsides and settles. The calmed room simply waits. What to do next? That's up to you, missis. Words from some long-forgotten historical novel, or perhaps from Mayhew, suddenly rising up to push her into action.

She goes out, leans on her gate, watches for the removals men. A compacted-rubble surface does duty as pavement. Heaped, broken sausages of dog shit foul the kerb. Bulky green and blue wheelie bins. Discarded cardboard packaging piled alongside. Bright yellow For Sale signs, To Let signs, in flimsy plywood, stick up at intervals.

A door clicks. Madeleine looks round. A woman emerges from the raised ground-floor entrance of the house next door. Small black eyes set in nests of wrinkles; grey-black hair cut in a bob. Her hairstyle and her lively face, her floaty black clothes, make her seem ageless.

She introduces herself: I'm Sally, ground floor, we're mostly council flats here. You're not council, are you? I hope you enjoy your little flat.

Thank you, Madeleine says: I'm sure I shall. Once the removals men turn up.

Sally says: come in for a cup of tea while you wait, why don't you? Meet my granddaughter Rose.

Rose is a thin, shining young woman of about twenty, quivering as though electricity jumps through her. Sharp, eager face. Pronounced cheekbones, short hair in a dark quiff, full, pouting lips. Tea, Nan? I'll get it.

Sally ushers Madeleine into the sitting-room. Glossy pale-green damask wallpaper patterned with silvery flowers. Matching curtains. A sky-blue carpet. Flatscreen TV. Madeleine sits down where she's told, in a plump armchair covered in grey velvet. Sally seats herself on the matching sofa, taps a cushion. This is where Rose sleeps. It's a sofa-bed, see, it pulls out. She's fallen out with her mum, that's my daughter, she's living with me while she sorts herself out. Wish I had a spare room, but there you go. Bless her, she doesn't complain.

Rose brings in a tray set with blue floral mugs, a plate of custard creams. Sally pours information at Madeleine: the whereabouts of the supermarket and post office, the times of rubbish collections. These were all private houses once, then the landlord sold them to the Council, they divided them into flats. Odd the way they did the basements. The tenant underneath me has to go down to his flat from the communal hallway here, but you next door, you've got your own entrance.

She pauses to sip tea. The street hasn't changed much on the outside, apart from the bomb damage down the end. Rose, where are those pictures?

Rose picks up some photocopies from a side table. Nan got these down the library.

Black-and-white photographs of women in little tip-tilted hats, narrow black frocks with bustles, walking in this very cul-de-sac. Sally shudders. I hate them, they make me remember I'll die, be like them one day, yet I can't get rid of them.

Rose tells Madeleine about wanting to become an artist. She left school at seventeen, works part-time in a local minicab office, draws and paints on Sally's kitchen table. Quite a few artists round here. I know some of them, up at the Elephant, the studios there.

An engine roars outside. Sally cocks an ear. There's your van arriving. Come and see us again soon.

August passes, smelling of turps and paint. Madeleine explores the neighbourhood's parks, markets. One of the pleasures of living in south London is jumping on buses and traversing the river in order to visit friends in the north; catching the bus back again late at night, sailing across Waterloo Bridge, or Blackfriars Bridge, or London Bridge. She feared she'd lost the river, moving here, but she hasn't, she relates to it more actively than before, not just walking along admiring it but leaping to and fro across it. One evening in early September, from Tate Modern's sixth-floor bar, celebrating a friend's birthday, she surveys

Queen's Wharf opposite, on the far side of the lively water, a stub of red brick above the indented dock, and marvels that she ever lived there.

She walks home, threading a path through backstreets. A nearly-full moon sails high above. Just as she passes the end of John Ruskin Street, she spots a big dog fox strolling ahead, making towards Walworth Road. The light from the street lamp gleams on its fur. It sees her, pauses. They gaze at one another. The fox obviously has no fear of humans. It trots on, towards a huddle of wheelie bins overflowing with empty pizza boxes.

Further along Orchard Street, just past the playground, something else gleams. More fur? Another fox? Fleet as a fox, certainly, skimming through the shadows. No. A youth striding towards her. Hands in pockets. Slender build. A voice says: hi! She pauses. Recognises those cheekbones. Not a boy at all. She's run into Rose. Even at night she shines: her dark hair, her brown eyes, her pouting red mouth. She stops: what you up to? Where you been?

They stand on the pavement under the plane trees, by the light of the moon, and talk. Rose is off scavenging: easier to rummage through skips this late, when no one's looking. Bits and bobs. Doors, you can get in some skips. Much better quality than the rubbish the Council has put on all our flats. I'd like to put better doors in, proper solid old ones, all down the street. Give everybody a nice old door, starting with my nan.

Rose is also after shelves, boxes, all kinds of wood. She's got storage space now. She's renting a room in the local community house, for a fiver a week, and she is going to take all the wood back there and fit up a studio. Build things. What kind of things? Dunno yet.

Rose balances back and forth on the soles of her trainers. They smile at one another, nod goodbye, and part.

Rose lopes off towards the end of the street. Madeleine walks on, feeling light: Rose stopped to talk, recognised her as a kindred spirit, a lover of the city at night. Rose is indeed like the fox, tawny and untamed, a swift, secret prowler, and in her tipsy state Madeleine speeds along the pavement, the lithe vixen scenting the air, part of a pack, all of them hunting for treasures, under the light of the moon.

THREE

Joseph

O N S O M E E V E N I N G S J O S E P H reached home by a circuitous route, cutting up towards Holborn from Blackfriars or Waterloo, depending on the day's business, then letting himself get sidetracked, letting himself wander.

Free: simply one shadow among many. From behind a wall a watchman might step forward, offering a smoke, five minutes' company. An invisible woman's skirts might rustle ahead. A hoarse female voice, exactly pitched to brush his ears, might sidle from an alley's mouth. London sighed and growled and shook itself, a dog burrowing through dreams, and Joseph dreamed too. Reaching his little house in Lamb's Conduit Street he had to jolt awake.

Sometimes, when he came in, the three younger children would still be up, would patter downstairs for a kiss, to be bade goodnight. Alfred, Charley, and Flora. Three little curly brown heads. Three white nightgowns bunched up round knees. Three little pairs of bare feet.

Tonight, the children were shouting two floors above. Eager to wash, first of all he needed to get rid of the green burdens he carried. He put the cactus on the floor under the coat-pegs, left the marigolds on the hall table. He undid the vile cloak Mrs Dulcimer had pressed on him yesterday.

Blue tweed, flecked with yellow and purple. Cape over the shoulders, tortoiseshell buttons down the front. Shrugging it off, he caught a hint of violet perfume. Ha. But the day was behind him now: he had reached home.

Milly, bless her, had lit a fire in the bedroom against his return, had also brought up hot water. Often and often he'd told her not to lug those heavy cans. Don't fret, Pa, Milly would snap: I can manage. If we had a servant she'd have to do it, and it would be just as hard for her. He'd kiss Milly's cheek: I'd help any girl struggling under such a burden, you know I would.

The steaming bath stood on the hearthrug, the empty cans beside it, their brass sides shining in the firelight.

Joseph unbuttoned his grey waistcoat. Inherited from his stepfather, a larger man. Expertly turned by his mother, to reveal the less-worn inner side, necessarily taken in as a result of the re-stitched seams, it ended up fitting Joseph exactly. He stroked the waistcoat as he took it off. Wool soft as his littlest one's face.

The children kept him in the healthy centre of his life. Gambolling and frisking, or whining and squabbling, they were innocent as cherubs. He wanted to show them all possible love: surely their good behaviour would flow from feeling cherished. Cara dwelled on the effort involved in goodness. You had to set your back against temptation. Resist it with all your might. Reading the newspaper, so full of horrors, made her tremble and cry out. This morning she'd reported to him an item about a woman who threw her three small children off Waterloo Bridge, then hurled herself after them. How could she do that? Cara sobbed. Joseph said: who knows what despair she felt? Perhaps she was starving. He stroked his wife's arm: hush, my dear one. This sort of thing happens every day, you know it does. Don't tear yourself apart fretting about it.

He unbuttoned his trousers and stepped out of them. He unloosened his necktie, took off his collar, rimmed with black from city smoke, and tossed it down. He undid his shirt.

Perhaps the father of those children had deserted that woman. Had they even been married? Hard for women of the labouring class to remain virtuous, Joseph had speculated to Mayhew two days back, given the overcrowding in their tenements. He'd stood in a Waterloo street recently and counted twenty people leaving one dilapidated dwelling, over the course of an hour, fifteen trudging out of the house next door. Little privacy in those slums for washing or for changing clothes. Men and women mingled freely in the beer shops, the street, worked side by side in the markets, on the pavement stalls. Was it in these circumstances of easy familiarity that so many females took that first, fatal, false step, crossed over from the daylight world into that other, shadier one?

Joseph had dropped into the *Morning Chronicle* offices that evening, as he sometimes did, to describe the day's work, the success or otherwise of his attempted interviews. After a brief discussion, he'd perch at a desk in the corner, write up his notes in the neat hand he'd perfected during his years at Bow Street, coaxing things into shape, sharper focus, for Mayhew to look over later. The great man, dark hair sticking up untidily, cuffs turned back, presided at a larger desk piled with notebooks and papers, cluttered with pens, inkpots, blotters, a tray of nibs and India rubbers. A brass bell stood on one corner of the leather surface, a peacock fan lay on another.

As usual, Mayhew had reminded Joseph who was in charge. Careful, Benson. I don't want you to understand people so much as study them. We have to keep a distance from the objects of our survey. Our scientific method requires us to remain detached.

He seized his pipe, leaned back and put his feet up on his desk, and began to pack the bowl with tobacco. He lit it, inhaled. You're still new to this work, of course. Let me remind you of my project's nature. Let me recapitulate.

Joseph studied his boots, silently addressing first the right and then the left: I know all this already! You've explained it to me a dozen times! The boots jumped up, did a brief dance, kicked each other, then sat dutifully still.

Mayhew emphasised his points by striking his pipe on the desk. Flakes of burning tobacco flew out, onto his pile of papers, adding scorch marks to ink blots, and he crushed them with the pipe stem. Joseph listened, and gazed at the half-eaten ham sandwich lying on a plate perched on a heap of files. Mayhew had had lunch, but he hadn't. Too busy pounding the filthy streets behind Waterloo Bridge. His stomach lurched, complained. He tried to ignore it, concentrate on his employer's words.

Mayhew waved his pipe. The main point we must bear in mind at all times, I insist, is simply to listen to the poor, record their own versions of their working lives. Or their lives of vice. Keep your opinion out of it. Just take down what they say.

Joseph had been on the job for three weeks so far. He sometimes met other researchers on the office stairs as they clumped up and down, notebooks clutched under their arms. Better born than he was, better educated, he could tell from their voices, their assessing glances. Would-be journalists, a retired clergyman or two. Hard-pressed chaps with copy to write, deadlines to meet, stopping just for a nod, a spot of chaff, then speeding on again.

He himself had been taken on as an investigator in the second division, his daily task to interview examples of the poor who chose not to labour but to exploit and rob their fellow men. An ex-police clerk, Mayhew had mused, interviewing him: used to dealing with villains, eh? Yes, I can certainly use you.

He's started Joseph off with stallholders. For his first two weeks he concentrated on the cheats amongst them. You fell into conversation; showed your interest; tickled their vanity. Amazing how quickly they trusted you, how they couldn't resist revealing their tricks: hiding bruised, near-rotten plums at the bottom of the punnet and displaying fine ones on top; bulking out packets of tea with dried grass underneath the Orange Pekoe; using false weights on their scales. Inwardly shocked, Joseph kept a bland face, took notes, reported back to the boss.

Now Mayhew had set him to collecting information on a different group of the criminal poor, in a particular part of town: the prostitutes on London's Surrey side, in the south-eastern districts lying nearest the Thames. You're the fatherly type, Mayhew remarked: you won't scare 'em off.

Joseph hoped so. He needed to hang on to this precious bit of luck. The attack of dysentery had done for him: too much time off work and Bow Street had given him his marching orders. The governor had been decent though: written him a reference, mentioned Mayhew, and so Joseph had pushed along to the *Morning Chronicle* office, introduced himself, bargained for a post. He'd try to keep his mouth shut from now on. Complete his probationary period satisfactorily. Their fortunes were on the mend, he'd promised Cara: his wages at the end of the month would prove it. All his savings had been wiped out by butcher's bills, grocer's bills, that single, expensive visit from the doctor. Just enough left over for day-to-day living costs, if Cara continued very careful with her housekeeping. Mayhew had been generous, understanding Joseph's straitened financial situation, advancing him plentiful expenses, telling him simply to keep an account of what he spent. Joseph wasn't making nearly enough. He should take on an additional job. Not yet, though. Give this one a chance first.

A starling flapped up outside, landed on the bedroom windowsill, struck its beak against the glass. Joseph yawned and stretched. So much freer with most of your clothes off. He stroked his belly, which was rounding out once more, after the dysentery had melted the flesh off him. He wasn't fat, but perhaps he should start exercising again. Boxing? Dumb-bells? Get back into good physical shape. Sharpen his wits. Recover all his former alertness. During that last conversation with Mayhew, two days previously, he had nearly blown it: offering a personal and unsought point of view.

Mayhew's pipe had gone out. He tried to get it going again, sucking it quickly, making little snorting, gasping sounds, then flung it down. He tapped his pen on his desk. Nonetheless, my dear Benson, what you say reminds me of something. We don't yet know enough about the actual living conditions of the criminal poor. Interviewing these girls on the street isn't enough. Have you visited any of their dwelling-places? You must do so!

Joseph relished his evening visits to the *Morning Chronicle*. The half-hour offered a chance to wind down after the difficulties of the working day, coaxing sullen, suspicious individuals into accepting being questioned. Seeing Mayhew both reassured and intrigued him. Plump Mayhew, in his heavy black suit, with his outflung arms and waving hands, crouched in his sanctum like a great dark spider, issuing gossamer threads in all directions, spinning a huge, complicated web, catching just the flies he wanted. Flies buzzed in a tussling rage, hurling themselves around the corners of the room, and criminals hurled themselves around the corners of the city. Capture them at the right time, Benson! Choose your moment! Was Joseph a spider too, or a fly? He wasn't always sure, although Mayhew liked to protest that all his assistants were invaluable: I may be the one initiating this work, Benson, but I depend upon you completely to help me. You are my eyes and ears!

His hot office smelled of coal dust, rancid butter and stale ham, and sweat. Windows tight shut against the foetid street outside. The great man directed all operations from his throne-like oak desk, thumping his domed brass bell when he required his scribes to run in from the next room. His *Chronicle* bulletins were meeting with great success amongst readers, his empire ever-expanding. Accordingly, to get his articles written on time, he employed, in addition to his band of informants, a team of secretaries, messengers and stenographers. He collated the information his scouts brought back, dictated and re-wrote and re-shaped. You handed in a report, and it became Mayhewed.

Joseph leaned on the edge of the bath, stood on one foot then the other, rolling down the knee-length stockings Cara had knitted for him, pushing them off over his heels. The wool was matted and damp with sweat. He untied the string fastening his drawers. The smell of his own semen rose up. Like fresh milk turned a little sour. Odd how other people's smells were always much worse than one's own. People farting on omnibuses made him want to retch. His stockings and drawers joined the heap on the floor.

Mayhew was the boss. Find out about tarts' lodgings! Jump to it! Accordingly, that same evening, after their discussion, Joseph had gone out again after supper, walked down to Mother Busk's on Waterloo Road, asked for Polly, the black-haired girl he'd met a year ago.

She remembered him, or pretended to: long time no see! Not dead yet, then? What can I do for you? And then last night he had visited Mrs Dulcimer's in Walworth, and been robbed for his pains. Damn the woman. She'd babbled excuses as she half-smothered him in that horrible cloak. All a mistake. Doll's one for taking odd notions into her head, d'you see, she took a fancy to you, obviously, and so she took your coat. She's not a thief. She didn't mean to steal, I'm sure. It just came over her, I expect. She's not a bad girl, really.

Doll was a bit touched, perhaps. On his way home in the jolting cab Joseph had decided to accept Mrs Dulcimer's tale. For the moment. Would Doll interest Mayhew? A simpleton who stole not from straightforward wickedness but for some other, twisted reason. What was her story? Well: they'd see.

Now he had a hold over the black lady. Possibly he could turn the event to his advantage, force the woman to reveal more of her trade secrets. What kind of place nurtured a being like Doll? Perhaps she hid keen wits under those daft looks. Those sensual, swinging hips. Perhaps she was a decoy. Probably Mrs Dulcimer knew all the back ways to all the local swag shops. Rather than get a warrant, go straight to the house with a constable, and have the place searched, too late by now probably, they should watch the canny black lady's comings and goings. What was she, exactly? Facts, Benson, facts!

He stepped into the bath, sat down, drawing up his knees. He reached over, took up one of the clean towels Milly had left out, folded it, placed it behind him to make a headrest, and lay back, basking in the clean steam.

Late this morning, still obediently pursuing Mayhew's latest instructions, he had visited a row of lodging-houses on Newington Road. How to tell which harboured decent working people and which sheltered prostitutes? He chose at random: two establishments, side by side, whose doors on to the street stood ajar. He knocked on the door of the nearest and went in.

The low-ceilinged basement kitchen was warmed by a steeply banked fire. Ropes suspended over the fireplace held drying shirts. A dozen or so men, shabbily dressed, clustered around an oilcloth-covered table, reading newspapers, eating fish breakfasts, drinking tea. All looked sour-faced with exhaustion. One had given up, slumped asleep, his head on his folded arms.

Some of these chaps had been hop-picking in Kent, the landlady explained, her thin lips parting over tobacco-stained teeth, and had walked a long way. Others, she indicated with a wave of her hand, were resting after dawn shifts selling fruit at the market, preparatory to going out again, for whatever casual work they could get. After their bit of bread and butter they'd be off. Her open mouth revealed gums clotted with white wads of half-chewed bread and fish. She put in a finger, rummaged, pulled out a fishbone. She looked at it, cast it onto the table. She swallowed, picked up another piece of fry in her fingers and bit into it. Grease ran onto her chin, which she wiped with her sleeve. Joseph tipped his hat and left.

The kitchen of the second house, peopled solely by women, seemed livelier. Here, the purple-gowned landlady was pouring out coffee for a group of half-a-dozen well-dressed girls of about Milly's age. Cheerful and healthy enough they looked, lounging in wooden armchairs by the fire, or at the big central table, laden with crockery, packs of cards, and candle-holders. Dresses, bonnets and petti-coats hung from strings looped all round the salmon-pink walls and over screens.

One young creature, smartly got up in a green jacket and skirt, her hair neatly coiled and netted, was sorting through a pile of silk and muslin squares in front of her. Cravats, scarves and handkerchiefs. Next to her, a more genteel-looking girl in pale blue was paring her nails with a knife, while another, wrapped in a red shawl, was mending a long tear in the hem of a white gown. They ceased their chatter as he came in, glanced at each other. The girl in green swept her hoard of flimsies onto her lap, stuck out her chin and gave him a bold look. When she bade him a merry hello, the others followed suit.

Joseph introduced himself, asked if they would talk to him about their lives. They shrugged. He searched for a tactful formula. The landlady was watching him. One clumsy word, one seeming allegation that she ran a dodgy set up, and she'd throw him out. How could he ask her lady lodgers to describe their bedrooms? Whether they ever shared them with men casually picked up on the street? How often they changed the sheets? Impossible. No. Avoid all mention of sleeping-quarters for the moment. Start with something less intimate. Assume these girls are virtuous, and gainfully employed. Begin there.

He cleared his throat. What jobs do you do, young ladies? Who employs you? How much do you earn per day, roughly speaking? How far do you have to travel to your place of work? What are your hours?

They stared at him. Then giggled. Hey, mister! Chilly out, is it? One of the girls pointed at his cloak, chortled, put her hand over her mouth. Another stood up from her perch on a settle drawn close to the grate. She flounced the cage of her crinoline backwards, so that it turned inside out, curved up around her like a great shell. Saucy as a parakeet flashing its plumage, she plumped down again, her back skirts over her head, her front ones drawn up to reveal her quilted pink petticoat, and a white one showing under that. Ta-da! she jeered at him, while the others laughed.

They were all, of course, thieves. Doubtless most of them were also prostitutes. Night-prowlers, going about the streets to plunder drunken men. Right! Exactly the sort of women Mayhew wished him to interview. It ought to be easy: none of them seemed the slightest bit ashamed. None of them, however, wished to talk to him. What! He was joking, surely. He could be a plain-clothes policeman. They tittered at each other, then bade him insolent good-byes. The parakeet-girl flapped up her petticoats again, squawking. The landlady jerked her thumb towards the doorway. She clapped shut the door behind him.

Joseph stood in the street, his cheeks hot. The bloody cloak's fault. If he'd been wearing his overcoat he'd have been treated with more respect. Watching boys catcalled, pointed and jeered, and he waved his fist at them. When a group of heavies in leather aprons rounded the corner and lurched towards him, Joseph made off.

He lifted his right foot out of the bathwater, balanced it on his left knee, and soaped his toes. From in between them he winkled out crusts of dirt, particles of grit. Astonishing what you picked up in a single day. Were his boot-soles worn to holes? Quite possibly, with all the walking he did. He plunged his feet back into the suds, gave them a good rinse.

During the afternoon, not wanting to give up, he'd paced more streets of the neighbourhood. The narrow thoroughfares stank of excrement, flowed with rubbish. No pavements: simply the road surface of packed rubble and puddling mud. Women hopped along it, hoisting their skirts well clear, showing their gaudy stockings. In some cases, naked legs. Bare feet thrust into cracked old shoes. Two small girls plodded past, wearing enormous down-at-heel slippers. Someone's cast-offs. Bareheaded mothers, their hair scraped back, slumped on chairs at the front doors of decaying tenements. Hard-faced, with gaunt cheekbones and hostile eyes. They slapped away the pestering children, slapped them again when they fell over and whined.

Joseph shifted down the bath, held his nose with one hand as he submerged himself, pushed his other hand through his hair. He sat up again, the soapy water sluicing his shoulders. He spluttered, wiped his cheeks.

Nathalie, pregnant almost immediately after their marriage, had still seemed like a child herself. So tiny and so delicate. Yet she brimmed with maternal tenderness, towards him as much as towards the coming baby. She would stroke his shoulders as he kneeled by her chair, his head against her belly, to feel the child kicking. He whispered his fears: that she was so narrow, that the birth would rip her apart. Nathalie would hush him: I'm young, I'm healthy and strong, just stop your fretting. He pressed her fingers to his mouth, kissed them one by one.

Labour set on unexpectedly, two months early, one wintry afternoon. It lasted all night. Quite normal with a first baby, barked the midwife. Sitting by the fire after his lonely cheese and pickle supper, listening to the yowls from upstairs, he daydreamed about lion-taming, the coming child somehow changed into a ravening beast cornering Nathalie and tearing her apart in its jaws. He fell asleep in his chair, woke cold and stiff to a crisping tumble of grey coals. At dawn, his sister-in-law Cara put her face round the door: a girl! What a little 'un! Strong as ever can be.

A little later, the doctor diagnosed Nathalie's post-partum fever. Cara came down, a squirming white bundle in her arms. She spoke of finding a wet nurse. He turned aside and grunted. If he opened his mouth he would howl. The world would collapse. Anything could happen if Nathalie could be taken from him. Grief was a landslide of rocks, mud, rubble, wanting to choke him.

Cara provided the obvious solution. She gave up her nursemaid's job, moved in, cared for Milly, took over the housekeeping. Fifteen years later, here she still was. Married to him, and now, aged thirty-five, the mother of three small children. How did women bear the agony of childbirth? Cara was stoic: you got something out of it; you got the baby at the end.

But we cannot afford any more children, my dear one, and nor should you be put through those travails again. Cara's health was no longer good, and Joseph worried about her. He did his best to be a considerate husband, to limit his caresses to once a week at most, to withdraw in time. Cara refused to insert a sponge soaked in vinegar beforehand, or douche afterwards: against her religion, she insisted. She didn't want Joseph to use a condom either. He didn't like them much, in any case: they dulled sensation.

Recently, according to the hints of the doctor, who'd followed instructions on post-dysentery diet with advice on limiting families, Joseph had been considering separate bedrooms. If only they had the space. Milly now slept in what had been his mother's room, and wouldn't want to give up her privacy. If he had his own room, all to himself, he could stay up as late as he chose, do whatever he wanted. Put up a shelf to display his collection of stones, butterflies, shells. Save up to buy a telescope, sit at the window, study the night sky. Track the constellations.

Touch the surface of the moon. The moon's face turned away. Her dark cheek. Scented with lilies.

Prickle of coldness on his skin. The water was cooling rapidly. Joseph lifted his head from the edge of the bath, took his flannel in one hand, the soap in the other, began to wash his balls, his cock.

In the slums south of the river that he had begun to visit, the evidence of unrestrained male lust was everywhere. Those worn women he had passed earlier today, their litters of puny infants pulling at their skirts, squalling and dribbling: the sight of such misery had distressed him so much that on his way home, rather than call in on Mayhew at his office, he had gone for a drink in the River Queen, one of his favourite pubs on the Strand. He'd write up his notes at home tonight, finish his report some time tomorrow. That would do.

The crowded pub smelled of fresh sawdust and spilled beer, pipe tobacco, perspiring bodies. He found a seat next to the bow window. He read his newspaper and smoked.

Slipping through the throng came a slender girl in a blue jacket, a striped blue-and-white skirt puffed out over a crinoline; the pink frill of a furled parasol; the scent of violets. Tendrils of dark brown hair escaped from under a blue straw bonnet. The girl hovered for a moment, then gestured, pulled up a stool next to him: may I? She sat down, took out a small cloth-bound book from her pocket, began to read with steady concentration, the tip of her red tongue showing between her little white teeth. She reminded him of Nathalie, that way she'd had of retiring behind her magazine, shutting out the world. Tears gathered under his eyelids. He got out his handkerchief and blew his nose. The girl looked up.

They fell easily into conversation. She showed him her grammar book: goodness, it is hard! A quick smile, a wrinkle of her brow. Italian, she said she was, from an immigrant family lodging in Clerkenwell. Seeing his interest, she described their lives. Parents both in work. Able to pay their rent. No debts. They seemed a fine example of industrious poverty: law-abiding Catholics who kept their heads down, attended weekly Mass at one of the embassy chapels, tried to fit in. My papa taught me to play the violin, but I'm no good at it. To earn a living, he mends broken instruments, he frames pictures. My mother keeps house and minds the little ones, also she mends and cleans clothes for the second-hand dealer down the street. Spruces up, you say? On Sundays, when I go home to visit, I do the cooking, to give her a rest. The rest of the week, I lodge near here, in Surrey Street. It's easier.

Easier for what, my dear little miss?

Her brown eyes sparkled through her black lashes. Guess!

She chattered on, describing her three elder brothers, street entertainers, the dances she went to with them. Polkas I love the best. Waltzes? We do not try those. She pattered out her broken English with a pronounced accent that only added to her piquancy, her charm.

He said: I know the answer to my question. I'm sorry for it. I'm sorry for you. I wish you could find some other way to live.

She pouted, fingered a dark brown ringlet. Don't be sorry. I'm doing very well, thank you.

When had she slid into prostitution? Why? What were her lodgings like? Should he ask her, then take notes? No: he wasn't in south-east London now. He could leave the job behind. Just sit with her. Enjoy her company. Enjoy the moment. A sweet girl. Forget she's a prostitute.

As a married man he'd remained faithful. For better, for worse. You made that promise, and you kept it. Except during that odd, brief period a year ago, when his self-control had broken. People said: I became beside myself with rage. Beside myself with sorrow. Hackneyed phrases whose truth he'd lived out. The grown-up Joseph ate, worked and talked as usual; next to him the child Joseph sobbed and fought. The small brown sickroom smelled of camphor and eucalyptus. He leaned over the bed, stroked his mother's hand, murmured to her. Come on, old lady: come on. The pillows half obscured her face; her breath rasped. She opened her eyes a crack, closed them. Cara, red-faced, expostulated. Your mother's dying, Joseph, can't you see? Leave her alone now, just let her go! He had bolted from the house, flung himself into the darkness of the night streets, blundered towards the river, fetched up in Waterloo. A gaudy lantern hailed him: he went in, expecting a pub. Mother Busk soon set him right: she diagnosed his trouble, brought him a remedy. Hello, sir. My name's Polly. Her loosened black hair tangled against him like seaweed. Diving inside her, he had been able to disappear, as into a cave brimming up at high tide with the incoming sea, and then gasping and crying he'd kicked out, towards the crests of green waves, surfaced, swum for shore, been borne back onto the beach. Half-winded, struggling up the shelf of shingle, returning to his changed life. He'd stumbled home, tearstained, at two in the morning, to a bewildered wife who'd chosen not to say a word.

He bought the Italian girl a brandy and soda. She thanked him gravely. She sipped daintily, all the time looking at him, with sharp blackbird eyes, over the rim of the glass. She leaned towards him and again he caught her violet scent. She whispered her invitation: shall we? You would like?

The gleam of a swift smile. She sounded so off-hand and friendly. He was trembling. He put his hands on his knees, to steady himself. He shouldn't. He shouldn't.

At least a week since he'd been intimate with Cara. Once they'd climbed into bed at night, the curtains rattling on their rings, falls of clean faded chintz swept open, swept back, she'd peck his cheek, pull the sheet over her shoulder, turn away. He'd press his mouth to the back of her soap-scented neck, that inch of flesh between nightcap and nightgown, then remain restless, wide awake. Somehow like lying on gravel. His self-control was laudable, yes, dear doctor, but almost unbearable too. The doctor had specifically warned against self-abuse, which led to degeneration, thence to madness. What was Joseph supposed to do?

Why not? Nobody would ever know. Absolutely nothing to stop him. Just this once.

The girl stood up, sauntered past the bar. He followed her. She took him out to the yard at the back, into the wash-house, she made it all so easy, fitting the condom on him, gathering her swoop of skirts in one hand, unlatching her drawers with the other. He swung her up, nuzzled her ear, drank in her pungent violet scent, then lifted her up and down, squirted deep into her. Such pleasure: not having to be careful, withdraw before he came. The condom didn't matter, could not dull this intensity, this ecstasy of letting go inside her. Thank you, he whispered: ah, you little darling.

He eased her off him, jumped her down. He held her in his arms, put his face against hers.

Deftly she re-fastened her underthings, checked the money he handed her, plunged it into her skirt pocket, darted away. He gave her a couple of minutes, then strolled back inside. There she was, ringlets smoothed and bonnet strings neatly re-tied in a bow under her chin, sidling up to the bar, managing to look so ladylike even as she ogled the men looming on either side of her.

The bedroom's fire sank with a soft crash. Joseph yawned, stood up, began to towel his hair. The cold bathwater had grey scum around its edges, like old scrambled egg. He stepped out onto the mat in front of the hearthrug, began to mop his arms.

Leaving the pub, Joseph had stopped at the flower seller's further along the Strand. Hunched on an upturned bucket, she sheltered under a blue umbrella. He bought a cactus, fleshy green leaves tipped with scarlet. Tomorrow he'd take it with him up to Highgate, put it on Nathalie's grave. The flower seller twirled a bit of newspaper round his purchase. Coarse red hands, grimy fingernails. There you are, dear. He leaned forward, lifted out a dripping bunch of orange marigolds from a tin pot. I'll take these too.

Walking on towards St Paul's, cactus and flowers pressed together in the crook of one arm, Joseph swung his stick and beat at shadows and tried to return to himself. That brief adventure was in the past. The girl had slipped back into the black stream of her kind, one slippery fish among thousands. He'd known her for just half an hour. Press on, press on. The girl's face kept surfacing. She refused to drown in the depths of his mind. Her lively eyes mocked him. She'd marked him. As though she'd thrown a can of paint at his back.

Somehow the encounter had to do with wearing the tweed cloak Mrs Dulcimer had thrust at him the previous night, all the while apologising for her thieving maid. He had gone out into the rain cursing them both. Somehow Mrs Dulcimer had nudged him off course. Call that episode just now her cloak's fault. Wearing it had changed him. Turned him into someone else. On his return home yesterday, meeting him in the hall, Milly had thought so too. Goodness, Pa, who'd you swap clothes with? You mountebank! Just ready for the panto! He'd raised a playful hand and she'd dodged, smiling and shouting, and Cara had darted up from the kitchen, ready to fuss.

He'd fobbed them off with a story of taking his coat to the mender's, to have a torn sleeve repaired, then borrowing the cloak from Mayhew. Cara had said: oh, Joseph, I could have stitched that for you, you're always trying to save me trouble, bless you. Saucy Milly had said: I don't think much of Mr Mayhew's taste.

Sometimes you kept an experience to yourself. If you told someone else about it, you lost it. That was the point of secrets. Something that belonged to you alone, a golden, unnamed fruit that dropped into your hands, which you hid in your pocket, took out when you were alone. You held off as long as you could, then dived in, bit the fruit, its juices splashing all over you. The encounter with the girl tonight belonged to him, and certainly not to Mayhew, who would thunder his disapproval and probably show Joseph the door. So keep quiet about it. Same thing with the trip to Walworth. He had failed with the black lady. What exactly was she up to? He needed to go back, talk to her again.

Joseph stood barefoot on the cotton bath-mat, softness pressing up against his soles, and finished drying himself. Warmth all round him, cradling him. He let go his breath, stood and stretched, feeling restored, healthy, he was clean, and the coals' heat played over his calves, his thighs. Suddenly he wanted to whistle and sing, but desisted, mindful of the little ones, whom Milly had presumably coaxed into sleep.

He took up a file, and began to smooth his nails. That girl in the Newington house, paring hers with a knife: how guileless she'd looked. Yet these girls let you do whatever you wanted. As long as you paid for it. Mayhew wasn't so much interested in the acts that the girls performed as the histories that preceded them. He wanted the girls pumped for their streams of explanations. Confessions. How they came to swerve off the track. Whereas Joseph thought he'd also like to classify what the girls actually did. Compare their poses and gestures to those described in certain publications you could rummage for on the barrows along Farringdon Road, or in the shops in Holywell Street.

Books that smiled at you slyly, beckoned you discreetly. That guide for tourists, published years back, to the high-flying prostitutes of the West End. Street by street; woman by woman; names, appearances, ages, specialities. Joseph couldn't afford to buy it. When he went back, to sample further chapters, the book had gone.

Black-hatted, black-overcoated men ringed the dank basement. They read silently, faces to the walls of volumes, concentrating and inward-turned, as though they were praying. At certain moments some of the books dropped into French, which was frustrating. Nathalie had taught him a few French words, endearments mostly, but the lessons never got very far. Hearing her speak French excited him too much. Tell me the French for buttons, for laces, for drawers. She whispered: *joli garçon, toi*.

Joseph flexed his fingers, pulled on his knuckles, cracking them. He examined his scrubbed nails, their white half-moons. Hands that had clasped the Italian girl's whaleboned waist. Her hands were half the size of his. Soft, well-kept.

Mayhew was interested in prostitutes simply because they were criminals. He'd said to Joseph: you've a particular know-how to contribute, I suppose.

Working as a police clerk, Joseph had developed a certain forensic glance. When miscreants, caught in the act, were hauled in to the station by the constables, he would swivel from his stool in the corner, read the villains' demeanour, study their physiognomies, the characters these revealed. The admission records, detailing the arrests, which he inscribed in his ledger, were necessarily factual and dry, lacking all emotion, but inside himself he invented a different account, made quick sketches in words. Here's a sullen-seeming woman with thick curls sprouting above a shallow forehead, slits of deep-set eyes darting fiery glances right and left as she searches out possible aggressors, gets ready to run. Here's a man with a hunched back, his head sunk between his shoulders, his collar turned up to try to hide the bruises on his neck. Here's a man with his long nose in the air and his eyelids lowered; shooting his ragged cuffs, drawling, as he affects indifference. Here's a half-bald girl sticking out her lip, her bosom, her foot; fists clenched.

So get on with the job. Begin again. Tomorrow he would go back south of the river, return to that Newington lodging-house. Find a way to make those girls talk to him, tell him the costs of renting beds, the costs of laundry. Doubtless offering them a drink would do it. Offer one to the landlady too.

Usually Joseph rummaged in the bedroom chest of drawers for fresh clothes. Tonight, clearly determined to display her starching and ironing skills, Milly had put out a clean shirt for him. A soft breastplate, it leaned against the buttoned back of the low chair. Calm as Mrs Dulcimer the previous night as she lolled on her gold satin cushions. The folded sleeves offered him a mute invitation to pull them apart. Seize them by the cuffs, crease them in his powerful fingers, let them wrap round him in an embrace. A lovely woman's arms. Some unknown woman, very well dressed, with an intricately arranged coiffure, a mischievous glance.

Mayhew had interviewed one such a week back, in a house off the Haymarket, and shown Joseph his account. She claimed to be heroically sacrificing herself, to save her children from destitution. Her out-of-work husband came to collect her late every afternoon, escort her home. Mayhew had winked. My dear Benson, so easily shocked.

Mayhew had not the slightest idea what Joseph already knew, had already experienced. Those few occasions in his youth. And then that time a year ago. Stumbling into Mother Busk's green-painted saloon, hat clutched in one hand, coat soon unbuttoned and cast aside. He sat at the little gilded table and mopped his tears. Polly the black-haired girl tapped his shoulder: come on then. Purple-draped cubicle, looped with threads of silvery stars. Bottle of brandy. Two glasses, which winked in the lamplight. Winked at each other; conspirators. Yes, we know. Yes, we understand. The girl's white thighs splayed apart, her black-fringed cunt, her rouged mouth. For a moment he forgot that he was paying her to pretend. She took him, held him, contained him, made him feel safe by calling time's up! She pushed him out, patting his arm. There you go, dearie. He tried to kiss her but she twisted her head aside. Nah, don't be daft. He went back a couple of times the following week, after his mother's funeral, had to make do with other girls, less appealing. Polly's laid up, one explained: she's expecting, she's feeling very sick.

The bedroom fire was burning down. Smell of coal and soap. Joseph stretched and yawned. He picked up the shirt, shook it out. A scorch mark decorated one of the tails. Oh, Milly. He wrestled on the burned garment and did it up. He took a fresh collar from the stand on the chest of drawers. He brushed his hair. As he did every evening, he opened the green leather jewellery case in which Cara kept his mother's few pieces: a tarnished gilt brooch and bracelet, a ring set with green glass. The gewgaws she and Nathalie had inherited from an aunt lay alongside: amber earrings, a string of white beads, a jet clip.

In a second box, covered in rubbed coral silk, lay Nathalie's glass-bead rosary, her little tin medallion of the Virgin. The ring woven of a lock of her own hair. He kissed the plaited circlet, closed both boxes, put them back in the drawer behind Cara's muslin envelope of pocket handkerchiefs.

His wife met him downstairs in the hall. A smile lifted her face back into girlish prettiness. She said: I've put the marigolds in the dining-room. Ah, you're sweet to bring me flowers.

She stretched out her arms for an embrace. Her brown weekday dress, trimmed with brown braid, had lumpy-looking sleeves, badly set, the whole thing too obviously home-made by an unskilled seamstress. Cara was so good. Saving on the housekeeping by sewing her own clothes, turning and refurbishing them year by year. Trying to teach Milly to iron. Memories burned into him; like the scorch marks on his shirt-tails. That dark-eyed minx staring straight back at him as he levered her up and down. The scent of her hair and skin.

He kissed Cara, put his arm round her. Let's get you a new frock soon, love. That one's past its best. Does nothing for you.

Cara flushed. He cursed himself for insensitivity. Dear Cara. She didn't yet know that he was planning a fine surprise for her. As soon as he'd received his wages he would pack her off, with the children, to visit her family in Boulogne. To hell with the bill for the piano, the bill for the sideboard: his creditors could wait. He'd planned this treat just before the dysentery struck; got as far as obtaining passports. The travel money had dribbled away on medicines. But now his first pay packet would bring Cara delight. She often lamented that she missed her family, especially when she received a letter from her mother. Sighing over its shortness, dropping a tear or two. She got Milly to write back, partly to make sure the girl kept up her French, partly so that she would retain a sense of having grandparents. Something might come of it. You never knew. Families were supposed to help.

Joseph patted Cara's shoulder. He slid his hand up to her neck, stroked it, tickled it gently until a new smile trembled on her lips. She had a nice mouth, pale and pink, like a flattened rosebud. He tipped up her chin and kissed her again. She definitely needed a holiday. And she really ought to hire a full-time servant. Her health would suffer even further otherwise. If they continued very careful, perhaps they could just about afford it.

It might be difficult to make Cara agree. She wouldn't admit that the idea of servants scared her. She had no sense of her own authority. Because she'd once been a servant herself? He forgot that; it was so long ago. Still, he would insist she got the help she deserved.

He kissed her a third time. Cara patted his cheek, twisted away from his arm. Milly's fetched in some chops, and there's some soup if you want it, and the leftover pudding from yesterday.

Milly shouted from the basement: dinner's served!

The three of them sat down around the table that filled the cramped space dignified by the name of dining-room. All the rooms had similar fine names, and all of them, squeezed into the small, thin house, were no bigger than closets. Hence the low rent. So cosy, Mr Benson, the landlord had said, showing him around: and the dining-room so convenient, you see, bang next to the kitchen. Everything to hand. That was true: Milly could fetch extra gravy in a trice, or more bread, or collect up dirty plates with one sweep of her arm and bowl them into the sink.

Tonight Milly had hurried in, cheeks shiny from cooking steam, slapped down the marigolds jammed into a jug. Next to the flowers she dumped the knives and forks, then picked up the cutlery again, polished it with a corner of her apron.

She said: I forgot to heat the soup. Never mind. The chops are done.

The over-grilled, blackened chops sat in a puddle of fat. Joseph winced. Unfair to criticise Milly. Or Cara. How could she have taught her stepdaughter to produce decent meals? Frenchwomen didn't understand cookery. He'd been so in love with Nathalie he hadn't cared that she couldn't recognise a suet pudding and spoke fondly of garlic. Cara did her best and that was that.

He'd picked up cooking from watching his mother. How to stretch a scrap of mutton with potatoes, carrots and dumplings. How to keep lunchtime's vegetable water for night-time soup, thicken it with rice. How to rub fat into flour. Ah, Joseph, you've a wonderfully light hand for pastry. With the trimmings from pies he cut out biscuits, made twists sprinkled with sugar. He wanted to be a chef when he grew up, but there was no money to pay for his training: off with him to the police station to act as messenger boy. From there he'd worked his way up to clerking. Thanks to the teaching at the parish board school he could write a fair hand, cover foolscap neatly, with scarcely a blot. He daydreamed as he walked home each night, imagined working behind the scenes in a smart food-shop, creating tarts and cakes. Copper saucepans and moulds; fluted silvery tins. Often in the evenings he'd push his tired mother into a kitchen chair, take over making supper. Ah, Joseph dear, you're good to me. When the Hoof came in, she didn't let on who'd cooked, in case he jeered.

Joseph forked out the chops, shaking off grease drips, served his wife and daughter, then took his own portion. Bone with a knob of fatty meat attached. He chewed the gristly lump in silence.

Milly kept her head down. Eyelids lowered, lashes brushing her cheeks. Straight white parting, brown hair drawn back and twisted in a messy knot. One long curl falling across her eye. Her right hand rested on the handle of her knife. Her left fiddled with something in her lap.

He said: what's that you're reading, sweetheart? You shouldn't be reading at table. Please! Put it away!

Milly scowled. She said: it's a physiology textbook, that's all. I want to know how bones fit together. I want to understand fractures and things.

She reached behind her chair and placed her book on the sideboard. He said: is that from the library? Oh, Milly. You'll have put grease marks all over the pages, most likely.

Fingermarks on white paper. The Italian girl's fingertips caressing his cheeks and lips. She stretched up to reach him, she stood before him on tiptoe, braced, ready to be lifted up, fitted onto him. Her hands clasping his shoulders, pressing them harder, harder, as they panted, fused, bones muscles sinews flesh a deep sweetness mounting, molten.

Cara said: what's the matter, Joseph? Is something wrong?

He jumped. Nothing! A touch of indigestion, that's all.

She said: you must have had a hard day, dear. You seem quite tired.

Once, in their hopeful, newly married days, she had plied him with questions about his working life. Then the children arrived, took up all her attention. She'd nursed Joseph through his bout of dysentery with devotion mixed with a certain briskness. Now she was content just to know he had a job again. Research for a well-known journalist who wrote articles for the national press: it sounded well. He didn't propose to tell Cara that research now meant eyeing up prostitutes in the street, tapping the chosen ones on the arm, accompanying them back to the low dives where they hung out, offering them rounds of drinks. She'd turn away, flushing. She wasn't supposed to know about such things. Nor did he want her to.

Cara said: the chops are a little bit tough, I confess. We'll do better tomorrow, won't we, Milly? She beamed at her stepdaughter: pure, maternal affection. She blinked shortsightedly at the cruet set: Milly, did you remember to grind more pepper?

Cara would seal off the troubling outside world by drawing the curtains around their bed. Inside this cocoon they made love, when they did make love, in the dark. She'd never allowed him to see her naked. She lay swathed from head to toe in frilled and pintucked linen, and to get anywhere near her he had to gather up those voluminous folds and roll them above her waist. Like rolling up an awning. Roll up, roll up. Circus parade of girls at Mother Busk's who shed their underclothes so easily, bright layers of silk petticoats, lace drawers.

Cara blinked again: where's the salt?

He'd blinked all right on that first visit to Mother Busk's, but then his eyes flew wide open, maintained a steady gaze. The spectacle glittered and flashed like a kaleidoscope: the tarts parading in the brilliant light of flaring gas-jets; wearing their painted faces like masks. Lifting their hands to swish their crinolined skirts from side to side, making them balloon and sway. Unbelievable glimpses of nakedness. Shock of those pink lips. Haloes of hair. Then the rainbows of crisp frills swept down and hid them again. The men leaned in, open-mouthed; fish drawn to those bright lures. Hooked, bloodied, gutted. Their money once twinkled out of their pockets, they'd be thrown aside. No use to anybody.

On his recent visit, two days back, dutifully following Mayhew's instructions, Joseph had bought Polly the black-haired girl a drink, then coaxed her to talk to him. I'll pay you for your time, of course I will. Early still: few other customers in. With Mother Busk's glance on her, Polly had to yield. She fiddled with her scarf, re-arranging it over her décolletage. She studied her fingernails. Talk to you? What about?

This felt more intimate than when they'd had their clothes off. He was unsure, in these new circumstances, quite how to address her. Courtesy was the key surely. And the drink certainly helped overcome shyness, his as well as hers.

I'm doing a spot of research, Miss Polly. Into, ah, your living conditions. So, for example, do you sleep here, as well as, er, sit here? What kind of accommodation is offered you?

Mother Busk might want to fold her girls up, like evening frocks, press them flat into chests of drawers in some anteroom behind the row of boudoir cubicles, but presumably they tottered up to an attic of an early morning. Three to a grubby bed, wiped out by gin.

Polly bared her teeth at him: you want to come up and see for yourself, darling?

He scribbled down her words while she tossed back her drink. Did she choose with whom to share a bed, a room? Well. It varied. Girls came and went. Decent sorts, mainly. Good friends with the others she mostly was: they looked out for each other. You hollered for help if a man turned violent, and your pal would holler back, bang on the wall. Mother Busk kept a cudgel to hand. When necessary she dashed in, sorted the punters out. The girls slept upstairs. In a dormitory, yes. They kept their private stuff in baskets under their beds. If somebody nicked something you usually guessed who it was and thumped them. They did their own washing, monthly rags included, hung it up to dry in the yard behind. Cheaper, see? If the house girl did it, Mother Busk docked their earnings, mean old cow. Joseph felt himself blush. At home no one mentioned those rags. On wash-days, Cara instructed him to keep out of her way. The house smelled of hot soap. Dinner was a bite of meat.

On getting up, the wine bottle emptied, Polly had offered him some parting words of advice. You should talk to Mrs Dulcimer. Not much she hasn't seen in her time. She knows all the girls. 'Course she does. Yes, so you should.

He'd written down in his pocketbook the address Polly gave him, gone home, composed a discreet note asking for an appointment. She'd replied the following morning: come this evening; and so off he went. Did the postmen ever imagine what kind of business they facilitated, as they flew hither and thither, criss-crossing the same street eleven times a day? Storks brought babies, he'd been told as a child: white bundles dangling from their beaks. Postmen storks brought bundles of bills, mostly. And then a note from an unknown woman, drawing him into her dark world. Tantalising at first; then disappointing. Why had he bothered travelling to Walworth? It had brought him only grief. A lost coat. A loss of self-respect as well as of precious money. A sense of having been fooled. But there was something there. Something going on. Worth finding out what it was, surely.

Milly dropped the serving spoon on the floor, and Cara exclaimed. Under the noise of her reproaches came a faint tapping sound from upstairs. One of the children, presumably. Out of bed, hopping about, looking for mischief. He'd send Milly up to check, once she and Cara had calmed down. Milly wanted just to wipe the spoon on the cloth and Cara was insisting on a clean one. He shut them out of his attention, chewed on the last of his chop.

Cara began listlessly to scrape and stack their plates. The sound from upstairs came again: this time a sharper rat-a-tat. Milly pushed back her chair. I'll go.

She banged out. Joseph said: Cara, you look so tired. We really must get a proper servant. Let's stop all this shilly-shallying and just hire someone.

He waited for her to list the difficulties involved. Hard to manage with someone living in, a maid would have to sleep on the fold-down bed in the kitchen, and that cluttered up the space. Girls these days were so insolent, so careless. And how did you know you could trust their references? They might be faked! They might be thieves, just winkling their way in!

No. Just find a strong, good-tempered skivvy who could clean the boots and knives, keep the house nice, stoke the parlour fire. Milly was prone to lounging in a chair, her legs swung over the arm, getting lost in a book, letting the coals burn too low. Just as the fire died, she'd start poking furiously at the red, twinkling mass, then sigh as she took up the scuttle and trailed off out to the shed for coal. If she wasn't reading she was wanting to get out of the house, to tow Cara to concerts at the library, to public lectures.

Who's going to pay for that, my darling miss? Kissing her cheek, tweaking her ear. D'you suppose I'm made of money? Milly would answer him back: so let me learn a trade! Let me go out to work! He had to remind her: your stepmother needs you at home, put on a smile, can't you?

Cara said: I'll think about getting a servant, I promise. Just let me take these plates to the kitchen. I want to see how the pudding's getting on.

He and Milly fought because they loved each other so much. They were so alike: hot-tempered, easily roused, relishing a skirmish. On those occasions of strife he couldn't explain to his frowning daughter, watching her fiddle her fingers through her untidy hair, re-twist and re-fasten it on top of her head, the ferocious tenderness he felt for her; this fierce need to protect her. As though she were a baby dove he cradled in his hands. The spitting image of Nathalie. For that alone he cherished her. He saw himself mirrored in her too, in her desire to explore the city, its churches and monuments. She shared his interest in the natural world, in history. She pored over the encyclopedia, listened to his explanations about ferns, minerals, butterflies, building materials, engineering. Then would fire up: let's go down to the river, let's take the ferry to Greenwich, let's go and see the Hospital, let's visit the Observatory. He couldn't spell out to her his fears. Some of the prostitutes he'd been interviewing, if you believed their tales, had started out just like Milly, wanting ardently to embrace life, and look at them now: ghastly imitations of youth, hair dyed, faces heavily painted to conceal their age. Raddled and haggard, diseased, utterly wretched. Finally awarded a bed in the workhouse, if they were lucky, followed by a bed in the paupers' graveyard on Redcross Way.

Cara came back in with the pudding, a jug of custard. Try some of this, dearest.

Milly's feet pounded back down the stairs. She flung open the dining-room door. She said: it's for you, Pa. Some queer woman. She looks foreign, somehow. What you can see of her, anyway. Perhaps she's a spy! Or an assassin!

Joseph said: you and your love of drama. You've been reading too many novels, Milly.

Cara pulled at her collar, settling it higher around her throat. Rather late to be paying visits, surely. Why not just leave a card?

He rose, put his hand on her shoulder. Now, now, dearest. She'll be someone collecting for some good cause, I have no doubt.

Milly said: perhaps she's the good cause herself. She looks like a widow. She's all in black.

Upstairs, in the dimly lit hall, the woman waiting just inside the front door wore a black-spotted veil drawn tightly over her face, a black hooded cloak. She was carrying a large carpet-bag, which she put down on the mat as he stood still and stared at her.

She lifted her black-gloved hands, pushed back her hood, revealing a close-fitting black bonnet. She unfastened the veil, threw it back over the bonnet's edge. No hair showed. Just the curving bones of her face. Her dark skin gleamed. She glanced at him from under her eyelashes. Those big brown-black eyes. His mouth felt dry. He greeted her: evening, Mrs Dulcimer.

She spoke in that low, controlled voice of hers: please forgive me for disturbing you at home.

If he didn't know better, he'd write her down as a mantua-maker travelling with her bag of samples. Standing here in his hall, meek and composed, she looked as respectable as any one of his neighbours. Those inquisitive matrons with their sharp eyes. God help him if they'd watched her approach, glimpsed the dark skin beneath the veil.

They'd soon waylay Cara: that nigger a friend of yours? Got herself up as quite the lady, hadn't she?

Tossed-back veil dewy with rain. Her features arranged to look soft and concerned. She said: I felt I must come, as quickly as I could. As you asked me to.

He'd got back late last night chilled to the bone and very upset. He'd drunk a glass of brandy to calm down, had fallen asleep over the fire's embers. Cara had prodded him awake and he'd stumbled upstairs.

Well, lady, so what can you do for me, hey? He swallowed the words back. Let her reveal her hand first.

Raindrops glistened on Mrs Dulcimer's woollen shoulders. How tidy she looked, in all her blacks; demure as a missionary's new convert. Did she feel nervous, crossing the river, coming north, arriving in a distant, strange neighbourhood? No longer the mistress of her own household but some kind of supplicant. Had she come to plead with him on Doll's behalf? To offer him a bribe? Unnecessary. What he needed was simply an informant, and very likely she'd fit the bill.

She pointed to the carpet-bag, slumped like a dog on the mat. Skin of bristling purple velour. Twisted fangs of brass. Your coat, she said: here it is. I decided to return it to you myself. I certainly couldn't trust that foolish girl.

No doubt about it: makeup, subtly applied, added drama to a woman's face. Mrs Dulcimer's kohl-encircled eyes and blue-shadowed eyelids made her positively alluring. In a flashy kind of way. She had painted her big, plump mouth a soft rose. Her brown cheeks glowed. The cold outside or a skilfully applied smudge of rouge?

She said: the silly child took it to the local pawnbroker's. All I had to do was go and redeem it. As soon as I got up. As soon as the shop was open. I was busy at home all this afternoon. I came here, I assure you, as soon as I could.

Where did she sleep? A boudoir, opening off her sitting-room, hung with swathes of scarlet brocade. A wide bed with a padded velvet headboard edged with gilt curlicues. Blue silk sheets, rumpled and tumbled like the waves of a summer sea. Her glistening black hair, coming loose from its night-time plait, curling across the pillows. Lace at the low neck of her nightgown. Warmth inside the sheets, the smell of her warm body.

He said: so where is she now?

She raised her brows. Doll? Safe at home, locked in the kitchen, crying her eyes out. I scolded her, of course.

Was that all? Doll should have been punished. Punished how? When Milly disobeyed him, or answered back, he couldn't bear that she had to be so difficult, couldn't just acknowledge his concern for her. He felt forced to send her to her room. She'd stick her nose in the air, stalk upstairs. Solitary confinement just meant more time for lying on her bed reading.

Mrs Dulcimer said: I can see from the look on your face you think I should have thrown her out. But I couldn't do that. Much too cruel. Doll's come to me only recently. She's had a sad history. But she's learning to behave. I'm seeing to it.

She bent down and twisted open the bag's clasp. She ripped open a brown-paper wrapping; lifted and shook out his coat. She held it up it with one black-gloved hand, and knocked it with the other, getting rid of the creases. He suddenly felt sorry for the coat, being smacked. It hadn't done anything wrong. It had got carried away, that was all. Not its fault.

Mrs Dulcimer said: the money's still there, in the inside pocket.

His face must have shown his surprise, his suspicion. She put out a gloved hand, as though she wanted to pat his arm, then quickly drew it back, turned it to and fro, as though inspecting the ruching at the wrist of her glove. She said: you can feel that they're banknotes, through the cloth. They've a particular crispness and crackle. Doll didn't notice, but I did. Please don't worry. The pocket's intact. The stitches haven't been tampered with. You can trust me.

Nathalie had given him the coat as a birthday present, six months before she died. Second-hand, obviously, but looking brand-new after her steaming and pressing. She'd filled the pockets with extra gifts. Small, ridiculous things, such as she knew he'd enjoy. A bag of liquorice sweets. A stick of sealing-wax. A blue cotton handkerchief. A watch-fob. Part of their game that morning had been his tearing open the stitched-up pockets, one by one, extracting the treasures, kissing her for each revelation. That night, in their bedroom, naked under the coat, she'd strolled up and down before him, lifting her hands to unloosen her hair, unleashing that torrent of brown curls, smiling at him over her shoulder, and he'd unbuttoned her, very slowly. Some time after she died, he placed the banknotes in the inside pocket, over his heart. The money he'd have spent on taking Nathalie and the child to France, to show the baby to her grandparents. He got his mother to stitch up the pocket again. A kind of little cloth tomb. Don't tell Cara, Ma. It'd only upset her more. His mother had winked at him. It's our secret.

Mrs Dulcimer smiled at him. A real smile, eye-crinkling, full of warmth. She sounded so eager; like a child wanting him to praise her for good behaviour.

Trust you? Joseph asked: how do I know I can do that?

She bit her lip. She smoothed the backs of her gloves, pulled the cloak around her. Every bit of her swaddled in black, only her face showing. Those dark eyes.

Just count the notes, she said: and then you'll know, won't you?

If she'd been a lady, he'd have apologised for doubting her word. But in fact she hadn't tricked him, had she? She'd redeemed the coat, brought it back to him. Honour among thieves. He wasn't a thief. Nor was she. Doll the maid was the culprit in this case.

He said: thank you. I'm much obliged to you.

Mrs Dulcimer drew her veil back down and fastened it under her chin. She pulled up her hood. She said: I must go. Like you last night, I've a cab waiting.

How neat she looked, her gloves buttoned tightly, the tips of her glossy boots showing beneath her black hem. She nodded at him, stepped towards the door. As she passed him with a rustle of skirts he caught a hint of her rose scent. It drifted close to his face, stroked his cheek.

He shut the door behind her and went slowly back downstairs, sliding his hands over the banisters. They ran smoothly under his open palms. Just as he re-entered the dining-room he remembered that he hadn't given the woman back her tweed cloak.

Why not tomorrow? He was bound for Walworth, in any case, to continue his research. He could drop in to Apricot Place after his weekly visit to the cemetery up in Highgate. Wrap up the cloak, take it with him along with the potted cactus, his gardening tools. Miniature fork and trowel stood ready on the tin tray at the bottom of the hallstand, ready to be slipped into the deep side pocket of his coat. Easy to carry a brown-paper parcel as well. Nathalie waited for him in Highgate. She wore a cloak too; not of tweed but of earth.

FOUR

Madeleine

DAWN LIGHT PAINTS THE bedroom walls a creamy grey. The closed white curtains make a soft screen. Like the one Rose-next-door and her artist friends hung up for the shadow-puppet play they put on last weekend in the community house along the street. Flat black profiles jerked back and forth. Jesus, a robed figure with jutting hair and beard, seated himself, raised his hand, forefinger pointing like a teacher's. The silhouette of a woman pushed in: Mary Magdalene; ripple of her flowing curls and cloak. Her limbs hinged; she kneeled before the Lord. Her hand dipped at her pot of ointment: she anointed the Saviour's feet.

Rose got Madeleine involved in the project over supper in Sally's kitchen: you write us an Easter story, and we'll do the rest. They were chopping parsley, mashing garlic, while Sally stirred sliced onions into hot oil. Madeleine said: heretic's version, OK? Rose lifted an eyebrow: no fancy words, thanks. Madeleine said: my grandmother Nelly called that swallowing the dictionary. Sally smiled at Madeleine: don't take no heed of Rose.

Madeleine began grating Cheddar. She said: Nelly was born near here, did I tell you? On the Old Kent Road.

She used to go shopping with her mother in East Street market.

Sally banged her wooden spoon: the Lane, Madeleine, it's called the Lane.

Still in her dressing-gown Madeleine stands at the open back door, drinks her breakfast coffee, eyes the pink-flowered hellebores at the top of the area steps. With the puppet play over, she feels restless. She needs another project outside paid work, something besides her recently taken job making cakes and sandwiches at the café on Walworth Road. But what?

Shelve the problem by going out. Thursday today. Maundy Thursday. Why not call it the start of the Easter holidays, go to the pub tonight?

Soon after moving in nine months ago, she began poking her nose into various locals. Mainly on her own: her north London friends don't want to cross the river just to get a drink. Toby's new post as a chef for a catering company keeps him busy most evenings. See you Sunday, maybe. Once or twice Madeleine has invited Sally. Always the same response: I don't go to pubs. I have a drink at home sometimes. If I'm in the mood.

Toby has pointed her towards the Adam and Eve, near Kennington: not yet a gastro-pub so you're safe.

Old wooden frontage; on a corner; properly full. The blue doors pump open and shut, the pub a body breathing in and out, the punters its air. One older one, blotchy-skinned, dyed red hair white at the roots, leaning on an elbow crutch, limps in and out to use the facilities in the Ladies, leaving her dog and wheelie bag outside at her accustomed perch, a bench near the kerb. The bar staff, a rota of kind young Poles, nod her through. Here you can make a drink last as long as you want. You can pick up a paper from the bar and read it. No one bothers you.

Thursday afternoons Madeleine's shift at the café stops at four. Back at home she decides on an hour's gardening out the back. Moving in here last year, sad to see the garden paved over like a garage forecourt, she heaved up its stone lid that squashed all green life, planted cheap shrubs lugged home from the stall on East Street, cuttings given by friends. Rose, needing to earn some extra cash, gave her a hand with the paving stones. For lunch they ate egg and cress sandwiches, sitting on the back step, and Rose showed Madeleine her photographs of the white-painted ghost bicycles, festooned with bouquets, marking fatal accident sites, that have begun appearing on local streets. Memorials put up by the dead bikers' friends.

Today Madeleine digs over a little waste patch to make a herb plot. Along with weeds she forks up tiny shards of bone, broken buttons, strips of what look like leather or cartilage. Garden treasure: not quite rubbish. What to do with it? Keep it for the moment. Sort it out later.

She tips this debris onto a folded newspaper, pours it into the turquoise pot she inherited from Nelly, patterned with sprigs of cherry blossom, dragons with curled tails. Nelly pointed out to her granddaughter the stubs of broken handles: that's why Mother got it cheap. That man on the stall down the Lane, he knew she liked nice things, he'd keep them for her, bring them out on Sunday mornings when we went there early. Then when I got married she gave it to me.

Where to stow her garden loot? Too much stuff already in this small flat. Finally Madeleine puts the pot on the shelf above the fridge and water tank, hiding in the hallway alcove behind a long lace curtain. She draws the curtain back across, goes to have a quick shower.

Hot water sprays her shoulders, her back. Flesh turned to a scented stream of warmth. Self melts.

A crash outside the bathroom. She jumps, wet soles sliding on slippery enamel, almost falls. Did she leave the back door open? Has it slammed in a gust of wind? Wrapped in a towel she goes to check. The back door is securely locked, just as she left it when she came in from gardening.

A noise from the basement flat next door, perhaps. Or from the flat upstairs.

She dons a knee-length grey pencil skirt, a skimpy grey leather jacket bought from the market stall selling designer samples with the labels ripped out. She picks up the hand mirror she inherited from Nelly, scratched glass in an oval frame of dark wood, and Nelly's gilt-backed hairbrush. Nelly was so poor when she died that she had scarcely anything else to leave. The turquoise pot. Her blue paisley headscarf. Madeleine's mother said to her daughter: go on, you have those little bits, I don't need them.

In the shadowy bedroom Madeleine's reflection swims hazily in the mirror. Her face gleams, much darker than usual, her eyes shine liquidly, almost brown, under arched eyebrows. Unnerving; as though someone else altogether looks back at her. She switches on the light. The image dissolves, re-forms. Her daily self reappears.

She puts up her hair, catches it with combs, dashes on red lipstick, pulls on her suede ankle boots, winds her red lace and linen scarf around her neck. Off she strolls. She bumps into Rose, togged up in a skimpy lime-green tweed jacket, short flared flowered skirt, thick-soled suede shoes. Brothel-creepers, Madeleine says: are they still called that? Rose cocks an eye: the Adam and Eve? What you want to be going there for? Madeleine says: you working tonight? Come with me, why don't you? Rose shakes her head. I'm working fewer nights now.

I'm doing my A-levels at evening classes. She jogs away: art homework to do! A few yards further on Madeleine meets Sally, pushchair piled with shopping: where're you off to, babe, all dolled up?

Through the council estate built round the grassed-over humps of the bombsites, past the parade of shops set back on a concrete plaza. Older blocks, high-rises chucked up in the sixties, loom behind. She crosses the main road stinking with exhaust fumes, dodges the bicycles skimming between lorries and buses, cuts through alleys, reaches the pub, just as the daylight begins to dim and the sun's warmth to ebb.

Fresh tobacco scent tickles her nose. On the narrow pavement, overcoated people pack in around small iron tables set with ashtrays. Grey smoke wreathes above the huddled groups.

Madeleine pushes open the door. The heat of pressed-together bodies flows at her, light from gold globes of lamps, a chime of voices. Drinkers throng the benches, stand at the bar, the mirror behind it garlanded with red plastic apples. She nudges in, people's arms and shoulders rub hers, so intimate, like getting into bed with a crowd of strangers. The same feeling as going to the cinema by herself. Wriggle her way along the row of knees, sit in the midst of a pack of unknown people in the dark, all of them held close in the hush and thrill of the start of the film.

She dives into a space at the end of a table, secures it with her bronze satin bag, throws her scarf down on the facing bench. She fetches herself a glass of red wine, settles back with it, opens her book.

She sips, half-closing her eyes. Ah, this first hit of the night. She learned to like wine on that exchange trip to Paris when she was thirteen. The father of the family kept pouring her more. We'll make a Frenchwoman of you yet! Madame thinned her lips and studied the silky pink wallpaper patterned with green-grey herons. White tablecloth set with white porcelain dishes, silver-plate serving spoons, black-handled knives. The nuns had made a mistake, said Madame's frown, her pure white hands throttling her table napkin: she'd been expecting someone more *comme il faut*, with proper manners and *convenable* clothes.

The wine soothed Madeleine's anxiety to get it right, see Madame smile. Half a glass of Chablis to accompany the creamed spinach crowned with poached eggs. Half a glass of Côtes-du-Rhône-Villages with the slice of bloody meat, with the wrinkled, oozing cheese. Monsieur's cheeks flushed crimson; his smell of eau de cologne. One Sunday afternoon he took her for a walk around the neighbourhood, pointed beyond the boulevard to the high walls shutting off what he said were nineteenth-century hospitals. Run by nuns, that one. Nuns founded the nursing profession, did you know that? Your Miss Nightingale worked there for a while, learning how to become a nurse. And that hospital there cared for mad people, hence the high gates. That's where they put all the bad girls who misbehaved!

This seat taken?

Green eyes in an enquiring, friendly face. Brown-grey crewcut. Deep-chested body stooping towards her. She shrugs. No, help yourself. He sinks down, lifts his pint, nods his thanks. He swigs his beer, catches her glance. He tilts his head sideways, reads out the title on the spine of her book: *La Cuisine Familiale*. Are you French? You look as though you could be.

Madeleine says: I think my mother would have liked to be French. She loved France. She taught elocution at the local convent school. A French Order. So we did lots of French dishes in Domestic Science.

The man rests on the bench, letting his wide shoulders drop. He listens, drinking his beer, nodding at her to go on. Madeleine strokes the stem of her glass. She says: when Mum died last winter, I inherited her cookery books. They're very old-fashioned, but some of the recipes are classics. Potage Bonne Femme, for example.

Good Woman Soup. The café's home-delivery customers don't care about Madeleine's dishes' French names. They just relish her turning up on the café's sturdy black bicycle and bringing lunch. She packs the foil boxes on the rack behind her saddle. People's names and addresses written on the lids. Heat the food in the microwave and serve up.

People recommend the delivery service to each other, or their relatives drop in to organise it. Some clients don't qualify for meals arranged by social services. Others just can't be bothered to cook. And then the ones who need the little extras, their hands held for ten minutes, their story listened to, Madeleine can give them that too.

One or two of the older gents loll with their flies open, when she arrives, offer her tips for a fondle, so lonely they are, and she shakes her head at them, gets them to zip up. Ah, Madeleine, don't be so unkind.

The newcomer lolls at Madeleine's side, taking pulls at his pint. His black jacket, finely ribbed corduroy, looks old and soft. The Monsieur in Paris wore a dark jacket on Sundays. Late-morning he would trot back from the patisserie, a beribboned box dangled by its shiny loop from his forefinger. After the grated carrots with vinaigrette, the roast veal and green salad, the cheese, the family wielded little silver forks, dug into rhum babas, coffee-cream eclairs. You had to choose one or the other. Madeleine wanted both. The Monsieur shook his head at her. *Petite gourmande.* Madame added: you must not get fat.

Madeleine says: my mother loved everything French. So she gave me a French name. Madeleine.

The man says: that's a cake, isn't it?

Madeleine says: some people say the cake's named after Mary Magdalene, the disciple of Jesus, and her cockle-shell-shaped boat. According to the legend, after the death of Jesus she sailed from the Holy Land to Provence. Other people say it's named after the first cook to make it, back in the seventeenth century. I like the Mary Magdalene derivation, myself.

She can hear Toby teasing her. Mrs Teacher! That cry from the playground: clever dick! Show off! She bends her head over her glass, finishes her wine.

The man says: Ah. I see. Mary Magdalene. Yes, a fine saint. Loyal, faithful. She stuck by Jesus when his other followers ran away.

He pauses. Gives her a wry look. My name's Emm. He glances at her again. Emm's short for Emmanuel.

One of the names for Jesus. Bit of a burden, that moniker, surely? No wonder he's shortened it.

Emm traces a forefinger through a puddle of beer then puts his hands flat on the scratched tabletop and stares at them, as though puzzled by his sturdy fingers, his clean nails. His white cuffs protrude unevenly from the black sleeves of his jacket, and she wants to pull them straight, pat them into place over his wrists.

His eyes shine green. He nods at their empty glasses: what are you having?

He plunges into the crowd. Madeleine studies a paragraph about various kinds of small cakes. For financiers you combine stiffly whipped egg whites with melted butter, sugar, ground almonds and flour. Do bankers in the

Bourse in Paris particularly relish financiers? Monsieur brought them home occasionally. He nibbled their crisp edges. He dabbed his lips with a silky white square.

Emm returns from the boil and hubbub of the bar, bearing their drinks, sits down opposite her again. He tilts his glass to his mouth. That's better. What a day. So intense.

He tells her about the counselling conference he's been attending at Westminster Hall. His green eyes snap. Outreach services planned to the inner city, beginning with the poorest parts of south-east London. Tomorrow, Good Friday, he returns to his parishioners in Surrey. He describes a 1930s vicarage with lawn and rosebeds. In a small nineteenth-century church with a leaking roof he preaches the love of God, leads his Anglican congregation in hymns. I'm retiring this year. This'll be my last Easter. But I'm going to continue my voluntary work, this mission we're planning for people hard hit by the recession. Poverty brings such emotional distress. We want to help with that. As well as offering practical support of course.

Bloody hell. A vicar. Just my luck.

She swirls her wine, sips it. He celebrates Easter. Does he believe that Christ rose from the dead? A literal truth for him, or a symbolic one? She remembers Piero della Francesca's image of the resurrected Christ, which she and William gazed at in Sansepolcro, thirty years back, on their honeymoon. The strong, beautiful man thrusting himself out of the darkness into the light; his muscular arms heaving up the lid of the coffin confining him; forcing his way back into the bright world.

Emm asks: you married? She says: I'm divorced. Ten years back. Emm says: I'm a widower. The community's been wonderful to me. The funeral was a very difficult day. People were unbelievably helpful and kind.

Madeleine says: if you read the mainstream papers, journalists' columns, I mean, you get the impression kindness is a form of stupidity. All that matters is being cynical and ironic. Cool. In control!

She pauses. Drinks more wine. She says: not the journalists' fault, I suppose. They're just reflecting the culture they live in. You're supposed to care only about yourself. Getting ahead. But not everybody's like that.

Emm says: people care a lot about their children. Want the best for them. Most people want to become parents.

Madeleine did once she met William. Night after night they made love: passionate, bawdy, intent, messy, blissful. Practising, William called it. Practising for what? For the next time, the next night.

Emm says: in my job I'm supposed to be kind. Kindness is what people demand of me. Suddenly it was the other way round. Parishioners kept turning up with casseroles. Offering to do my laundry. Weed the garden.

He glances at her. She feels he wants to go on talking about his loss. She wants to savour her wine, not his sorrow, certainly not her own. She queues at the bar, buys them both another drink, then smiles at Emm and picks up her book. He gives her a smile in return, a nod, pulls out a newspaper.

Half an hour later she decides it's time to go home. She bids Emm goodbye. Happy Easter, he says.

The cold air slaps her out of tipsiness. A woken dog whimpers as she passes. His owner's dark shape sags on a bench, her wheelie bag nearby. Where will that woman sleep tonight? Madeleine's boots spring her along. Skirt hitched up above her knees for ease of movement, bag clutched under her arm. Strung amber beads of street lamps. Shadows flicker in front gardens and behind parked cars.

A stitch slows her; she halts, a hand at her side. The wind wraps a cold metallic ribbon around her bare neck. She claps a hand to her shivery flesh.

Behind her someone shouts. She jumps. A male voice stirs the darkness. Madeleine. Wait!

Emm rocks up to her, panting. He holds out a soft droop of material. You left this in the pub.

She winds her scarf around her neck. Instantly it blots the cold. He says: I'll walk with you a while, if I may. Hands shoved into his jacket pockets, he jolts along by her side. She says: but you've hurt your foot, running. I'm so sorry. No, Emm says: I did that at the weekend. Just blisters. I've taken up walking in the countryside, and I'm still breaking in my new boots.

They pass under a row of plane trees, their lopped branches ending in black knobs, clustering fans of leaves. Two-dimensional shapes in the shadowy night. Like cut-outs. Almost abstract. Flat as Rose's shadow puppets that so delighted the children. But Emm, tilting gently along, his arm brushing hers, is not flat. Solid chest under his jacket. His face curved towards hers. The pace of Madeleine's heartbeat suddenly increases. Blood thumps at the back of her throat; in her ears.

They turn into Orchard Street. Red cigarette tips glow in the darkness of the little park, a bottle crashes, some-one swears. They swerve round the jumble of overflowing rubbish bins, between the cracked, drying coils of dog turds. Madeleine waves a hand at the spearhead iron rail-ings marking the corner of Apricot Place: I live along here.

They reach her gate. She halts. Why not take a risk? She says: come in for a glass of wine, if you like. Sorry I haven't any beer.

Clutching the cold handrail she goes ahead of him down into the area, her feet in their flat boots feeling for the edges of the wedge-shaped steps. She fiddles her key into the lock, opens the door.

A dry, woody fragrance rushes out. Brandy. How on earth? Anyone would think she'd been at some cheap cooking tipple, getting drunk, upending the open bottle onto the floor.

She says: can you smell brandy? I don't know where that's come from. I never drink brandy!

Emm breathes in. No, I can't smell it.

She shakes her head, tells herself to forget it. Out of the corner of her eye, as she opens the cupboard, gets out a bottle and glasses, she watches Emm survey the small sitting-room, its dusty, grey-painted floorboards studded with stalacmites of books, its two blue basket chairs with dented cushions, its packed bookshelves, its pictures. A cobweb veils one corner. Madeleine does her housework just before friends are due to visit. Unexpected guests have to accept the presence of apple cores in saucers, drifts of papers, scatters of pens. What Nelly called a heap of tack, Madeleine names lovely mess. If you leave clearing it up as late as possible then you really notice the difference.

Madeleine puts bottle and glasses on the table, which bears a laptop at one end, wedged in between a chipped pink soup tureen, a pile of stencilled yellow soup plates, a big blue willow-pattern bowl, a stack of unironed pillow-cases. Scarlet tulips flare and contort in an orange jug encircled by fallen petals. Emm gives an almost imperceptible shrug.

Madeleine says: I expect you employ a cleaner, don't you? Or do the ladies of the parish fight over whose turn it is to help you?

She's being sharp with him because she suddenly feels shy. She fiddles with her scarf, unwinds it, throws it over the back of a chair.

She says: those bits and pieces were my mother's. Not the laptop, though. Dad died ten years ago, then Mum died this January just gone, six months after I moved here. I couldn't bear to get rid of her stuff all at once, so I kept lots of it. Even the things I don't like.

Emm's green eyes gleam in his creased brown face. So much loss in your life! I'm sorry. Being alone is really tough.

Madeleine starts. I've got plenty of friends, thanks very much. Good neighbours too. The people round here are really friendly. Well, most of them.

The older ones, especially, like to stop for a quick chat. Madeleine greets everyone she meets along her little street. You're my neighbours and so I'll say hello. Some, resentful, mumble at their feet and stride past. Mad bitch invading their space. Others nod and greet her back.

Emm says: I'm sorry. I didn't mean to be patronising. That was clumsy of me.

Out on Walworth Road, anywhere you pause, a stranger may smile at you, crack a joke, complain humorously about this or that. At the bus-stop, at the newsagent's, in the market queues. Passers-by briefly join themselves together: a wry look, a shared grimace at someone's antics, something odd happening, a few words exchanged; then off they swirl again. Moments of human contact: a startle of warmth. Sometimes she meets Rose loping along, foraging for sculpture materials. Eyes darting left and right. A scavenged plank balanced across her shoulders, a couple of old posts under one arm, or the side of a chest of drawers, she's a bird flying on wooden wings, an angel walking on wooden stilts. She's always available for talking. I'm moving out from my nan's, Madeleine. My friend Jerry's squat up near the Elephant, they've got a room come free.

Madeleine says: I feel lucky, living in this neighbour-hood. It's run-down in lots of ways but it's got soul. I love it.

She uncorks the bottle. The waft of brandy has faded. Replaced by the dark tannin smell of the red wine she pours into their glasses.

Emm looks down. I was speaking from my own experi-ence, I suppose. We can all feel vulnerable sometimes. We all have losses to bear, don't we? Some people are open about them, some aren't.

Counselling bromides. Not the right technique for talking to someone you've only just met. A way of keeping a distance; keeping control. Madeleine also wants to keep control. They're circling around each other like fighters, on their toes, fists bunched, weighing each other up.

She tastes the lovely austere red. How can she possibly tell a stranger, however sympathetic, how she feels about her mother's death? That dislocation, the world unhinged, flapping loose, and herself too? Emm obviously means well. Perhaps he's a skilled, helpful counsellor when he's on the job in some impersonal consulting-room. Now, he's just a nice-looking man with a weathered face, green eyes. A concern for people who suffer. A love of weekend walks.

OK, I'll play. Just start the game in a different place. She selects a bright, clipped voice: how's your foot? Why don't you let me have a look at it? A foot massage might help.

Emm's face tightens, then relaxes. She watches him decide to trust the moment, see what it brings. He discards his black jacket, tosses it onto a chair. She dims the light, pulls up a low wooden stool and perches in front of him. She unties his laces, takes off his brogues, unpeels his blue socks. She lifts his foot, the sore one, into her lap. He leans back and closes his eyes. She tips a few drops of

94

rose geranium oil into her hand, starts to stroke, carefully avoiding the reddened skin around the pierced white flap of the empty blister. Her fingertips and palm massage his instep, push over and around the ball of his foot. Gently she pulls at his toes, one by one, easing her finger in between them, searching out the rough, dry patches, feeling the edges of the nails. She touches and kneads in silence, she presses her thumbs into the arch of his foot, and his skin softens under her fingers, and he grunts, and relaxes. She takes up his other foot and repeats the process.

Emm's voice sounds blurry. Wonderful. The pain's completely gone. His eyes flick open: you're a witch.

The room smells of rose geranium. So calm. Just the sound of their breathing in the semi-darkness. Madeleine sits back, puts her palms together, letting the residue of sweet oil sink into her skin.

Emm sits up. What happens next, Mrs Magdalene? I'll have to guess.

She smiles at him. In the Gospel story, after anointing the feet of Jesus she wipes them with her hair. As I'm sure you know perfectly well. But in my version they have supper. I'm hungry. Are you? Would you like to eat something?

At daybreak, she floats and rolls in towards shore on currents of dreams. Light streams in around the edges of the white curtains. She stretches, sits up, yawning. Soft boulders of pillows surround her. She draws back her fist and punches one.

A female voice begins to speak to her. Distinct as the chit-chat of birds beyond the window. Don't take on so. Don't fret. Come on, duck, get up. Time for breakfast. Hot cross buns? Why not? Although those nuns at your school believed in fasting on Good Friday, didn't they? A bit of fish for your dinner and that was that.

Her grandmother Nelly. Warmth rushes through Madeleine. But Nelly's been dead for over thirty years. Once as close as this quilt, and as comforting. That astonishing gift she gave the child: taking her seriously, bothering with her. Ticking her off, teasing her, chatting to her.

A little bit of what you fancy does you good, Nelly says: and enough is as good as a feast.

Madeleine says: whether there's anything to eat for breakfast is a matter for conjecture.

Last night, she served Emm and herself their food by candlelight. She cleared a space on the end of the table, flung on a cloth. They wolfed the mushroom soup she'd left ready for her return from the pub. They sat back, drinking wine, talking about walks they'd taken: the Ridgeway, the Gower peninsula. They mopped their plates with the end of the loaf, polished off the cheese. Emm said: thank you for your hospitality. But I mustn't intrude any longer. I must be off to my hotel. It's not very far from here. I'll walk.

Madeleine scoops up her green linen dressing-gown, lying across the end of her bed, dons it. She darts bare-foot, soles flinching across the gritty lino, into the kitchen to make coffee. Waiting for it to bubble up, she tucks her arms inside her thin sleeves. Garment green as the vest-ment worn by the parish priest in her childhood when he said Mass on weekdays. On special joyful Sundays, such as Easter, he wore white.

Shivering in the pale yellow light seeping around the edges of the white calico blind and scalloping the fall of its cord strung with plastic pearls, she runs her eyes over the open shelves, looking for biscuits, for Ryvita, for anything at all. She's got flour, butter, sugar, lemon, eggs. Very well then. Whisk up some madeleines. She'll eat a couple for breakfast once they're done, take the rest into work. Display them on the tiered glass cakestand on the café counter.

Ten minutes beating everything together, dripping melted butter onto the mixture, folding it in, and the tray slides into the oven. She opens the back door, treads up the four steps. Sunlight fills the courtyard garden. Clutching her cup of coffee she bends to check the nasturtium and sweet pea seedlings, the green tendrils of jasmine and honeysuckle. The lilies of the valley poke up their pale snouts, and the roses and daisies are in bud, glittering with dew.

Cool air on her face and throat. She can have breakfast outside, if she wraps up warm enough. Will Emm, in a few hours' time, be preparing for the Good Friday ritual? In her childhood that meant the church shrouded in darkness. No flowers or candles. The priest chanting Christ's reproaches from the cross: my people, what have you done to me, answer me.

What sort of service will Emm lead? High or Low? What will he wear?

Preparing to leave, he got up from the table, looked about for his black jacket. He smiled at her. His green eyes gleamed, as though they held tears. You're so nice. I wish I could stay longer, get to know you better.

He hesitated. Madeleine sat still. He tugged the black sleeves up over his arms. Fished in his jacket pocket, brought out a wallet, a phone. Hesitated again.

He blurted: but do you do this a lot? Leaving your scarf in the pub like that, a bit obvious, wasn't it? And d'you offer a massage to all the men you bring home?

He was fingering his wallet, preparing to open it. Madeleine blinked. She said: d'you want me to charge you for services rendered, then? So that I can turn into a repented prostitute, and you can convert me! Is that it? You Jesus me Mary Magdalene. You really are a stickler for that story, aren't you!

Emm stiffened. That's not fair. That's unkind. I wanted to show you the photo of my wife I keep in my wallet, that's all. Don't be so defensive. I'm not reproaching you for anything.

Madeleine muttered: yes, you are.

Emm said: no. Not at all. Please don't be upset. I'm really sorry. I think you're a lovely person. So free! My wife has … had, I mean … fair hair too, long and curly, rather like yours.

Madeleine said: why are you talking about your wife? What d'you mean, your wife has long curly hair?

Emm wrinkled his mouth in a sad smile. He opened his phone. Will you give me your number? I'd really like to see you again. If I may.

Tears of wax dripped down the candles. The room smelled warmly of soup. Their empty bowls, butter-smeared plates, stood on the table. Bread crusts, rinds of cheese.

Madeleine got to her feet, folded her arms. She's not dead at all, is she? You made that up.

Emm bent his head. His voice cracked. She may as well be dead. I've left her. We were very unhappy together. We're separated.

His mouth had greasy crumbs at the corners. The Monsieur in Paris, that fastidious man, had lifted a napkin to his lips. Emm hadn't bothered to wipe his. Disgusting. Like encountering loops of slimy milk skin when you drank your cup of coffee. You recoiled; involuntarily spat.

Madeleine said: I certainly don't want to see you again. You lied to me. You can have a dozen wives for all I care. But you shouldn't tell lies.

Emm's face hardened. You're very happy, taking the moral high ground, aren't you? You like being in the right, don't you? Real life's not that clear-cut. Haven't you ever found life complicated, difficult?

Madeleine moved towards the hall doorway. She kept her voice calm. She said: going out with married men is not a good idea. I did that often enough, when I was young, to have learned better.

Emm seemed to bunch, to become all muscle. But we were making friends. How can you be so unfair? Let me explain.

Madeleine said: you don't need to. You'll probably go back to your wife, see if you don't. That's what usually happens.

He gave a cry, loomed over her, reached for her. She twisted away, ran into the front hall, held open the door. Get out.

Emm pushed past her. You smug, self-righteous bitch!

The fury in his voice knocked her back. He shouldered out into pre-midnight darkness and cold. She banged shut the door, locked it.

Standing in the morning light in the garden, she sighs. Fool.

No, not a fool. Just a woman who misses sex. She didn't stop to think, just rushed ahead she reached out towards Emm yes she did. Oh, Mary Magdalene. In the garden, by the tomb, the risen Jesus says to her: do not touch me. But Madeleine didn't heed his warning, did she? Who was Emm, really? Narrow escape? From what? No idea.

She steps deeper into the green enclosure. Barefoot, hopping across the flat stones set in the green stream of plants. A blackbird sings chink-chink, like the ringing of metal poles when scaffolding falls in the street. A thrush yammers away, hidden in the silver-white bushes behind the spread of pale yellow primroses.

Never say die, says Nelly: plenty more fish in the sea.

The warm, buttery smell of baking, hot sugar, entices Madeleine back indoors, to check on the cakes rising in the oven.

FIVE

Joseph

H IGHGATE CEMETERY LAY TIDY and calm in
cloudy autumn light, paths weeded, fallen leaves
raked into heaps. Graves in rows; beds in a green dormitory. Only the Last Trump would waken these sleepers.
Did Joseph believe that? The lid of this garden whistling
up and the dead flying out, restored, perfected? White
shrouds fluttering and swirling in the crisp air.

As usual, he read the inscription he had had chiselled
into the stone. Nathalie Benson – beloved wife. Departed,
but never forgotten. His mother's and stepfather's grave-
stones alongside simply bore their names and dates. His
mother deserved a bit of poetry but he had run out of
money.

Overhead, trees tousled their branches together, the wind
shaking them sounding like rushing water. Nobody was
about, nobody watching him. He put down the parcel and
the cactus that he carried, kneeled, leaned forwards, propping
himself on his hands, and kissed Nathalie's covering earth.
He wanted it to hold the taste of her mouth. He wanted to
lay his face flat against the ground and press his ear to it. To
hear her singing among the worms, defying them.

She roamed the underworld. Some kind of topsy-
turvy heaven. Did he believe in heaven? He wanted to.

A place where no one suffered. If Nathalie lived there now, at least she was free from the burdening flesh; his airy, cloud-skimming spirit. Try to believe that. No longer in pain. Milly, swelling and kicking, had tethered her to earth. The umbilical cord cut, Nathalie had soared away. She'd never grow old. Never get slack-bellied, wrinkled, coarse. She remained exquisite.

From his coat pocket he took out a small trowel and fork, a pair of garden scissors. He cleared away the withered stalks and leaves of the chrysanthemums he had left last time. He tore up the green and yellow ivy that had appeared from nowhere, tugged out the white roots of the bindweed, threw them into the bushes. He wedged the cactus pot into the tin vase at the base of the headstone. He rubbed off the traces of moss that threatened to blur the grooves of the lettering.

All around him stood figures leaning against headstones. Long-haired women clasping urns or harps, cherub-children stretching out their arms, angels perching on earth just for a moment before darting heavenwards again. Nathalie was one of those angels.

The sun came out; flashing patterns of light and shadow that waved and blinked over him, making him part of itself, the sky transforming itself to sea, flowing over his shoulders like blue water. Splashing him. A blessing.

Blue streams. Something blue wavered on the path a few yards away, shook him back into awareness of the green spot where he knelt, stroking the letters spelling his wife's name. Another mourner? Joseph reared up, not wanting anyone to observe him. In the dazzle of sun the blue fragment dissolved, re-composed itself. Blue lace-cap flowers blowing on a hydrangea bush. A woman dressed in a flowing lavender-coloured skirt, which swirled about her as she turned and looked in his direction. Her face in deep shadow. Bonnetless. No gloves. Curly fair hair twisted up on top of her head.

He said: Nathalie?

Could it be? He tried not to move, lest he disturb her, frighten her away. The sun went on flickering on the dancing green leaves of the bushes and the woman shimmered in the light. The brightness made his eyes water. He shut them, mopped them with his handkerchief. When he opened his eyes again the woman had disappeared.

Of course it hadn't been Nathalie. Impossible. Anyway, he didn't believe in ghosts. He was a rational man with a living to earn. He shoved his gardening implements back into his coat pockets and made towards the cemetery gates. He'd tidy up his parents' grave another time.

He descended the hill to Camden Town, climbed aboard an omnibus heading south. Muddy, damp straw underfoot. Huddling his shoulders round to avoid touching the overcoat of the man seated next to him, who stank of stale tobacco and days-old sweat, he scanned the list of questions he'd scribbled. Too pompous and rigorous. How those girls had sniggered at him yesterday when he'd enquired about their means of earning a living.

Better by far just to chat to these streetwalkers; see what came up. Get help where and when he needed it. Starting with Mrs Dulcimer.

In the light of morning, Apricot Place looked almost rawly modern: clean neatly pointed brickwork; miniature evergreens in pots in the front areas. Someone had swept the pavement and steps outside Mrs Dulcimer's house. The front door shone buttercup yellow, the brass doorknocker gleamed. A different maid let him in, a heavily pregnant, scrawny girl with mousy hair and jutting, shiny cheekbones, a wide mouth. Where was the thieving Doll? Hiding in the kitchen, perhaps. Or packed off back home.

This one was an awkward little skivvy all right. So what's your name, then? She twisted her red fists in her apron and mumbled. Betsy, sir.

Joseph held his parcel in one hand and took off his hat with the other. Your mistress in? The girl hesitated. I don't know. It's early for callers, sir. He waved her aside. No need to show me up. I know the way.

Light fell towards him in dusty shafts from the casement on the landing. On the window seat stood a pair of women's boots in pale brown canvas, their white ankle buttons splashed with dirt and streaks of something red. He bent closer. Had Mrs Dulcimer been out to the butcher's already, this early in the morning? Or perhaps she'd trodden on some runover creature, squashed under a carter's wheels. These south London streets swirled with vermin: stray dogs; foxes; feral cats. Just before turning into Apricot Place he'd paused on the main road to watch two terriers fighting over a rat, its dark coat sleeked flat with grease, one gripping it by the back legs and the other by the head. They tore it apart, a mess of purple clots, then shot off in opposite directions, jaws clamping the gobbets of bloody flesh.

He knocked at the sitting-room door. After a moment, Mrs Dulcimer's voice bade him enter.

The curtains parted and pulled back, the blinds up, faint yellow sunshine flowed in, sharp as lemon juice. A fire burned in the grate, Mrs Dulcimer's chair set close to it. She was older than he had first supposed. Easily fifty, in this light. Creases around her dark eyes, fine lines on her brown throat. She hadn't yet put up her hair: her black locks coiled in two curly braids over her shoulders. She was wearing a robe of thin blue wool, made high at the neck, the sleeves turned back over her slender wrists and the bodice tied with a twisted blue cord, and she was holding a newspaper. She glanced at him coolly, said nothing.

Why didn't she smile? Last night, delivering his coat, she'd acted the supplicant, reaching out to him. Now she'd withdrawn, into this powerful silence. She was the hostess: she ought to speak first. She ought to make him feel welcome, particularly as he had brought back her wretched cloak, sweating across town with it on a cold morning, plodding down from the common through half a mile of mud to reach her house.

He searched for politeness. I'm sorry. I should have let you know I planned to call on you.

She glanced at the tray on the little table drawn up next to her chair. A blue coffee-pot patterned with yellow flecks, a matching cup, a dish of butter curls, a pot of yellow jam. An empty toast rack stood next to a basket of rolls. Toast crumbs scattered a plate.

She folded her newspaper, making a fat little packet of black print. She said: your convenience does not match mine. You should have thought of that before just turning up and assuming I'd be available. When in fact, as you see, I am still at breakfast.

He felt like a schoolboy, a grubby ten-year-old scolded for forgetting a point of grammar. A detail of manners. Stand when your teacher enters the room and don't answer back. None of your cheek, you ignoramus!

He said: you should train your maid better, madam. She let me come up!

She considered this. I wouldn't say she's my maid, exactly.

Fur-edged low-heeled mules, with pointed toes, clung to her slim feet. Bare brown ankles. Blue woollen folds sweeping over her knees. Her soft shape. No corset, surely. Under that blue gown was she naked?

The scene spun before him, the radiant pattern made by a kaleidoscope. A long-stemmed silver jam spoon. Small bone-handled knife. Puddle of apricot jam, a brown fruit-pit nestling in the fringing gold flesh. The lace-edged white cloth covering the table. A vase of orange-speckled pink lilies. An open book, bound in half-calf, lying next to it, the pages weighed down with a fat dimple of green glass. Her glistening black hair, those childish pigtails tied with blue ribbon. The newspaper, which she was tossing to the floor.

She said: now you're here, why not pull up a chair and sit down?

He held out the parcel containing the tweed cloak. Your property, ma'am. You forgot it last night.

Mrs Dulcimer shrugged. She pointed to the half-moon table bearing the vase of lilies. Put it there, would you?

The fresh smell of her coffee lingered. She'd had a light, delicious breakfast. Hard, dewy butter, obviously straight from an earthenware cooler, not melting and oily, as so often at home. Rolls smelling new-baked. Why couldn't Milly learn to make bread instead of pestering him to allow her to attend nursing classes? Why won't you let me? Because they don't exist, my sweetest girl! Milly had glared at him. In France they do. Grandmère said so, in her last letter. I asked her to find out for me. The Sisters of Charity run them, at their hospital in Paris. I could go there! I could learn nursing!

Don't think of Milly here. He stared at the turquoise pot on the mantelpiece. The conviction rose inside his mind: Mrs Dulcimer is an artful, conspiring, corrupted wretch. No: that was what he'd imagined on his visit two days ago, watching her study the sturdy container. Its glossy surface had caught his thoughts, held them, and now gave them back to him. It was alive. A sort of idol, squatting there, round-bellied, grinning at him.

Mrs Dulcimer plucked her napkin from her lap and leaned over the tray, folded the little square of linen on top of the bread basket. Here, then, as at home, a napkin did service for several meals. Mrs Dulcimer, for all her tinselly ornaments, was probably in need of money. Indeed, the daylight showed up the carpet's faded red and blue, its bald patches only half-hidden by the little gilt chairs placed over them. The pink-and-blue-striped curtains had the sheen of cheap silk. Mrs Dulcimer's blue robe looked quality enough, though not perfectly clean. As though she'd worn it for a month. It would smell of her. Perspiration mixed with the scent of lilies. The robe had fallen open a little way, as she stooped, revealing her throat, the edge of a frilled white chemise. Ah, so she wasn't completely naked, after all.

The turquoise pot leered at him. If his thoughts could stay behind in the room when he left it, attached to objects, to ornaments, then they no longer belonged to him. They flew about, like pet canaries released from a cage. They hid, like nightingales in a thicket. When she and Cara were growing up in Boulogne, Nathalie told him once, pacing arm in arm with him along the riverbank at Richmond, they'd linger late in the little local park on summer nights, first to hear the nightingales sing, and then to hear their mother calling them home: *méchantes filles méchantes filles!* The sensible, practical mother had encouraged their quest to find work in London. Plenty of rich English people travelled to Boulogne for summer holidays, hired French nursemaids for their children, took the maids home with them. The mother had blessed her daughters' departure: good luck in the country of the *rosbifs!*

Joseph said: I don't know why, exactly, but I could fancy myself in France. Your breakfast, I suppose. Not so much as a boiled egg you get given over there, I've been told. They like sweet things. Brioches and that.

On Sundays, Nathalie had served French breakfasts, bread and butter and coffee, using the coffee-service he'd bought her as a wedding-present, knocked down cheap because it lacked a sugar-basin. She'd dip her bread into her cup and hold it to his mouth, so that he gulped hot buttered aromatics.

Mrs Dulcimer folded her hands. Still a good-looking woman. Those egg-shaped cheeks. Those deep-set eyes, those black eyelashes. She said: I spent some of my youth in France. They have their own customs. No better or worse than here, but different, certainly.

He said: you have travelled abroad?

He and Cara had once got as far as the coast, when his parents had rented rooms in Herne Bay one July; before his stepfather died. They took Milly, and Alfred, the toddling baby, Cara's firstborn, down with them, to stay with the old people for a few days, feast on oysters. He and Cara collected wild flowers on cliff rambles, shells and dead starfish along the beach, netted butterflies on walks inland. Milly organised paddling, the building of sandcastles. Back in London she helped Cara lift the dead blooms from the press and stick them into the album, wire the sea treasures onto a shallow wooden tray, pin the butterflies to a board.

Mrs Dulcimer said: I worked in Paris for a while, after I met my husband. We ran a little hotel. Much liked by English travellers, because we spoke their language.

Nathalie and Cara were the first Frenchwomen Joseph had ever met. Not at all the painted houris of popular repute. Just two nursemaids, nicely turned out in indigo frocks, plain straw bonnets, taking their charges for an airing in Hyde Park. They had paused to buy milk from the old woman who milked the cow tethered by one of the main paths. She glowered as he drifted up, drawn by the charming picture of the children holding out their pale-blue china mugs produced from Nathalie's basket. My cups not good enough for you, young madam, I suppose? Nathalie lifted her brows: we don't like to drink from tin, and they don't look so clean. The milk-seller rattled them back into the bowl of washing-up water underneath the stand, settled herself on her stool, bucket at her feet, drew on the cow's teats. The children gazed, round-eyed, at the foaming pail. In Nathalie's clear, direct glance Joseph was reborn. A small, delicately made woman. Glossy brown hair twining under her bonnet-brim. Slim waist and tiny feet.

He saw immediately he'd have to take on her older sister too, in order to spend time with the young one she guarded and obviously adored. So from the start he included Cara in his conversation, paid her compliments, invited her to accompany him and Nathalie on their brief, illicit walks. From time to time he and Nathalie escaped Cara's vigilance. Boating on the river, that afternoon at Richmond, mooring under a willow tree, kissing under the tickling green fronds.

Mrs Dulcimer said: I liked France, but I missed London. So when my husband died, I decided to return to England and try something similar here. A boarding-house, I mean.

Joseph said: you have no family of your own to help you? No one at all?

She confirmed: no one.

She turned her head aside. She sighed out the words. That last cholera epidemic. Here, on this side of the river, it was especially bad.

Joseph said: yes! The papers were full of it. A terrible time.

Daily, he knew, he courted danger, wandering through the south London slums. All too easy to pick up an infection, bring it home. All Londoners had to endure living in bad air, but some districts were worse than others. Joseph took the family up to Hampstead as often as possible, made the children run about in the fresh, sweet breezes of the Vale of Health, open their lungs and draw in deep breaths of cleanliness. Hoped that would see them through the week. Then they plunged back down into the odours and overflowing drains of Lamb's Conduit Street.

What had Mrs Dulcimer's husband been like? A black man? Black or white, you had tender skin, which shivered or warmed, which felt the touch of another's hands, yearned for it, or flinched away. He'd not yet touched Mrs Dulcimer. He'd shake hands on leaving. Clasp those black fingers in his own. Surely they'd feel just like any other woman's. But she wasn't like any other woman. She seemed in no hurry whatsoever to get on with her domestic duties, for a start.

Mrs Dulcimer said: returning here, I studied the situation. I saw that many young working women had no families to return to at night, for whatever reason, and stood in considerable moral danger as a result. Particularly when in between jobs as domestic servants. Great numbers of young women in that situation are homeless, Mr Benson, did you know? Often their poverty leaves them little choice but to sell themselves and so earn the money to pay for a bed for the night. I decided to take a small house and run it as lodgings, in which my female tenants could feel safe and secure.

Translating her hints into facts, Joseph grew hot. How could he have so misunderstood the situation? He looked down, to avoid her eyes, and surveyed his trouser knees, green with the grass and moss he'd kneeled on earlier. He covered them with his palms. He said: you mean you're rescuing fallen women?

Black women were not benefactresses, surely. They received charity, rather than dishing it out.

Mrs Dulcimer sat up straight, began to turn down her sleeves, unrolling them to cover the backs of her hands. She pulled them over her fingertips, as though she felt chilly. Black folks disliked the cold particularly, he supposed. Even when they were born in Deptford? He didn't know.

Her voice became brisk, less carefully genteel. I am not rescuing anybody. I do not go about scooping up found-lings, or stray dogs, or strayed girls. My tenants are all either in work or about to be so. You misunderstood the nature of my establishment on your first visit, didn't you? You obviously still do.

A wave of heat rushed up into Joseph's face. Mrs Dulcimer was looking amused. Big dark eyes wide open. One brown foot swinging a slipper. Enjoying herself pointing out his foolishness.

What was she playing at? She could have set him straight, right away, on his first visit. Rather than correct his error, rather than take offence at his misconception, as she ought to have done, she'd gone along with him. Acted being a madam while in fact running a refuge. She had deceived him. What kind of a woman enjoyed such tricks?

He said: so you're a philanthropist, ma'am. You shouldn't have pretended otherwise.

Mrs Dulcimer looked pleased with herself. And no wonder. She'd caught him on the hop, she'd put him firmly in the wrong, so now she paused, and surveyed him, as though she felt sorry for him.

She said: no. Not at all. You still don't understand, do you? I'm just a businesswoman. I provide a service, and expect to be paid. I understand that some of my tenants, in between live-in domestic posts, may fall behind with their rent. I subsidise them for a certain period if necessary, so that they do not feel obliged to leave and find themselves on the street. But they always repay me. That is part of our agreement. Certainly, I help them find jobs if I can. That is one small thing I can do for them.

Joseph said: you are generous, ma'am.

Mrs Dulcimer shook her head. No. The arrangement suits me. I like the company. In the evenings I drink tea with my lodgers, if I'm in the mood. Sometimes I help them write their letters, if need be. Or we play cards, or we read plays together. Shakespeare, for example, is a firm favourite. His cheerful works, at any rate. At the moment we're reading *Much Ado About Nothing*.

A black woman reading Shakespeare! A joke, surely. She read plays? Joseph had never seen a play by Shakespeare. Hardly ever been to the theatre. Once with Nathalie, in the early days, before her pregnancy showed. English music hall hadn't impressed her much. Nothing to compare with French gaieties, it seemed. Still, she'd been pleased to get out. She arranged her hair in a new style, a crown of plaits, walked very gracefully, taking neat steps, her head up, her hands lifting her full skirts. She smiled to herself, obviously pleased with the admiring glances cast her way, demurely pretending not to notice. Joseph relished other men admiring his wife's sparkling eyes half-veiled by her downcast lashes, her rosebud mouth and delicately flushed cheeks, but their appraisal made him uneasy too. He gripped her elbow and steered her along. Just so, as a boy, had he tried to take care of his mother, when they went shopping. Often she'd jerk free: ah, stop your fussing! Leave me be! Nathalie would shake her head at him: I'm not going to fly away!

Mrs Dulcimer continued. And then on Sunday afternoons, in fine weather, we walk in the pleasure gardens here in Walworth, or we go out into the countryside. We ramble down to Camberwell, to visit the farm, or we go up Herne Hill with a picnic, and make our reading party in a meadow.

She twisted her mouth. Don't look so surprised. Some of my lodgers can read and write. And those that can't, and wish to, are learning. I teach them, because I enjoy it. And so we keep each other going.

She put a light stress on her final word. Joseph felt the hint, as though he were a horse in harness and she had touched him on the shoulder with the thong of her whip. He could see the creased leather harness, its straps and buckles. He could feel a metal bar across his tongue.

He wanted to summon the right words. He seemed to have few left. Like opening the chest of drawers of a morning and finding no clean shirts. No clothes at all. She'd given him his coat back, and he'd returned her cloak. They had exchanged clothes. She'd taken all of his. He shivered, naked; he wanted to pick up her loose, hanging blue wool sleeve and lift it to his face.

He said: I should like to talk to you again. I still think you may be able to help me. You could perform some invaluable introductions for me, I am sure, if you chose to do so.

Mrs Dulcimer raised her arms and gently flapped her sleeves, as though they were wings. The gesture released her scent of warm bread, warm skin. She said: not this morning, though. I am busy. Come back tomorrow, if you like.

She rose from her nest of gold cushions, and so he got up too. Those dented silk mounds would be warm. He bowed. Should he shake hands? She folded her arms inside her loose blue sleeves.

His knees felt damp. He looked down again at the green stains on his trousers, the green debris that clung there. She looked too. Unceremoniously she bent, and brushed off some bits of grass and twig. The kind of gesture Nathalie would have made, dusting him down, laughing at him. When Mrs Dulcimer straightened up, her rosy mouth was very close to his, half-open, inviting. Again he caught her scent.

He said: I must be off, ma'am. I bid you good day.

At the end of Apricot Place, on the corner of Orchard Street, he paused. A clamour of carts and barrows, jolting over the cobbles, a noise of hammering. A flourish of canvas awnings, their sides flapping in the wind. A market seemed to be setting up on the main road. People surged about, their shouts banging back and forth. To avoid them he cut up through a back street running parallel. He strode between rows of fine new houses fronted with long gardens, tidily planted with young laurels, beds of pink and red cyclamen, mauve Michaelmas daisies. He headed north, towards the common.

Mayhew had criticised him for a lack of objectivity, had stressed proper research, properly organised. Very well, sir! Joseph had made a careful plan for his morning's work. He would stick to it, whatever happened. He would not be swerved off course.

Step one: establish the background. Discover the terrain. He needed a clearer sense of these neighbourhoods; their boundaries, their approaches. No more wandering haphazardly, as he'd done at first, depending on chance encounters with gay ladies willing to chat. No chatting today. Confirmation of the city's south-eastern layout. Urban geography, pure and simple.

Accordingly, map in hand, he spent a couple of hours tramping around the squalid district between Waterloo, London Bridge and the Borough, checking the names of the main roads encircling it, the side streets branching off.

Each time he stopped, or dawdled, a woman slid up to him: all on your own, dearie? Shall I show you a good time? He shook these girls off, one by one, made a quick note on his map, marking the site of each encounter with a cross. Information that might come in handy, at some point. Did street prostitutes work their own particular patches, or roam more widely? How far from their lodging-houses was it economic for them to go? If one girl strayed onto another girl's stamping ground, did they fight? Summon their bullies to do the fighting for them? He'd begun pondering these questions two days ago, when first visiting Mrs Dulcimer, hadn't he? Only two days! At some level he felt he'd known her all his life.

He tripped on a dead cat. He steered past a mound of dung. His map blew in the breeze, cracking and bellying out like a sail, and he struggled with the canvas-backed folds that wrapped themselves around his arm. Trying to hold it, read it, mark it, all at the same time: almost impossible.

He paced up and down, halting every so often at the mouths of alleys, checking them against his flapping map. Most of them were unnamed. He peered into narrow openings between warrens of ancient, dilapidated buildings. From time to time the newspapers fulminated against the conditions in which the poor were forced to live: these massed rabbit hutches thrown up centuries back; to be demolished one day, presumably, when the authorities got round to it, and their inhabitants moved on, from one small city of slum tenements to another, from one net of secret ways, unknown to cartographers and government surveyors, to the next.

Such invisibility: handy for prostitute-thieves slinking out at night to ply their trade. Armed with their false charm, their brittle smiles. A phalanx of painted girls flaunting ringlets glossy as wax, tight-waisted jackets and flimsy cloth boots, their ballooning skirts swung over their arms for quick getaways.

Foxes had their runs, leaving beaten-down lines in meadow grass; even dogs did. Women scurried along their own night-time ways like rats, lured by the smell of male flesh, male money, they scampered around your feet. Bit and nipped you.

The rats prowled inside him, gnawing his stomach. Hunger. Church bells rang out a chime for mid-day. Time to eat. Good excuse not to have to plunge alone into any of these mazes of courts and paths, get lost most likely, encounter God knew what villains armed with clubs, no compunction whatsoever about whacking him over the head, stripping him of his watch, most of his clothes. He'd finish up his morning's work somewhere indoors, relatively quiet, mark down particular street openings from memory.

He stopped at a chophouse in an alley off Borough High Street, drawn by the bustle of customers surging into the paved yard. A sign chalked on a blackboard promised beefsteaks and meat pies. People yelled their orders through a hatch, then found seats.

Here you are, darling! A hand bearing a plate shot over his shoulder. A damp armpit pressed his nose. Fresh, salty tang of her sweat. She whirled round, darted off again. Blue check skirts over a wide arse, limp white bow of apron strings.

Steam rose from the central hole in the scalloped-edged pie shining with glaze; piping hot mashed potato, forked up in crests, to the side; the whole encircled by a neat moat of onion gravy. The crisp shell of raised pastry enclosed melting golden meat jelly, chunks of pork made savoury with plenty of black pepper, a hint of sage.

He ate swiftly. This afternoon he would embark on step two of his plan, which was a development of step one, but altogether more ambitious. The printed street map of London he was using, published just a few years ago, was already out of date. It showed Apricot Place, for example, near its edge, but few of the newer developments of terraced houses north-east of Walworth, alongside the warehouses, following the curve of the river; few of the raw side streets being built on the south axis down towards Camberwell.

If he were properly to include Walworth in his research, he would need to make a sketch of the entire area as it stood today, to fill in the gaps on his map. This afternoon he'd walk the district, from north to south, from east to west, making notes as he went. A kind of beating the bounds of the parish, but done according to strict scientific principles.

The pastry tasted deliciously of lard. Fattiness on his tongue. He swallowed the last rich morsel, picked up the crumbs, pressed them to his wetted finger, and ate those too.

He began doodling on a blank page of his notebook. What would his life have been like if he'd managed to do as he originally wanted, cook for a living? He might have worked in an establishment like this one, a whitewashed, beamed interior pleasantly dark behind small windows of thick, blurry glass, crowded with oak tables, settles and benches, a fire burning in the grate at one end. The drover's cart from Kent had set down somewhere nearby, perhaps. His mother would have struggled out, counted her bags and bundles. The small boy clutched her hand. Don't fret, Joseph. We'll stop here for a moment. The landlady let the woman sit by the fire, brought the boy a cup of milk. She patted his shoulder. There you are, my love, get that down you.

What would his life have been like if he'd been able to train as a cartographer, actually understand the principles of geometry, trigonometry, if he'd been able to travel these districts with set square and compasses, produce exact to-scale versions of these neighbourhoods? Impossible to imagine. He'd done very well, getting to where he was now. Useless to envy those with more education, better prospects. He'd show them, that was all. Surprise them with what he came up with. That includes you, Mayhew.

He looked at his doodle. The rough pencil strokes baffled him for a moment, before he saw. An apricot in section. As in a botanical engraving; as in a textbook on gardening and husbandry. Two curves of flesh around a fringed oval stone. Like a woman's secret mouth, secret lips. Her apricot place.

A tide of warmth spread from the back of his shoulders down his arms, into his hands. A kind of ache. Pleasurable. Strong. It pushed through him. His cock stirred, lifted.

Some of the books in the Holywell Street basement provoked similar effects. For example that guidebook to the exquisitely dressed, upmarket whores of the West End. Street by street. Shamelessly straightforward. What they cost and what they did.

Why shouldn't he do something similar for south-east London? Compose a beyond-the-Thames almanac of pleasure-for-sale? Had he known, somewhere deep down, he wanted to do that? Was that why this morning he'd begun marking the sites where girls dawdled and wheedled male passers-by? So why not pursue that particular line of enquiry? Interview the girls, get their names and addresses, find out their specialities, their favourite games and tricks. List these beauties by type, as greengrocers would arrange fruits on trays. Catalogue their glistening skins, downy bloom, fragrant smells, sweet tastes. Find a willing publisher, an unshockable printer. Duodecimo size; just right for slipping into your pocket. Elegantly bound, pink half-calf, say, with stamped gold lettering, silk headband, silk bookmark. A cheaper, cloth-bound edition for poorer punters. Advertise discreetly. Hey presto, his fortune was made. Pay off his debts, buy Cara some new frocks, squire her and the children to Boulogne to visit her family. Then what?

His cock subsided. The dream faded. It had led him down a blind alley. A cul-de-sac. Mrs Dulcimer leaned back on her golden cushions and surveyed him from under sleepy-seeming eyelids. She licked a streak of glistening butter from her fingertip. He'd lean forwards, take her hand, lick her fingers clean.

Start again. He picked up his half-empty tankard, gulped beer. Rush of bittersweet hops. Rush of clarity. Forget the lure of quick easy money. Something else was summoning him. It tugged at his sleeve. Murmured to him. Listen. Listen.

Why not compose a journalistic account, authoritative and sober and complete, of the sexual underworld, the secret city, here in the south-east? Go far beyond Mayhew's requirements. Out-Mayhew Mayhew! Include all sorts of information: thumbnail histories of the girls, exact descriptions of where they hung out, in houses and along streets, diagrams of their rat-runs, tables of what they charged, the particular services they offered, whether they worked freelance or were controlled by bullies. Describe a bully's role, the cut he took. Finally, present the material to Mayhew and the *Morning Chronicle*.

See his own words in print. A series, running week by week. His own name in full under each article. Mayhew acknowledging him as an authority.

Cara? She would be shocked at first by his subject matter, but then, surely, she'd understand? Feel proud of him, even. Milly would too.

He took a piss in the limewashed privy in the backyard. It didn't smell too bad: must have been emptied recently. Horses neighed from the other side of the red-brick wall. A whiff of manure. Horses tossing their heads, stamping their feet. The Hoof used to braid their manes. He'd lay his arm along their glossy necks, rub his cheek up and down them, murmuring, while Joseph cowered at the stable door.

Returning to his table, he began writing his overdue report to Mayhew covering the work of the last couple of days. Descriptions of tarts' lodgings. He rubbed his head, sighed.

As a police clerk he'd been a master of the tidy, succinct account. Recording interviews in the station with suspects, witnesses, ne'er-do-wells of all sorts, safely seated on the other side of the table from these miscreants, he had translated their grunts, cries, pleas, broken sentences, into something coherent. Subject, verb, object. Commas in the right places. Correct grammar kept everything tidy, just as the police tried to create order in the city.

Writing for Mayhew, however, making sense of these pencilled notes jotted down while Joseph was out and about, felt different. Mayhew demanded clear narrative structure. It sounded so easy. But the words Joseph chased had an energy of their own, just like criminals, they rose up and jumped about, tried to evade control, hid themselves, then suddenly roused up again and Joseph pursued them trying to capture them but so often not succeeding.

In fact narrative demanded a gun: pick off the facts one by one. Hang them up neat as shot pheasants in the game-butcher's. Alas: Joseph had never learned to handle a weapon. The Hoof had had to shoot a diseased horse once. Off went the flopping dead creature on the back of a cart. Later on, hacked into joints perhaps, the meat sold for pies in the poorer establishments, where the punters didn't enquire too closely into what they were eating. Places like this? Let's hope not.

Finished, have you, dearie?

The serving girl whisked away his plate. Her thumb in a smear of brown gravy on the china edge. Shining red face. Brown-lashed eyes. Breasts straining behind her apron. He said thank you but she hardly acknowledged him, veering to the next table to collect more dirty crocks.

He abandoned his report for Mayhew, turned a page. He wanted to write something for this new project he'd dreamed up. Start by describing Mrs Dulcimer. His black muse. His Walworth Beauty. Follow with an account of this morning's patrol, his encounters with the prostitutes who'd accosted him. He'd dealt with those pleading women by waving them off. Now he summoned them back, one by one. China-blue eyes. Lemony scent, mismatched boots. Smell of stale sweat, rotted teeth. Rain-draggled pink silk skirt. A purple bow above her ear. A bonnet nodding with daisies. Later he'd match these jottings with the crosses marked on his map. Then he'd join up all the crosses, see what winding lines they laid across the printed grid of streets.

After a while he yawned, checked his watch. Time to be on the move again. He tore out the doodle, and the sheets of his new writing, wanting to keep them separate from his work notes, and put them in the right-hand pocket of his jacket. He put his notebook in the other. He pulled on his coat, pushed open the chophouse door, crossed the cobbled yard. The air in the street smelled of coal and apples, cooled his warm cheeks. He strode back towards Newington.

The mid-day pause had renewed him. He plunged in and out of the foul warrens off the main road. He shouldered aside importunate beggars, tambourine-players, passing sellers of bootlaces. He looked for landmarks, scrawled quick notes, dashing down how one back lane connected to another, wove into the criminal web. He paced down towards the cricket ground at the Oval, back up into Walworth, around the common.

By late afternoon, his feet aching, he'd had enough. He cut off towards Blackfriars Bridge. In its centre he halted, leaned on the parapet. He looked north towards Holborn, south towards Walworth, down at the tumbling river that separated them, the low warehouses lining the muddy shores. The fading light dissolved everything into greyness: the stinking waters, the clouds, the sky.

The river behind him, he pursued his route through familiar streets. More than familiar. He even loved them. They led him out towards adventures. Then they summoned him home again.

Yet Holborn wasn't his true home, though he'd lived here for so long. A temporary resting place, that was all. Somewhere to lay his head at night. Somewhere to leave in the morning. He slowed, considering this.

He passed a row of iron columns bracing a pub. A line of gas lamps rose up. Blink, and columns and lamp-posts became massing plane trees, turning green and gold. Tall as the trees rustling around the edges of the fields in Kent. A certain touch of the wind on his cheek and he was suddenly there. Three years old, newly put into trousers, his long curls cropped, trudging along a hedgerow lane threaded with pink and cream honeysuckle. The smell of his mother's sun-warmed skin. Blackberries tightly red,

hawthorns and hips swelling on the prickly branches leaning down. Such paths lay deep below his feet even now,
he tracked his past as he tracked along beside the Fleet,
towards Smithfield, the drovers plodded past him whipping their cattle forwards, the birds whirred up disturbed
from their nests, his mother called to him not to dawdle,
come on, dearie, not far now. Sheen of perspiration on her
freckled face, can of milk in each hand. They'd been to
the farm, and were coming home. Soft grass shone on the
steep banks they walked between, over dry ruts, the mud
whitened by the sun, and the scent of manure, warm earth,
rich as yeast.

He made a detour westwards, to the stationer's shop
on Southampton Way. He chose a new notebook bound
in sprigged cotton, with a black silk bookmark. Cheap,
because grimy with shop-dust and dog-eared. He bought
a pot of glue, a small brush. He paid for these items out
of the money Mayhew had advanced him for expenses,
arguing with his conscience: this was for work all right.
Just for work he couldn't yet show the boss. He came out
with a brown paper parcel, nicely twirled up with string,
tucked under his arm.

He should get back to Lamb's Conduit Street, greet
his wife and children, eat supper. Review his scribbles on
his map; paste his new notes and the doodle into his new
notebook. Yet he wanted to pause, also. Stay outside the
enclosing walls of his house a little longer. Reflect on the
work achieved, the work dreamed up. So why not drop
in to a pub? He could have another try at his report for
Mayhew, summing up the last couple of days. If he just
concentrated, he could write the whole thing in one go,
then deliver it to the *Morning Chronicle* office on the
Strand. Yes. And afterwards enjoy a quiet evening with
Cara and Milly, by the fire.

He turned towards the Strand. He made for the River Queen, sat over a pint, remembering the Italian girl. A long moment, somehow coloured yellow – yellow-amber as a stream of beer or a woman's hair. Nathalie had had amber-brown hair with yellow lights. At night she'd let it down, shake it loose, swish it like a tail. He wanted to bellow and holler: where are you, Nathalie? For on their honeymoon weekend she'd embroiled him in certain antics. How did she dream up these games? Being French, was it? Surely too obvious. Lots of Frenchwomen didn't like playing, from everything Nathalie had told him, laughing. You think we're a nation of harlots, don't you? Easily seduced, lacking all morals – but I assure you, it's the opposite, dear Lord, nothing could ever equal the boredom of my parents' home on Sundays, like being stifled in layers of flannel, those dreary long lunches with the priest visiting, then in the afternoons nothing to do but the mending, oh that tiny brown sitting-room, I hated it.

No. Nothing to do with Nathalie's Frenchness. She was still a child in some ways, that was all, and she'd liked games, the ones you invented freely, on the spot, between you, when you went to bed in that funny little board-ing-house, cheerful after a tolerable supper, a few glasses down, still awake enough to want to romp. Nathalie, his true love. Her knees up, her legs apart, her aureole of curling brown hair, the fleshy lips kissing each other, how gently he put his fingers there, into her juice, how Nathalie flowed for him, he buried his face in her suck-ing her so juicy sweet and ripe, he licked her until she shouted out. Then they'd change places. She invented such foolish larks. Tonight: pirates. Aha! You are my prisoner! She boarded him, she captured him, she stole his heart and soul away. She picked up his discarded necktie and tied it in a bow around his upstanding cock. Glory glory!

Maypole! Oh, you English! She fell over on the pillows, laughing.

The barmaids' reflections moved, refracted, against the mirrors, in the light of the gas lamps. Reddened mouths opened, cried, joked, cursed. He looked at his brown-paper parcel, sighed. Those fresh white pages would have to wait. He drained his glass. Another? The trouble with drinking was that it tempted you to drink more. He ought to resist, hurry back to Cara. No. First of all obey his self-imposed deadline. Then, and only then, call it a day.

He shouted for pen and ink, fetched himself a brandy and soda, paid for it out of his expenses cash. He'd reimburse the boss at the end of the month, out of his wages. Right. Just sum up what he had learned about prostitutes' accommodation in Waterloo, the Borough, Newington. Apartments or rooms rented or not. Beds shared at such-and-such prices. Costs of washing and so forth. A sober, dull account. But one that Mayhew would approve.

He'd gleaned so little information so far that he'd have to fudge it a bit, expand guesses into reported speech. Well. All right. Get on with it.

After a while he forgot his surroundings, was just a flow of words, a hand moving steadily back and forth across small lined pages. Thoughts arrived, one connecting to the next, all seemingly in the right order. He finished, signed his name, tore out the pages and folded them in three, ready for delivery. He stretched and yawned. He hardly noticed the change in the light, the shadow falling across the table, until someone bent over him, murmured in his ear. Hello, dearie. Lonely, are we?

He raised his head. A girl had swayed up to his side. Fresh from the farm she looked, wholesome as a newlaid egg. Barns, and crackling straw, and sunlight in long shafts. Thick ginger hair. Her skin glowed almost golden.

Freckles, and a rosy, pouting mouth. A direct glance from her amber eyes. What's all that writing for, then?

She would clasp his hand, wrap his arm around her waist, lead him upstairs. Kiss him with those soft lips. Good as a country supper of strawberries and cream.

Hunger could be relished. Sharp. Almost exquisite. You could put off satiety, enjoy anticipating it. With Nathalie, on that rapturous weekend of honeymoon, he had taken his time, because from now on she'd always be there, she'd keep offering herself freely, giving him herself completely.

Cara had done so too. Not her fault if the babies kept coming. If now they had to hold each other at bay.

The girl whispered: I'll make it a real treat. You'll see.

Her voice, slow and rich, pulled him towards her. He hesitated. He was on the wrong side of the river for work. But hang on. Surely Mayhew wouldn't object to his doing a spot of compare and contrast. See whether lodgings on the Strand differed much from lodgings in Walworth. Or not. Discover the price this little beauty charged, discover whether a girl here cost a great deal more than one on the Surrey side. What had he paid the little Italian girl? He couldn't remember. An illicit expense, which he hadn't recorded. Mayhew would frown as he flipped through Joseph's accounts. These don't add up. Where exactly did my money go, Benson? Explain yourself, if you please.

Think about that later. He shoved his notebook and report into his pocket, put his parcel under his arm. The girl glanced back at him over her shoulder. Her feet, moulded in tightly fitting boots, tap-tapped up the staircase. He followed her.

The lit gas burnished the girl's hair. Like light shining through a glass pot of marmalade. She threw down her plaid shawl. Nice little place, isn't it? A real home from home.

A bare, wood-planked floor, a strip of grey matting near the bed. A pink quilted coverlet. A white nightdress flung over a plywood screen in one corner. A bunch of feathery green herbs in a brown jar on the windowsill, next to a pot of scarlet geraniums. Keep the flies out, don't they? Ma taught me that.

Lazy drag of vowels. An accent with a burr in it. No wonder she attracted him: sounds he knew; deep in him. Part of his flesh. From Kent, she must be. If he took notes, would she go on talking to him or would she feel too shy? He hesitated, then dug in his pocket for his notebook and pencil.

She began unbuttoning her blouse. Deft brown fingers with blunt nails.

Don't, he said: please. You've misunderstood me. I didn't come up here for that.

She went on undressing. Now she was unloosening the back fastening of her skirt. Easing it off, over her hips. Didn't you? What did you come for, then?

How pale the flesh of her upper arms, contrasting with her sunburned face and neck. White chemise, gathered at the yoke, flowed to her knees. From underneath it her white petticoat fell to her calves. He wanted to look away but couldn't.

I'd like to talk to you, he said.

She lifted an eyebrow. Talk, then.

Begin with Mayhew's questions, to put her at her ease. Then move on to the details that really interested him. But she was the one at her ease, wasn't she? Calmly folding her clothes over the footboard of the bed, patting the sleeves of her blouse to lie flat. Whereas he could feel himself sweating. He plunged on. I'd like to know how much rent you have to pay, how often you change the sheets, how you get your washing done.

Was she listening? She perched on the near side of the bed, unlaced her boots, kicked them off. She sighed. Ah, that's better. They were killing me. She wiggled her feet. Stockings dark with damp at the toes. Joseph said: and I'd really like to know where you're from, what brought you here. Won't you tell me?

She let out her breath in an explosive puff. You're a queer one. Oh, my poor feet.

She bent down to touch one of her heels, winced, cupped it in her hand, soothing a blister perhaps, then sat up again. She spoke to the bedpost. You're a real nosy-parker, you.

Joseph prompted her. You're from Kent? I'm sure you must be, from your voice. My family came from there too. Do you miss it? I know I do.

She seemed to soften. Well, the farm failed, didn't it. We was all thrown off. Nothing for it but to move up here.

She balanced on the grey matting, flexing her toes, looking down at them, then straightened herself, came to stand close to him. Her breath smelled of the mint leaves she must have been chewing earlier. That fresh green scent: his mother propped up in bed to sip mint tea, steam shadowing her face. That late, halting conversation. You can't know how hard it was for me, Joseph, coming to London, leaving everything I knew. You were so little, just four, you were worried by the change, you didn't settle for a long time. Your stepfather called you the Silly-billy-bawler. First time you met him you burst into tears.

Did this girl have brothers, sisters? Where were they now? He said: I'm sorry you've had such troubles. I'm sorry your life is so hard.

She said: let's stick to business, shall we?

She put a hand on his arm. He stepped back a pace. Such fresh skin. London hadn't yet tarnished her. She glowed in the cheaply furnished room like a flower at sunset, as though the last of the sun had got inside her, deepening her colour. Her low, warm voice slid over him. Then the sense of her words scratched him. So what would you like, then? Come on, get on with it, I haven't got all night.

She could have been weighing out sugar in a shop. He could play that game. Choose from his list of gestures, of poses. His shopping-list.

He could turn her on her side in a flurry of petticoat pleats, enter her from behind, grasp the bedstead with one hand, caress her breast with the other, jerk at her rhythmically, the bed creaking under them. They'd both heat up, she'd release more scent. Something aromatic, spicy, that she'd dabbed on her neck and behind her ears. Below that: something darker, more animal. He was in that Kentish farmhouse kitchen, reek of warm blood, newly slaughtered chickens piled at one end of the table, a woman, her back to him, was bending over a bowl, whisk and wooden spoon lying nearby, she broke eggs into the bowl, separating them, beating them, the whites frothed and mounted, the sheets on this girl's bed would furl up round him beaten egg white her white chemise crumpled on the floor he'd shoot into her. Joseph flinched, heard himself groan: Nathalie.

What's up with you? Hands on hips, the girl stared at him. Frayed linen straps of her chemise. He touched her cool freckled shoulder. I'm sorry.

She frowned. He searched for a get out. I've had too much to drink. Another time, perhaps.

The girl wheeled away. Just clear off, mister. You've been wasting my time. Here I've been, taking everything off, and now I've got to put it all back on again. Plus those bloody boots.

I'm really sorry, Joseph said to her back.

She stepped to the window, plucked a sprig of mint, tore off a few leaves and put them into her mouth. She turned, chewing, folded her arms. She spoke through her mouthful of leaves. Hey ho. A change is as good as a rest, I suppose. You'll have to pay me, anyroad.

Of course, Joseph said: certainly.

He fished in his trouser pocket. She waited. The whole space of the room between them. The air somehow bristling, the light of the gas lamp sliding away behind her halo of golden-ginger hair.

She shivered, reached for her blouse, pulled it on. She bent her head, concentrated on her buttons. She flung on her skirt, put her hands behind her waist, fastening it. She faced him again. Right.

He opened his leather purse, counted money into her outstretched hand. She checked it, pocketed it. The identical moment with the little Italian. Briskly shaking out the coins in her palm. Businesslike shove of money into its hiding-place.

The girl sat down on the edge of her bed, hands on her knees, and stared with hatred at her boots. He was a boot. She hated him. He bolted out, ran down the stairs.

Dark sky, melting into fog. People in masses, shoving back and forth. Bumping into him, jolting him aside. Fifteen minutes later, his report safely delivered to the *Morning Chronicle*, walking up Lamb's Conduit Street he felt even hungrier than before. The grumpy-looking clerk had rubbed his hands and yawned: you want to see Mr Mayhew, sir? He's still here. Working late as usual. Joseph had shaken his head, thrust out his written pages. Just make sure he gets these.

He stayed up after Milly and Cara went to bed, telling them he needed some peace and quiet for thinking over the day. Milly smiled at him: and for smoking a nice cigar, eh, Pa?

He took down his little portable desk from its perch on top of the bookcase, unlocked it. He unwrapped his parcel, took out the new notebook.

That girl tonight. Herself. Her own distinctive face, form, history. Memories of a childhood all her own, whether unhappy or happy. Now a hapless girl cast upon the town, part of a tribe of streetwalkers. A race? Ethnographers classified races, the white, the brown, the black, as scientists classified plants or butterflies. Could you really classify women too? Mayhew thought so, didn't he. Poor, labouring-class women, at least. Good women. Bad women. The work-shy criminals. Female pickpockets and thieves, exploiting their reputation for tender, maternal femininity, luring little children round corners, stripping them of all their clothes then legging it. Night-flying prostitutes netted like moths: classes one, two, three. For some men prostitutes were flowers. A nice fresh rosebud for your lapel. When it faded, dropped its petals, you tossed it away and bought another. That girl tonight had been robust as mint.

He pasted the torn-out notes and the doodle into the new notebook, locked everything up inside his desk, which he hid behind the piano, pushing it behind the heap of children's toys as far back as it would go.

He'd never tried to write down his thoughts about Nathalie. He couldn't keep her inside a notebook, inside his desk. She belonged in a different space: some kind of oval frame, wreathed in twining stems and buds. Like the Virgin on her little tin medal. Next time he visited her in Highgate he'd take her some fine autumnal blooms. Chrysanthemums perhaps. He whispered to her: goodnight.

SIX

Madeleine

WET, SHIVERY LUNCHTIME IN May. After only a few hours in Highgate Madeleine wants to bolt. The mansion's gardens, planted with laurels, imprison her. Rain patters on leaves. Light as the touch of that hand early this morning, stroking her hair.

She stiffened. Lay rigid, eyes closed. It's not true it's not true. Someone breathed quietly, very close to her. Warm breath on her cheek. Someone was leaning over her, waiting for her to wake.

The hand flitted over her hair again.

The alarm clock beeped and she jumped. Nobody there. Of course not. Get up. Go to work.

Standing on the gravel path near the grapelike clusters of wisteria blooms, she ticks herself off: you've come to Highgate to give Toby a hand, just keep your head down, do your work, do what Francine tells you, all will be well.

The soprano notes of invisible Francine start up. Come and see the potting shed.

Toby's voice, dark cello glissando, sounds an echo: oh, do. Such a treat for the hired help! A Highgate potting shed is like no other!

Just over here, cries Francine.

Madeleine ducks under the wisteria roof of the pergola, through a low arched doorway, into a grey interior smelling of earth. Springy planked floor underfoot. Small gothic windows diffuse pale light.

Wooden shelves lining the plastered walls bear stacks of upturned old terracotta flowerpots packed close together. A frieze of antique aluminium watering-cans and buckets runs round underneath. A blue bench holds multiples of plywood seed-trays, rolls of green twine, china beakers stuck full of plant labels, wicker baskets of wooden-handled trowels and dibbers. A row of folding metal chairs leans under one window in a grey concertina.

Toby brushes his palm over his close-cropped head, his long eyelashes, flicks wet from his lapels. Madeleine sidles nearer, and whispers. It's like a stage set.

He purses his full, pale lips: straight out of a style mag. Nostalgia-chic. Boho-sheds. Lady Chatterley lives! Enter Mellors, chewing a straw.

Madeleine wanders over to a wheeled clothes-rail, its burden covered with a white sheet. She pokes at it: what's this?

Francine swivels her white, powdered face. Her dark red lips compress as she shakes her purple nylon umbrella free of raindrops. She says: those are the costumes for tonight. Anthony decided to go Victorian. This will be the green room.

Underneath the rack, tumbled on the ground, lie a pair of handcuffs and a truncheon. Props for Shakespeare's comic constable, presumably. Dogberry, that's it.

Toby says: pity it's *Much Ado* and not panto, Francine. You'd make a nice principal boy.

Francine sleeks back her short black hair. She wears a skimpy black tunic over black leggings, a wide black leather belt with silver studs slung round her hips. Her fur-cuffed black ankle boots with thick crêpe soles seem just right for a housekeeper who has to run up and down stairs all day long, in and out of a chilly, sopping garden. Madeleine, optimistic in long blue crinkled-silk skirt and T-shirt, skinny cardigan, wet soles sliding in her summer sandals, has no weatherproof clothes with her, no umbrella. The sun was out this morning when she left her flat, the street warm and humid, but she ought to have known it might rain.

Francine says: I did audition for Hero, but I didn't get it. No worries. I'm hopeless at acting! But I'm going to be the prompter. And I'll probably give them a hand with the bar in the interval.

Madeleine hangs her bag on a wrought-iron obelisk and bends to examine a display of mouse-traps. She says to Toby: I used to teach *Much Ado*. Part of my course on comedy.

Some of her students disliked Shakespeare on principle. Boring. Incomprehensible. Irrelevant. Coaxed to a performance at the Globe, they succumbed to stage magic, if not to all aspects of the plot. Afterwards, in the coach going home, they argued over it. Beatrice hadn't got a boyfriend, was therefore desperate. OK. But why did it matter if a girl talked out of her bedroom window to a bloke standing underneath in the garden? Why would anyone care?

Francine says: Anthony's a very experienced director. Just because we're an amateur group doesn't mean we haven't got very high standards!

Toby gives the potting shed a final dismissive glance. It's just for show! Completely useless! Francine flushes pink through her white makeup. She says: not at all. The owners do use it.

Her phone burbles. She claps it to her ear, listens, nods. She turns towards the oblong of rainy brilliance filling the doorway. The delivery's arrived. Give me a hand?

She goes out ahead of them through the pergola, turns left onto the path, snaps up her brolly, plunges into the drizzle. Madeleine, following Toby's grey raincoated back, pauses for another look through a clematis-hung arch at the steeply terraced kitchen garden clinging to the slope to the right.

Strands of red plastic tape, hung with a Keep Out sign, bar entry. Beyond this barrier apple trees, espaliered against the brick walls, show fruit beginning to swell. Peas and beans twine up rows of bamboo wigwams. Low box hedges, sheared into billowy, overlapping cloud shapes, reach up the short, ladderlike slope, bracing stepped beds of artichokes and asparagus, strips planted with spinach, cabbage and chard. Climbing roses, spiralling over willow trellises, tie the whole place together. The blown clusters of roses shower down white petals in the wind.

Toby turns round, waits for her to catch him up. One hand grasps the handle of his umbrella. Rain sheens the tops of his black leather shoes. He sniffs. Most of this place is over-the-top nonsense, but they can do vegetables OK. Sid would have loved it.

Toby's pale cheeks wrinkle up like a bulldog's, into folds of velvet, as he grimaces, and his lips compress to two lines, and his eyes to shining blue slits. Wet white petals, blown down from the roses, encircle his head, his fair curls that are just beginning to show again. Madeleine strokes off the little patches of white, like confetti, displays them in the palm of her hand. You've been wearing a wreath!

They follow Francine back along the way they've come, brushing between raindrop-laden gooseberry bushes. Down the tumbling zigzag of stone steps into the court-yard. The house presents its golden back.

Right, says Francine: let's sort this lot out.

Rain-darkened cartons pile on the gravel. Curving ruts of tyre marks scooped in the course of skittered stones show where the delivery van reversed in the space, turned on top of the skid marks left by their own arrival some hours previously.

Francine checks her watch: two o'clock, still plenty of time.

They load trolleys with boxes of bottles and glasses, bags of ice, pull and bump them up the steep steps, back past the potting shed and the kitchen garden, up to the cedar-wood verandah right at the top of the property. Bloody hell, Toby complains: you could do with a funicular.

Francine stoops over a carton, eases it off the trolley. She says: Anthony'll be up sooner or later. He'll want to know how we're getting on.

She starts to tear open the boxes, lift out bottles. Toby smokes, pinching his roll-up between thumb and forefinger, while Madeleine stands on the edge of the verandah, scans the view once more. Antique urns sprayed gold, planted with white geraniums and petunias, rear in front of them. Mown camomile drops away, a green waterfall rushing down to the roofs and courtyard below. She says to Toby: nice, eh. Toby says: you can't like it. It's all so vulgar.

He grinds his cigarette underfoot, bends and picks up the mashed stub, looks around for a rubbish bin. She follows him in. He turns and gives her a quick, smoke-scented kiss on the cheek. Sorry I snapped at you. Madeleine waggles her thumbs at him: fainites, fainites. He picks up an egg whisk, flicks it against the black slate countertop.

Francine's menu comprises a cold buffet preceded by canapés. Following her instructions, Toby and Madeleine have stuffed shop-bought mini Yorkshire puddings with pre-cooked pink shreds of roast beef, topped with horse-radish, have dropped hardboiled quails' eggs into nests of shop-bought croustades topped with hollandaise sauce out of a jar, arranged all these on black glass serving plates. Now Toby begins to unmould the country *pâté*: at least you allowed me to make this from scratch. Honestly, Francine. Madeleine fetches the salmon mousse: shall I turn this out? Toby waves her aside. Leave me be! Get on with the salad.

He rang Madeleine the previous day. Are you around tomorrow? Some theatre group's putting on a play in the grounds of a mansion up in Highgate. They've booked me and another chap as caterers, but he's rung in sick and nobody else is free on a Saturday.

Mansion? asked Madeleine: who owns it?

Couple of film directors, Toby said: the company's sent them butlers before. Fantastic house, apparently. I wouldn't mind seeing what it's like.

Madeleine had just begun trying to juggle this quarter's income against newly received bills. She said: done!

She set the alarm for eight. Its beep rescued her from her dream, shook her into the reality of daylight. The baby in the flat upstairs was crying again. Footsteps crossed the floor. Heels knocked on floorboards. Up and down. Up and down. The baby went on wailing. Madeleine returned to bed with a cup of tea. She picked up her library book, plunged into it, to distract herself from the anguish over-head. A volume of local history: descriptions of her part of Southwark as it used to be, from medieval times onwards. Maps showed the growth of the streets, the pockets of development around the market gardens, the coming of the railway. Here was Apricot Place, abutting fields. Did Mayhew, or his researchers, ever get this far?

Leaving the flat, she found a bunch of flowers lying on the threshold. A few white daisies, well past their best, clumsily wrapped in white tissue paper. The edge of a white card poked up amongst the brown-tipped petals. Scribbled across it in biro was a phone number, and a message. *You know you want to. Don't be shy. I'm here for you. Love from Emm.*

She winced. She ran up the area steps, threw the card into the rubbish bin, closed the lid, laid the bouquet on top of it. Let some passer-by take it? She certainly wasn't up to offering it to Sally, explaining its provenance. She wouldn't insult her neighbour with half-dead flowers, either. So throw them away. She opened the brown garden-waste bin, dropped the daisies into it.

Walworth Road felt sleepy, some shops still shuttered, few people about. The scent of warm spice, yeast and sugar drifted out of the Caribbean bakery. The newsagent's door swung open and shut. She plunged westwards, through cramped backstreets of nineteenth-century artisans' dwellings, each with its little bootscraper on the pavement just outside the front door. She headed towards the Imperial War Museum rearing in the distance.

The tap of a boot on paving stones; the flying ribbons on a bonnet. Women walked out of the pages of books and accompanied her. Mary Wollstonecraft, briefly domiciled, as a young woman, in Walworth, fretting about what to do with her life. Closer into town, Mary vanished with a wave of her hand, replaced by Elizabeth Gaskell strolling up to Hampstead for an evening picnic. Thick boots, my dear, that's the answer.

Madeleine couldn't match those ardent walkers. At Charing Cross, when the rain began, she gave up and sank into the underground. At the other end, popping up in Highgate, she felt she'd become a mole, and started smiling. There was Toby, her fellow mole, smiling back.

Francine arrived in her jeep, roared them further up the hill, through tunnels of green branches. Beads of water dashed down the windscreen. Good of you to come at such short notice, Madeleine. It's so important to work with an agency I trust, and of course they vouched for Toby and Toby vouched for you. I don't like hiring strangers. They could be anyone.

Toby said: foreigners, you mean? It's so hard to get the servants these days, isn't it?

Francine said: oh look, a magpie!

Toby turned, rolled his eyes at Madeleine. Shouting above the noise of the engine, Francine went on explaining: the owners only decided quite recently to make their garden available. But Anthony's coped brilliantly. Just one rehearsal on site, and the dress rehearsal yesterday, and the tech., that was all he needed.

They approached the top of the rise, high brick walls running along on either side of the narrow road. Wasn't Highgate cemetery near here? Madeleine should have arrived earlier, gone in for a ramble around the necropolis: overgrown paths winding past tumble-down monuments wreathed in ivy, Egyptian-style mausoleums, battered stone angels. She'd first visited the creeper-covered labyrinth as a student, wheeling her bike; books and sandwiches in the basket. A spring day, when blackbirds shook themselves into whirling patterns overhead in the strong wind. She studied cherubs' heads, ornate crosses, weeping female figures, angels gazing heavenwards. She read the names on tombstones: the title pages of condensed books. Biographies bound in granite. Madeleine copied down some of the names in her notebook; the ones that took her fancy. Nathalie Benson. Beloved wife. Departed but never forgotten. Frederick Benson and Amelia Benson, buried together in a stone double bed quilted with moss. Next to them lay Joseph Benson. Madeleine brushed away dusty earth, sat on Joseph's grave to eat her sandwiches. You don't mind, Mr Benson, I hope.

Francine's jeep smelled new. Leather and air freshener. Madeleine said to Toby's back: I haven't come this way for years.

She was temporarily lost. A pleasurable feeling in London. She didn't expect it. Though perhaps to miss her way in the cemetery itself would be less beguiling. Shadows stretching out to drag her back into the thickets of ivy, black clouds rising up, the big iron gates locked. No way out.

Francine said: quite a way from the tube, isn't it?

How will Madeleine get back later on? Home so distant that the connecting cord stretches too thin, snaps. Spend the night curled on a tomb half-buried between the roots of a tree. Bats tangling in her hair. Close her eyes so that she won't see the flickering shades jumping from tree to tree, getting ever closer. Ghosts fastening themselves onto her like lost skins returned. Hey, she reminded herself: I don't believe in ghosts. What about Nelly, then? Speaking to her whenever she feels like it? Nelly isn't a ghost. Just Nelly.

The jeep swung to the left, along a paved lane. They nosed under overhanging green branches. No other cars. Francine said: my employers like it here because it's so quiet.

They halted in front of a high wooden gate. Francine pointed her remote, and the gate swung open then shut behind them. The short gravelled drive, bordered by flowerbeds, swept them round a stand of yellow-speckled evergreens glittering with rain. Francine slowed the jeep. Here we are!

An early Victorian house built of golden stone. A scaled-down version of an Italian original. Austere shapes of windows, columns, capitals. The harmonious proportions conjured an illusion of weightlessness, made the house seem to float. Round to the left Francine drove them, to the servants' entrance. From its porch they collected the overalls and caps laid ready on a stone bench. They climbed up the vertiginous approach to the verandah kitchen, surveyed the teak workbenches, the cooker and fridge-freezer crammed into the tiny space.

As they donned their overalls, tied aprons on top, Francine spelled out a time-table. As much prep and cooking as possible to be done now. Quick break for a working lunch, then I'll show you the garden. Special guests for the private supper, our sponsors and patrons, will arrive at 6.30 p.m. and be given a tour of the grounds. At 7 p.m. they will come up here for Prosecco and canapés, followed by dinner. Then they will go back down to join the rest of the audience. The actors will be performing on the lawn, against the backdrop of shrubs and trees, it's a perfect stage set. But the spectators will be under cover, Anthony's hired a three-sided marquee.

She tore open plastic-wrapped trays of aubergines and courgettes. Toby plumped up his round white cap, flapped his chef's apron, pinched up its hem between fingers and thumb, pointed his toe. The play must go on!

Madeleine swung her tea-towel, wanting to become Beatrice, saucy and witty and rude. Toby said: we did *Much Ado* at school. I played Hero. Nice costume, all muslin drapes. Masses of rouge, and a wreath of lilies, and silver sandals. He stroked his head, its delicate cap of fair hair. No need for a wig, though, with my darling curls. I grew them long, specially.

Francine said: Anthony wanted to do something a bit grittier at first, but he was overruled. People coming for a night out, our sponsors especially, they prefer comedy.

Some of Madeleine's female students, watching Hero slandered and shamed, witnessing her father's willingness to kill her for dishonouring her family, had nodded in recognition. At school they'd been called slags if they had sex. If they didn't want to do sexting they got called prudes.

Toby patted his groin and squeaked: oh, sir, you do me wrong – I am a maid! Madeleine retorted: strumpet! whore! Toby threw a blue tea-towel over her head: enter the ladies, masked! They capered in the space between the cooker and the fridge-freezer, squawking. A pavane! cried Toby. Mind my veggies, said Francine: calm down!

After eating their lunch of cold ham on the verandah, gazing out at the rain, they strolled with Francine round the garden. They noted the marquee being erected on the lawn, inspected the shell-lined grotto, the carp pond, re-mounted the steep steps to admire the vegetable plots, the potting shed.

Back in the hilltop kitchen, wine boxes unpacked, Toby's cigarette break over, Francine checks her phone again. 2.15. Plenty of time to get everything done.

Traffic noises erupt somewhere below. Gravel crunches. Heavy-sounding vehicles chug in, rev and hoot. Francine blinks, says nothing. Madeleine assembles cartons of eggs, packets of sugar and chocolate. Toby says: shame we're not allowed inside the house. Mean wretches. Madeleine says: I reckon we should break in, take a peep.

Francine frowns. Let's get on! Black sleeves rolled above her elbows, she piles grilled slices of aubergine, peppers and courgettes into miniature towers, sticks pennants of basil on top. Toby shrugs at this mélange: airlifted! Chilled. Grown on polystyrene granules I have no doubt. Completely tasteless. You've got a potager bursting with produce. Why on earth don't you use that? Francine says:

everything's had to be brought in specially. Anthony's using the garden for free, but that's as far as it goes.

Francine slices mozzarella. Toby points his whisk, clots of cream plopping onto the counter: that's not even the real thing. It's not buffalo. Francine seizes a sponge. She says: the guests won't mind. They're nice, polite English people. Not foodies like you. Even if they do notice they won't complain. They'll say everything's lovely.

Madeleine's chocolate mousse mixture bulks up. With a rubber-tipped spatula she scrapes the bubbly blackness into white porcelain ramekins, stows these in the fridge, next to the clingfilmed bowl of whipped cream. All done, she says: and it's only three. What shall we play now?

Toby says: I need another cigarette. Come and keep me company.

The three of them stand on the verandah, faces lifted to the fine rain blowing in. Madeleine stretches out a sandalled foot, to capture wetness on her toes. The dome of a yellow umbrella bobs up the stone stairs towards them. Francine unties her apron, bundles it aside. Here he is!

Enter on cue Anthony, the play's director. He bounds up the last step, pauses. The rain intensifies colour: olive green Barbour open over a round-necked grey T-shirt; blue jeans. Curly brown hair flying round his face. Tall and lean. Brown eyes under dark brows, big nose, mobile mouth.

Toby puts his mouth to Madeleine's ear. Oh, handsome! She murmurs back: he's gorgeous. He's like a sculpture. A god!

An eighteenth-century version. One of those elegant stone figures decorating the balustrade of an Italian villa's terrace, posed lolling and amused. He needs a lyre, though, not a brolly. Anthony's gaze sweeps across Madeleine, halts for a moment at Toby, stops at Francine. He leaps up the couple of wooden steps onto the verandah, casts his dripping umbrella to the floor.

He grimaces. There's been a bit of a disaster. In fact, several.

Deep, warm voice. Madeleine wills him to speak more. Vowels that roll over you like honey. Is this how Beatrice feels, listening to Benedick? No wonder she's so rude to him: she needs to provoke him, needle him, make his words flow back at her, pour over her again and again.

Francine stretches out a hand, looks tender. She commands: explain!

He keeps his tone playful. He's obviously upset, and at the same time he's mocking himself for making a fuss.

He raises a finger. Firstly, he explains, three large lorries have just arrived and parked down in the courtyard. Apparently there's going to be some filming going on tonight in the house. No one has told Anthony anything about that.

Francine says: oh, I'm so sorry. The problem is, the owners are finishing up a film, and the schedule won't let them wait a single day. It won't affect us, I promise you.

Secondly, the young woman playing Hero has collapsed, weeping, with violent toothache. Thirdly, the cast don't have understudies. What's a man to do?

Francine pushes Anthony into a canvas chair, picks up the umbrella and closes it, leans it against the wall. Water trickles along the oiled teak floor. Let's get you a cup of tea. Madeleine, would you put the kettle on? Quick as you can, please.

Madeleine brings in the tray. Black pottery teapot with big gold spots, matching cups. She pours tea, serves Anthony.

His gaze settles on Toby. He narrows his brown eyes. I say, would you mind standing back a little?

Madeleine watches Toby decide to play. Pause. Music. Enter Toby. He glances at Anthony from under his eyelashes, turns away, glances back. Their gazes intertwine. Yes, exactly like Claudio catching sight of Hero for the first time. And she of him. Split second of wonder. Captured. Enchanted. Toby looks down modestly. Applause, Toby.

Toby poses like another graceful statue on a balustrade, a young shepherd, or a faun, Bacchus himself perhaps, holding not a wine-pitcher but a milk jug. His look unblinking. Anthony stares back at him. She wants to laugh, but can't. Something this intense and solemn hushes her. The air seems to turn solid. Everything goes very still, all movement, every breath. The two faces. Nobody speaks. Crashing in the undergrowth. The god approaches. Beware. Oh, beware.

Francine's eyes follow the direction of Anthony's. She hesitates, seems to sink. She is obviously scrabbling for the correct gesture, the relevant speech. She clasps her hands: Toby knows the play, he was saying so earlier.

Anthony sits back, frowns, becomes again the capable director alert to new talent. He says to Toby: it's a tiny part. You could learn it in five minutes. Hero scarcely speaks at all. And she's always accompanied by her ladies, so they'd be able to move you about. Really all you'll have to do is get up a few lines, smile and look pretty.

A veil, please, in that case, says Toby: I insist on a veil.

Francine's lips part. Flash of little white teeth. She straightens her black tunic. Her fingers grip its edges. Well, thank goodness we've got that sorted out! Let's get on, shall we? Lots still to do.

She gathers the mugs back onto the tray, vanishes with it into the kitchen. Clatter of china. The rush of tap water. The chug-chug of a dishwasher.

Anthony will now show Toby down to the garden-stage, block out his moves, lend him a copy of the play, procure him a private place where he can rehearse his lines undisturbed. We'll fix you up with a costume later, with Francine's help. There's a blonde wig somewhere. And we'll find you a pair of shoes.

With a flourish and a flurry it's all over. Anthony tucks his arm into Toby's, whirls him off down the hillside.

Francine returns, unrolling her black sleeves. Madeleine, you've time for another break. Nothing more we can do up here for the moment. I need to go and check on what's happening with the marquee. I'll see you later.

Fine, says Madeleine.

No worries, says Francine.

Exit Francine, humming, under her purple brolly. Off she hurries, drops down the steep path, not seeming to care whether she skids or trips.

Madeleine plumps up the cushions on the canvas chair. Perhaps she should make herself a fresh pot of tea. No. An urge for a drink. To hell with it. Too late to sack her for pilfering. She can give Francine the money later on. She unscrews the cap on a bottle of Chilean red, pours herself a large glassful. Nelly pipes up behind her shoulder: oh, you sad creature. Madeleine turns: and who was it who drank bottles of stout every day in pregnancy on doctor's orders? Nelly scolds. Get on with you. Pinching drink. Oh, you tinker.

Now Madeleine wants her book. She'll curl up, read, drink wine. Where's her bag? Of course: she's left it in the potting shed. A handy place for reading on this rainy afternoon: dry, peaceful, and, as prospective green room, pleasantly imbued with theatre magic. Down she goes, bottle tucked under her arm, full glass in her hand, rain falling into the wine, puckering its surface.

Rain-percussion; gentle drumming on her shoulders. Fudge of sand and grit squidges under her feet. She enters the pergola, stops, with her free hand brushes water from her hair. The gesture recalls Toby's earlier, smoothing a fringe of raindrops from his eyelashes. Speaking of Sid. Trying not to weep. Now he's got Anthony's arm round his shoulders, Anthony's gaze searching his own, Anthony's voice murmuring to him. Toby will learn his part in a twinkling, he'll be a great success, at the cast party on stage after the show he'll flirt with everyone but especially with Anthony and then they'll vanish together into the wings for as long as they choose and Madeleine will envy them, yes, she will, and toss back another glass of wine.

She stoops under the lintel of the potting shed, half-closes the door behind her, so that light can reach into the blue shadows, just enough to read by. That earth smell again. It rises up and surrounds her, wraps her in a shawl of humus.

There's her bag, hung over the back of the obelisk near the workbench. She pushes aside the stack of seed-trays, sets down her bottle and glass.

Something white flickers in the shadows opposite. Flutter of a white hand.

Her insides burp and curdle. A ghost escaped from the cemetery. No. I don't believe in ghosts, remember? Not the cartoon sort, anyway, the ones draped in white sheets moaning whoo-hoo. Other sorts then? Perhaps. Yes. As of this morning I do.

A whimper stabs up. Somebody there, over by the wall opposite. A human shape huddles on the ground beneath the costume rack, next to the little pile of Dogberry props. A pale scarf wound around her head, the lower part of her face. One hand clasps it in place, the other holds her knees as she rocks to and fro, giving out little bleats of pain.

Madeleine says: oh, you made me jump!

The young woman's wrapped in some sort of dark cloak. One slender foot thrust out. No shoes.

Madeleine says: you must be Hero. I mean, the one with the toothache. Oh, I'm so sorry. Is there anything I can do for you?

The girl dips her head, shakes it. She lowers her scarf a fraction, and croaks. It just hurts so much.

Coloured shapes glimmer. The sheet on the clothes rack has been half torn back, trails along the ground, revealing a press of fancy garments: a flounced green crinolined dress, crimson bodices and jackets, pink petticoats, dark overcoats, tweed trousers. Feathered bonnets bulk out, a lace collar, a couple of gilded masks. Fur-cuffed black ankle boots lie on their sides.

Madeleine says: Francine. Oh, Francine.

Pink face blotched with patches of white, dark red lipstick smeared along her cheeks, mascara leaking black runnels. Francine weeps afresh.

Madeleine hovers over her, squats down. Francine stares at her from bloodshot eyes, puts out a hand to push her away. She gives another snivelling sob, blots her face on a tissue pulled from her sleeve. Cadences of woe: I could have played Hero. I thought. I thought we. That he.

She averts her face, folds herself over her lap. Her sodden tissue, a pulp of blotted black mascara, bulges from her fingers. Madeleine fiddles a handkerchief from her pocket, hands it over. Francine blows her nose, wipes her eyes.

Words blurt forth mixed with tears. I started helping with DramSoc. We'd go for coffee. Go to the pub. He said what a good listener I was. Hadn't known him before. He told me he was bisexual. I said no worries. He said I was his right hand.

Francine gasps, snorts, clutches her balled handkerchief. She wipes her eyes again. With her heavy white makeup gone, she looks very young.

Madeleine says: oh, I am so sorry.

Francine glares at her. Don't patronise me! You don't know what it's like. You can't understand.

One classic remedy available. Madeleine gets up. Come on, let's have a drink. A glass of wine will do you good.

She pushes the clothes rack to one side, kicks away the piled props, fetches the bottle from the potting table. She sits down on the ground, next to Francine, their backs against the wall. She tops up the glass. Here. Think of it as medicine.

Lengths of silk and velvet swing near her face, brush her cheeks. She reaches up a hand, hauls the sheet completely off the costume rail and wraps it around their legs, covering their feet. If your feet stay warm, the rest of you does. Francine rubs the back of her hand across her mouth and nose, drinks some wine. It works like medicine, yes, because she stops crying, and also it works on the roughed-up psyche like oil. Words can flow out smoothly from the hurt throat.

Toby's not even good-looking. And giving himself such airs. Why does Anthony like him so much? All he's done since he got here is criticise. And now they've gone off together! Easy to see where they'll end up. You can't fool me.

Toby and Anthony behaved freely: immediate recognition of desire, willingness to act on it. Madeleine behaved like them when she was young, didn't she? She still would, given half a chance, wouldn't she? Oh sweet Francine.

Madeleine says: I suppose Toby's honest. At least he says what he thinks.

Francine takes a swig of wine. She says: when I'm at work here I can't say what I think. I'm paid to keep my trap shut.

Francine yawns. She sits up, takes another glug of wine. She shudders, coughs. Madeleine says: easy! She pats Francine's back. You drink even faster than I do. Let's make it last.

The shed feels warm now. In the shade of the costume rack, they loll shoulder to shoulder, passing the glass back and forth between them, sipping. The wine tastes of cherries spiced with cinnamon. Drinking wine, as opposed to stout, in the afternoon, she wants to explain to Nelly: well, it's like being a student again, lying on the grass by the river, picnicking with friends. Read poetry and plays to each other, talk and daydream. Nelly taps her novel borrowed from the mobile library. Just as long as you don't bring trouble home.

Madeleine tilts the last red drops into the shared glass. Their breath smells of ripe fruit. Their breaths mingle, just as Toby and Anthony's glances mingled earlier. She slumps further down, her edges softening, melting. Warm inside, the warm-earth air of the potting shed, the wine tastes earthy, red earth, she's a fat grape ready to pop, scatter her little black pellets wherever they want to fall.

Francine combs her hair with her fingers. She says: Toby doesn't know how the owners of this house make so much money. His precious Anthony doesn't know either.

She leans to one side, picks up the handcuffs. Aluminium, leather-edged, on a chain of wide links. She reaches for the truncheon. From further behind her, she draws out a small whip. She puts them in her lap, along with the handcuffs, as though she's tidying up a child's toys. She says: they make porn films. That's what this place is for. It's where they shoot the films. They started off with bodice-ripper type ones inside the house. Gonzo porn. Whatever. Then Lady Chatterley-type stuff in the potager and in here. Now they make porn for women.

Scripted by women? Madeleine asks.

She reaches out, strokes the fur edging a velvet robe. Her fingers enter its silkiness.

She says: I like reading novels with sex in, when it's well done. But I don't know much about visual porn. I'm a porn-film virgin!

Francine folds her arms. She says: what you need to understand is, all young men use porn. And now young women do too. Francine's voice has taken on the pleasure of telling an older woman things she doesn't know. That's why they've let Anthony put on his stupid *Much Ado*. They're going to film it so they can intercut tiny bits of the footage with their own stuff. They didn't tell him in advance in case he kicked up a fuss. And the special patrons: they're all the marketing people. Stupid Anthony hasn't even guessed.

Francine gleams, brittle and shiny as a shell, one of those fluted cockle cases covering the wall of the grotto in the garden below. Pleated, like a half-open fan, sharp-edged, cemented to the wall, part of an ancient design. Once, as a child, she wriggled in her bed, in sunlight, rolled naked in grass, she nuzzled and bit her mother and sucked her and licked her, she wanted to stroke and be stroked, her father tossed her up teased her tickled her and she screamed with delight, she ran down the hill in the darkness, she swam in the buffeting rough sea, she fought with her best friend twisting over and over on the kitchen floor, she smelled her mother's skin the enticing sweet-fish scent underneath her skirts. Whose memories are those, Madeleine's or Francine's?

Francine stills her face. The moment stretches around them, flimsy, taut, like a silken tent keeping the rain off. Keeping too much feeling out.

Madeleine gazes at the empty glass. She says: my generation of women believed in free love. The Pill freed us! But we believed in passion, too. And I still do. So there, Francine!

Francine says: that sod Anthony. Kept going on about how much he liked women, how much they liked him. What does he know about women? Fucking nothing!

She digs for her phone, takes it out, checks her messages, while Madeleine waits. Francine snaps her phone shut, catches Madeleine's glance. She says: times have changed. Nowadays, with phones, everybody who wants to can shoot their own porn, shoot themselves having sex, post it on the internet.

She pockets her phone. The owners here are afraid of going bust. They're cutting down on staff. I'm out of a job as of Monday. So what the fuck does any of it matter?

She grimaces. She gathers herself, puts her hand on Madeleine's shoulder, levers herself up, unwinding the cotton sheet from around her legs, beating it aside. Madeleine stays sitting on the ground. Francine stoops, steps into her fur-cuffed boots. She stands up straight. The brisk housekeeper once more. Cold and strong as Mrs Danvers in *Rebecca*, efficiently torturing the new bride.

She says: come back up in good time, won't you? There'll be all kinds of last-minute things to see to.

At the door of the shed Francine pauses, turns: thanks for the wine. Let's go halves on it.

Madeleine keeps silent. Silvery-grey wood walls make a box holding the scent of dust. They look at one another. Air between them, separating them. Memory of their bodies close, shoulders touching, the smell of makeup, everything loose and runny, tears, sweat, wine, words.

Francine hurries out, through the screen of rain. Tap tap tap of her feet across the tiled floor of the pergola.

Madeleine gets up. She punches a top hat, a red silk waistcoat. She smothers the costume rack with the sheet, smoothing it well down over the robes, the crinolines and overcoats. The stage manager making the curtain descend, sweeping the actors from view.

There's time for a walk, surely. If only she had an umbrella. She could go to the cemetery. Re-visit those Victorian graves. See if a ghost turns up.

Who or what is a ghost? One answer, given in a book read long ago: middle-aged women lacking a sex life believed in the paranormal as consolation. Ghosts wanted them even if men didn't.

Definitions seal things off. Like the lids of tombs. Then in the middle of the night the lid creaks, lifts itself up, and flocks of new meanings flurry out. Uncontrollable. Poets are grave-robbers, making dead words live.

She jolts across the path. I must be drunk. I don't care. She swerves along in the rain, which trembles onto her feet.

Perhaps ghosts represent the possibility of stories. Something unfinished, that needs recounting. In the cemetery the ghosts run back and forth, holding out their arms and weeping, wanting to meet someone who won't be frightened but who'll listen. I'll go and sit with some ghosts. Tune in to their stories. Ask them to tune into mine.

Her phone warbles. Toby, sounding exuberant. Where are you? Get your ass up here! We've got work to do.

SEVEN

Joseph

THE HOUSE REEKED OF kippers. Cara always cooked fish on Friday mornings; a nod to her Catholic upbringing. Why could she not remember that he hated kippers and always had?

The lodging-houses of the poor stank of fried fish. He didn't want the poor following him home. Kippers *à la* Cara were grilled, not fried, he reminded himself. No good. Halibut poached in milk he could just about stomach for breakfast, but not these creatures flat as boot-soles, flopping yellow-brown and greasy on a purple-flowered plate, their black eyes glistening in wrinkled sockets. He stared back at them. Mere relics of fish; wizened and mummified; like those relics of saints Nathalie had told him were kept in Catholic churches.

Cara, wrapped in her grey cotton dressing-gown, a white cap tied on over her curl-papers, turned in the dining-room doorway. Eat up while they're still hot, dearest.

Children wailed two floors above. A door slammed. Joseph said: won't you sit down and have breakfast with me, my love?

Cara flung up her hands. Impossible. I must go up and give Milly a hand. She can't manage on her own.

Joseph prodded his kipper with his fork. Footsteps thumped. Milly yelled from the hall: down in just a minute. Save me some coffee!

Cara said: oh, goodness, I forgot, I left the coffee-pot boiling on the stove. And the loaf from yesterday warming up. Just let me go and see how it's doing.

Joseph mangled the crinkled, gold-black fish enough to make it look as though he'd eaten some of it at least. He ran upstairs, found his hat and coat, opened the front door to let out the odour of over-grilled kipper and over-boiled coffee and to let in the smell of the street. Bacon frying, rain-wetted dust, rotting fruit, sweating animal. Fresh, steaming heap of straw-packed horse dung: the milk-cart must be on its rounds.

Sunlight washed over the house fronts. The postman, walking up from two doors along, hailed him, thrust out a bundle of letters. Joseph took them, nodded his thanks. The postman tipped his fingers to his hat, made off.

Joseph drew the front door almost shut. He thumbed open the first three letters, scanned their contents. A terse note from the landlord, enclosing another copy of his last quarter's bill for rent. A dunning note from the furniture shop where he'd bought the sideboard. Another from the auction house, enquiring about payment for the piano. He thrust them into his trouser pocket.

The fourth envelope bore Mayhew's handwriting. That characteristic black scrawl of his thick-nibbed pen. Joseph's stomach somersaulted. If this was the boss's response it was swift work. On reading Joseph's report, delivered yesterday evening, he must have dashed off his reply immediately, caught a late post.

Cara came up, pink-faced, from the kitchen: but you're not staying for the bread!

Her wrapper was faded, her brown slippers down-at-heel. He would buy her a new dressing-gown for her birthday, and some new slippers. Mules, perhaps. Why not? Something dainty, trimmed with fur, and to hell with the cost.

Cara wiped her brow with her sleeve. She said: I've decided you're right. I absolutely must find a maidservant.

Joseph said: at last! I'm very pleased to hear that.

Cara put out a hand and brushed a scrap of thread, silky-looking and golden, from his lapel, twiddled it between her fingers. She said: we could advertise. That's how we found Kathleen.

So that was the name of the Irish girl who sauntered in weekly to do the scrubbing. Joseph had caught sight of her once or twice, hunkered down over her brush, singing to herself as she worked. A pair of heels, an aproned bum, an outstretched red hand. Grey soapy water sluicing across the floor, a filthy rag draped over the back step.

Cara said: Milly and I can go to the newspaper office this afternoon. That will make a nice walk with the children.

She began twining the gold thread round her finger; a soft ring. Joseph said: no need for you to bother with newspaper offices. Much easier for me to attend to all that, while I'm out. I know the very place to begin making enquiries.

Cara pulled off the gold thread, thrust it into her pocket.

Where had he picked that up? From a tassel, it must have been. From the braid on those fancy gold satin cushions in Mrs Dulcimer's drawing-room. Yesterday. He'd leaned back on those cushions fat as the pillows on a newly made bed. She'd sat there, wrapped in blue wool.

He tore open Mayhew's letter. The boss's writing was decipherable, just, despite being dashed off with a scratching pen that left a trail of ink blots. Heavy black scorings-out, underlinings. The words jumped up and hit Joseph like fists. Incoherent. Not clear. Over-involved and over-subjective. These notes are of little use and these interviews must be repeated.

The sour smell of burning erupted from the kitchen below. Cara cried: oh heavens, the bread! She rushed to the basement stairs.

Joseph fetched his notebook from his desk. He picked up the new notebook too. Safer taken with him than left at home. He slammed the front door behind him and made off down the street.

He strode south towards Blackfriars, weaving in and out between other pedestrians. Women in crinolines churned along like paddle-steamers, knocking him with their shopping baskets, their umbrellas, then glaring at him. Excuse me, ma'am, he repeated: excuse me.

One woman strolling towards him slowed her pace to let him pass. Lively grey eyes. No bonnet, no gloves. Curly fair hair piled up loosely on top of her head. Long blue skirt of crinkled silk. Memory flared: that woman spotted in the cemetery yesterday. A trick of the light she'd been, a phantom composed of shadow and dazzle. Yet here she was again. As they came face to face she caught his eye, gave him a quizzical glance. Was she going to speak to him? Instinctively he put out a hand to halt her but she wheeled away, she was lost to him, the crowd behind caught him, carried him along.

He'd walked too fast. His chest tightened, a powerful hand clenching him inside, squeezing him. Damn Mayhew and his fiddle-faddle criticisms. Just you try and do better.

The wind pushed across his shoulder-blades, almost blew his hat off. The smell of Smithfield Market assailed him: meat grease and fat, warm blood, bones. He skirted a toppling heap of refuse, ripe and stinking, walked on down through Farringdon. Gutters strewn with yellow-green leaves of watercress. The fruit stalls were setting up, men hefting big baskets, building pyramids of apples. Workers shouted overhead, lowering containers of rubble from scaffolding. Ladders lifted themselves, fell.

Barging past the bottom of Ludgate Hill, hearing St Paul's bells boom out the hour, Joseph looked up at the great smoke-blackened façade. On impulse, he turned towards it.

Climbing the five hundred-odd steps to the Golden Gallery restored him. The cold, fresh air blew about his head and calmed him. He stood among the clouds lively with bird's wings, seagulls swooping and cawing. He looked down.

Still early enough for clear, pearly light to remain. London not yet covered over by smoke. Long queues of omnibuses, miniatures, like the tin toys he'd played with as a child. Crowded with tiny dolls climbing on, climbing off, jerking their arms back and forth. Rounded fat shapes like sugar mice: the rumps of brewers' drays. London was an engraving, black lines that moved. Black dots: people hurrying along in opposite directions. A scribbled black mass, swaying to and fro: carts and cabs, every driver intent on his business.

This high up, from this lofty perspective, he could find detachment. Blackened breakfasts became grey pencil-shading, then faded. Rubbed out completely. Bills, Mayhew's letter, floated away on the wind. Lean over the parapet, survey that mass of anonymous people, under-stand how at the same time each man in the crowd was an individual, struggling for existence, grabbing for life, determined to survive. Mayhew floated like a black-suited angel above the city. Mayhew cherished each of those individual black-dot lives, wanted to hear each person's story; like some master novelist giving expression to all human beings. You could only do that by getting this high up, taking this distant perspective. Surveyed from this lofty eyrie, your material calmed, became manageable. Back down on the ground you got lost amid other men, no longer in charge of your vision, the crowd of humanity surged and knocked. Too many shifting points of view.

The bells chimed the quarter-hour. Joseph corkscrewed down the staircase from the dome. Back to earth, he told himself. Ready to start afresh.

He hailed an omnibus. What would Mayhew make of this ruffian driver, stove-pipe hat at an angle, pipe clenched in his teeth, hollering and cursing at other conveyances getting in his way as he coaxed his team along? Or that booted and caped inspector, standing there in the mud, watch clasped in one hand, notebook in the other? Whereas to others of Mayhew's class they were invisible as the souls of the dead, to Mayhew they shone with purpose, with meaning. They formed part of the mighty army of working men who kept London alive. So get on with your own job, Joseph. That meant travelling to Walworth, to Apricot Place.

Betsy opened the door, peered out, one hand on her swollen belly. Her face dull, her attention inward-turned. Where was her husband? Perhaps he worked away, re-joined her on Sundays. Joseph smiled at the girl, and she jerked, and leaned back.

Mrs Dulcimer's sitting-room held the scent and heat of a crackling fire. This morning she sported a crimson walking dress. Her black hair was a tied-up mass of curly plaits. An earring of blue turquoise chips bunched onto tiny gold wires clasped one ear-lobe. On the side table lay a straw bonnet adorned with a curling red feather.

She said: so you're back.

He returned: yes, I'm back.

She raked the red mass of the fire, settling it. She picked up her gloves, a little red bag that matched her walking-dress. Another badly chosen moment to visit! I'm on my way out to the market, to buy dinner. I must get to the butcher's in good time.

But she herself had suggested he call today! How would he ever pin the woman down? Butterfly fluttering hither and thither. His Walworth Beauty with flickering wings. Tantalising him, flying out of his reach. Joseph tightened his grip on his stick. I was hoping for a brief conversation.

Mrs Dulcimer shook out her crimson skirts. Why not accompany me? We can talk as we go.

She put up her hands to her hair, patted it, smoothed it behind her ears. Her fingers touched her earring, held it for a moment. Still twiddling an escaping tendril, she looked around for her bonnet. She said: it's not far. Just along the main road.

Joseph used to watch Nathalie re-arrange her hair. Slowly, eyeing him eyeing her, one by one she would pluck the combs from her ringlets, unfastening their high twists and loops. She shook out her thick, wavy brown mane. She faced him and preened, lifting her long curls, teasing them around her fingertips.

Mrs Dulcimer's spicy scent reached him. Carnations? Roses? Some fancy pomade. Her black velvet eye-shade lay on the side table, next to her bonnet. Nathalie was kissing the back of his neck. He wanted to capture her fingers: let's see what we can do with this.

The crisp frilled edges would tickle his face. Nathalie would tie the knot behind his head with a firm hand. He'd have to guess, in the plush darkness, quite what she was up to. She'd sit astride him, her nightdress up round her hips, her thighs, slippery with sweat, gripping him, releasing him. Soft as summer grass her sweet-smelling hair would fall onto his face, sweep across his mouth. Deft fingertips would flick it aside, the hair acting like a brush, swishing to and fro over his skin. He was a canvas and she was painting him. Shivers erupting all over him. Her mouth seizing his, long languorous kisses, she rocked up and down until he could bear no more, shouts of animal joy ripped out of him, she'd flop forwards onto him, her arms around his head, the fingers of one hand threaded into his hair. She'd reach for the knot, untie it, draw the mask away from his face. They would lie together, their legs interwoven, his head on her breast.

Are you coming or not? Mrs Dulcimer threw a veil over her bonnet, picked up a red shawl with a blue and yellow paisley border. Shall we go?

He followed her down the stairs. Daylight splashed from the landing window behind them onto the top of her bonnet, her red-draped shoulders. The bloodied boots he'd spotted yesterday had been removed.

In the hall Mrs Dulcimer took up a large wicker basket, slid its glossy plaited handle over her arm. She said: remind me, won't you, I must stop at the stationer's stall. I've run short of paper, and of ink.

The buttercup-yellow front door shut behind them. From over the wall at the end of the cul-de-sac the green breath of the countryside brushed Joseph's nostrils again. Under the bitter-smelling pall of London smoke crept the scent of warm earth, of blackberries ripening. Wheatfields cut close and golden, stubble heating up in the sunshine. Trees bowed over with reddening apples, with swelling pears. He blinked, returned to the London street. Late October, sun and cool wind touching his cheek.

Mrs Dulcimer lifted her skirts clear of the muddy ground. And then, if there's time, I'm going to the library.

Passing under the archway they turned out of Apricot Place, into Orchard Street, thence into the main road. Two hundred yards further on and the market hubbub beat up at them. Bawling street-sellers thrust forward their wares, purchasers jostled each other to get through. The throng parted a crack, and Mrs Dulcimer dived into the space opened up.

Her red-feathered bonnet bobbed ahead. He scrambled in her wake. Stalls displayed tin saucepans, glossy blue and yellow crockery, towers of water tumblers, japanned tea-trays, roasting pans. One establishment showed off blue check shirts and red handkerchiefs hung on lines above its door. Another had headless dummies, dressed in fustian jackets, lining both sides of the pavement, with rows of secondhand shoes underneath them. Small boys wriggled through, holding up strings of onions. A confectioner pushed along, hoisting a tray of boiled sweets, striped and whorled like marbles.

Joseph found his breath, his balance, called to Mrs Dulcimer: my work began with all this!

A leather-aproned youth thrust a bucket of whelks at her face. She pushed the boy off, turned to study yellow haddock laid out on crushed ice on a marble slab. She sank her voice under the din, sending it out like a low note on a flute: you're in business? You're going to open a shop?

A donkey cart backed, heaped with a slide of green and white turnips. The donkey released a stream of knobbly turds and the greengrocer stallholder summoned Mrs Dulcimer with a high whoop to look at his pickling cabbages, his potatoes.

Joseph shouted: it's a collaboration. My colleague's idea. To record the lives of the labouring poor. I'm concerning myself with those who will not work. The criminal classes. One particular sub-section thereof.

A gang of urchins took up the cry. The criminal classes! The criminal classes! The children squawked and danced. Mrs Dulcimer forged on. Joseph lurched along behind, banging into a brown-shawled woman proffering bunches of parsley, dodging a chorus line of pastry cooks in white aprons holding out platters of curd tarts.

Mrs Dulcimer pointed. The butcher's down there. She turned into a side street, where the crowd lessened a bit. Pheasants hung on hooks; strings of partridges and quails. A grey-haired woman building a pile of wooden crates called a greeting. A couple of overalled girls flogging walnuts stopped shouting long enough to shake hands. Another, sweat-darkened hair escaping from her shabby bonnet, shaking a pierced roasting pan full of chestnuts over a red-glowing brazier, screamed out hello from across the road. Their glances roamed over Joseph and passed on.

The butcher's shop counter, opening onto the street, was piled high with slabs of red and white meat, towers of fat cuts reaching almost to the first-floor windowsills. A small boy, flourishing a bunch of yellow feather dusters, shooed away the bluebottles that buzzed about.

Mrs Dulcimer surveyed a mounded pink coil of sausages, a white enamel dish glistening with kidneys, flanked by another of white squares of tripe. Handkerchief clutched to his nose to keep off the stench of dead flesh, warm blood, Joseph managed to go on speaking. It can be hard work cajoling wrongdoers to accept being inter-viewed. Money helps. Or drink.

The butcher's assistants roared out the prices of saddle and flank. Neighbouring stallholders competed, advertis-ing chickens and rabbits. Mrs Dulcimer ignored the din, pointed to the meat she wanted.

Mind your backs! Joseph jumped aside as two cows lumbered past, driven by a gaunt crone wearing a man's overcoat fastened with twine. He shouted: I try not to judge them. I just record what they say.

Mrs Dulcimer battled forwards again. She paused, began choosing leeks, fat ones with white snub ends. She held out her basket for the vegetable-seller to tip a stream of orange carrots into it. She turned her head, glanced a question.

He said: prostitutes, I mean. They're very wary, most of them.

Mrs Dulcimer said: they have reason to be wary of you, perhaps.

He took the basket from her: let me carry this. She walked on ahead, but kept stopping, so that each time he bumped into her and had to apologise. She bought a ream of paper from one stall, a bundle of nib-holders from another.

She said: for them to talk to you freely, they would need to trust that you were a true well-wisher, a true friend.

She fingered the silk scarves looped up, fluttering like streamers, in front of a hat shop. She conferred with the stallholder over the price of artificial anemones. Joseph leaned against the wooden post supporting the milliner's canvas awning. Lengths of lace and ribbon blew in his face, tickled him.

Was she mocking him? Nathalie would tease him rather than mock him. She'd seize a pillow and pummel him with it. Let go, let go, I need to get dressed. After a few protests, mind the baby, we must be careful of the baby, she would yield, he cried out I love you, he shuddered, he came. She held his shoulders and whispered: I love you too. Five minutes later she'd be up, hunting on the floor for her stockings. Silky black scraps. *Sainte Vierge*! There's a great hole in the heel of this one. Oh, curses. They were meant to last until New Year.

They emerged from the market at the top of the main road, where the common began. Mrs Dulcimer said: there! We're done! Her red mouth curved. Her teeth shone in her dark face.

Joseph said: there's a lodging-house near Newington Causeway I need to visit again. In order to complete an interview. Would you accompany me? I think the inmates might talk to me if you were there too, to reassure them I mean no harm.

She hesitated. Oh. All right. I suppose so.

She turned under the massing trees, towards Newington. Joseph plodded along at her side. The invisible sun, burning through the smog floating overhead, pressed heat onto the shoulders of his overcoat. Too many layers of wool. The laden basket, too large to carry easily, bumped his thigh.

He said: I need your help with something else as well. I'm looking for a maid of all work for my household. I thought you might know someone, given what you've explained to me of the nature of your lodging-house, your tenants.

Mrs Dulcimer paused, stood still. A bee alighted on the edge of her bonnet. A golden-brown stud of fur. Quivering. She raised her hand, brushed it off.

Joseph said: I've decided, by the way, not to press charges against the girl Doll. I accept that there were mitigating factors, which you hinted at, in her case. Some distressing circumstance, which made her behave, let us say, irrationally.

He heard himself sounding prosy as a solicitor's clerk. Mrs Dulcimer was smiling at him, as though she thought so too. Golden-green leaves rocked and fluttered down. One landed on the red shoulder of Mrs Dulcimer's cape, stuck there, like an epaulette. She said: that is good of you. I owe you a favour now, don't I? I should like to help you, and I think I can. Doll is in fact seeking a situation at this very moment. She won't re-offend. She's a good worker, I can assure you, with solid references from her last job.

Two dogs, barking and chasing, fled up to them, did a figure-of-eight in between them. Perhaps lured by the smell of the beef in the basket. Joseph kicked out and the dogs sprang away, made off across the green. Tails flying, legs stretched; a flow of muscle under brown skin. References written by whom? Joseph wondered. What kind of job? Pickpocket? Thief's moll helping out in the swag shop?

Mrs Dulcimer said: Doll was in service until some months ago. Her employers gave her a good character. I'll send her over to see your wife this afternoon.

She caught his glance. I've still got your note, with the address on it.

That first meeting. So exotic she'd seemed. Her black skin, her big dark eyes. But in fact she was quite ordinary. A bustling housewife, a kindly patroness of housemaids, doing her best to help the deserving poor, exactly the kind of people Joseph was not meant to be studying. And now she'd got him bogged down in shopping.

Mrs Dulcimer said: you'll be giving Doll the chance to put sad things behind her. Once settled in a decent family, she won't look back.

An experiment in rescue, was it? He was going to take on a girl with a criminal past, see what happened. Cara's worst fears come true? On the other hand, Doll might prove a helpful source of information about the under-world's living arrangements, at the very least. Easier to pump her once he'd got her at home. Those gravel-grey eyes looking into his. That bow-shaped mouth releasing stories of bullies' doss-houses and thieves' kitchens.

He said: I want it to be a surprise for my wife, that a servant might turn up so quickly. She won't be expecting one to arrive so soon.

How to ask for discretion? How to explain that there was no need for the females of the Benson household to know exactly whence the prospective maid came? Cara hadn't liked the idea of a strange woman calling at her house at an unusual hour, and he'd had to lie, claiming that Mrs Dulcimer was the clothes-mender's wife delivering his coat and wanting to be paid on the spot. While as for Milly: she was too sharp for her own good. Liable to put two and two together and make a thousand.

Was he looking worried? Mrs Dulcimer seemed to read his expression. She nodded at him, as though to say: yes, a surprise it shall be. Don't fret. It will be all right.

They reached the far side of the common, edged with white-painted wooden rails. You could sense the river, flowing along on the left, invisible behind these massing warehouses. Stinking, sucking tide, burden of excrement. He and Mrs Dulcimer glanced at each other at the same moment, grimaced.

They trudged past a row of shops selling second-hand furniture, second-hand waistcoats, second-hand fire-irons. At the far end a tall, thin house wedged itself in next to a stables, its door painted apple green, its white doorstep patterned with dusty footprints. Tied-back grey-and-white-checked curtains framed the front window, a notice advertising Beds to Let.

Sweat trickled down Joseph's back. He paused, swapped the basket from one hand to another, took out his hand-kerchief and wiped his forehead. Mrs Dulcimer's brown face looked friendly and concerned. She said: that's too heavy and awkward to carry any further, isn't it?

She gestured at the green door. Let's leave it here. I know the owner. Mrs Bonnet and I are old friends. She'll look after it for me. I can collect it later, on my way home. Or her boy will take it for me, on his barrow. Let's go inside for a moment, and drink something, and then continue on our way.

Darkness and coolness. A room almost bare of furniture, smelling of scrubbing soap. Three straw-seated chairs pushed back on the damp tiled floor. Mrs Dulcimer! The landlady, coming in, stepping over gleaming wet, sang out her greeting. Auburn hair, lighter than Joseph's own, under a twist of lace-frilled white linen. Eyes green as gooseberries; creamy, freckled skin. A rounded figure under her muffling grey apron. She nodded and bobbed at Joseph with perfunctory politeness. Her concern was directed at her friend. Ah, my dear. Draw up a chair, do, never mind the floor, it's nearly dry. What can I fetch you? I've no fresh water, pump's failed, but I've lemonade. That do you?

Mrs Dulcimer tweaked off her gloves. She settled them on her knee, stroked them to lie flat. Joseph took off his own gloves, stuffed them into his frock-coat pocket. He removed his hat, and placed it on the seat of a nearby chair.

Mrs Bonnet returned with a brown pottery jug, poured streams of lemonade into glass tumblers. She said to Mrs Dulcimer: you look well. And that's a nice earring you're wearing. Have I seen it before? But surely it's one of a pair? You've lost the other on the way here. Oh, what a shame.

Mrs Dulcimer touched the little gold-strung cluster of turquoise beads that hooped one earlobe. Oh, Hetty dear, I lost the other years ago. And I don't wear this one every day, you know. You wouldn't recognise it, necessarily.

She stroked the other earlobe. She looked over at Mrs Bonnet. Strange, isn't it, the power an ornament has to affect your mood? Mornings I decide to wear this I feel half hopeful and half sad. Or perhaps it's not so strange. I can't wear a particular earring in the wrong state of mind, that's all. But which comes first? The choice of ornament, or the feeling? The one seems to be the same as the other, when I think about it.

Mrs Bonnet puffed out her lips, blew a little cloud of airy sound. For heaven's sakes! Blowed if I know! Ah, you do go on!

Mrs Dulcimer shrank a bit; folded her hands in her lap, studied the tips of her boots. Glancing at this withdrawal, Mrs Bonnet seemed to regret her sharpness, to want to humour her friend. She touched her own earlobes, both of them bare and pink; black pinholes where earrings would jab in. Mine have gone for a walk again. Coming back on Monday we hope. It's terrible, the exercise they have to take. To and fro, to and fro!

Mrs Dulcimer recovered, sat up. She said: never mind. That's a nice bit of lace you've got there, Hetty. It suits you very well.

Mrs Bonnet lowered her voice. So. Everything all right? Mrs Dulcimer gave a tiny shake of the head in Joseph's direction, setting the red plume on her bonnet nodding, and replied: all right. The other woman said: Annie's getting along? Mrs Dulcimer confirmed this: yes, she's getting along. Her friend Betsy's with us now, turned up just recently, and so they keep each other company.

Mrs Bonnet sighed. She drew up a chair, sat down, leaned back. She stuck out her booted feet in front of her, rubbed one hand over her rounded chin. She gazed at the floor, spoke to the damp red tiles: ah, poor Annie, it was hard for her. She sat up straighter, cleared her throat. Well,

I'm stopping at home all morning. Of course I'll mind the basket for you. We'll put it out the back, in the cool.

Mrs Bonnet leaned forwards. A kindly face, wasn't it? It would show concern at children falling over, scraping their calves, wailing; at tenants needing nice hot dinners. She might, at a guess, be willing to answer some questions. Silently Joseph rehearsed them. Do you ever let beds by the hour rather than the night? What do you charge? How large are your rooms? How often do you change the sheets?

Mrs Bonnet looked past him, to Mrs Dulcimer. Tell me more of how Annie's doing. She's improving, I suppose.

Mrs Dulcimer returned: yes, certainly. We've come a long way from beef tea. We're onto soups now, and rice pudding.

She pointed to the basket. And stew, as you see.

How long were they going to sit gossiping? They seemed set for the rest of the day. His arms and legs felt too long, folded up in this small room. He fidgeted, tipping his chair backwards. He reached for his hat, hooked it over his knee, smoothed its glossy top.

Mrs Dulcimer turned, gave him a faint smile, and nodded. To Mrs Bonnet she said: we're heading to Newington Causeway this morning, this gentleman and myself. He has a mind to visit the lodging-houses, one in particular, I'm sure you can guess which. A business matter. I'm going along to smooth his path, as you might say.

She made him sound like a debt collector. Or worse. The auburn-haired woman folded her arms over her plump aproned belly. Ah, you won't find her. Nobody in. The police was round there earlier today, tipped off it was a swag shop. She got a hint of it, they say. Some plain-clothes man poking about yesterday, asking questions, she got the wind up her. She done a runner in the middle of the night. Her girls too. Place cleaned out, all the bedding and crockery they could lift, and the month's rent not paid. My boy Bertie came past this morning, told me. He was down there on a delivery. Heard all about it.

Joseph smacked his fist into his palm, causing his hat to fall to the floor. So this expedition has been a complete waste of time!

He stooped to pick up his hat. Damnation. Damp stains on the brim. Mrs Dulcimer got up. Dearie, we must be off. Can you spare your barrow for half a day? If we're not going on to Newington, I'll take my shopping home with me immediately. And the basket's very heavy.

Certainly you may have the barrow, Mrs Bonnet assented, rising from her chair: I'll send my boy over to fetch it this evening. No, better that he goes with you now. Then he can bring it straight back.

She touched Mrs Dulcimer's arm. You take care.

Back in the street, Mrs Dulcimer turned to Joseph. Our conversation got interrupted, didn't it? Why not come home with me now? I'll give you lunch, and we can go on talking.

He said: thank you. I assure you, a slice of bread and cheese is all I require.

She said: that's what Mrs Bonnet likes, too. She works so hard, she's the midwife for all round here, as well as keeping her lodging-house, she doesn't always have time for a proper dinner. Sometimes she comes over to me for supper, and that way I make sure she gets something decent to eat.

Past the common, they took the back way, parallel to the main road, to avoid the market crowds. They walked silently side by side under the plane trees, Mrs Bonnet's boy following behind with the loaded barrow. The sun's warmth pressed down through the grey clouds veiling the sky. Mrs Dulcimer was lifting her face to the gusting wind, the whirling leaves, smiling faintly. Left to himself, Joseph calmed. I've wasted an entire morning. Am I sulking? Yes.

The breeze tickled the back of his neck above his collar: Joseph, you're absurd! He jumped. Who was that? A female voice, amused and low-toned. To hell with it. He offered his arm to Mrs Dulcimer, and she took it. They swung along, under the trees.

At Apricot Place Joseph flicked Mrs Bonnet's boy a farthing: good lad. Off with you now, straight back home and no lingering! No getting into mischief!

The boy shrugged: you won't be there to see, though, will you, mister? He skipped off with his barrow, smirking.

Joseph stroked his soles over the bootscraper, leaving curds of mud, then followed his hostess down into the area and under the stone porch formed by the steps going up to the front entrance. She unlocked a blue-painted door, led him into a kitchen with whitewashed walls; windows back and front. A range stood in the chimney breast, saucepans and ladles hanging from a rack above it, shelves to either side. Opposite, a dresser held a grey pottery bread crock, an array of blue and yellow plates, jugs and bowls. The same china he'd seen on sale in the market. There stood her blue, yellow-flecked breakfast cup, the matching coffee-pot.

Mrs Dulcimer halted by the deal table. She said: let me take your hat and coat, and find Doll and send her off, and check on Annie, then, if you don't mind, I shall cook while we talk, so that I don't fall behind. I shan't be a moment.

He heard her running upstairs, calling for Doll. A female creature flying away from him, promising to return. He just had to wait. He didn't mind. Observe, Benson, observe. So far, Mayhew had interviewed no household servants, seemed not to require descriptions of kitchens and pantries. Domestic life too dull for him to bother with? No villains here? Not in Cara's view: she knew all about cooks filching sugar and tea, hoarding more than their fair share of leftovers, watering the wine. Life on the street had more snap and fizz, certainly. Nonetheless Joseph paced about, taking measurements with eye and foot.

A clock ticked somewhere. Cool air reached him from the open window. Pigeons cooed in the green garden wreathing beyond the glass panes. The back door dangled an array of aprons, presumably graded for different levels of work: heavy baize, sturdy linen, fine cotton.

Wheelbacked oak chairs, tucked well in around the table, a yellow-painted stool laden with books, completed the furniture. Pots of preserves, their pleated white paper caps secured with string, massed on a shelf. A second shelf held brown pottery jars with labels tied on: salt, flour, sugar, rice, tea. Mrs Dulcimer's handwriting: he recognised the flourishes on the tails of the consonants.

Her particular way of forming her letters cropped up again on a piece of card propped on the dresser: a scrawled list of menus. Tripe with onions. Apple tart. Beef rissoles with carrots and cabbage. Caramel rice pudding. Neck of lamb with suet dumplings. Raised mutton pie. Plum turnovers. Vegetable curry.

A pile of books teetered on the three-legged stool. *The Art of Cookery Made Plain and Easy* by Mrs Hannah Glasse. A complete Shakespeare. *Frankenstein*, by Mary Shelley. *Jane Eyre* by Currer Bell. A book of household hints. A book on home doctoring.

Above him, the front door banged shut. Doll departing for Lamb's Conduit Street, presumably. Footsteps sounded at the top of the stairs. He closed the medical textbook, shoved it back underneath the Shakespeare. When Mrs Dulcimer entered the kitchen he was lifting out the bloodstained paper-wrapped package of meat from the basket, looking round for a plate.

She had put off her bonnet and walking-dress, had donned some grey and green garment, a sort of sack, in a striped pattern. No cap. Her knot of black plaits glistened. Again he caught the scent of her pomade. She reached down an oval platter: here, put it onto this.

She tied on a linen apron, blue with cream stripes, hands behind her back twisting a swift bow. Nice neat waist she still had, despite her age. She pulled out a blue kerchief from the apron pocket, tied it round her head like a turban, with a rakish bow over one eye. She saw Joseph watching her, and smiled. My uniform!

Transformed into a cook, she obviously knew her business. She moved in her small kingdom deftly, confidently. Everything seemed to be in the right place, ready to hand: pot-holders, trivets, long-handled iron hooks. She took up a thin-bladed knife, with a ragged edge. With this fine weapon she chopped the beef into red cubes that she dusted with flour. She slashed off leeks' whiskery ends, sliced them thinly, cast them into a little pot with butter and salt, set them to soften. She peeled and sliced onions and carrots, threw them into a wide, flat pan with a larger knob of butter, a spoonful of oil. Ah, just a moment, I must go outside for some herbs.

He took the frying-pan and wooden spoon from her: here, let me do that. Mrs Dulcimer pursed her lips. You know how to cook?

He pushed aside the browning vegetables, tipped in the meat, moved the pieces gently to and fro over the flame. I certainly do!

Mrs Dulcimer nodded. My husband enjoyed cooking, too. He was the chef in our hotel. He was so gifted, he could make food the way French people liked it.

Foreign dishes. Nathalie had got him to try eating steamed globe artichokes. Oh, Joseph, plenty of English people eat artichokes, I know they do. He poked it. But this is a giant sunflower bud! No, it's not. She showed him. Tear off the leaves, one by one, dip them into the hot cream sauce, draw them through your teeth, the nutty base of the leaf resting on your tongue. There. See? Later he undressed her, layer by layer: my sweet artichoke.

Mrs Dulcimer returned from the garden with a fistful of thyme and sage. She fished dried bay leaves out of a jar. We'll flavour the stew with beer, as well. When I lived in France, we used wine of course. The beer's over there. Will you fetch it?

She gestured towards a cloth-covered jug on the windowsill. She sat down and began to peel potatoes. She said: so. To business. I understand that you wish to talk to prostitutes, for your research, or, I should say, you wish to get them to talk to you. I can certainly introduce you to some of the local women. You'll need to be respectful, mind. They are used to being lectured by well-wishers, and can grow very resentful.

Joseph took up the jug of beer, poured a brown stream into the pan. The puddle of meat and vegetables hissed and frothed, then settled. He stirred gently. He said: please go on. I'm listening.

Mrs Dulcimer selected another potato. She cupped it in her brown palm. May I speak freely? I think you may be making a mistake in how you approach your study.

Where did she learn to speak so fancy? From the visitors to her hotel, it must have been. That husband of hers, egging her on to talk nicely to their guests. Or perhaps all that Shakespeare. All those books she read. You didn't expect a black woman to sound so educated. More educated than he was! Blimey.

She went on. Men like you define street women, prostitutes, as completely cut off from their respectable sisters. Yet, from my point of view, they are just girls who take up that trade at certain moments in their lives. They may not stay in it. They may move in and out of it, as circumstances dictate.

Joseph said: trade?

She hailed from Deptford, didn't she. Ships sailing into the docks from the East Indies, the West Indies. Spice trade. Sacks of nutmeg, cinnamon, mace. To flavour fruit cakes. Mincemeat. Savoury pies. Bite into the pie, stick your face in it and eat. Stick to the recipe. Tried, tested, proved. Stick to the facts. He gripped the handle of the pan, tilted the welter of meat and beer from side to side, sluicing the skidding carrots and onions with juice. Where was the pepper? This needed pepper.

He said: there may be something in what you say. I must think about it.

Trade in female flesh; young bodies weighed out like chunks of sugar, costed, paid for. But also trade meaning job. Meaning skill. Learned over years of apprenticeship. Women apprenticed to learn feminine arts. How to draw men in. A sly bit of flirtation, flattery, when you started out courting, eyeing them up, that was one thing. That was what nice women did. Coquetting. Tarts cold-bloodedly employing those self-same charms to impose on men, get money from them, he recognised that but he didn't have to approve of it. He'd gone along with it recently, yes, that little Italian, because he was only human, he had very strong needs, he hadn't been able to resist.

A stitch suddenly attacked his side; like someone poking him. Whispering. Oh, go on with you! A jab at his ribs again. He bent over, coughing.

Mrs Dulcimer held the potato in one brown hand, turning it round and round as her blade slipped over it. Long curl of brown peel. Peel her clothes off and she'd be brown all over. A brown bush.

She remained silent and yet he felt she addressed him. Admit it, Joseph. You long for what they offer. Their succulence. Their taste. The promise of: what? Water rose in his eyes, streamed down his face.

Mrs Dulcimer said: oh, those onions. They're very strong, aren't they?

He mopped his eyes. Her hands were becoming covered with earth. Fingernails clotted with black. She'd have to wash those potatoes again once she'd finished peeling them.

She began skinning another potato, shaving off brown-white lengths with rapid flicks of her knife. The peelings shot away, fell onto the table. She held up the potato: top and bottom lopped, sides carved into curves, making a barrel shape. She said: that's how I learned to do it in France. All food, when it was served, had to look beautiful. Even potatoes!

She nodded at her handiwork, tossed it into the waiting pot of water. With his wooden spoon Joseph lifted his pieces of meat, turned them, mixed the onions and carrots back towards the beef.

Prostitutes. Potatoes. Potato-women hawked in markets. Dug up from good Kentish earth, lugged to London, sold to connoisseurs. Now, this one's nice, no bruises or black eyes, just firm white flesh, very tasty. Earlies, sir. They're the best.

My dear brethren. Beware. A vile, debased simulacrum of the sacred marriage act. The preacher's voice spluttered in his head like a wet potato dropped into hot oil. Mrs

Dulcimer swept the peelings into a tin bucket. These are for my chickens. I've a cockerel and six hens out the back. Good layers so far.

She suddenly laughed. I had three cockerels before. Too many. Forcing themselves on the hens non-stop. So I wrung the necks of two of them, and made *coq au vin*. A nice little feast for the lodgers and me.

She came to stand next to him at the stove. So close they almost touched. Her spicy carnation scent mixed with that of her sweat, the rich perfume of the meat simmering with herbs. She stirred her little copper saucepan of leeks, sprinkled flour into it, a dollop of cream, a crushed bay leaf, scooted her wooden spoon back and forth. This is a dish I often have at mid-day. You'll share it with me, I hope. We'll leave some for Doll, when she returns. Betsy's feeling poorly, she's near her time, she's gone back to bed. And Annie's fast asleep. I'll take them up some food later on.

Joseph skimmed a layer of fat off the top of the stew, spooned it into a basin. Sheen of yellow, the fat congealing as it cooled. He smiled to himself. You could apply the scientific method to everything. Yes, Mayhew. Certainly to cookery. Exact amounts and mixtures. Precise temperatures. He could have run a food shop, yes, he could. He could have conjured up cheese puffs, devilled kidneys; he could have poached fish dumplings, baked glistening hams, poured fresh aspic over sliced hardboiled eggs. He'd bought a cookery book once, on a second-hand stall, pored over it: mouthwatering juicy stuff. Ah. Now there, dear Mayhew, were classification categories that made sense. Service *à la Russe*. Service *à la Française*. Entrées. Removes. Luncheon dishes. Supper dishes. Fifty recipes for eggs. Fifty types of sauce. As a boy he'd dreamed of inventing a new sauce, named after himself. If he invented one now he'd make it a variation on s*auce brune*, flavoured with bay, a drop of Madeira, a pinch of black pepper, a spoonful of cream, name it *Sauce Dulcimer*.

Mrs Dulcimer lent across, prodded the stew with her spoon, bent over it, sniffed it. Yes, that will do. She clapped a lid onto the pot, put it into the oven. She set a pan of water to heat.

She said: prostitutes provide a service. To men. If there were no demand for their services, there would be no prostitutes.

Ah, lady, in a perfect world, perhaps. He licked the juice off the wooden spoon, tapped it on the tabletop. Once, twice. He agreed with her and also he didn't.

He took up the vegetable knife and ran his fingers along the blade, clearing it of earth. Mrs Dulcimer fetched two eggs, cracked them into cups, tipped them one after the other into the boiling pan wreathed in steam.

Joseph said: I called you a philanthropist, before. Now I think you're an impossible idealist.

The pot's water shuddered, frills of white frothing up inside it. He said: you should have put some vinegar in that.

Mrs Dulcimer said: and I forgot the salt, too. She laid her hand, wrapped in a cloth, on the handle of the sauce-pan. She shook it gently to and fro, tipping in vinegar, a pinch of salt, then released it.

She said: love between men and women should be free. No monetary transaction involved. Human beings should not be bought and sold.

She did not utter the word slaves, but he heard it. She toasted and buttered two large slices of bread, spread them with leek puree, slipped a poached egg on top of each one. Joseph ate in silence. Mrs Dulcimer sat opposite, similarly quiet.

You had to like someone to be able to eat in their company. Some people filled you with disgust as you heard them chew and swallow. Watched them! The Hoof, eating and talking at the same time, long loud breaths sucked in whistling through his teeth, before he spat out words, bits of gristle and bone.

Joseph licked the last vestiges of egg yolk off his fork. Clotted yellow on the tines, sweet on his tongue. He said: you understand these girls, don't you? You understand their lives.

Mrs Dulcimer said: I'll tell you about my own life, if that will help. If you want to listen!

She fetched a dish of greengages from the pantry. Mine is a common tale. One that you must have heard several times already, in the course of your research.

She plucked a greengage stone from between her lips, dropped it onto her plate. She licked her fingertips. Little pink tongue neat and swift as a cat's. She put her elbows on the table, cupped her face in her hands. Making space for herself; keeping him at a distance; her elbows as barricades.

She said: all young people want to find a sweetheart, to get together, to mate. You meet someone you fancy, you want to touch them, you court them. So I fell in love with a handsome young fellow. A porter in the docks. But we couldn't marry. His family was dead set against it. I was broken-hearted, him too, but what good did that do us? So he went off, and I got away too, I moved to the City, I found work washing floors in a hotel. I met my husband there. He worked as a cook, as I told you before. He had some money put by, and so we took a gamble, we moved to France. And there we were able to make a life.

She moved her elbows, sat up straight, began to brush crumbs into her palm. And what about you? What about your life? Are you going to tell me something about it?

He said: I've little to tell. I had a wife I loved, and she died. Now I'm married again, to a good, kind woman. I've got four children. A house, a job. I'm very fortunate.

Mrs Dulcimer sat quietly. He said: please. Go on with your story.

She leaned forward, making a little pile of the crusts of her toast. Her grey and green sleeve fluttered at her wrist. She said: I was one of the lucky ones.

She pushed away her plate, dabbed her mouth with her napkin, crumpled it between her hands. I got my child into the Foundling Hospital. They draw lots because there are too many babies to take in. It's like betting. Win or lose, you have to submit.

She smoothed the napkin, rolled it up, tied it in a knot. She touched her bare earlobe. I left an earring with the baby, as a token of who I was, who she was. We were allowed to do that. My idea was that I'd come back and claim her one day, and that way, the earrings matching up, I'd be sure. They wrote down my name when they took her in, but not hers. I was going to fetch her back one day, you know.

Joseph said: but it didn't happen?

Mrs Dulcimer said: no, it didn't happen.

She put the knotted napkin into her palm and balanced it there. Tilted it back and forth. She rocked the tiny white bundle in her hand. She addressed the tablecloth. Just before I got married, I told my husband, that's to say my husband-to-be, that I had a child.

Joseph corrected her: that you'd had a child.

Mrs Dulcimer corrected him back: she was still my child. Even though I'd given her away and couldn't see her.

She tipped the napkin from hand to hand. She gave it away, she took it back, she gave it away. She said: being a moral person, a churchgoer, my husband-to-be was very unhappy at my news. He made me go down on my knees and pray. He prayed with me, oh, yes. As a Christian, he ended up forgiving me, but he decided that if we were to marry we should leave the child where she was. I'd made a fresh start, and she should be allowed to continue with hers.

Mrs Dulcimer closed her hand over her knotted napkin. A white tail poked up out of her fist. Like one of those shapes his mother used to make to amuse him, twiddling her fingers in front of the candle-flame. Shadow-animals projected onto the wall: rabbits, dogs, crocodiles. Ghosts of creatures. Ghosts of babies. Mrs Dulcimer said: I chose my husband over my child. How else would I have survived? I couldn't find work. Nobody would employ a black girl with a bastard child in tow. My family was poor. They all worked long hours down in the docks. I believed they couldn't help me. I suppose I was too ashamed to ask them. Perhaps after all they would have taken me back in. The thought torments me so you can't conceive.

Mrs Dulcimer opened her fingers, let the squashed napkin drop. She said: my husband was a good man, in his way. He had small experience of the world, and so it was easy for him to be clear about right and wrong. It was brought home to me that I had made a grave mistake.

She spat out the words as though they tasted bitter. She was trying to hide her suffering. Joseph wanted to put his arms round her, comfort her. He said: I am beginning to understand how easy it is for women to make mistakes. Men do not always help them.

Mrs Dulcimer grimaced. She spoke in a grating voice. You don't understand at all. The mistake I refer to was getting married.

She stood up. I'll bid you goodbye. I've work waiting.

He walked slowly, wanting to kill time. Three o'clock. Such a dead time of day. He drifted north towards Blackfriars, crossed the river, wandered towards Holborn. He too had work on hand, a report to draft, but where could he settle to do it? Too early to go home, cope with his wife and children bouncing about calling to each other, clattering the fire irons, banging the door, interrupting him with offers of tea, shouting to one another to hush, Papa's writing. Intolerable, today, even to contemplate going to Mayhew's office, using that corner desk, sitting under the old man's beady eye.

He dropped into the Purple Empress in Red Lion Street. Just one glass of brandy. Make it last as long as he needed.

The simpers and flapped eyelashes of the two gaudily dressed women hovering at the bar, leaned in on by half-tipsy men, seemed banal; much too obvious. One gay creature wore a cape of emerald lace and carried, under her arm, a pug dog, which she was extravagantly kissing and caressing. Her sister tart wore a bonnet topped with a heap of fake cherries, and made a great show of tapping the clustering men with her frilled maroon-and-white-striped parasol as she laughed.

He shifted his chair, to avoid seeing the pug-woman's wide red mouth snapping open and shut like a purse. He took out his notebooks, but could find no words to put down. Mrs Dulcimer's had crowded his out. Yet he had to persevere. He absolutely had to make a go of this job.

Therefore write for Mayhew what Mayhew wanted. Joseph began sketching a plan for the revised report. Paragraphs numbered one, two, three. He drew a margin down the left-hand side of the page. He wrote the date. He sucked his pencil end and sighed.

A slender girl, brown-haired and pale, wrapped in a brown mantle with a reddish velvet trim, tripped by, pretending not to notice his glance at her neat little canvas boots finished with blue bows. She paused, turned back. Afternoon, sir. Mind if I sit here?

Not at all, Joseph said, closing his notebook: charmed.

He was, too. Bright brown eyes, dark lashes. A lady fox, chestnut fur nicely groomed, plumy brush curled out of sight. She wore a plain, close bonnet covered in dark pink silk, with white ruching inside, adorned with a single knot of pink ribbon. A cast-off from an employer, perhaps.

She plumped down next to him, gave him a faint smile. She was simply one of the poor, neither virtuous nor vicious. Yes, Mrs Dulcimer, all right, I'm listening to you. Perhaps she'd been a lady's maid at one time. The band of delicately frilled muslin at her throat was of good quality, as were her boots. In her mittened hands she held a bobbin, strung with a bunch of bright beads on white threads. She worked at her lace while darting glances at him, her fingers flying to and fro. Don't mind me, darling! You make your mind up what you want, and I'll get on.

Pretend she's not soliciting. Don't shout at her to be off, don't get her into trouble. Taking a long, considering look, he put her down, finally, as a former dressmaker's assistant, fallen on hard times, augmenting her meagre savings as best she could, in the only way she knew, all right, Mrs Dulcimer, I'll grant you that. Don't go on at me! I've taken your point!

The minx dropped her heap of needles, bobbins, white tracery. She shook her wrists, rubbed her fingers: ah, they ache. So stop here with me for a while, Joseph suggested: rest your hands. Talk to me.

She shrugged: buy me a drink and sure, I'll talk to you. But I've little to tell. I'll have a gin-and-water, with some sugar, if you'll be so kind.

Since he was not on the Surrey side, this wasn't a work interview. He'd just keep the girl company for a while, see what the conversation brought.

He spoke gently. Will you tell me about yourself, about your life? Can you read, for example? Can you write?

She answered readily. She described going to school as a child, learning her letters, learning the Creed, a couple of prayers. Taught lacemaking by a neighbour. Taken out of school at eleven, set to work minding the neighbours' babies, then employed as a seamstress in a big establishment over at Whitechapel.

Eighteen last birthday. She had a child of three, by one father, and one of one and a half, by another. Her mother cared for both. Mother's crippled and can't go out, but she does what she can. There's a boy in the street brings her bundles of waste paper, to make spills with, which he takes away and sells. Or she'll mind children for the neighbours, when there's need. She ties them to the bedstead with string, and that way they can toddle about but not fall down the stairs and hurt themselves.

She put both hands round her glass and stared at its wet rim while Joseph remained still, not wanting to halt her flow. Her mother lived this side of Whitechapel, in one rented room, paid for by the daughter. One bed for the mother and the two children. Nowhere to cook, so the neighbour boy carried meals in when he brought the waste paper. Easily portable food like buns, bruised fruit sold off cheap, a cone of fried fish now and again. Privy out the back in the yard, shared with twenty other people. No father? Joseph ventured. No father, assented the girl. She downed more gin-and-water. He died after an accident on a building site. We got no compensation, though we tried.

Joseph asked: and your children's fathers?

Ah, the girl said: the first one died of consumption, poor fellow, and the second cleared off a while back. Work on a ship, he said, but I've not heard from him since. He may be dead and drowned, poor boy, who knows? He was my sweetie all right, but off he had to go.

She stopped, and looked at Joseph with hot eyes. She dropped her end of the tidily patterned talk they wove between them like cat's cradle. She grabbed her scissors and slashed it. Cries, anguished words, flying up out, seized by her and smashed back down. And then I couldn't keep my job as a seamstress, not with the children. You have to sew all night if there's a big order on, and the baby wasn't weaned, and then some tittle-tattler told them I wasn't married. That was that. Out!

She shut herself up with a swig of gin. She set the glass down, passed her hand across her face, resumed her calm expression. She relaxed, settled in her seat. Well, the pub was warm, wasn't it, and she was soothing herself with the drink in front of her. Perhaps, in fact, both he and she felt similarly. Wary. Not yet defeated. Their two pairs of elbows on the table; not far apart. Their faces turned towards one another. Their eyes meeting. Like two thrushes searching for food. Checking the territory. Assessing any possible danger.

You're a long way from home, here, Joseph suggested: wouldn't there be employment for you nearer Whitechapel? So that you could live with your mother and see your children?

The girl's voice hardened and sharpened. If I can't be seen I can't be talked about. Mother and I decided that was best. So that if ever I'm able to leave off this work I can go back and no one'll be any the wiser. I'll be able to start over.

The girl's face, as well as her voice, dared him to pity her. Come on, then. You've had an hour of my time. That's worth more than one single bloody glass of gin.

He gave her a handful of coins, which she counted. There's enough here to pay for an hour and a half. Want the extra, do you? Come on, then. I lodge just next door, above the coffee-house.

She reminded him of Doll. Yet another pretty young woman. Spirited. Intelligent. Ordinary. So many prostitutes looked completely ordinary. All right, there were extremes. Bejewelled courtesans at one end, gutter drabs at the other. As in Mayhew's classification, dear Mrs Dulcimer. But in the middle was this vast group of women selling themselves as though they were simply pounds of butter, packets of chops, baskets of fruit. And if you didn't know they were doing that, you'd take them just as normal human beings, trotting about their business, loving their little ones, performing the small acts of kindness that kept the world going. If only all prostitutes wore green lace capes, garish wigs, vulgar bonnets, he'd know where he was!

Well, he said: goodbye. Good luck.

She stared. You don't want it?

Thank you, he said: for talking to me.

Getting up, he paused. I don't suppose you'd tell me your name?

No, she said: I bloody wouldn't.

At home, the hall smelled warm and stale. A thread of scent wound up from downstairs: a tang of mutton simmering. The children squealed to him from two floors above where, presumably, Milly was putting them to bed. Cara cried a greeting from the kitchen. Added something about the water for his bath being already upstairs. He groaned. He should have been here sooner, to help. He peeled off his coat, ran up to his bedroom.

Pouring the tepid water over his shoulders, he winced. Like being back at school, where duckings in the horse trough punished you into manliness and sometimes, to make extra sure of your capacity for endurance, you were held down, choking. Screaming when you came up for air, screaming when finally you were released, the bullies howling with amusement. Mummy's boy! Mummy's boy! After a year of being ducked and beaten he'd managed to get himself removed, by dint of falling ill. His mother wrapped the doorknocker in straw, so that people coming to the house wouldn't disturb him. At the time he wasn't aware of it. Later, when she told him about it, he felt her care. She'd wanted to wrap him in straw. Stop him being knocked. Being picked up and flung back and forth. She had tried.

He finished dressing and wandered downstairs. Cara, swathed in a white cotton apron, was setting out plates and cutlery in the dining-room. Her brown ringlets poked out from underneath a wide white bandeau. She swivelled to greet him with a hasty kiss.

He seated himself, patted the chair next to his. Sit down, love. Come and talk to me for a minute.

She began: oh, for heaven's sake, there isn't time. Then her smile answered his. She released her fistful of forks and spoons to stream across the cloth. She lowered herself onto his knee, settled herself, touched his cheek. Her hand smelled faintly of mutton and strongly of carbolic soap. He reached up, took her hand in his, held it in his lap. He stroked her fingers, one by one. An old game that they hadn't played for a long time. He felt her calm, relax. The skin on her hand was rough and red. Tomorrow he'd buy her some lotion. Something really fancy, scented with carnation, with roses.

She leaned her head on his shoulder. She said: a girl turned up early this afternoon, wanting a place, saying you'd sent her. Thank you, Joseph. I didn't think you'd manage to see to it, with all you have to do.

He squeezed her cushiony waist. Well, you were wrong, weren't you?

Cara continued: she had proper references, she looks clean and sober, and so she's coming back with her things this evening, to get settled in. Tomorrow I'll start her off on the sideboard in here. It sadly needs polishing.

How could it be more polished than it already was? Red wood, all curlicues and inlays, like the crimson meat marbled with white fat he'd seen on that butcher's stall this morning. Cara's choice. Her pride and joy, she named it. He'd bought it for her as a wedding anniversary present. He thought it might be hideous, but he wasn't sure.

He stroked her starched shoulder. Clean apron, smelling of ironing. Milly must have done some laundering today. He shifted, put both arms around Cara, held her contentedly, enjoying the plump feel of her. Ah, but that poor girl. He should have gone out into the street and bought her a sandwich. She'd probably be there herself now, earning the money to pay for it, plus her next glass of gin. He sighed. Cara patted his face. You're tired, dearest. All that walking you do.

His stomach growled. Cara laughed, squirmed, levered herself up. I must see to my stew.

After supper, which he praised valiantly, bringing a pleased flush to Cara's cheeks, Milly proposed leaving the washing-up for the new maid to attend to when she arrived. I'm having the night off! She made tea and brought it up, then played for them, stiff-backed, drilling conscientiously through a Scotch jig. Cara took out her mending-basket and began darning. Wrinkly grey wool travelled in and out of his grey sock. He smoked, gazed at the fire.

Cara put down her needle and drummed her thimble finger on the arm of her chair. Keep in time, Milly!

Joseph said: play us a song now, sweetheart.

Milly thumped the keys afresh and sang. I know where I'm going,/ and I know who's going with me./ I know who I love,/ but the Lord knows who I'll marry.

Not that old thing again, Cara grumbled.

Milly said: I like it anyway. You criticise everything I do! You can't appreciate beautiful songs!

She took herself off to bed, banging the door behind her. Cara shook her head. She's getting to be even more of a handful, that child.

All girls are a handful at her age, surely, Joseph returned: they're growing up. Weren't you ever like that?

Nathalie was suddenly hovering in the air between them. Cara pressed her lips together, gave him a glance he couldn't read. She darted her needle through her darn; up and down. She had taught Milly to sew. And now Milly wanted to learn how to sew flesh, how to stitch up wounds. Probably she'd be very good at it. Women were so much less squeamish than men. Well, of course. If you could go through childbirth you could go through anything. Oh, Nathalie.

Cara put on a tinkling voice: ah, there's nothing like an evening at home by the fire. Why don't you fetch a book and read to me?

Because I'm not in the mood, my dearest one. Worried about Milly. Worried about my debts. Worried about how I'm going to explain my expenses to Mayhew.

Also, walled in by chairs and piano. Restless in his acreage of hearthrug. He stepped across to his wife's chair. He leaned over her, traced her jawline with one finger, tipped her face up, kissed her. Let's go to bed early ourselves, shall we, dearest?

Cara flinched. Her hands twisted the sock in her lap. Oh, Joseph, no. The new maid's not arrived yet, I must wait up to let her in, and anyway I'm so tired. And remember what the doctor said.

She was flushed and nervous. He knew what it cost her to speak openly. She was brave, he'd give her that. Cara blurted it out. No more children. Not yet, anyway.

I'd be very careful, Joseph said: you know I would. Please, Cara.

She'd been brought up to obey: father, priest, husband, doctor. You can't please all of us at once! Which one will it be? He knew, of course.

Cara bent her head, muttered. I don't want to risk it. I'm sorry, Joseph.

He made his voice as light as he could. I'm sorry too. I shouldn't have asked you. Don't upset yourself. I'm sorry. Everything's all right.

He moved away from her, put his hands in his pockets. Two paces forward across the rug, two paces back. He turned, addressed Cara's stabbing needle. It's too hot in here. I'm stifling. I think I'll go out, get some air. Don't wait up. Leave the door for me. I'll lock up when I get home.

Cara pressed her lips together again, continued darning.

EIGHT

Madeleine

L AMB'S CONDUIT STREET IN Holborn channels a flow of blue June weather, dust and pollen floating under the trees. Madeleine idles along between the flat-fronted, sash-windowed buildings set back from the pavement on both sides. When she steps on the edge of a broken paving-stone it tilts up, like a trapdoor entrance to the underworld. So just fall down into it.

An underground kitchen, dimly lit. Two aproned women toil, one scrubbing a saucepan, the other shaking out heavy-looking sheets. Irons heat on the range. Smell of burned onions. In a dark corner: a girl's muffled sobs. The woman swilling the blackened pot swivels towards her, sighs. Be all right, Dorothy. I didn't mean to shout. No, Mrs Benson, blubs the girl.

A man yells. Madeleine comes to. A passing bicyclist is berating a group of tourists blocking the middle of the street while they take photographs. Madeleine steps round the trip-up paving slab, wanders on.

On gable ends the ghosts of nineteenth-century signs, stencilled in faded black, advertise chocolates and hosiery in flowing script. Modern signs flourishing above the newly gentrified shops point Madeleine towards leather bags, French furnishings, organic vegetables, designer face cream and children's clothes. At the top of the street, green branches above a white stuccoed wall mark the boundary of Coram's Fields.

Wedged open, the door to the Lamb funnels in sunlight to spill along the bare, planked floor. Late morning, almost empty, just a couple of men leaning side by side nursing pints. Behind the bar, a woman wipes drips from a beer tap with a blue rag. She sells Madeleine a tomato juice. On your holidays, are you? Sort of, Madeleine says: I've just lost my job. The man standing next to her says: drowning your sorrows? Better make it a Bloody Mary, then.

Madeleine shakes her head at vodka, nods yes for ice, red pepper sauce. She says: I was working in a café in south-east London. It changed hands, the new owner wanted young people working for him, that was that. So now I've got plenty of free time.

She tucks herself into an alcove seat padded in green leather. Safely distant from Emm's offering found earlier this morning. Getting up, hearing a sound in the hallway, she flung on her dressing-gown, went to check. Thorny dark stems thrust in through the flap of the letterbox, choking it. She opened the front door, wrenched free from the outside a bunch of dead roses. Shrivelled leaves and withered red blooms, petals dangling, accompanied by a scrap of paper scrawled with a message: *My dear Madeleine, why haven't you got back in touch? Much love – Emm.*

The flowers looked like something he'd fished out of someone's rubbish. She threw them into the brown garden-waste bin. She peered up and down the street. Quiet as usual. No one about.

The flat felt flimsily walled; a paper box. So find refuge elsewhere. She dressed, picked up her little ruck-sack, slammed the front door behind her, strode out of Apricot Place. She walked north, ended up in Holborn, in Lamb's Conduit Street. Safer; anonymous amongst the crowds.

She and Toby had parted in Holborn, close to here, after they left Highgate. They caught the night bus down the hill; climbed to the upper deck, sat in the front seat. Toby, arms folded, eyes half closed, smiled to himself. A streak of tawny greasepaint above his eyebrow. Mouth still tinted red. The bus swerved around a corner, throwing them against each other. He murmured: that Francine. Guess what she did. Sleepy Madeleine said: goodness knows. So tell me.

Toby said: she crept up on us having sex in the grotto, and filmed us on her phone. She came over and told me just before the start of the play. But I told her: it's too late to put me off my stroke! All I've got to do now is walk on stage and look languishing. So fuck off!

Madeleine said: she wanted her revenge. Oh, Toby.

Toby said: her idea was to post the clip on the internet. Shame her beloved Anthony for evermore.

The bus slowed, stopped, stuck in jammed traffic. Passengers behind them groaned, swore, growled into their phones. Blurred haloes of blue, yellow, orange lights swam in the dark glass windows.

Toby said: unfortunately for her, as I pointed out, neither of us was recognisable. Anthony was wearing a mask and I was in a long blonde wig and a veil. I told her to go ahead. Publish and be damned! In any case, it would all work as a brilliant souvenir of the production. Here we are, darlings, in the un-dress rehearsal! I don't know what she did in the end. I didn't bother checking.

Madeleine asked: you planning to see Anthony again?

Toby said: certainly.

Madeleine said: and Francine?

Toby shrugged. She'll get over it. She's a survivor, that one.

Madeleine leaves the pub, meanders eastwards from Lamb's Conduit Street towards Gray's Inn Road. Sandwich bars and solicitors' offices front the soot-blackened Georgian buildings. She spends the afternoon nosing into side alleys, turning along every branching street she doesn't know. She zigzags north, finds herself near the Angel. Here, in a charity shop, she buys a sleeveless dress in red broderie anglaise. Italian, well-cut, knee-length. Very pleased with her bargain, she keeps the dress on. She rings Toby, tells him about losing her job. He says: time you started claiming your state pension, surely. Madeleine says: that feels so weird, somehow. I don't feel old enough inside. Toby sounds impatient. What does that matter? You're owed it. He proposes an early evening drink. For once, he's not working. See you at six, then.

In golden light, she walks back down into Bloomsbury, slants into Marchmont Street. Virginia Woolf slouches ahead. Loose duster coat over a long cardigan, shapeless blouse and skirt. She slipped out hours ago to buy a pencil and is still peacefully roaming. Just ahead of her stroll Charlotte Mew and Hilda Doolittle, arguing about poetry, making for a Corner House: cup of tea, poached egg on toast.

Toby's wearing old blue jeans, a black leather jacket. Grey-blond curls encircle his head. He hugs her. Nice rag. Haven't seen you in red before. Glass of red wine to match? Madeleine describes her route. Showing off about the distance she has tramped. Joking: would you say I'm a *flâneur*? A *flâneuse*?

Toby tips up his pint. These days everybody's a *flâneur*. What they mean is, they've just popped out for a breath of air.

Madeleine says: I think women can be *flâneurs*, but no one notices. They think we're just out shopping.

She smooths her red dress over her knees. Of course, sometimes we are.

Toby says: I never think of women as *flâneurs*. Only men. Nineteenth-century chaps like Baudelaire.

Madeleine says: men strolling alone were *flâneurs*, women strolling alone were street-walkers. Tarts. A complete double standard!

Toby pushes out his lip at her. Blah-blah-blah!

Madeleine says: I'm living in a nineteenth-century house, and I love it. I can imagine the lives of the housemaids, the cooks, from all the reading I've done, but I've no idea how it felt to be a London woman in those days, walking alone along a street like this one. I read Mayhew, but it's his researcher giving his version of what women say. There's Flora Tristan, but she's an observer, like Mayhew. And in novels of the time women's experience in the street is hardly ever mentioned. Only in passing.

So write some fiction, Toby says: imagine it. You don't know what it's like because you haven't written it yet! If you invent it you'll find out!

Madeleine fingers the cut-out pattern of her red dress, the ridges of red stitches surrounding the flower shapes. What would Toby make of the Emm business? Suppose it gets worse? Suddenly she wants to tell Toby about it, ask his advice. She looks at him, opens her mouth to speak. A phone cheeps. Toby claps his hand to his pocket. He gestures sorry at her, turns away to talk. Perhaps it's Anthony. Madeleine stares at the red wine stain at the bottom of her glass. She leaves him to it, goes to buy another round.

Later, at home, she clears a space on her table cluttered with bank statements, tax forms. The envelope containing her council tax bill: payment demanded for street-cleaning, rubbish removal, bin emptying. Start with a description of a street. Here in Walworth? A front door. What's behind it? Think of Nelly, her rush of tales. She was Nelly's rapt audience. So go forward, up the steps, bang the doorknocker. She turns over the envelope, scribbles on its torn flap stained with coffee-cup rings. She turns over the rest of her mail, writes on the backs of all the envelopes. She transfers her words to her laptop, writes some more.

She stops when she feels hungry. She looks up at the black windowpane. Three hours have passed. She forgot herself. Result: happiness.

She dons the red dress on her mother's birthday in early July. Anniversary needing to be marked. Go wandering again. Back up Lamb's Conduit Street; through the green expanse of tree-filled Brunswick Square. She reaches a cul-de-sac; car-free shaded by planes. Under their rustling canopy a cluster of silvery metal tables and chairs, set in the dust, defines a café space, black iron railings on two sides, children shouting in the nearby playground. To one side, stone steps lead up to the eighteenth-century house sheltering the Foundling Museum.

She studies the displays of photographs, documents, registers. She reads the official accounts of impoverished women handing in their babies, leaving tokens with the children, in case later identification and removal should ever be possible. Nineteenth-century relics laid out on glass shelves in glass cases: a chipped mother-of-pearl button, a tiny punched-metal tag, a hooped gold earring strung with turquoise beads. A blackened hatpin. A fragment of jet.

She sits outside under the sweeping branches of the planes. She scribbles in her notebook, eats a plateful of spiced fish, tomatoes and beans. The Moroccan chef, white apron laced about his slender hips, offers her a glass of wine, as she's his only lunchtime customer. People here only eat sandwiches! He tells her about his mother, who sends him home-made harissa in the post.

Madeleine gestures at the white gauze dressing taped to his forehead: what happened to you? He says: I got punched last night at a club in Hoxton. Some man didn't like me looking at his girlfriend.

Would Rose describe herself as someone's girlfriend? She acknowledges her new lover casually. Jerry. My friend. I've mentioned him, haven't I? One of the artists up at the studios. Yeah, he's OK.

Madeleine wears the red dress to go to the theatre with Toby a few weeks later, one evening in late July. He rings her: I've got a spare ticket for a show transferring for one night to the Great Hall in Bart's. Day after tomorrow. Interested?

Madeleine asks: Anthony coming too?

No, says Toby: that's why I've got the spare ticket. Bit of a crisis. His stepmother's been taken into hospital. He'll ring me later, when I get home.

A warm late afternoon. She'll walk to Bart's. She dons the flat red satin pumps, with thick rubber soles, in which she can stride easily.

Before leaving she steps outside to water her pots of pelargoniums in the front area. Scarlet, salmon-pink, fuschia-pink, magenta. The clashing colours that her mother liked. That she chose in her mother's memory.

Something not quite right. Green and yellow fronds curl above her. Greenery dangling in the wrong place. A wreath twined round by a black streamer hangs on her gate. Long twists of ivy, secured with a black bow.

She goes up the steps. A small piece of paper pokes out from between the ivy leaves. *Please don't force me to say goodbye. You will regret it. All my love – Emm.*

Ivy torn from a neighbour's front hedge perhaps. The black ribbon binding looks to have been cut from a rubbish sack. She pinches up the wreath, dumps it in the brown bin.

A crackly-looking plane leaf drifts down, lands on the tiny flowerbed Madeleine has planted around the tree's base. Marigolds, asters, fuchsias and nasturtiums. Yellow marigold petals almost the same shade as the For Sale sign that has recently appeared, strapped to the railings. Who's planning to move out? Perhaps the couple overhead with the screaming baby will leave. Good. But perhaps someone even noisier will move in. Toby has to endure a neighbour who watches internet porn half the night, grunting and yelling as he comes on the other side of a flimsy wall.

She addresses Emm's lurking presence out loud. Fuck off!

She strolls over London Bridge, cuts across to St Paul's and St Martin's Le Grand. The sun, shining all day, hazy now behind golden mist, has brought out the pedestrians, dark buds just waiting for light and warmth in order to burst into bloom. The City streets flower with young women in bright summer clothes, men who've shed jackets and ties and unbuttoned their collars, massing on the pavements outside wine bars.

She goes through Postman's Park, turns down Little Britain towards Smithfield. The narrow lane becomes an alley, debouches into a circular piazza. The market looms up opposite, a hefty shed. White neo-classical façade, metal struts painted red-purple-blue. On her right, the arched gateway of St Bartholomew the Great. She turns left, follows the wall round, through the high doorway into Bart's courtyard.

On the phone Toby warned her about the play: it'll be a strange piece. Possibly audience participation. I'm going to wear drab clothes and keep my head down.

Madeleine said: audience participation sounds like an encounter group. Scary!

A large crowd, three hundred people or so, buzzes about the stone portico of Bart's Great Hall. The evening light gleams on the ornate pediment over the closed wooden door. Burnishes fair hair, a gold signet ring. Toby, standing to one side of the throng, putting up one hand to scratch his ear. White T-shirt and grey jeans, clean and well-ironed. One forefinger hooks his grey linen jacket across his shoulder. Bright blue eyes in his big pale face. Alert, light on his toes; ready. She kisses him on both cheeks. She says: excuse me, sir, but I'm afraid you don't look drab at all.

Toby grins, preens. But I'm trying to blend in!

No time to tell him about Emm's ivy wreath: the door to the Great Hall cracks open, revealing a young man with black hair and a chin-fringe of black beard, wearing black jeans and a black T-shirt. He balances a clipboard. He surveys the crowd. The buzzing subsides. He waits. Another beat, and another.

The man clears his throat, raises a forefinger. He calls: the audience will be separated into two groups, according to gender. The men will please line up here and the women over there. I shall take the men in first.

Toby rolls his eyes, glances goodbye. He joins the trousered cohort. The young man ushers them through the stone doorway.

After five minutes or so, the young man reappears. He beckons the women to follow him through the doorway, into the entrance hall. Madeleine sees again those 1940s photographs in the Foundling Museum: a line of cheery orphan boys in shorts marching diagonally across a court-yard, swinging their arms. A line of meek overalled girls behind a long table, heads down over their sewing. Her heart jolts. No, don't be daft, we're not orphans, we're not abandoned, we're here of our own free will.

Too late to flee. Hemmed in. They ascend a wide stone staircase with ornate iron balusters, which leads up around two left-angled turns, transporting them into the air under the stone vaults high above. They surge past a vast wall-painting on the first half-landing. No time to hang back, dawdle to study it: their guide urges them forward.

Narrow double doors, brown as hazelnut shells, split open, as though cracked with a hammer. They enter a long, high-ceilinged room. On the right-hand wall, dangling strips of white canvas veil what must be a series of tall windows, reaching down to the floor. In front of these banner-like hangings, parallel to them, stand rows of brown benches. The young man directs the women to fill these seats. Briskly he sweeps them in. Keep moving. Look sharp. Madeleine spots an empty place at the end of a nearby bench, darts into it.

On the far side of the Great Hall, directly opposite the benches, tiered cinema-style seats clamped onto a metal ramp hold the men, already in position, a separate mass, in gloomy shadows. A blur. No individuality. No Toby visible.

The women continue filing in, clutching cardigans and bags. Subdued nervous laughter. A hum of talk. Someone nudges in next to Madeleine. She scarcely notices. Just moves up a little. Like being on the tube: you can ignore other passengers. She goes on preferring the bus, where people still sometimes talk to one another. The theatre's a bus, whirling them towards the unknown.

The lights dim further. The shadowy block of male audience opposite dissolves into pure blackness. A yellow glow illuminates the women's side. Presumably the ranked men can still see the women, but the women can't see the men. No more face to face: they've gone.

Flashes of pale movement. Here and there figures in long grey dresses, white pinafores, are taking their places among the host of female Londoners in their jeans and short skirts, fitting themselves into the gaps. Like watching an oil painting develop: dabs of lavender, grey and white laid onto masses of black, of dark blue.

At the far end of the Great Hall, opposite the door by which they all entered, a tall shape appears from the shadows. Corseted: hard outlines of waist and hips. Tidy black gown, white apron and white cap. She glides into the wide space of the floor separating the men's and women's places, stands still, waiting for them all to notice her, pay attention.

Some kind of nineteenth-century hospital matron? We're in Bart's Hospital, after all. A play about hospitals? Doctors and nurses? Aged five Madeleine played that all right, with her little friends. Pulling down each other's underwear; peeping; showing.

The aproned woman says: you need to understand how things are run here, so that we can coexist in harmony. She draws a small book from her pocket, begins to read aloud. The women will. The women will not. The women must. The women must not.

Rise, in silence, at such a time. Retire, in silence, at such a time. Eat, exercise, scrub floors, work in the laundry, pray, sew.

Not a hospital matron. The Mistress of Postulants instructing would-be nuns? The superintendent of an asylum? Of a ward for female prisoners?

A bunch of keys on a black ring dangles from a chain at her belt. Yes: a sort of jailer. A maternal one, to some degree. She seems to care about her charges' well-being. She looks over the edge of her book and studies their faces with a keen glance, as though she wants to understand them.

The woman is an architect. She changes the meaning of the Great Hall. She makes spike-topped walls rise, impossible to scale, puts bars on the windows, secures the entrance. No longer can the wide door in its stuccoed frame split apart into two narrow ones: locks and bolts prevent its opening. The Great Hall vanishes, along with the oil portraits in their gilded frames, the marble busts, the heraldic shields and plaques. The woman summons a bleaker building. A blank place with no art, no decoration. An institution structured by hierarchies, built on principles of clear distinction between categories. Like the Dewey Decimal System for libraries. So here I am, amid the lunatics and gypsies.

The woman lists punishments for disobedience, insolence, self-assertion, loss of self-control. So many days in solitary confinement. So many days on bread and water. So many dunkings in cold baths. Do you understand me? Do you understand what I have said? Put your hand up if you have understood.

Everyone puts their hand up. The woman nods. Good. You may put your hands down.

A light pressure on her left foot startles Madeleine. She's got neighbours. She's seated in between two other women. Strangers. But this one's not obeying the rules. Once the performance has started you should keep yourself to yourself. Don't be a nuisance! Don't cause trouble!

She smells her own fresh sweat, coursing down her armpits. The touch repeats itself, shy, polite. Delicate as a mouse's paw, someone's foot nudges hers. A conspiratorial foot. Sly. Pretend it's not happening? Cautiously she turns her head. A young woman in a long grey linen dress, collar and cuffs fastened with black buttons, topped by a white sleeveless overall, perches at the very end of the bench, next to her. Close to her. Too close. Black hair in plaits tied behind her head. Pink mouth. Rosy cheeks. The black-haired girl smiles. Eager, appealing curve of her lips. She has stretched out her foot in its little brown boot and is pressing it on Madeleine's red satin pump. Much too intimate. What's she up to?

Intense gaze. Over-intense. As though they know each other, as though she's trying to transmit some secret message. Madeleine almost chokes. An inmate of this prison-like place. She's sitting next to a prisoner. A lunatic prisoner?

Sweat springs up again, flows down her sides. The young woman lifts her foot away, sits still, hands folded in her lap. She keeps smiling, as though to reassure Madeleine. A pleading smile. She whispers: my name's Polly. What's yours? She reaches for Madeleine's hand, clasps it: Muddy Lane? Maddylane. That's an odd name. Never heard that one before.

Audience participation. OK. Be brave. Go with it. She says: yours is a nice name. Polly beams, fondles her hand. Finger circling her palm. Like writing. Not unpleasant. She just wants human contact. She just wants a bit of affection. Polly seems very young in her grey frock with its high collar and long sleeves. Demure as a trainee nun.

Polly says: I like the red of your dress. Wish I had one like that. We're not allowed colours in here. When you come in, they dish you out the uniform and don't care whether it fits you or not. Same with the boots!

Curses, curses. Why didn't she do as Toby did and put on a quiet colour? Because she liked how the dress made her feel: sensual, happy. Her red flag. See me! She wore it for Toby, to say let's have a cheerful evening, enjoy ourselves, and now he's been taken away and set apart with all the other men, invisible witnesses to this beginning drama. Too late. Red fish in the theatre sea. Polly's trying to hook her. Reel her in. What will Polly do with her? Just keep swimming in these waves. Ripples of murmuring voices. Here and there in the massed rows of benches, other whispering conversations have begun, a stir of mutual interest, delicate nets being spun. She can't push Polly away, tell her to shut up. Too unkind. She can't walk out. Too rude.

Take a deep breath. Keep calm. It's all right. Polly means no harm, just wants them to recognise each other. She forces herself to smile back. Horrid little smile it must be, tight and wrinkled as a dried-up chili pepper.

One by one, the young women in their grey frocks stand up, speak to the audience. Polly joins in. They toss out broken sentences; dislocated images. The smell of his cigar. A shilling in my palm, he closed my fingers round it. Good girl, be a good girl. The bottle of brandy by the bed. His beard, so soft. Fringed yellow curtains drawn. The smell of cold fog, of coal. Blue cushion. Ma shouted for me, but I hid. Jam tarts and sponge cakes, lemonade. The stopper flew out the bottle exploded all over the pantry floor. His cum all over my face. Piano music.

Polly's voice, distinctive, with a little crackle to it, a little croak, rises above the chorus. The attention of the audience swerves, holds her. Madeleine crouches into herself, absorbing each contralto note. Oh, my baby boy. My pretty little one. I wash him, I feed him, I sing him to sleep. Naughty rascal. Fingernails like pieces of the moon. His darling willy. His naughty tricks you wouldn't believe!

Polly turns, grips Madeleine's hand, tugs her to her feet. Have you got children, Madeleine?

Her eyes plead. Join in, please join in. Help me out. Don't let me down. Come on, you can do this.

Not an instruction. Just a request. You can say yes or no. She feels she must say yes. Cooperate. Be kind, be helpful, be nice. That was the rule for women in her family. Deep in her as a bone. How could you ever say no? Her open mouth makes no sound. Try again. The hall, packed with people, waits. Look, there's Nelly, sitting in the front row, turning round to nod and smile: go on, child, have a go, it won't harm you. White hair knotted behind her head. Blue-flowered crêpe blouse, blue cardigan buttoned over her heavy bosom. Nelly rests her elbows on the table, tips her tea into her saucer and blows on it, tells me tales of her childhood in London. My heart full of her words for ever. Shivers up and down my spine, along my shoulders. Enchantment: the past returns, glimpsed through a street doorway, and I'm walking towards it, I'm in the present and the past both at the same time, one delicately folded around the other.

Madeleine says: no, I've got no children.

Unknown women at parties sometimes ask her this. Often, perhaps shocked or embarrassed by her curt negative, they answer her with pitying looks. One woman mused: I really don't understand how someone can not want children. Madeleine should have said: well, I'm sorry for you, because that just shows your lack of imagination, doesn't it? As usual, she thought of the riposte too late. *L'esprit de l'escalier.* Thinking of something to say only when you're on your way out.

Madeleine used to think *l'esprit de l'escalier* meant a ghost on the stairs. Ghosts liked transitional places; cross-over spaces, where metamorphosis can happen; they floated from one level to another. She has passed the threshold, climbed the stairs to arrive in this vast dark cave full of phantoms. Is Polly a haunting from the nineteenth century? Her dress suggests that; the swaying gathered skirt, the pleated yoke. You can't touch ghosts. The flesh and blood actor Polly clasps Madeleine's hand. Sorry I spoke! You look sad. Your eyes talk, d'you know that?

Madeleine says: I wanted a child with my husband, but it didn't happen. I had a couple of miscarriages. So after a bit I just accepted being childless.

She rarely speaks of this. So long ago. Easier to speak of it now, in this context of theatre. A frame put round pain. Polly caresses her hand. We'll be friends, shall we?

All over the women's side of the hall the voices continue to spring up. They mutter, halt, intertwine. Come with us! The young women in grey pull their chosen companions into the central space in front of the benches. A dozen or so Londoners, stumbling, ducking their heads, blushing. Thirteen women, perhaps. A baker's dozen in Nelly-talk. Polly's fingers close around Madeleine's. They cajole. Don't resist me. Jump up. Take a risk.

She hesitates. Get on with you, child, says Nelly: if you come a cropper, so what? Madeleine rises from the wooden bench. Linked to Polly by their clasped hands, she follows. She steps out of the safe anonymity of the rows of female audience, onto the gleaming wooden floor.

Enormous space. The lights pinpoint her. Too visible. The floor takes her far away. Far out of safety. Into another place altogether.

The young women in grey sit the audience women down in the centre of the boards, take their own places in the ring. Legs tucked to one side, skirts smoothed over booted feet. You're our guests! Usually we have to stay mum when ladies come, they talk to us and we listen. But tonight we're allowed to talk.

They turn from one audience woman to another. Where do you live? And you? When did you leave home? How d'you earn your living? Are your parents still alive? What did they teach you as you grew up? Do you believe in God? What do you believe in?

The audience women flinch. They hunch their shoulders round, let their hair fall over their averted faces. They mutter in turn. No. Nothing, really. No.

Polly, still grasping Madeleine's hand, turns to her: and you? Do you believe in God?

A coaxing look. Their plaited fingers: a friendship knot. Polly's oval nails, polished pearl, her face-powder, vanilla-scented, her own sweat. Madeleine says: no, I don't believe in God. I used to, but not any more. Not since my adolescence. Polly's black eyes shine. She asks: so what do you believe in now?

Everybody waits, hushed, for her reply. Madeleine remembers her walk through Smithfield, where heretics were burned alive, and she remembers her walk through the Borough, skirting Guy's Hospital, where Keats trained as an apothecary. The silence and stillness of the Great Hall let inspiration rise. She lifts her face, calls out to the dark, listening masses of audience: I believe in poetry, and in what Keats said about the holiness of the heart's affections, that's to say I believe in the love between friends, and in the power, the sacred truth of the imagination.

Blimey, says Polly: that's some speech. Don't mind us, will you?

She releases Madeleine. Men friends? Much good may they do you! Screw you and hop it, most of them.

Madeleine insists: no, I mean real friends. Men and women both.

Polly says: whew! Go for it, darling! But we don't read poetry in here. The matron reads us sermons. Three times a day, at meals. And we're so wicked we have to say our prayers three times a day as well. Polly blows her nose. Now, what about this funny name of yours? What's it mean?

Madeleine says: it means Magdalene.

Polly claps her hands, screeches with laughter. We're all Magdalenes in here! You've come to the right place, darling. Welcome to the Home for Sinners. Welcome to the Refuge for Magdalenes. At first I thought you was one of the ladies on the committee but now I see you're one of us. One of the ladies of the night! We're all night-flyers in here!

Madeleine begins to understand. She and the other women in the audience are visitors from another time; from the future; summoned by Polly and her companions. Polly's not a ghost. She's living in the here and now. Madeleine and all the others are ghosts, avatars, from the twenty-first century. They have somehow materialised inside this locked-up penitentiary, whose inmates have met them, befriended them. The women in grey study their strange guests, look into their faces, question them, listen to their replies. The rules of hospitality in this bleak salon mean that the guests must join in.

Hard going. The group of audience women huddle in the centre of the shining floor, heads down, mouths clamped. They twiddle their hair, fidget with their bracelets and rings. Yet under the yellow lights Madeleine relaxes. Odd situation, but she feels easy. Like being back out on the street. Those casual encounters with passers-by that she so relishes. Drawn in. People wanting to make contact; reaching out to her. How can she not respond?

A bell rings. The matron declares: our Home is a benevolent place. We treat our penitents as human beings. And so now it's time for recreation.

The women in grey start dancing, chanting rude verses, singing out nonsense rhymes. Madeleine joins in. Word-wings flare out behind her. Transported, into another world. Land of imagination: utterly real. She's not herself:

she's larger, different, she's someone else. Possessed by angels and demons both. Flying and floating in a golden bubble outside time. Running and sweating and laughing she's the red bead in the grey necklace she's in their gang.

Crack! Halt! The matron re-emerges. Dark hour-glass. Dark sand runs out. She claps her hands. Time's up! Enough of this carnival!

The audience women hover. The women in grey, chattering, shoving, fall in around the matron. They form a line, Polly at its end, near Madeleine.

Polly steps away from her sister inmates to face Madeleine. We shall have to go soon. You will have to go soon.

She leans forward. Madeleine, there's something I've got to tell you. It's a secret. Don't let anybody hear.

The matron clasps her hands in front of her corset-breastplate. The deep frills of her cap shadow her face. Her head swivels back and forth. She's keeping them under surveillance; up to the very end. The young women in grey stay in their line but lean against each other, floppy, as though they're very tired. The audience women stay huddled together, their arms folded.

Madeleine and Polly remain together in the centre of the floor. The whole hall seems to settle; the breath of the invisible watching men to be expelled in a collective sigh. Here comes the leave-taking, and then we're done.

Polly puts out a hand. Nice little girl, taught by the ladies' committee how to say a proper goodbye. Madeleine's mother schooled her child in French manners. Madeleine had to kiss everyone hello and goodbye, willy-nilly. Allow herself to be kissed by whichever uncle wanted to plant wet-lipped smackers. Once she left home she spent years rebelling. Invisible cords bound her, had to be broken. She roamed the streets, talked to strangers. Outside her parents' house it seemed easier to discard the rules, approach people gently, speak freely.

Polly says: I wish I could go with you. You've cheered me up. I hate it in here. I can't tell you how much I hate it. And it's going to get worse.

Sheen of water over her cheeks. Her mouth trembles. Her voice too. She drops her crackly voice to a whisper. Something bad's going to happen. I don't know what to do.

The matron bends forward, listening. Like the priest in the confessional, all those years ago. Get it over with. Endure it; like the uncles' kisses. Ritual of humiliation repeated every Saturday night.

Polly says: the gentlemen who fund this place, they get rid of us, regular. It's called giving us a fresh start. So they've decided they're going to send me to New South Wales, like they did with the others last year. They're going to put me on the boat next week. That's it. I'll be done for. I'll never see my little nipper again.

She presses their joined hands. She looks suddenly charged up; electric. She says: Madeleine, I need to escape. Take me with you. Don't leave me here.

Madeleine goes on trying to wrench her hand away. The lights brighten. The end of the play? Silence. The other audience women retreat, scurry to their places on the benches. The women in grey hover, alert.

Madeleine waits a moment. Polly's eyes plead. Madeleine says: yes. All right. But we must leave right away. I'm going now. I can't bear this. I can't stay here a moment longer.

Polly shouts: come on! The young women in grey run up, join on, hands linked, a long, wavering line, they scamper in great loops up and down the hall, a grey and white rope untying and re-tying itself, and the matron chases them, she joins on the end, pulling them one way, they tug her another, they dance out of one of the floor-length windows, suddenly open, its blind flapped back, onto the wide balcony outside. As though they've fled into the night sky. They pause here, catching their breath, flexing their feet, shaking the energy back into their arms and legs.

Polly puts up a hand and pulls at her plaits. A wig, which she plucks off. It tumbles to the ground, revealing her dark crewcut. She scratches her scalp, shakes her head, dashes the tears from her cheeks.

Polly embraces Madeleine. Laughing. Thank you! She's out of breath, hot, smelling of sweat, makeup. Madeleine blinks, wipes her eyes on the back of her hand. Polly says: my name's Maria. Please stay behind afterwards, I'd love to talk to you, I want to tell you about how we made the play, all the research we did, it's been an amazing time.

She kisses Madeleine again, then back in they all run, hands linked, to the applause, and they take a bow and don't let go of Madeleine and she has to take a bow too. Then she breaks away and darts back to her place in the audience, sinks down, so that she can become one of the watchers once more, so that she can applaud the actors, their young male director. The young man in black who brought them into this place: there he is smiling and bowing. She leans her head forward over her knees, gulps air, hauls it in. Corkscrewing down through dark clouds, from some other world, falling back into this one, the ground jarring her feet. She picks up her bag from underneath the bench, finds her handkerchief, blows her nose.

Scarper. Don't wait for Polly-Maria. She joins the flow of people tipping out down the curve of the stairs, men and women mixed together again. She presses out of the great door under the portico.

Toby's waiting outside the main gate. He hugs her. Bravo. Well done. You did really well.

He links her arm into his, draws her out into the piazza. The meat market looms opposite, a dark hangar beyond the traffic lights. White gleam of a few parked butcher's vans. People dissipate along the street. Toby says: shall we go for a drink? There's a pub just round the corner. She shakes her head. No. Sorry. I need to keep moving for a bit. I need to walk.

Toby embraces her again. Warmth, and the beat of his heart. They stand there together. Dear Toby. Go home and ring Anthony. She kisses his cheek, turns away. He shouts after her: you've torn your dress at the back with all that cavorting. She shouts back: goodnight.

Blessed darkness cool on her hot skin. The ripped slit of her dress makes walking even easier than earlier in the evening. She heads away from Bart's, north through the shut-up market, its puddled concrete floor smelling of cleaning fluid, up St John Street, along Clerkenwell Road, back up Lamb's Conduit Street, round the edge of Brunswick Square, to the Foundling Museum. She stands in front of the shallow flight of steps mounting to its locked doors.

Would a young woman like Polly-Maria have handed her baby in here? Or somewhere more discreet, round the back? Were the babies wrapped in blankets? In shawls? In pieces of sheet? Did they howl as they were taken from their mothers' arms? Did the mothers cry too or did they hurry away and do their crying somewhere else? Or were they coldly dry-eyed with relief? A suffering woman can hide heartbreak behind a hard-faced mask. Then people call her a little unfeeling slut, shake their heads. We wash our hands of you, Miss Slut.

Madeleine starts the long trek home. After half a mile she changes her mind, makes for the bus-stop at the bottom of Southampton Row.

The chilly night bus, half-empty, sweeps her across the river. High tide, the water slapping up, tipped with wavering zigzags of light. The bus hurtles them from stop to stop, racing to beat the lights, swerving and tilting around corners. A woman sprawling at the very back recounts a story-lament: her release from prison, her drinking problem, how she's lost her way has no money what bus is this what time is it? The other passengers ignore her, stare at their laps.

She gets off when Madeleine does, a couple of stops past the Elephant. Curly brown hair, bruised red face. She stands at the bus-stop, swaying. Madeleine says: d'you need a hand? You OK? The woman says: hey, petal, which way's the church? St Mary Something. I'm looking for the refuge. The vicar there, he told me I'm always welcome. He's a lovely man. So kind. They've beds, and breakfast in the mornings. Dinner too, on a weekend night. I'm not too late for a bed. I could do with my bed right now.

Madeleine points. I think the church is over there, towards Kennington Way. I think I know the one you mean.

The woman's face sharpens. She eyes Madeleine. No, I've changed my mind. It's the pub I need first. Spare us some cash, love. Go on, be nice.

Madeleine hesitates. She opens her bag, digs into her purse, gives the woman some change. She says: I'm not sure the pubs are still open. Will you be all right?

The woman says: why not come with me, then? Buy me a pint of lager? Coward, aren't you? She laughs and scowls at Madeleine's shake of the head. She blows her a kiss. Bless you, darling! I love you, so I do! She turns back, sways into an alley, disappears.

A cat yowls at the far end of Apricot Place. The street lamps glimmer on pale bits of paper blowing along the kerb. A white window-blind. A white collar. A dog collar. Emm? Madeleine whirls round. Nobody there.

She searches the fridge for food. An open jar of anchovies. A bowl of leftover green beans. A slosh of olive oil, a slice of bread. A glass of wine. She needs a drink just as much as that woman did.

Plate on her lap, she sits on her back step, feet planted in the area, under the canopy of the dark sky. Rock music plays two gardens along. A plane growls high overhead, a police helicopter buzzes to and fro. Sirens wail. She spears slivers of salty fish.

What did the people who lived here before her eat for supper? Soup? Stew? What did the servants eat? Grace Poole in *Jane Eyre* opted for toasted cheese, a roast onion, a pint of porter. The characters Mayhew described, out on the street working, bought takeaways: fried fish, ham rolls, buns. The young women selling sex were generous with their money. Mayhew's researcher reported them treating their fellow night-workers to drinks, to a share of their sandwiches.

Madeleine puts her empty plate aside. She goes up the area steps into the garden, to the flowerbed at the end, leans over to draw in the scent of the stocks. Straightening up, she looks back towards the house. Dark windows, except for one on the top floor, where light glows. A pale, girlish face. Hands splayed flat against the glass. Chin tilts up. Mouth opens wide; a silent cry.

The fall of a curtain or a blind. The window goes black.

Madeleine falls rapidly asleep. She dreams of being buckled into a grey sacking dress stiff as a straitjacket. A pair of shears comes at her, Emm's hands grip her shoulders, the matron cuts off all her hair. She hands Madeleine a sack. Here's your babies. Take them away and bury them.

NINE

Joseph

POLLY THE BLACK-HAIRED GIRL, naked, pink as a boiled shrimp. Salt smell of sea-juice. Blue-green coverlet of the bed rumpled like waves. Joseph leaned forward, put his hands on her knees, pressed her thighs apart, bent his head. Hold still. She squawked. A floorboard squeaked. He woke up, rubbed his face. Brilliant light cut in through the gap between the curtains.

Full moon, which saw him home earlier last night, full of beer. Slices of currant pudding to soak it up. Slabs of cold butter on top of the hot suet sponge; no wonder he dreamed. Though at the time delicious: crunch of gritty sugar, fragrant grease flowing smoothly across his tongue. Plump fruity mouthfuls. Moonlight like melting butter.

Next to him, Cara slept, pale brown lashes two lines of stub. She gave out whuffling breaths. His head lolled, enormous. Iron tent pegs pinned his splayed limbs to the mattress. Throat scraped with dryness. Parched. Empty water glass. Damn. He'd have to go downstairs.

He concentrated, sat up. Heaved one leg over the side of the bed, then the other. No need to light a candle. He pulled on dressing-gown and slippers, opened the bedroom door, trod gently across the landing. Milly was a light sleeper. Don't wake her. Moonlight emptied itself onto him from the small window, streamed down the stairs ahead. Scoured and rinsed his brain. Now he had a headache, too.

Concentrate. Don't rouse the household. He swivelled through the shadowy hall. In the dark basement he felt his way jumpily, gloomily. Why had he drunk so much? Never again. His skull tingled, as though it were shrinking. Doorknobs roamed past his fingers. Chair legs knocked his shins. Empty carafe on the dining-room sideboard yawned. Go and pump up some water.

Pale gold light underlined the kitchen door. As at Mrs Dulcimer's, on that first visit, when he approached her sitting-room. Going in, he'd stumbled, almost fallen. Flat on the floor at her feet.

Hand on latch, he stopped. Curses. He'd forgotten. The new maid slept there now, in the wicker bed that folded down from the side wall. Doll of the grey gravel eyes. She'd been due to arrive yesterday evening and presumably had done so, after he'd gone out. He'd not caught a glimpse of Doll: he'd come back late, letting himself in with elaborate quiet, locking up then easing the bolt across, weaving upstairs, edging into bed beside the sleeping Cara. How had he reached home? Safely, at any rate.

He shouldn't have drunk so much. He shouldn't have gone out in the first place, but he'd been desperate. Putting Holborn behind him, he'd charged south towards Charing Cross, fetched up in a pub in Villiers Street. A shadowy vault packed with people smoking, shouting, laying bets. After a couple of beers, he felt restless again, shouldered his way out, set forth once more. He turned towards Piccadilly.

Gas lamps fixed to the fronts of buildings sent up tall flares, glittered on the brass ornaments of horses' harnesses, the buckles finishing the leather straps of carriage doors.

Drivers flicked their whips and bellowed at the stuck traffic, cabs and omnibuses halted athwart each other. Children darted between the wheels to beg, skipping barefoot over fresh dung, their cupped hands reaching up for coins. People leaned down and yelled at them to get off and Joseph wanted to yell too. You should be in bed!

He turned down towards the Haymarket. Mayhew had mentioned one of the dolly-houses there, hadn't he, a while back? Joseph had never witnessed the Haymarket spectacle. Now, tonight, suddenly he was in the mood to do so. Facts, Benson, facts!

The wide street was jam-packed, throngs of men swaying and shoving up and down the pavement. Joseph held back, found himself studying these watchers: dark shapes in frock coats and tall hats. Some of them were obviously youngsters up from the suburbs for a spot of fun, others clearly habitués of the track, eyeing the talent with a world-weary air, taking their time choosing which fillies to summon, which bar to patronise. Nonchalant; hats tipped back; hands in pockets. A casual demeanour that masked excitement, surely. Some openly avid: necks craning forwards, mouths half-open. Shouldering their way to the front to get a better view.

The gorgeously dressed tarts strutted back and forth, curvetting and prancing like circus ponies, hands on hips, best foot forwards. Parade of shining satin-wrapped merchandise. The purchasers prowled up and down and surveyed them. Good tits. Too fat for me. Nice haunches on that one. Nice plump calves.

Two young mashers near him were eyeing each other, bristling and tentative, as though ready to toss a coin, hazard a throw. Yes. Here. They vanished into a brightly lit saloon, a haze of cigar smoke wreathing through the haloes of gas.

Joseph loitered in the crisp cold; part of the anonymous crowd. Scents of fog, horse manure, other men's breath; the soft blackness of woollen frock coats and silk-covered hats; the mud beneath their feet. Just dissolve. Forget himself. Impossible: the mob of men had its teeth in him, shook him to and fro in its jaws, wouldn't let him go.

Some of the parading girls wore boots with stacked soles, to raise them above the pavement filth. They tilted up their crinolines, showing off their brightly stockinged legs. Crinolines like pleated curtains, raised by a string. Frilled frames for cunts.

People pushed him this way and that, trod on his boots, poked him in the back. Other men's faces loomed up, white Japanese lanterns swinging close to his own then vanishing back into the crowd. Voices blared and hollered. Music wailed from an invisible organ, out of tune, and a woman's voice quavered along, trying to catch up with the beat and failing. How long would the performance keep going? All night, presumably. Until the revellers fell over in the gutter and the police turned up to clear them away.

He turned eastward, towards St-Martin-in-the-Fields. Suddenly hungry, needing to eat. A chophouse, luridly lit, packed with people taking supper after the theatre. Cut-glass mirrors, reflecting back and forth, on the green walls. Red-painted benches, squares of red leather serving as tablecloths. Re-heated meat pies, fried slices of pudding, glasses of beer.

The suet lodged heavily inside him. The basement closed round him. Clammy and dank, it still reeked of yesterday's kippers. Joseph shivered, wrapping his dressing-gown more firmly round him, retying the cord. The tiny hallway at the bottom of the stairs held cold as a well holds water. Should he just go back to bed? Pull the clothes over his head. Sleep as soundly as presumably the new maid was doing on the other side of the kitchen door.

He yawned, gazed at the thin gold line tracing the sharp angles of the doorframe. Then woke up fully: the gold line meant that Doll must have fallen asleep with her candle still burning. Very dangerous, that. Should he creep in and snuff it out? She might wake up and scream to find a dark male shape looming over her. No. Better to go back upstairs, rouse Cara, get her to come down. Unfair? Poor Cara, she needed her sleep. But she'd see to the girl all right, scold her, put some sense into her about extinguishing lights. Poor child. Pity to get her into trouble on her very first night here. Perhaps he should rattle the latch to alert her to his presence, open the door just an inch, call in to her. Then she could get up, and while she was at it could pump him some water. No. Best to let Cara deal with it.

He hovered. A draught crept under his nightshirt and tickled his bare calves. Just as he turned to go back upstairs, a voice struck up behind the door. Hesitant, hoarse. What was Doll up to? Talking in her sleep? He hesitated. What to do?

A second voice responded. Murmuring, low. Entertaining a follower on her first night in a new place? She'd have to be mad.

He stooped to the keyhole underneath the latch. A golden gap; filled with candlelight from the kitchen beyond. He kneeled down and applied his eye to the golden opening.

Moonlight, from the unshuttered window, fell across the floor; candlelight a golden bubble. Inside the feathery golden globe, two human shapes bent towards each other. Two young women, their hair in night-time plaits dangling under their night-caps' ruffles. Doll, in her little bed, narrow as a shelf, hinged to the wall, leaned one elbow on her thin pillow, a grey woollen shawl pulled around her shoulders. Cara's, inherited from his mother; presumably taken from the hook upstairs in the hall. Milly, in night-gown and plaid dressing-gown, perched nearby, on the edge of the kitchen table, her slippered feet resting on the seat of a chair drawn up close to it. The candle burned in a tin holder set on a stool between them, flame flicker-ing inside a hazy halo of light, and lit their profiles. The golden light separated them, and joined them.

They were still; rapt in listening and talking; Milly with her hands thrust into her sleeves, Doll looking back at her. A woven-straw bag sat next to the fold-down bed. Doll's, presumably. A curled rag of handkerchief lay on the brown blanket. So she'd been crying. Milly, that light sleeper, must have heard her and trotted down. Must have wrapped her in Cara's shawl, to comfort her.

Their voices, pitched low, rose and fell. Snatches of their talk floated to him. Bag of apples. Across the river. Forgotten. Scared of the dark. Black beetles. Doll seemed to be explaining, and Milly interrupting her and putting more questions. That's my Milly! Always wants to know everything!

The words whispered themselves forth. Brothers and sisters? Five. I miss them. Where, exactly? Rotherhithe, miss.

Should he go in, interrupt them, get his water, dispatch Milly back to bed? He straightened up slowly. Stiff back. Too cold to hang about here much longer. He wanted his warm bed, his warm, sleeping wife.

Doll's mournful voice piped on. Dad's a warehouseman. In the docks. I went into service. Then Mrs Bonnet, at the boarding-house in Newington.

Milly's tones, a little louder than before. What? Who?

Doll responding. So then Mrs Dulcimer.

He jumped. Put his ear against the doorjamb. Cool wood, a bit greasy. Doll raised her reedy voice, obviously wanting Milly to understand.

Mrs Bonnet. She helps girls in trouble. If you go to her early enough. She gets rid of it for you. Girls who need to, who need help, go there. Then I come to stay with Mrs Dulcimer, until I was better. She keeps a room spare, for girls who need it. Little Annie she's got in there at the moment. She come in from Brixton.

He couldn't bear it. The high voice speaking calmly of such horrors. As though she were describing picking bedbugs out of a mattress and drowning them in a bucket of water.

The childish voice went on. Mrs Dulcimer? She's the lady sent me here, when Mr Benson asked her to.

Joseph banged on the door. He clicked the latch, pushed the door open.

Two faces swivelled, white and shocked. Doll jerked the shawl over her head, huddled inside it. Just as he'd done as a small boy: if I can't see you then you can't see me. Milly straightened herself, sat upright. She said: it's all right, Dorothy, it's only my pa.

She was tense and trembling. She shouldn't have to know about such terrible things. She was still a child. So, he saw, was Doll. He said: Mrs Benson wouldn't like you wasting good wax candles. Blow that light out now.

Doll's hand crept out, like a little mouse. She pulled the shawl away from her face. Red, swollen eyelids. She crouched, sniffing into her sleeve. She whispered: I didn't mean any harm, Mr Benson, when I took your coat. Mrs Dulcimer said she'd make it all right with you.

Milly stared at him. He ignored her, spoke to Doll. There's no need to be frightened of the dark. No rats down here. No black beetles. The range is still alight. Open one of the oven doors, and you'll see the glow. There's nothing to be scared of. Now go to sleep, and you, Milly, get back to bed.

He drove Milly up the two flights of stairs. She gathered up her nightgown, scampered ahead of him. On the landing, hand on the latch of her door, she turned. Her bright eyes scanned his face. Mrs Dulcimer. She's that darkie who came to the house the other night, isn't she? She must be. How d'you know her, Pa? Is she a friend of yours?

Joseph pushed her into her bedroom. None of your business, miss. Be quiet. I'll speak to you tomorrow.

He'd forgotten to bring up that glass of water. He crept between the sheets, stretched out under the quilt, next to Cara's soft bulk. Grit seemed to be scraping the inside of his eyelids. They wouldn't close. A different light began to leak between the curtains. Dawn, bluish-white, like souring milk.

Girls killing their babies. Having them killed. Women willingly and consciously killing unborn babies. He knew it happened. He read the papers, didn't he? He recognised, in a theoretical way, the desperation a girl might feel, getting pregnant out of wedlock. Are you listening, Mrs Dulcimer? He supposed he understood, by now, the difficulty a girl faced if her lover scarpered, refused to marry her. She'd be turned out of her place. Very likely turned away by her family, too. Yes, he realised that.

That didn't make it right. Murder was murder.

Mrs Dulcimer, damn her, had got inside him, kept on talking to him. So what would you prefer? That a girl should help herself, by the only means she can, or that she casts herself into the gutter and hopes to be found by some well-meaning person like yourself before she starves, freezes to death?

Yesterday, as she talked, her cheeks had flushed, her voice hoarsened, the words tipping out of her. Then she had pushed aside the table, the flap of tablecloth, and stood up. She had work to do. She'd wished him a good day.

Good day. Day. Daylight filled the bedroom. He rolled over, reached out a hand for Cara's shoulder. Nobody there. She was already up. He must have gone back to sleep after all. He'd overslept.

He didn't want to encounter Doll or Milly or talk to either of them. Leave it be. Let sleeping dogs lie. For today at least. Just get on. He had business to complete.

Overnight, while he slept, something had clarified. Now he must see Mayhew, and lay these new conclusions before him.

Mayhew worked all through the week. On a Saturday morning he'd be in his office, surely. Strike while the iron's hot.

Cara had left a jug half full of cold water on the washstand. Joseph splashed his face and hands, pulled on his clothes. He'd get breakfast out, on his way to the Strand. From the hall he shouted a goodbye down towards the clattering of pots in the basement, then hurried out of the house.

Mayhew's empty office smelled of yesterday's coal fire, the ashes not yet raked from the grate. Papers piled haphazardly on the desk, as usual, books and pens scattered higgledy-piggledy. The clerk put his thin, long nosed face round the door. Mr Mayhew, sir? I believe he's gone to the Turkish baths. Or it may be he's gone first to the gymnasium. Some matter of a boxer he wanted to interview.

Joseph's stepfather had passed on to him a single skill: how to punch another man. Joseph might display a gift for boxing, earn his living that way. You don't seem to have any other talents, my little mollycoddled nodcock! To start with, the Hoof had wanted to get Joseph trained to work with horses, become a groom like himself. As often as he was hauled there, however, the boy could not be forced to linger in a stable. Pointed towards a broom, a heap of filthy straw, he would flee as soon as he could from those lips drawn back snarling over enormous yellow teeth, those vast rumps, those stamping nailed shoes. Resignedly, the Hoof had decided to teach him to box. Joseph practised alone, outdoors, the little yard as ring, using a makeshift sandbag. He found he was light on his feet in that constricted space, could dance and feint and bob. The Hoof put up his fists: come on! Joseph landed well-aimed blows with right and left. Three sessions in, his stepfather had called time, patted his shoulder. You'll do. Off to school with you now.

On his first day, when a boy walked up to him and hit him in the face with no warning, Joseph punched him straight back. Both of them poured blood. The master asked: who started it? Joseph stayed silent. Both boys were punished: three cuts to each palm. Both blinked back tears. The other boy looked out for him after that. It wasn't enough to guard against a whole gang of louts deciding to wash off your mummy-smell in the horse trough, but it helped.

He ran his employer to ground in the Turkish baths in Ironmonger Row. Mayhew had obviously just come out of the cold plunge pool. He was sitting in the anteroom on a bench, a towel wrapped around his loins, while the assistant rubbed him down. Too early yet, apparently, for other clients to have wandered in: the pillared alcoves all round were empty, curtains pulled back to reveal leather-padded couches, bolsters with embroidered linen covers. Tall brass pots of green ferns stood about. A mosaic of blue and turquoise tiles, waist high, encircling the room, gave the effect of an underwater cave. Mayhew bent his dripping head and grunted, while the man massaged his big white shoulders, mopped them. Folds of white belly. Dark curls on his chest.

Mayhew took the cloth and began to dry his thick black hair. That'll do. You can leave us now. We'll have to talk later. Benson, do stop hovering. Sit down, man. I confess I wasn't expecting you. Explain yourself, if you please.

Joseph hitched up his trousers and seated himself on the mahogany bench opposite, trying to place his feet out of the way of the pools of water puddling and shining on the blue-tiled floor.

Mayhew, pale as a codfish, was wiping the water streaming down the sides of his face, his neck. He spoke through muffling folds of towel. Since you have interrupted me just as I was about to begin an interview, I assume you have something important to say to me.

Cut the crap, Mayhew. Pomposity doesn't work when you've got no clothes on. You're threadbare, man, you're threadbare. Joseph spread his hands, palms up. Loaded with invisible documents, notes, reports. He said: I believe I have.

Collect your thoughts. Put them into the right order. Come on, you can do this. One fact after another, arranged in logical sequence. Difficult, as always. Almost impossible when you had hardly slept and had a head lined with lead, a stomach that kept convulsing.

He saw himself like a caricature, hands waving then squeezed together, cheeks flushed, mouth opening and shutting. Just begin. He said: I received your letter yesterday morning, and read it with great care. I respect your criticisms of my approach. In obedience to your instructions I shall continue trying to find out more about the living conditions of prostitute women. But before I continue with any more of that research I must lay before you what seems to me a fundamental error in our way of thinking.

Mayhew raised his eyebrows, gave a soundless whistle. He cast aside the wet cloth, got up. He plucked at the towel fastened around his hips, unloosened it, dropped it on the wet floor. He stood and yawned, stretched. Tall, firm-fleshed man. Fat but solid. His white belly curved over his penis. White mushroom dangling inside a curling nest of hair. Somewhere under his plumpness hid muscles, strength. Joseph's stepfather had been similarly tall and well-built. How agile was Mayhew? Challenged to a fight, would he lumber around or balance eagerly on his toes? Floor him with your argument, Joseph. Concentrate.

Mayhew stroked his chin with a large white hand. My good fellow, your disclosures must wait a few minutes. First, let me get dressed. Then let's go next door to the barber's. I could do with a haircut and a shave. You certainly could, too.

He vanished through an archway, left Joseph kicking his heels. All right! Round one to Mayhew. Get your breath back. Flex your muscles. Begin again. Perhaps I know a dodge or two you don't, old man.

Re-emerging, Mayhew swept Joseph before him, out into the street, down an alley. Two dark openings, side by side, one with a dangling sign marking it an hotel. A red-and-white pole hung out above the other, fastened to the wall by gilded wire. The open hotel door revealed stairs ahead, curving upwards out of sight. Mayhew swerved aside, entered the second doorway. Joseph followed, into an emerald-tiled cave smelling of almond hair oil.

Two barbers, in red waistcoats and white aprons, received them. In a moment, they were seated side by side, white cloths tied over their chests and round their collars, and were tipped back, scalps covered with froths of soap. Mayhew and he had become twins. Mayhew's crown of white suds must mirror his own. Very well: while they remained equal, while brisk fingertips lathered them both at the same tempo, Joseph insisted on speaking. He had tried to prepare his speech. Awkward. Stuttering. But he must deliver the rest of it before he forgot it altogether.

He said: I have come to the conclusion that prostitutes are not simply lazy, work-shy, immoral exploiters of gullible drunken men. Indeed, I no longer consider that they should be classified as criminals at all. To see them as straightforwardly and coldly committed to a life of vice is to misunderstand the nature of what they are about.

He turned his head surreptitiously, watched Mayhew sigh, shut his eyes, purse his lips. He hissed at the ceiling. And what is that?

Hard fingers rummaged behind and inside Joseph's ears, across his forehead. He blinked, as soap stung him. He said: they offer for sale something that men wish to buy. In that sense, they are like costermongers selling fruit, pastry-merchants selling biscuits. They are actually in full employment.

Their barbers worked in tandem. Tipping warm water over their heads, ruffling their hair as they rinsed it, then towelling them half dry. All right, gents! Sit up just a little, if you please. Hands got busy with comb and scissors. Flick of cool hard tortoiseshell, stroke of cold steel blades.

Joseph said: in addition, these women work for their livings in a way that benefits mankind. They perform a useful service. Doctors have long recognised that consorting with prostitutes saves young unmarried men from having to resort to self-abuse. However, prostitutes also benefit married men. They allow a married man to discharge his superfluous animal energy in a way that protects his wife from what might otherwise be considered his excessive demands.

Mayhew's booted feet began to tap on the footrest of his chair. Joseph hesitated. Tilting his chin, he glanced up at the ceiling's cracked carapace, its pattern of brown stains spread like flower petals. Water overflowing from a hotel room above, presumably. Some careless chambermaid knocking over a bath, causing a minor flood. Places such as this ought to have proper systems of plumbing, pipes fitted to swirl away the overflows. Scandalous that they didn't, in this day and age.

He said: doctors would call it a question of hygiene. Moral hygiene. Just as modern experts in engineering propose a complete overhaul of our city's sewage system, so I propose a complete overhaul of the way that we think about prostitutes and label them. The so-called vicious practice of prostitution actually supports the sacred institution of marriage. Most men would admit that, if they were honest.

Mayhew stuck out a hand from underneath his bib-like covering and thumped the leather-covered arm of his chair. This is completely absurd. You cannot expect me to take you seriously.

Joseph said: please try to understand what I am saying, Mr Mayhew. My discovery turns our classification system topsy-turvy. If prostitutes are no longer to be placed in the category of those who refuse to work, this alters our ideas of what labour entails. We shall have to re-think some of our research.

Mayhew began spluttering, as though he'd swallowed soap. Our research! Our research! You mean my research, Benson. I will not have you interfering with my methods of conducting it, and certainly not with my system of classification.

The barber leaned in close, to clip his sideburns. Mayhew could not move, as the shining steel blades danced so near his skin, but his eyes glittered under his tufted black brows. Joseph caught his furious glance in the mirror and hastily looked away. Mayhew's voice was cold as the water trickling down Joseph's neck. I have run out of patience with you, Benson. I have explained to you time after time how I wish you to proceed. I have given you chance after chance to learn how to write a proper report. I have reached the conclusion that you are not so much unfortunately stupid as wilfully stubborn and obstinate. Your probationary period is hereby terminated. I've no more use for you.

The barber brought up his hand, flourishing a foaming brush. He worked soap, in quick circular motions, over Joseph's cheeks and neck. Then picked up his ivory-handled razor and began delicately stroking under his chin. Long deft sweeps. Rasping and scraping. Joseph clenched his teeth, and froze. Just endure it. Don't move. Don't make a sound. The dentist was as nothing compared to this. The dentist hurt you as he ground and scraped, but the pain eventually stopped. The barber could slit your throat in a flash. Don't get into a strop, Benson. Ha.

Mayhew shed his swaddling towels, studied his reflection in the mirror. Call into my office and my clerk will pay you the wages you're owed. At the same time you can deliver your account of your expenses. After that, I must beg you to bother me no more.

Curled, oiled, scented, they stood up side by side. Donning hat and coat, Mayhew nodded. I wish you a very good day.

He strode away. At the mouth of the alley, he turned off towards Fleet Street. Joseph leaned against the barber's shop doorframe. His skin seemed to have loosened, his muscles to have turned to strings of melted cheese. He was shaking. As though he had a fever. His legs would not stop trembling. This was like getting sacked from Bow Street, all over again.

His boots forced him along. He stumbled to the food-stall on the next corner, bought himself a well-sugared cup of coffee, a jam sandwich. Sweetness revived him. Even rancid butter consoled him, calmed him. The thickly sliced bread stopped his insides churning. What should he do now?

Go home? Tell Cara what had happened? His stomach twisted afresh. Jesus, all those bills she didn't know about. She'd start talking about selling her jewellery. And Milly. She'd never respect him again. They'd have to turn off the new maid, and the slavey. Milly would want to help. She'd insist on going out to work.

People surged past him, bumped into him, cursed him. Move, damn you! Get out of the way! He put his head down, shoved himself along. He hurt, as though he had a bloodied nose. Mayhew had smashed his face to pulp. So find somewhere quiet to sit, recover. Write out his invoice for the wages Mayhew owed him. The money might tide them over, just, while he looked for a new job. A dray jolted past, piled with milk churns. The acrid air of the street assailed his face, settled around his shoulders like ash. He continued walking in the direction the crowd was going. Hard to see. Soot got under his eyelids. His eyes streamed. He felt in his frock-coat pocket for his handkerchief.

Keys. Purse. Nothing else. A shape of absence. He'd left his notebook at home. The new notebook, too. Where? On the hall table, where anyone could find them, read them? Coming in so late last night, drunk, had he just cast them down and forgotten them? He must have been even drunker than he thought.

Surely he'd have noticed them this morning, though, even as he left in such a hurry. What had the hall table looked like when he went out? Covered with a pile of unironed laundry, that was it. Last night, swaying on the doorstep, he'd emptied his pockets to find his keys, hadn't he, come in clutching all his bits and pieces. Perhaps he'd dropped the notebooks onto the hall table. Perhaps someone had thrown down that mass of linen on top of them. In that case he'd better get a move on.

The hall smelled of onions frying. Voices sounded downstairs in the kitchen. Cara's. Doll's, answering. Chiming against each other predictably as church bells.

He hung up his coat on the hallstand, bowled his hat onto the rack above the row of brass hooks. The hall table had been dusted, polished. The scent of beeswax sprang at his nostrils, made him sneeze.

Milly's voice said: hello, Pa.

He wheeled. Her boots at eye level. Her ankles in grey wool stockings. Skirts pulled well down over knees. She was sitting halfway up the stairs. She'd barred the top of the space behind her with a broom and a mop, presumably to keep the children from coming any closer, falling down and hurting themselves. To keep them off her. Tiny lions rampaging and his daughter bored with lion-taming. The cross cubs stamped and howled invisibly behind her, safe in their attic enclosure. Later he would go up and play with them, but not now.

Milly posed like some goody-goody schoolgirl, one hand propping up her chin, the other displaying her textbooks spread across her lap. See, teacher. See me read. See me study. See me peep at Pa's secrets. His notebooks. The dark blue cover of one, the sprigged cotton cover of the other. Ties of black ribbon dangling. Knots undone. The black strings hanging loose. Uncorseted books, revealing

233

the body-thoughts inside. The drawing of the apricot. His musings during the halts on his journeys from one orchard, one fruit tree, to another. The orchards of Waterloo, Holborn, the Strand.

Milly picked up the new notebook and brandished it. That fake, sweet voice she put on when she wanted to annoy him. Funny lot of writing, Pa. Didn't know you were a poet!

He clenched his fists. Stay calm, stay calm. He found some dull words. Did he believe them? They'd do to hold back the boil of blood. He said: those are my private papers! How dare you rummage in what's private!

He had liked having a secret, the secret life he'd begun to live inside the new notebook. A safe house. Milly had wrenched open the door. Blown his house down.

Milly dropped her bravado. Now she looked puzzled, uncertain. What's all this writing about? Why are you writing about that Mrs Dulcimer?

Cara, clad in a pale linen apron, blundered up from the kitchen. Mopping her streaming face. She must have been peeling onions. Her weak eyes always reacted extravagantly, her eyelids staying red and swollen for hours. She was blowing her nose, pushing her limp hair back under her cap. Joseph, what are you doing back home so soon? We're all at sixes and sevens this morning. Dorothy's got everything to learn about her work, and Milly's all behind with the ironing, and the children have been quarrelling so you wouldn't believe. If you want lunch, I'm afraid you'll have to wait. Milly's very upset about something but she won't tell me what. I can't get a word out of her. And I'm in the middle of showing Dorothy how to make onion sauce, and I mustn't leave her too long or she's bound to let it catch and then it'll burn.

He cried: be quiet! She turned pink, compressed her lips. Milly sat immobile on her step, looking down her nose at him. Fire rose inside him. He shouted: give me those notebooks and go to your room.

Fierce joy in losing his temper. A red tempest scorched through him and he just let go into it. Freedom and release: saying exactly what he thought and not caring. All his life he'd longed to and now finally he could let rip properly. Power flowing through him. Nobody could push him around. Lord in his own home. Current of life rushing through him, hot and pure.

Cara looked ready to burst into tears. The first time he'd ever shouted at her. But he couldn't apologise. Not yet.

Milly glared. It's not fair! I didn't know they were private! You left them lying around, it's your fault!

Her very ringlets bristled with outraged virtue. She spoke through tears. What Ma hasn't told you yet is that the landlord's been round looking for you. A whole quarter's rent owing, he said. He's coming back later for the money and if he doesn't get it, he'll have us put out on the street.

Cara said: I told him that couldn't be right. We always pay our rent on time!

Done for. Nothing for it but to keep blustering. Hold on to rage as to a mast in a storm, deck leaping up and down beneath his feet. Joseph addressed Milly. You stupid, interfering little girl!

Cara started to blub. Gulping into her handkerchief. He turned on her. While as for you! What have you got to cry about, may I ask?

She hiccupped, shoulders heaving. She stepped towards him, timidly touched his arm. Oh, Joseph, don't take on so. The landlord must have made a mistake, that's all. I'm sure Milly didn't mean to misbehave, reading your notes. I don't know what it's all about, but I'll find out. Let her go upstairs now, while you calm down, and I'll have a word with her later on.

He flung off her hand. Don't tell me to calm down! I know how to discipline my own child! Be quiet and let me deal with this!

Cara shuddered, turned rigid. She gazed at him as though she hated him. He'd gone too far. He knew it. He wanted to say sorry but couldn't.

She threw back her head and let out a wail. She's not your child. Why else do you think my sister married you? The only reason was so that her child would have a father.

The words flew up, hovered in the air above his head. Like vultures circling. Razor beaks. She wanted to peck out his eyes. Aim, fire. The words thudded down, spattered him with blood.

Cara screeched on. She and I planned it between us. I said to her, go on, he'll be up for it, you'll see. What else could she have done? She was desperate.

From her judge's seat high on the stairs Milly hurled the notebooks into the hall. They bounced on the bottom step, skidded over the floor, bumped at his feet. He bent over and picked them up, smoothed their splayed pages. Very careful movements or something might break. The dead birds, wings spread, bled red ink. He stowed the corpses in his trouser pocket. Someone was making a horrible noise. That woman with the red eyes and greyish apron and the open black pit of mouth. She smelled of onions and he needed to get away from her. She was gabbling out some tale or other. Explanations. Excuses. He wrung the tale's neck. Another dead bird. Look at it some other time. Get back to your onion sauce, you harpy disguised as a wife.

He went into the sitting-room, put the notebooks into his little portable desk. He locked it, put it back under the piano, pocketed the key.

Later, he could not remember leaving the house. He knew he had walked about in the drizzle for several hours, slipping in the mud underfoot, banging into people, shouldering them out of his way. Mind where you're going, chum. Mind your manners, you. Oh, look, Mama, that man's crying. At one moment, when drizzle changed to rain, soaked his shoulders and arms, he began shivering, realised he'd left his hat and overcoat at home. No wonder passers-by, shooting up their umbrellas with a crack of taut fabric, darting at him with black spikes, regarded him as though he were a madman. One woman turned, tentatively put out a hand. Curly fair hair. Swirl of blue skirts. Intent grey eyes. Her again. He blinked, and she was gone.

Where could he shelter? The rain drove him into a church porch, somewhere deep in the City. Bells clanged, smartly dressed people under a fluster of umbrellas began processing through the churchyard, two by two, between the graves. They halted, spotting him, flinched away. Red, well-fed faces. White nosegays in two little girls' mittened hands, white flowers in the men's buttonholes. A wedding, was it? Let me warn you. Let me tell you. He tried to speak, but choked. Wild and desperate he must look: did these gentlefolks take him for a beggar, a thief, about to rob them? A black-frocked verger appeared, chased him away: you can't stop here, my man, be off with you.

He leaned on a bollard, panting. He had hurt Milly so much. Why had he done that, lost control like that? Poor Milly.

Don't think of Milly now. Think about her later. Work out what to do later.

His sodden jacket clung to him, his waistcoat and shirt were solid rain. Water poured down his collar, seeped up, thickened with mud, into his boots. He weaved down a side alley, over greasy cobbles clotted with filth. As long as he kept going he'd be all right but he didn't know where to go, that was the problem. This journey had no beginning and no end. No map for it. No sketch. He was a bit of scrap paper the wind tossed to and fro he was waste paper sodden pulp. Keep walking. Just keep walking.

Somewhere near Waterloo he paused, gave up. Feet squelching coldly in his boots. Just find somewhere to sit, think things over. Not a pub. Too many bodies. Find somewhere else. The dark buildings pressed him between themselves. Meat in their sandwich. Black streams of people in the black rain. He couldn't breathe here. He turned off the Strand, down a narrow side street, rounded a warehouse, ducked inside a brick archway.

Water dripped from the curved vault above him, pooled round his feet. He was under some kind of viaduct. Tarry, sour smell of the river, thick with sewage. Just go down to the river and fall into it. Open your mouth and swallow it. Your bitter medicine your sleeping draught.

He leaned against the wall, slid down it rather than sat. He slumped against the sooty stones, his feet in a puddle. His head lolled onto his chest. Wait here for a while. Sleep for a bit.

The two young women who spotted him were on their way to work, they told him, seizing his shoulders and shaking him. Giddy up, mister, you'll make us late, stir a stump, wake up! Their concerned faces, bright with rouge, loomed close to his. Reddened lips exclaimed. He's a goner. No, he ain't. Feel in his pockets, quick! No, don't. Ruched velvet cloaks, black lace mittens. Gently they slapped his cheeks, hoarsely they ticked him off. You'll catch your death! One of them produced a flask and tipped brandy down him. He spluttered, shook his head, snorting. His throat burned. His stomach burned.

The women argued across him. He can't stay here. Why bother? The others'll be along soon. So? They'll have him turned over in a trice, poor devil. So what? So we better take him along with us.

They hauled him to his feet, frogmarched him into the street. His arms around their necks. Breath smelling of peppermint cachous. Hair and skin smelling of oranges and flowers. His legs wilted: stems of grass. His boots trailed after him. Up a muddy slope they half-walked, half-dragged him, panting, swearing. Back into the Strand, choked with people and traffic, the din of iron wheels on rough paving-stones. Where've you got to get to, ducks? Where's home?

Joseph shook his head. His escorts clicked their teeth. Come on, come on, spit it out. Joseph mumbled. Walworth. Right you are. That's the ticket. Got some money to pay your fare? Show us your purse, dear. Off you go, then. They flagged down a passing omnibus, shouted to the driver, checking it was going south, pushed him on board. As the bus lurched forwards, one woman threw his purse after him and the other held up the shilling she'd filched from it. Both waved and shouted, their red lips glossed by raindrops. They ducked out of sight into the crowd of passers-by.

Joseph jostled through the group of men clinging to the platform rail, managed to get inside, forced himself onto the end of a seat. The woman next to him gathered her cape round her, ostentatiously shrank away from his damp body. Sorry, missis, Joseph said. She turned her head. He must look a mess, must reek of sweat. He dozed, words loosening themselves in his mind, dancing to patterns of nonsense.

Later, looking back, he thought perhaps he'd even slept, because suddenly he jerked as someone shouted, yanked him to his feet. Walworth! Chap here for Walworth! Eventually he had arrived in Apricot Place, banged on the yellow-painted door, been admitted by a thin, fair-haired girl clutching a dishcloth. She draped it over one arm and whispered: yes?

He held out his hands. Come on hands: talk for me. The girl gaped at his soaked sleeves, his mud-clotted boots. Why had he forgotten his outdoor clothes? He couldn't think. It didn't matter.

He hadn't completely lost his memory, though. He said: you must be Annie. I've heard about you. The girl jumped. Took hold of her apron edge, began to pleat it. She said: so what if I am? Who are you, then? What d'you want?

Joseph said: I'll go up. Don't bother announcing me.

Annie tried to block his path. The mistress is busy. She can't see you, whoever you are.

He pushed past Annie, her open mouth squeaking protest, went on up the stairs. His boots must be leaving wet, dirty marks on the treads. Nothing he could do about that. He didn't knock. Just barged straight in.

She was wearing the green and grey striped sack dress. Shawl round her shoulders, a green scarf twisted around her hair. Sitting in her chair pulled close to the fire. Pen in her hand, a board in her lap. Drift of paper. Eyes cast down. Scritch-scritch of her nib.

As he banged the door she jerked. She frowned, gave a little shake of the head, sighed. As though he were waking her from a daydream.

He lurched forwards. Put out a hand, clutched the back of a chair. She rubbed her forehead. What do you want, Joseph? Annie shouldn't have let you in. I am working.

The chair back propped him. Pull yourself together, Joseph. Breathe.

He said: working? What do you mean? What are you doing?

Mrs Dulcimer tapped her board with one brown hand. I am writing. Well, I was. Until you came in.

Writing her tenants' letters home for them, presumably. She'd told him she did that sometimes, hadn't she? Accounts of floors scrubbed, meals eaten, walks taken, sermons heard? So spice it up, lady. Add a new anecdote. He said: I'll tell you a funny story, shall I? Make you laugh all right, this one will.

He hurled it out. Falling in love. Betrayal. He was destroyed. Punchline: he'd lost his wife he'd lost his life.

Had he gone mad to speak so? Button your lip, shouted the Hoof: you little whinger. He was shaking. Yes, he must be mad.

She got up, put her writing materials on the side table. She said: you're wet through. Come to the fire and get dry.

Someone began wailing. A little corkscrew of noise, piercing Joseph's heart.

Mrs Dulcimer lifted her head. She said: Betsy had her baby last night. Luckily Mrs Bonnet got here in time. I must go upstairs in a minute and see how Betsy's doing.

She turned to Joseph. You seem to have lost your handkerchief. Let me fetch you one.

She moved to the side door that he had guessed led to her bedroom. She opened it, disappeared into the interior. Her contralto voice called: just a moment.

Just a moment. Wait. Not now. Later. That's what women so often said. Poor Cara. Not her fault! Only Nathalie hadn't said wait she'd said yes yes yes. All through that honeymoon weekend. When two months later she began saying no it was because she'd fallen pregnant. Too early to tell yet, surely, he'd said. Nathalie said: I just know. He'd swallowed her lies. Knives pricked his belly. He wanted to howl.

He got up and followed Mrs Dulcimer in. The curtains, only half pulled back, the blind raised a little way, let in a dim light. Her coiled black hair. The curve of her spine under her loose green and grey dress. She bent over, pulling open a drawer.

She turned, a folded handkerchief in her hand. She contemplated him. He wanted to say something but could not speak. He swayed in the doorway. She said: you'd better lie down for a bit, Joseph. Rest.

He stumbled to the bed. His knees gave way. He fell against the soft tumble of quilts and pillows. Someone lifted his knees, pulled them up. He lay back. Hands pulled off his boots, drew the covers up over him. The curtain-rings rattled and clicked. The light narrowed, vanished. He slept.

TEN

Madeleine

ROSE RINGS UP EARLY one evening in mid-August, wanting pictures of what she calls the olden days. It's for a model I'm making, of Apricot Place. People's clothes, I need, mainly. I can get them off the internet, and down the library, but I'd like something more personal, too. You got anything I could use?

With the back door propped open to let out the smell, Madeleine is poaching mackerel *au blanc*, with a bay leaf, a splash of vinegar. You serve it cold, with mayonnaise. Her mother's recipe. Nelly, watching her daughter-in-law whisk egg yolks and oil, would joke: why did the lobster blush? Because it saw the salad dressing. Why did the lobster blush again? Because it saw Queen Mary's bottom. The child Madeleine, not understanding these antique puns, would smile politely.

She tucks her phone under her chin, pushes at the fish with a wooden fork: my family photographs go back to the early 1920s. Nothing earlier. Will that be OK?

I've got some early stuff, Rose says: those photocopies from my nan, that she showed you before. So 1920s will do fine.

Madeleine says: come over now, if you like. Where are you?

Next door, with Nan, Rose says.

Madeleine turns off the heat under the saucepan, leaves the fish to cool in its scented bath. Rose wheels in her bike: d'you mind? Don't want it to get nicked.

Rose is wearing a 1960s sloppy jumper over tight, tapering pedal-pushers. Hair backcombed into a beehive. Heavy black liner flicked up at the corners of her eyes. Like a character from Nell Dunn's *Up the Junction*: ready to go!

She says: I found a dead rat just now, right outside your gate. Its head was half off. A fox must've been at it.

Madeleine jumps. Bloody hell.

Rose says: it's OK. I picked it up with a plastic bag that was lying around and chucked it in the rubbish.

Madeleine tries to sound brisk and sensible: I suppose it's no wonder if there's an occasional rat. All these over-flowing bins, the food and stuff spilled on the pavements.

Rose nods. It drives Nan mad. She's always cleaning up the mess.

Why did it choose to die just outside Madeleine's gate? Did Emm put it there? Don't think of Emm. Don't let him into my mind.

Rose looks around the sitting-room: you've cleared it out a bit. Looks much better.

She lifts the lid of the pink soup tureen, touches the edge of a blue-and-white-striped tea-towel. She opens a cookery book, glances inside, lays it down. With a finger-tip she traces the edge of a mottled blue and white enamel soup ladle.

Madeleine says: I kept the things I really liked. I gave the rest to the charity shop.

Nelly had her prized collection of miniature souvenir jugs, but she didn't need them in order to remember her past. She turned her memories into stories for her granddaughter, recounting her tales as they popped up, jumping freely from incident to incident. George threatened to send her back to her mother, because she cooked so badly when first married. I couldn't work out how you got all the dishes ready at the same time. Some things boiled dry and some went cold waiting on the table and some were only half done. Perhaps Nelly's glass-fronted cupboard full of tiny china pots represented a dream of order: rows of tidy dinners, smoking hot; rows of tidy husbands who didn't knock fiery shreds from their pipes onto the best embroidered tablecloth and burn holes in it.

Madeleine pulls down from the shelf the photograph album she inherited from her mother, a couple of art books. They take them out into the back garden, with the tray. Beer for Rose, wine for Madeleine, a bowl of black olives. They push aside dangling loops of nasturtiums, juicy long stems flinging themselves up the trellis, trailing along the ground. Flowers of pale yellow, apricot, salmon-pink, orange, red.

Rose studies the two French café chairs, iron patched with rust and peeling white paint. Don't tell me. From the junk market. You do like old things, don't you?

What do you like, Rose? Madeleine asks.

She seats herself, shrugs. I like whatever takes my fancy! Street design. I like streets, I like thinking about how people use street space. That's what my model's about.

She levers off the beer cap, pushes away her glass, takes a swig from the bottle. She says: I like computers. I'd like to have one of those computers that design and print in 3-D. That would help me make my model, all right. Dream on!

A fat pigeon bounces through the boughs of the ash tree next door. The leaves have begun to look dry, grey-green, ready to fall. Next year, tiny ash saplings will appear all over the garden and have to be rooted up. One of the guerrilla gardeners down the street collects them. He sneaks them into derelict brown-field sites, hoping for ash groves.

Rose describes working with the sheets of cardboard, cast-off packaging, that she finds thrown down in the street. Cardboard's better than the wood she tried using before. Less durable. Like the prefabs they used to have down the street, see, it won't last. She cuts it, fits shapes together in different ways. Constructing the cul-de-sac's house façades demands constant experiment. She fiddles, destroys what she's made, begins again. Should the passers-by be made of the same material as the road surfaces? Should they flap up from pavements, fold up from area steps? Do they have to coexist in layers: layers and layers of all the people who might have walked in Apricot Place?

So what's behind the house façades? Madeleine asks.

I don't know, Rose says: nothing. I'm not interested in the interiors. This piece is about the street.

She turns the album's thick pages, gently lifting, with a fingertip, the tissue-paper sheets that separate them. Tiny triangles of dark, thin card hold each black-and-white deckle-edged photograph at the corners.

She says: hideous clothes, the women had. They must've bound their tits to flatten them.

Madeleine points. There. That's Nelly. My grandmother. The one who grew up along the Old Kent Road.

Nelly poses, in her pale frock, bang in the middle of the group of sisters. Ivy, Mabel, Lily, Frieda, Maud. Heavy-fringed, dark-browed, squinting at the sun, they sit up straight for the camera, feet in strapped and buttoned shoes pointed to one side, hands clasped in laps. Black-and-white photograph, and yet Nelly's powerful presence demands that Madeleine tint her in: brown hair bobbed and waved, pink cheeks, yellow beads round her neck. Behind, hands on their girlfriends' shoulders, stand the men, grinning or frowning, hatless, their ties cast off. Nelly winks at Madeleine. I was wondering when you'd turn up. Well, come on then, girl. You're just in time for tea.

Madeleine leans back in her chair under the exuberant flower stems. She develops the photograph, impromptu, into a story she tells Rose. The landlady of their Herne Bay boarding house has lent Nelly and her pals two baskets for their picnic. Bottles of beer, sardine sandwiches, hardboiled eggs, watercress, jam tarts, a fruit cake. George sets to, lighting the spirit lamp, boiling the kettle. Myrtle unpacks teacups, a bag of sugar lumps, a few sticks of celery kept fresh in damp newspaper. The sisters spread a rug on the ground, put the food in the centre, sprawl round the edges. They take off their shoes and massage their toes, moan about their corns, accept cigarettes from the young men. George sings to Nelly silently you're the one you're the only one. She lounges, sorting the shells in her lap. Stockings rolled up and stuffed in her pocket. While the others paddle, she and George saunter into the sand dunes. Later she will find sand in her hair and inside her drawers but she won't care. Next day George will buy her a miniature jug: A Souvenir from Herne Bay.

Rose sips beer, frowns at the bowl of olives, pushes it away. She says: I could use your story. You write it out, then I'll paste it up onto the front door of one of the houses in my model. Girls don't always want to come back home, do they? Sometimes they want to stay out for good.

She pauses. A different story for every front door? Would you do that?

Madeleine says: OK. I'll have a go.

Start with a story about someone arriving. A worried mother searching for her lost daughter? No, a man. Link it to what she's already written about someone approaching along the street.

She shivers. Nelly whispers: someone stepped on your grave.

Rose glances behind her at the house. You've left the back door open. Shouldn't do that. It's how rats get in.

Madeleine opens one of the art books, a catalogue of a Royal Academy show. Degas's ballerinas, his paintings juxtaposed with late-nineteenth-century film stills and photographs: can-can dancers, acrobats, gymnasts. She says: more costumes for you to look at.

They flick over the pages. One particular picture halts them: an image of a theatre's proscenium arch, enclosing the dancers on stage. Tiny, far-off figures in frilled white muslin skirts, delicate and gauzy. Neon-bright streaks of lurid green, turquoise, rimmed by black. Black profiles; black silhouettes of men in top hats, fur collars; gloved hands holding cigars. They gaze down at the butterfly-dancers. Who's capturing whom?

Rose closes the Degas catalogue. So where's the Royal Academy? Somewhere near the Haymarket, is it? You ever been in the Life Rooms there? Jerry says they're full of casts and statues from two hundred years ago. Don't suppose they'd let me in to have a look, would they?

Madeleine says: I think you'd have to get permission.

Rose says: one day I'll get in there. If I get into art school.

Toby and Anthony gave Madeleine the Degas ticket: we're not coming. We've seen it three times already. Anyway, we're busy cooking. Francine's coming to supper. Sole Véronique. Cream, white wine and grapes. Nothing but the best for our Francine.

Madeleine gaped, gripped her phone. No! After what she did? Toby sounded amused: we've forgiven her. She loves Anthony, which shows her good taste. She may or may not ever love me. Anyway, she's got a new job, she's coming over to tell us all about it.

Madeleine says to Rose: one thing that particularly struck me in the Degas exhibition was the tiny, brief films they were showing alongside the paintings. Dancers, acrobats. It suddenly seemed odd, seeing dead people alive and moving on screen. With photos it's odd too. Everyone's stilled in photos. The living and the dead look just the same. Death gets cancelled out.

Rose says: women often died young in the olden days, didn't they? Too many kids. You'll have to write me a story about that.

Madeleine says: and so many children died young, too. Perhaps you should include a hearse in your model. It must have been a common sight on these streets.

Her eyes feel wet. What is it? She sits up straight, blows her nose.

Rose balances her phone on her palm, flips it open. You want to see the passers-by I've done so far? She strokes her thumb across the dark surface, tilts it so that Madeleine can see the flow of pictures. Cutouts. Silhouettes in white against black. A woman in a wide skirt. A man in top hat and frock coat. A child in a frilled dress and pantalettes. Rose sighs. They're no good. They look like that card game Nan had. Happy Families.

She closes her phone. Madeleine plays Tinker Tailor with the olive stones. Tinker Tailor Netsurfer Emailer. Rose blurts: d'you think people in those days fell in love like people now say they do? Lot of rubbish, I sometimes think.

True love, true love. On the phone Toby said: Anthony and I are so lucky, we've found each other. Francine's got no one. If she wants to make it up with us it's no skin off my nose!

White petals from the nearby rosebush topple, drift to the ground. One lands on the tabletop. Curve of white: a tulle sylphide skirt. Those hardworking ballerinas in Degas's pictures. Under soft gestures and graceful poses they hide their strength: the ruthless determination to become artists.

Madeleine looks at Rose's still face. She knows her well enough by now to recognise some difficult feeling struggling behind the blank façade. Something else she wants to say, but needs prompting on.

When d'you take your A Levels? Next summer, is it? How's it all going?

Rose stares at her lap. I'm thinking about dropping out. Dunno whether it's worth even thinking about art school. The money's going to be a problem.

Madeleine says: well—

Rose interrupts. I know, I know, in your day there were grants, further education was a right. Don't say it! Times have fucking changed!

Madeleine says: you'd be eligible for a bursary. They do exist.

Rose shrugs. If I get in. If I do go. I don't know. I know you have to be organised. If you really want to do it. Jerry's lot are, for sure.

In her squat up at the Elephant, behind the artists' studio complex, the household, men and women alike, takes turns: shifts in childcare, shifts in working. Madeleine visited those converted nineteenth-century workshops on one of their open days. Through a wide doorway, into a cobbled yard. Old terracotta pots planted with olive trees; piles of stones; crates. Garlands of bright green ivy looped along the brick walls between the workshop thresholds, trailed above the low lintels. Children ran and played and yelled. Rose showed Madeleine the studios, approached up narrow rickety stairs with dipping treads. Wood-burning stoves; shelves full of bric-a-brac; walls covered in paintings, drawings, embroideries. The squat was tucked away behind; a former warehouse turned into a ramshackle home.

In the pub afterwards Rose said: it won't last long. They're going to change the law on squatting pretty soon, make it more difficult. We could get thrown out any day.

Rose's feet in their Doc Martens tap against the table strut. Madeleine, I must go. Got to get to work.

Madeleine says: Rose, what is it? Something else is bothering you but I don't know what.

Rose gets up. I think I'm pregnant. I don't know what to do.

She addresses the ground. Jerry doesn't want a baby. Says he's too young to be a father. He wants to have some more fun first. So if I keep the baby we'll probably split up.

She scoops up the Degas catalogue, the albums. Can I borrow these for a day or two?

She marches down the garden steps, through the propped-open back door, goes ahead of Madeleine into the hall. The front door, opening, lets in a draught of cool air that blows through the flat. Rose drags her bike out, up the front area steps. She pedals away, vanishes.

Madeleine wraps her arms around herself. How could I have been so completely crass, so insensitive, talking about death, mentioning dead children? But I didn't know. Why did I do that? Oh, Rose, I'm sorry.

She returns to her galley kitchen, takes up a slotted spoon, lifts the dripping mackerel out of the pan. Four gleaming fish in a row. She's cooked too much food again. Hard to cook just for herself. One of life's pleasures: making food to offer to others. She'll invite Sally to supper. Does Sally know Rose is pregnant? She must do.

She lays the mackerel on a board, slits them open, teases out the spines. For over a hundred and fifty years other cooks have stood here before her, perhaps filleting fish just as she's doing, scraping off blue-black skin. Where did they store food? A built-in larder? Where did they throw waste? How often did the dustmen come round?

She carries the mackerel on their plate towards the fridge in its alcove, draws back the lace curtain. Shimmer of blue china on the shelf above: Nelly's turquoise pot that she shoved there months ago. She should sort out the contents, decide whether or not to get rid of them. She strokes the curve of the lid. Coated in dust. More neglected cleaning. Some other time. She pushes the plate of fish into the fridge, claps the door shut.

Now she'll read. Back to Mayhew, back to that volume of local history, to find more inspiration for stories for Rose. What will Rose do about her pregnancy? Don't interfere. She'll find her way.

Loud footsteps erupt in the silence. The tenant next door thumping downstairs to his basement flat adjoining hers? Must be. Crashing down over the bare treads. He's got an inside staircase, she remembers, down from the communal hallway. Sounds carry, even through these sturdy walls and ceilings. That baby upstairs, wailing morning and night. The mother tramping to and fro, trying to quieten it, sometimes wailing herself. Oh you little bugger will you shut up. So many people crammed in here. All of us intimate witnesses to each other's lives whether we like it or not.

So many of us. Layers and layers of people who lived here before. Who walked along this street.

Somehow she's drifting. What time is it? Her shoulder-blades tense, the skin there tightening, tautening. The air quivers, tingles. The back of her neck twitches, as though moist fingers are touching it. Someone breathes heavily, just behind her. Sweet smell of perfumed oil.

Somebody in the flat. Not a bad dream this time. She's awake. Someone got in through the open back door while she was saying goodbye to Rose at the front?

She wheels round. No one.

She checks her bedroom, the bathroom, the sitting-room. Each time she moves, steps forward or back, she senses a corresponding movement behind her. A shadow attached to her that she can't see. When she turns her head something jerks behind her.

The hallway darkens. Cloud blotting out the sun. Clammy atmosphere; like blundering into a vast cobweb. A skin fastening onto her, sticking to her, that she can't shake off. It wraps itself over her mouth and nose. Tightens. Binds her. She twists, wrenches herself to and fro, flails her elbows. Get out. I must get out. She's choking. Dying. Keep moving keep moving.

Something splits, tears. The passageway convulses, squeezes her. Pushes her. She thrusts herself towards the back door, falls outside, onto the garden steps. Hauls herself up them, into the daylight. Fresh air slaps her. She gasps, breathes.

ELEVEN

Joseph

JOSEPH WOKE INTO DARKNESS. A quilt floated around him, wrapped him lightly. Cool air stroked his face, the back of his neck. He pulled the quilt even closer, lay lapped in this warm nest of down. The half-open door let in golden light from the room beyond, the whispering and crackling of a fire. Burning wood smelled apple-sweet. Out there a chair creaked, papers rustled. He ought to get up. Too drowsy. Stay safe. Stay hidden. No one knew where he was. No one could find him.

Hide-and-seek: the game he played as a seven-year-old with his mother. She called for him to carry the scuttle of coal, to sweep the yard, and he vanished; nowhere to be found. Oh, you monkey! Come here this minute! Tucking himself into the larder, he curled on the cold floor, shut his eyes. Where did he go in those states of escape? Not quite sure. His mother's words for it: he just dissolved, into thin air.

His hidey-holes changed from week to week as she discovered them, exploded them. Under her bed in the room next to the kitchen. Below the brass hook in the passageway, inside the drop of overcoats. Outside, in the privy. Upstairs, in the box room where he slept. The box room doubled as linen-room, where washing hung to dry on wet days. Sent up to fetch the pillowcases for ironing, he would stand between the lines of damp sheets, listen to her call: oh you rascal, you scallywag.

Aged eight, he learned to read and write, to tell the time. Hiding, finding secret places, became more than a game. His season, his element, which soaked into him, formed him. Solitude gave him the freedom to daydream. He filched a stub of pencil from a kitchen drawer, scrawled pictures on torn squares of newspaper. With a stolen piece of chalk, he drew sparrows and blackbirds on the walls of the yard, cranes and ships.

One morning he turned the kitchen table into his house. The skirts of his mother's dressing-gown, thrown on over her chemise and petticoat, swishing to and fro, curtained the opening on the far side. The rough underneath of the table, yellow and raw, formed his ceiling. He squatted against the wooden pillar of the leg at the corner. His mother's slippered feet inched closer to him. When she stood still, his fingers flew out, hovered, stroked the felt that covered her toes, just lightly enough that she wouldn't feel his touch. Her invisible hands rattled kitchen tools, dumped pans. Her slippers tramped away. Clang of iron as she shook the frying pan. The thick, salty smell of kippers beginning to sizzle.

A chair scraped on the floor. Backwards, forwards. She yawned and burped, planted her feet apart. He gave her time to settle, then pinched up the hem of her dressing-gown, lifted it, crawled in, under the tent of her petticoat. He curled up between her open thighs, facing her, his head bent, one cheek resting on his drawn-up knees, his arms clasping them. Crisp brush of newspaper: his mother turning over a page. Her legs gleamed palely in the calico darkness. She wore no stockings, and no drawers. He'd got inside the house of her skin, her alluring scent, sweet-sour and fishy. If he leaned forward her curly brown muff would brush his forehead, tickle it. If he raised his head, approached his mouth to her? If he put out his tongue and licked her and tickled her?

She didn't move. Surely she knew exactly where he was? Surely she liked him being there, wanted him to stay with her. No Hoof tramping about, whistling, shouting for his tea. Just the two of us. Just the fish puckering and seizing in the pan. Breathe quietly. Breathe on her very softly, and feel that secret mouth breathing back.

Rush of cold air as the door banged open, the Hoof's voice sang out hello, his mother jerked up and away, sang back: sweetie!

Joseph retreated further under the table, as a pair of boots backed a pair of slippers towards the angle of wall and floor. Her giggle. Silence. Rustle of cloth. Her low, throaty voice: not now. Jo-Jo's hiding under the table.

Molly-coddler! Come here, my little nincompoop! A giant hand hauled him out, swung him by the collar. Half-choking, legs scrabbling in the air. Joseph squawked and kicked, and the Hoof laughed. Little dummy! He let go. Joseph tripped. The hearthrug's dusty cotton knots smacked his face.

Acrid smell of burning fish, red flame leaping, cloud of black smoke, his mother shrieking. Boots and slippers trampled towards him, pulled up the rug, tipped him out of it. Flare of red tongues. Rug flung over the blazing pan. Smell of scorched cloth. The Hoof hurled the black mess outside and his mother seized Joseph, ran him to the inner door, thrust him upstairs. Sobbing, feeling the flames lick him, singe him. Burn holes in him. Later, his mother hugged him, scolded him. The Hoof banged out to the pub.

Widening slice of gold light, as the door opened. Here came Mrs Dulcimer, carrying a basin, a towel over her arm. It's late afternoon, Joseph. I've brought you some warm water, look, in case you want to wash. Come next door when you're ready, and we'll have some tea.

He splashed his face and hands. Still groggy. Something bad had happened. What? He couldn't remember. He found his mud-caked boots beside the bed, dragged them on. No jacket. Had he lost it somewhere? He glanced in the little square mirror hung above the chest of drawers. A wild man, with troubled dark blue eyes, rumpled chestnut-grey hair, stared back. Big beaky nose. Another of the Hoof's names for him: Beaky. Leaky Beaky the Silly-Billy Bawler. Collar undone and crumpled. No cravat. Who was that fellow? No idea. A changeling, perhaps. Someone had sidled in while he slept and exchanged him. They were welcome to him, whoever they were. This new, unknown self would do for the time being. Until he got his bearings, discovered what he should do next. He splashed his face again, dried it on the soft towel.

He trod into the sitting-room just as Mrs Dulcimer entered from the other door, carrying a tray of tea things. Her long brown fingers clasped the plaited-brass handles. A red weal blistered the back of one hand. Her dark face turned, surveyed him. Eyes gleaming under the curve of her eyelids. Sculpted brown cheeks. Scarf twisted around her black hair. A draught swept in behind her, the smell of hot butter and cinnamon. She stretched out a slippered foot from under her green and grey skirts, kicked the door shut. He held the tray for her while she cleared the little table, sweeping up her pile of manuscript and setting it on the floor, perching pen and inkwell on top. Her brown hands plumped gold satin cushions, turned chairs to half-face the fire.

The blue Chinese pot smirked at him from the mantelpiece: how are the mighty fallen, eh? Near it, a dark, sack-like thing hung from the corner of the marble ledge. Here's your jacket, Mrs Dulcimer said, taking it down: it was soaking wet, so I brought it in here to dry. Joseph put it on, seated himself, while she poured tea.

She set a plate of bread and butter in front of him, a pot of anchovy paste, a cup of tea. She took up her own cup, began to drink from it. Eyes lowered, fringe of black lashes. Off in her private thoughts, allowing him time to recover his wits. A black jagged hole in his mind. Piece of jigsaw. The one missing bit.

The black gap shone darkly at him. Began to jump with light. Transformed, a star-shaped opening, now gold in the darkness. Just put your eye to it: peep through. Child stuck to the keyhole: the bedclothes humping and writhing. Last night, at home in Lamb's Conduit Street, he'd looked through the keyhole in the kitchen door. What's going on? I don't know! He wanted to cry and laugh both. His back ached; his throat convulsed. The speed with which Nathalie had married him: surely a clue? He'd pressed his lips to her soft cheek: why such haste, darling? She'd seized his big hand between her two little ones, pouted, whispered. I want to stop looking after other people's children. I want to start looking after you. She'd tickled his palm with her forefinger. Round and round the garden, she sang. Up the bleeding garden path more like.

Mrs Dulcimer propped her feet on the fender, leaned back, nursing her cup between her hands on her lap, the grey and green folds of her dress. The sweet smell of the apple wood burning mixed with the bitter one of coal. You could taste both: ripe fruit; sourness like soot.

The heat around the fireplace contrasted with the coldness of the rest of the room. He sneezed, groped for his handkerchief. A lace-edged square of white cotton printed with blue spots. Whose? Mrs Dulcimer's. She'd pushed it into his hand before he slept. He blew his nose into it. Yawned. He rubbed his face. Began to focus. The heap of white manuscript pages bore a few fragments of ash blown from the grate. He leaned down to brush them off. Lines of black writing, scribbled over, crossed out.

He said: I am sorry. I interrupted you earlier on. When I came in. I shouldn't have done so.

Mrs Dulcimer placed her blue and yellow cup back on the tray. She said: I finished my work while you were asleep. So you didn't disturb me after all.

He began to sip his tea, smoky-tasting, aromatic. He said: that is kind of you. Thank you.

She shook back her sleeves, turned her palms over, regarded her ink-stained fingertips. She put up a hand, pushed at her scarf, her bundle of black plaits, toppled to one side. She brushed crumbs from her cuff. She said: so many words describing untidy women begin with S, have you noticed? Sluttish. Slovenly. Sloppy. Slatternly. Slack. Slipshod. Slummocky.

She rolled the epithets over her tongue, relishing them like a nursery rhyme. She spread her inky hands in the air, looking pleased as Punch. A childish streak in her. Perhaps that was why he didn't feel ashamed that she'd seen him in such a sorry state. At first, certainly, she'd been annoyed at his intrusion, but now she seemed to accept that a person could arrive at her door in total disarray, his soul half torn from him. He ought to gather himself up, say something brisk and authoritative, shoot off into the hurly-burly street. He didn't want to move. Soothed by the hot, fragrant tea, by the steady ticking of the clock. His heartbeat slowed to match it. He took up a piece of bread and butter, spread it with anchovy paste, bit into it.

Coldness and saltiness. Springy fresh bread. She'd lopped off the crusts.

She said: nicer without crusts. I keep them for bread pudding. I've one baking in the oven now. It provides an economical supper.

Joseph said: I used to help my mother make that. Stale bread soaked in sweetened milky tea, with raisins and beaten eggs and a sprinkle of rum.

Mrs Dulcimer glanced at the red weal on her hand, sucked it. She must have burned herself on the stove. What did her skin taste like? Honeyed. Nutmeg, vanilla sugar, sultanas. Wasn't that what you put in bread and butter pudding? Wobbling pale yellow custard held inside soft white ramparts. Cara used to bake that for the children. One of the recipes she'd learned from his mother.

His shirt and waistcoat had dried on him while he slept. Dirt-stiffened. Never mind. The fire-lit room held him in warmth, which folded round him, like the quilt on her bed. So peaceful here. If only he could stay, rest. Somehow stop time, linger in this moment. Just flow out, be part of it. The ticking and crashing of coal against wood embers, red and glowing.

The edges of furniture softened as darkness began to gather in the corners. Mrs Dulcimer got up, drew the curtains against the misty dusk outside.

Flames like tiny red women kicked up their legs. Why hadn't he let himself suspect what Nathalie was up to? Because he was a well set up young fellow, with a decent job and prospects, a good catch for any children's nurse. Lucky to get him, wasn't she? Her lack of fear on their wedding night he'd accepted as a grateful virgin's compliment on his expertise. Rather than recognise it for what it was: the compliance of an experienced and cunning woman. Probably she'd been laughing at him behind his back the entire time.

No. Not true. Don't believe it. His thoughts were knives, scraping his insides. Perhaps, if you really loved a woman, you got over your jealousy. He might have. If he'd been given a chance. If she'd lived. Would he have wanted to marry her, though, if he'd known the truth? No. Was that true? Perhaps he might. How could he tell now?

The heap of wood and coal burned lustily, crisping and crackling in the grate. Mrs Dulcimer drank her tea and watched the flames. He should go home. Face the music. What music? A funeral dirge. The knives withdrew, leaving him cleaned out. Hollow. A blown egg. Pierced, sucked dry. Fragile shell. Easily crushed.

Sometimes sparrows built their nests in the high, windswept house gutters along Lamb's Conduit Street, and sometimes in the mornings, going outside, he came across fallen fledglings. Stretched-looking pale bodies. Grotesque, with broken, flopping necks. Featherless. Fatherless.

Joseph said: you said S for slut and so on. For me the letter S stands for Stepfather. I resented mine. Clumsy sort of chap. I couldn't see why my mother ever married him.

The fire glowed red and clear, sinking a little. You could cook on it. Make toast. Hold out the extendable fork with its long, thin tines piercing the slice of bread, turn it, you crouched close to the fire, felt your cheeks thicken and redden at its heat. You sat with your mother, watching her knife out dripping from the pot, spread it over the browned square. Bite into that earthy, silky taste of meat jelly and fat. Eat as slowly as he liked, no one chivvying him to hurry up, get back to his chores. The Hoof had gone out before Joseph got up and wouldn't be back until mid-day. Time alone together. After their shared late breakfast, his mother tidied up the remains of their meal, began preparing her husband's. She put a brace of kippers into a pan, set it on the stove. Joseph hid under the kitchen table.

The memory burned him all over again while Mrs Dulcimer looked on. She leaned forwards, put out her hand and jiggled a fallen bit of branch, its end glowing crimson. She used it as a poker, to stir the flames. She patted them; unruly children. She sat back, placidly regarding the heap of twinkling coals, flaring twigs. She breathed quietly. So he breathed too. He breathed out.

Keep still. Undo his life's red tangle somehow, smooth it, make it usable. Like helping his mother prepare her knitting. He held the skein in a wide loop between his outstretched hands, thumbs up to keep the wool in place; she seized the dangling free end and began to wind; the long thread of yarn ran back and forth between his spread fingers, criss-crossing the air, as she wound it into a globe. There! She held three red balls, began to juggle with them. She tossed them to the Hoof. That's for your new pullover. Robin Red-Breast! The Hoof crossed the room, arms full of red wool, kissed her, and she smiled.

Mrs Dulcimer refilled their cups. She said: hard for you, perhaps, having a stepfather. Your mother saw some good in him, I suppose.

She'd picked up his thoughts again. She was at home inside his mind. She went on: my mother didn't have much time for us, she worked so hard. She'd raise her fist when we got under her feet, she'd holler at us then we'd skedaddle. When she cried I would go to her and lick the tears off her face. She said I was her little comfort. Comfort was my middle name! She taught me to read and write. On Sunday nights she'd hear us say our prayers and then she'd tell us stories. Hair-raising, some of them.

Joseph fidgeted. The fire quivered, fragile suddenly, sticks about to collapse, more kindling needed to get it going again, she ought to ring for more coals.

He put down his cup. He said: my mother came to live with us, at the end. She was already ill, but she didn't want to let on.

Wrapped in her grey shawl, his mother sat in the kitchen, huddling close to the range. She wrote out recipes for Cara, she worked her way through the darning basket, she helped with the little ones. She fended off Joseph by not attending to him; always busy with counting stitches or measuring out flour. She'd flap her hands at him: out of the kitchen! Shoo!

Joseph said: children shouldn't question their parents, but I wanted her to explain why she'd ever married my stepfather, given how dull he was. Solid. Almost stupid.

He lowered his glance, talked to his teacup. At one time, as a boy, I believed she wasn't really a widow. That in fact she'd never been married to my father at all.

He gulped breath. Illegitimate. Terrible, shameful word to say. Like wearing a label tied round your forehead for all the world to gawk at. Despise you. You're not like them. Dirty son of a dirty mother. People stared, pointed, hissed. You live apart, outcast, you scratch a living in the wastelands, like a gypsy. Maimed, sick. Nathalie must have believed that, too.

He said: my mother told me, in one late conversation, that after marrying my stepfather she lost two babies. Two in three years. At the time, of course, I didn't know. She hid it from me. To protect me, I suppose. I was too young to understand about such things.

Mrs Dulcimer sat up straight. Her face softened. She said: losing two babies, well then, that was sad for her, wasn't it.

Only when you wanted the babies, lady. Those girls who visited Mrs Bonnet, what did they feel? Little more than children, if you considered Doll, and Annie. Desperate, presumably. Mrs Dulcimer fixed him with a direct gaze, as though to say: and how did they come to fall pregnant in the first place, Joseph? Did they do it all by themselves? And why should they tell you anything about how they feel?

Joseph said: I didn't want to understand, when she finally told me.

A spring morning, Saturday, a sharp wind whipping the new green leaves in Brunswick Square at the top of the street. Cara had taken the children out for an airing. Left alone with him in the kitchen, cleaning the brass while he watched, his mother had given halting replies to his questions. Her fingers closed round her stinking yellow rag. Speaking of the children she'd lost, she shut her face, blinked, turned her gaze away. She began to heave up from her chair. She said: I think I'll take my rest now. Will you help me upstairs, Joseph?

He gave her his arm. They crept up the two flights from the kitchen to her room. She wheezed and panted. She sat down on the bed, feet dangling, to allow him to remove her slippers. Billowy swollen ankles. He turned his head aside, dropped a slipper on the floor. Ah, you're a clumsy boy, Joseph. She slumped back against her pillows, heaped up to ease her breathing. She seemed to be falling asleep, her eyelids fluttering. Deeply fissured skin of her cheeks. Wrinkled throat. She was tender and soft as a sheet of tissue paper.

She murmured: stop fretting me. I married your step-father because I fancied him, d'you see. As a young man he was so beautiful, Joseph. No one to touch him, in his beauty. Such charm he had. Wicked, glinting looks.

Always promising something but never telling you what. I wanted him more than anything. There. Does that satisfy you?

His mother closed her eyes. Dreamy expression. A smile. She began to whisper in a hoarse voice. Such an appealing gaze he had. He was like a flower with some petals torn off.

Joseph pulled the bedclothes towards her chin. She chanted on. The brown throat the muscles of him the taut brown skin the lean frame the red mouth. The pleasure we had together, Joseph, I didn't know such pleasure could exist, I could never get enough of him, can't you understand that?

He sat with her, and soon she slept. Next day, feeling weaker, she did not get up.

Restless after work, unwilling to go home, he began taking evening strolls through the city streets. Long walks, criss-crossing the river, back and forth between prisons and palaces, following the curves of the brown serpent leaping past wharves and warehouses, wallowing between mud banks, biting London in two. In the blue glimmers of dusk he became an anonymous wanderer, carried hither and thither by the crowd, pushed down unknown alleys, back courts, tiny squares. You fled along, swept by the wind, by the pressure of people, by your desire to understand this monstrous, filthy, voracious town and your own place in it, you pursued the smell of money, of sex, of death. A young woman flitted ahead of him, hawking her cheap buttons. His mother. The Hoof waylaid her, took her for a drink. Your kid won't miss you for an hour or two. Come on, sweetheart, keep me company.

His mother was dying. Mother Busk's on the Waterloo Road flashed like a lighthouse. Sailor, beware the rocks. Mother Busk's rescued Joseph from drowning. He swam inside, summoned by the gold-spangled red and green glass panels of the lantern above the entrance. Thin Mother Busk had a tired, painted face, eyes like apple pips, wore a billowing dress of striped black and purple silk. She summed him up, summoned Polly, the black-haired girl. Polly lolled back, smiled as he arranged her. He lifted the lace edge of her chemise to lie just above her cunt. Plump thighs curving above her black stocking-tops. Her springy black hair tight as a sheep's fleece, curls clustering over his fingers. He kneeled, parted her lips, kissed and licked her.

He said: I should be going. I've trespassed on your hospitality long enough.

Mrs Dulcimer said: you've no coat and hat. I'll lend you my husband's, if you like. I've kept them all this time, thinking I'd sell them at some point. You're welcome to borrow them.

As he levered himself from his chair, the latch clicked. Annie, red-cheeked, pushing wisps of hair behind her ear, peeped round the door. A message, missis.

She hung back. Doll, dressed in a brown bonnet and brown cloak, stepped past her, carrying a large parcel and her straw bag. She halted just inside the door, shifted her feet, as though her boots hurt. Annie behind her bobbed from side to side, presumably to get a good view of what was going on. The draught whistled in from the passage, lifting the edge of the carpet. Just as on his first visit. Only a few days ago.

Doll's little face, framed in brown buckram, looked white and tight. She glanced at Mrs Dulcimer, received a nod, which seemed permission to speak. She faced Joseph, took a breath, lifted her chin and pushed words out, as though she were reciting a speech in some unfriendly classroom. Mrs Benson told me to bring you your coat. Miss Milly had a pretty good idea of where you'd be. Mrs

Benson didn't believe her at first, then she looked in your papers, and found the letter from the missis, with this address. So she told me to come straight over.

He'd locked his desk, hadn't he? He could see Cara forcing the lock with a sturdy knife, lifting the lid, trying the interior drawers, one by one. Rummaging through his private papers. Her flushed face, pursed lips.

Mrs Dulcimer leaned forward, lifted the lid of the teapot and peered inside. Annie, would you fetch us some more hot water, please? Shut the door behind you, there's a good girl.

Doll put down her bag, held out her parcel. I couldn't manage your hat as well, Mr Benson. I had to leave it behind.

He took the parcel from her, dropped it on the ground. He clasped her mittened hand. She was shaking. She smelled of the street: coal smoke and sweat. She lifted her face, rushed the words out. Mrs Benson's gone away. To her parents in France. Miss Milly too. I went with them to the station, to help them with the children, to see them onto the boat train, and then I come on here.

They'd done a runner. When in doubt: bolt. He couldn't fault it as a strategy.

How would they manage? Such inexperienced travellers. Flustered Cara, best bonnet thrust on, the three little ones tied to her wrists by ribbons, tangling and whining. Milly with a hastily packed bag in each hand. Climbing up into a third-class compartment, forcing their way into the packed space, finding room on the wooden seats. He should have been there to help them. To help them leave him.

Joseph stepped back from Doll, but kept hold of her hand. It lay stiffly in his. Damp wool, cold fingertips. Doll's mouth trembled. She pressed her lips together. She was obviously trying hard for self-control. He squeezed her hand. She did not squeeze back.

Mrs Dulcimer got up, walked across the room with a swish of skirts. She pulled forward a third chair. Low, like a chair for nursing a baby, it ran on little casters, its oval seat and back upholstered in faded yellow velvet, fastened with tarnished brass studs. Mrs Dulcimer put a gold satin cushion on it, patted it. I'm glad you found your way safely, Doll. Come and sit down and get warm.

She picked up the tray of crockery. I must just go upstairs and cast an eye on Betsy and the baby. Then I'll go down and help Annie make some fresh tea. I daresay you're thirsty, Doll, after your journey. I'll bring you up some tea, shall I?

Joseph held the door open for her. She said: it's dark now, and you've a long journey home. If you want to stay the night, I've the space. Doll can go in with Annie, and you can have the little room next to the kitchen.

She'd offered it before, hadn't she? Mocking him. Playing some game. This time he wanted to believe her, that she was serious, that she meant him well. Why not believe her? She'd taken him in, she'd let him sleep, given him tea, time to recover himself. How did you recover? He was a long gaping wound. His wife-skin torn off. Raw red flesh.

He said: thank you.

She nodded at him, glided out. Straight-backed, upright as a queen, the green-grey striped sack billowing out behind her. She vanished into the cold gloom of the passage. Closing the door, he heard the tap of her slippers, the clunk of the tray as she set it down somewhere, her contralto voice calling out to Annie to bring her a light.

He turned to his maidservant. Doll stood still, her brown outdoor things clutched round her. She chewed the tip of her glove. Pinched pale face. She peeped at him, looked as scared as she had done last night, when he caught her and Milly swapping confidences in the kitchen.

He rubbed his chin. A sigh blew out. Go on, then. Get yourself warmed up. Doll sat down abruptly on the third chair, which Mrs Dulcimer had placed between the other two, immediately opposite the fireplace. She made a bustle of taking off her damp things. She drew off her gloves, and chafed her hands. She undid her cloak and threw it behind her, so that it hung off the back of the chair. She untied her bonnet strings, discarded the bonnet, which fell aside onto the floor. Her lower lip sticking out, she fixed her glance on the red mass of the fire.

Her downcast gaze: sorrowful and puzzled. She was trying to spare him something. What?

He said: Doll?

She jerked her head in the direction of the doorway, where the parcel she had brought lay tumbled on the carpet, next to her bag. You better take a look, Mr Benson.

Joseph picked up the package, brought it over to the fire. He sat down, tore off the string, pulled away the brown paper wrappings. He lifted out his coat, unfolded its smooth woollen length. He unfastened the buttons, held the collar in one hand and slid his other between the lapels. His fingers slanted across the cool, soft lining, searching for the ridge of doubled-over silk marking the secret opening. His hand plunged into a hole. The stitches fastening the deep pocket had been cut through, and the banknotes removed.

Doll said: Mrs Benson found the notes this morning, after you'd left, when she picked up the coat, and was brushing it. She took them because she hadn't any money. She said she didn't know how long she'd be away for, so she took her jewellery too. Everything in the green box, and in the red one.

She blurted it out just as Milly would. Both defiant and scared. She sank back onto her seat. Her arms flopped, hung down at her sides. There, her pose seemed to sigh: now you know.

Joseph beat his fists on the arms of his chair. He said: hats off to Cara! She was always thorough, wasn't she!

He rolled the coat up, threw it down by the side of his chair along with the brown paper. He pushed the whole lot, crackling, behind him, away out of sight.

The fire was sinking. He got up, kneeled in front of the grate, scrabbled in the gritty bottom of the coal bucket, bringing out the last pieces of fuel. You had to fiddle delicately with the fallen, glowing lengths of wood, poke carefully so that they did not fragment, disintegrate into red cinders. The half-burned lengths settled, and he balanced coals on top, one by one. Flames sprang and danced.

He rose, dusted his hands on his trouser knees. His legs trembled. Seasick sailor cast adrift again. Tossing along over black waves under a black sky. No: Cara was the one who'd taken ship. The winds of rage behind her, filling her sails as she steered towards Boulogne.

First time the little ones had been out at sea. What would they make of it? One thing to paddle at the edge of the beach; quite another to stand at the rail and feel the deck lift and fall under your feet, shove you this way and that. They'd cling to Milly, whimpering, and she'd coax them not to cry, her curls streaming, her skirts whipping up.

Well, Milly had got what she wanted. Off to France, and as soon as could be, no doubt, she'd be making her way to Paris, to train with those nursing nuns. Sped on her way by the money he'd put aside for her and Nathalie all those years ago. Fair enough, Mrs Benson! He'd wanted Milly to benefit, and now she could. What would Cara's parents make of her visit? When would he see his wife and children again? Had Cara deserted him for good?

He sat down. Doll gave him an anxious look from her gravel-grey eyes. Poor child: what reversals for her to fathom. He tried to find a cheerful, encouraging voice. You did very well, Doll, making your way back here all by yourself. You were very brave. I wouldn't like Miss Milly to have to make such a journey all alone.

Doll gave him a flinty look. She said: I'm used to going about by myself, sir. I've had to be, from an early age.

She reached her hand backwards and patted her cloak pocket. Mrs Dulcimer showed me how to keep a hatpin handy, in case of need. You hold it inside your palm, and then, anyone who bothers you, you whip it out, stick it in his privates.

Nathalie had owned three hatpins. One black, tipped with jet. Two painted white, with fake pearls stuck on the ends; anchors for her wedding bonnet, ornaments emphasising her scrap of lace veil fastened to the confection of cream-coloured straw lined with pleated white silk. She'd trimmed the bonnet herself, adding a bunch of artificial white daisies, long white ribbons that streamed in the breeze. To bury Nathalie, they'd dressed her in her best gown, the one she'd worn for her marriage, and her wedding bonnet. The two white hatpins held the little straw poke over her curls.

And Mrs Dulcimer drew me a map, Doll went on: before I come over to you yesterday. She put arrows on it, for me to follow, and the numbers of the omnibuses.

After they had laid Nathalie in her coffin, leaving the lid leaning for the moment against the wall, Joseph had bent down, cut off one of his wife's twining locks. Later, Cara had plaited it into a ring for him. When Cara left the room, to open the front door to the undertakers, Joseph leaned over his wife, stroked her cheek, kissed her mouth. The men came in, hammered down the lid.

Joseph said: my notebooks. Do you know what happened to them?

Doll addressed her boots. She spoke sorrowfully, as though the boots had inexplicably misbehaved, and she had to chide them. But she loved them too and hoped in time that they'd improve and do better. She said: Mrs Benson burned them, sir. She threw them into the kitchen range. She threw in all of your papers that she could find.

Click of the latch, a rush of cold air. Mrs Dulcimer returned. She handed Doll a cup of tea. Brisk demeanour, a smile, which said: don't fret. None of this is your fault. Eyes fixed on her cup and saucer, Doll drank.

Little cave of firelight. The burning twigs shifted and sent up red sparks. Downstairs a door opened, slammed shut. Overhead, a baby began crying. Mrs Dulcimer said: I forgot to bring candles. I'll go and fetch some. And I'll bring up some more coal at the same time. Then I must start on the supper.

Joseph wanted so much to stay that he could not bear it. Slide downstairs, find that kitchen again, that bed next door to it, fall onto it. Just one good night's sleep and he'd be restored.

Much too easy. He had to prove he was capable of decision right now, that he could act. So get up, man. Pull yourself together. He said: please don't bother on my account. I need to be pushing off home. Put your things back on, Doll. We must be off.

Doll lowered her head, placed her cup on the little table. She crossed her arms and addressed the hearthrug's blue-grey tufts. Mr Benson, I'm sorry, sir, you can't go home. You're locked out. The landlord come back round again, lunchtime, he took the keys off Mrs Benson as she was leaving, you can only go back in once the rent's paid.

Joseph jumped to his feet. He can't do that! He's got no right!

Doll shrank in her chair. Joseph clenched his fist, roared. Doll ducked, threw up an arm to shield her face.

The tide cooled, ebbed. He gripped the chair back. He said to Doll: I'm sorry. I'm not angry with you. You've done nothing to make me angry. I'm sorry I frightened you.

Mrs Dulcimer put her hand on Doll's shoulder. It's all right. Go downstairs and sit with Annie for a bit, dearie. I'll be down shortly.

Doll picked up her straw bag, her cloak and bonnet, tumbled out. The door clapped shut. Mrs Dulcimer gathered up Doll's peeled-off gloves, which had fallen near her chair. She turned them the right way, smoothed them, rolled them into a neat ball, put it into her pocket. Joseph breathed heavily. His chest rasped and hurt. That poor girl. She'd laboured all the way across London, bringing him his coat, and he'd yelled at her. Not her fault she'd had to bring him bad news. Not her fault, any of this mess.

He sat down again, rubbed the back of his head, stared at his feet. Brown boots crusted with darker brown mud. Leather tops discoloured with milky stains of wet. At home the slavey or Milly cleaned the boots. He'd have to do it now. He'd done it as a child, sitting on the back step, a newspaper across his knees, brush in one hand. Knife off the dried clots of dirt. The Hoof's boot still damp with sweat. His mother's smaller boot, laces trailing. That pair of pale boots on the landing windowsill here. A girl beginning to miscarry, being offered comfort, a clean bed. Nathalie gasping, pressing her hands to her belly: it's beginning! Oh, Joseph, it's beginning.

He put his hand across his eyes, to hide his tears. So what if Nathalie had lied to him at the start? She had to. She hadn't lied to him in bed. He knew that, he felt it, her body-truth. Her flushed, serious face turned towards his, her hands gripping his shoulders, she squeezed him, commanded him, shut her eyes, opened them again, wait, wait, yes, he waited, kept moving, their fierce gentle dance, the long cry came from her. Had he dreamed it? No. So long ago, those rapturous encounters. Tears leaked through his fingers, ran saltily into his mouth.

Squeak of wood. A cupboard door opening and shutting. Clink of glass. The powerful fragrance of brandy. Mrs Dulcimer's voice said: I'll leave this with you.

The door shut behind her. He sat in the darkening room, sipped the brandy, stared at the sunk red mass of the fire.

TWELVE

Madeleine

BLUE SKY AND GOLDEN air. September warmth over-laid with coolness. Madeleine screeches the gate shut. Sally waves from her front window: where you off to, then?

Just for a walk, Madeleine calls back: such a beautiful day.

She's lying. She keeps on needing to find excuses to leave her flat. Escape that whatever-it-is. Philip Larkin would have called it a toad.

Once across the river she lets her feet decide. She strikes towards Covent Garden.

Years ago she passed through it on the day it closed as a wholesale fruit and vegetable market, emptied itself of working life. Piles of shallow wooden trays leaned against walls. Crumpled sheets of soft blue paper drifted along the straw-scattered cobbles. Hosed down, slippery with wet. A makeshift notice cut from the side of a carton dangled from string: goodbye from Vic, John and Reg. Now crowds of sightseers mill about near the tube, dawdle down towards the boutiques in the colonnades. Clowns pedal unicycles. Someone belts out an aria from *Don Giovanni*.

Madeleine weaves through the tourists, across the Piazza, dawdles eastward along the Strand, past the River

Queen, one of her favourite pubs. She crosses Farringdon Road, goes straight ahead, up Ludgate Hill, towards St Paul's cream-gold façade. Another crowd here, people jostling about, chattering, eating ice creams. She's caught in a swarm advancing from behind, pushed forward.

Her phone thrums and beeps. Toby sounds hurried, also mocking himself for being so. So much to do! So little time!

Madeleine plants herself at the foot of the steps leading up to the cathedral's great brown wooden doors, closed fast. The tides of visitors eddy towards the corner, towards the smaller entrance there. Others loll on the wide stone steps, stretching out their bare brown legs, drinking water from plastic bottles, checking their phones.

I'll help, Madeleine says: I could organise your transport, and a driver.

Is it worth it? Toby asks: such short distances. We could get the bus, surely.

He and Anthony have moved in together to an ex-Council flat near Waterloo Station, on the ground floor of a 1950s block set in a side street leading between shabby tenements and Victorian industrial buildings. They have ripped up the decking at the back, carted in sackfuls of earth, planted a garden. A vine, a row of lavender, an apple tree. On summer nights they'll sit out and drink gin and listen to the trains clattering in and out of the terminus. Now, in autumn, they perch, wrapped up in coats and scarves, on a bench set next to the short, promising stem of the climbing rose, which Madeleine brought, and watch the scudding clouds, the moon.

After Sid died Toby told Madeleine he knew he would never feel joy again. But now he does. He laughs. He dances. He writes poems to Anthony, cooks for him, talks about him all the time.

Madeleine says: and I'll bring a cake as well. What sort of cake would you like?

I don't want to know, Toby says: I'd rather have a surprise.

Some of the tourists outside St Paul's are eating burgers and chips from cardboard boxes. A bin at the edge of the piazza overflows with bottles and cans. Empty food boxes litter the ground nearby. The radical youths of the Occupy camp, a few years back, were tidier: ecological warriors who picked up rubbish. Sudden blossoming of tents tightly packed in, pitched on gravel not grass, their green curves echoing those of the dome above. The protesters festooned the surrounding wire fence with ribbons and necklaces, hung it with drawings and cartoons, handwritten messages. They made speeches against the Church's collusion with City corruption and greed, sang, handed out bowls of stew. St Paul's barricaded itself against them, its dignitaries skulking behind bolted doors.

Some Londoners treated the tent-city as just another spectacle; like Borough Market or Covent Garden. They passed by, shrugged, walked on. Others muttered about filthy shanty-towns. Journalists and bankers strolled through the camp, got involved briefly in debate, wandered away again. Tourists retreated behind their phones, holding them out like the powerful relics of saints to protect against contaminating evil. They shuffled along as though blind; miraculously able to see once they framed shots on their tiny screens. After a while the carnival drifted away. The cathedral went on standing firm.

Toby says: are you listening? I said, so we're all sorted. I'm doing the flowers and the food. Anthony's in charge of décor and music and our outfits.

I'll see you in a week's time, then, Madeleine says: I'll pick you up from home, take you to the civil ceremony, and then to the church and then to the party.

She stands back for a gang of Italian schoolgirls uniformed like a dance troupe with red sashes. Toby says: I know what you're thinking. But Anthony's a practising Anglican. If he wants a blessing in church he can have it. With a vicar in his best frock thrown in, and a choir singing the Bach Magnificat!

Next day sunlight wakes her, and footsteps overhead, the whimper of the baby. Troubling dreams withdraw, a dark tide drains out, leaves a residue, uneven marks that stain the morning. So snap out of it. Get up. Invent a treat. Buy a new outfit for Toby's do.

Sally catches her, emerging from her front door just as Madeleine is closing her gate. Smart Sally, in knee-length black boots, black beret. You off up the Lane? I'll walk with you. I'm going that way myself.

The leaves of the plane trees lining Apricot Place have begun to fall. Crackling brown debris silts up against the asters and fuchsias, still in bloom, that Madeleine planted in early summer around the roots of the tree opposite her flat. The yellow of a solitary marigold poking through the heap of fallen leaves matches that of the estate agent's Sold sign leaning against the railings.

Part of the tiny flowerbed has vanished. Overnight, someone has ripped up the climbing nasturtium plants she trained to scramble around the trunk, has dropped them on the pavement near her gate, withered leaves, wilting pale tangerine and apricot flowers. Watch where you put your feet! Sally yelps, points. Wet dog mess slumps out at one side of the piled greenery.

No long, lavish coils. Someone has torn up the juicy stalks into short lengths then dropped them on top of a heap of fresh dog turds where any passer-by, or Madeleine herself, would tread in it. Emm? She swears under her breath. Impossible to prove it.

Bloody vandals! Sally plucks short branches from her hedge, helps Madeleine sweep the mess over the kerb.

The sun sparkles on cast-down metallic snack wrappers, glitters on tarmac. Wafts of hot frying fat from the open doorways of kebab shops, aroma of burnt coffee from the cafés, sweet spiciness from the Jamaican bakery. Stink of oil and petrol from cars and buses.

Sally thrusts her arm through Madeleine's: don't want to lose you!

How is Rose? She can't ask. Leave her alone, instructs Nelly: don't interfere. Yes, Nelly, yes.

A metal arch frames the entrance to the Lane. On one corner a man sells wedge-heeled espadrilles and gladiator sandals, leftovers from summer sales, and on the other a woman offers plastic bags of nuts, birthday cards, children's books. They shout at one another over the heads of their customers, lob their conversation back and forth. She didn't! She bloody well did!

Madeleine sighs. I love coming here. It cheers me up.

What d'you need cheering up for? Sally asks.

Oh, Madeleine says: you know. Life. Sometimes it feels tough.

Tell me about it! Sally says.

That means: don't. Madeleine wouldn't know how to, in any case. The words won't form. They stay somehow underground. Muddled together. Nudging her, but invisible. Something wants to be said, but what? No answer, came the bold reply, quips Nelly. Madeleine wants to yell at her. Lay off, will you? Just leave me alone!

A tall, white-haired man, big and muscled, hollers the excellence of tubes of mustard lycra, tents of pleated azure viscose. A makeshift counter offers gold-threaded silks and satins, lurex and lamé, reels of glittering braid. Polystyrene legs clad in black-lace stockings dangle next to moulded bras in red, green, purple. Skimpy nylon thongs mix into heaps of frilled flowery knickers. Women throng in front, shouldering each other, heads down, intent on bargains. Their hands dive in, rummage, toss the gauzy scraps into the air.

Piled bunches of coriander, parsley, mint, form a fragrant green barrier. The butcher's, set back on the pavement, sells skinny-throated chickens, pimpled and pale, beaks and scaly yellow feet still on, and chunks of goat, and cows' legs with hooves intact. People hover at the fishmonger's stall, eating from mini tubs of cockles and whelks, checking over the crabs and prawns, the buckets of fish heads and spines.

Madeleine pauses, making Sally pause too. Look over there. That cartoon figure. I always salute her when I come past.

A plywood panel on the side of a haberdashery stall has been painted with a huge-eyed, impossibly wasp-waisted girl batting her feathery eyelashes. Hair tied up in a spotted red bow, she hoists up her pink T-shirt just high enough over her pointy breasts to reveal her sharp nipples. Sun and rain have softened her colours but not dimmed her coy grin.

Sally says: I knew the fellow who did that. Painted quite a few of the signs round here. Dead now. That's not the sort of art our Rose wants to do! But at least he earned a living from it.

A CD stall belts out reggae. An ironmonger chants the praises of saucepans and woks. His neighbour offers artificial peonies and fake-onyx vases and gilt-framed pictures of Mary and Jesus, apple-cheeked, their blue and red robes held open to reveal their sacred bleeding hearts. Sally raises her voice above the racket: because how will Rose ever make a living from art? She won't, will she.

Madeleine says: she could go on with her job at the same time, couldn't she?

Sally turns her head towards Madeleine, her black earrings swinging. I suppose part-time worked for me all right. While my kids were at school I ran the coffee stall at the London College of Printing, up at the Elephant. Nice lot, the students. We used to have a good laugh.

She presses Madeleine's arm. Some of them were designing cardboard boxes. I never knew boxes had to be designed. Now, every time I pick up bits of packaging for our Rose, for her model, I give it marks for how easy it is to open and fold flat.

In the middle of the market, the flower-man displays ranked geraniums massed by colour, wide swathes of scarlet, pink and crimson shining in the sunlight, and next to them bands of white petunias, yellow poppies, pots of green ferns. The last days of summer, carols the man: come on, girls, refresh those balconies, refresh those pots!

And then only a couple of days ago, Sally says, she told me she's thinking of destroying the whole thing and starting again. Says it's not right.

I'm supposed to be writing her stories to go with it, Madeleine says: I should be getting on with them.

At the beginning, when she was all fired up, writing seemed so easy; poured out. Now, as she advances further into it, every time she has a go she immediately feels bored. Language flees, replaced by a suffocating aimlessness. Why bother trying to write? You're rubbish at it. She rattles inside her room. After an hour's thrashing about, tugging her hair, drinking tea, gazing out of the window, she pulls the loneliness round her. My cloak; now called solitude. She settles down, dashes a few words onto her screen. Nelly hosts these beginning stories. You don't know how to start? Just admit you can't do it. I don't know how.

I don't know how. Write that down. Language begins to flow. Later on she can re-read, edit, re-write.

They reach the second-hand clothes racks, lined up two deep on either side of the road. Like the wings of a theatre: you come off-stage, shed one costume, don another. A little hat of black feathers with a spotted black veil? A dark grey 1940s overcoat? Sally says no. You're not going to a bleeding funeral, are you?

In the end Madeleine buys a man's collarless dress shirt with flopping cuffs. Sleeves, lower part and back in fine white cotton, bib front in what seems white brocade. Right. Now I need a bit of decoration.

A stall opposite displays costume jewellery: wide trays fatly striped with flashing rainbows of brilliants. Next to it: second-hand finds. Boxes of broken gilt chains, strings of faux-coral twigs, tin brooches, tarnished Our Lady medals. The stallholder, a lively-faced woman with hennaed hair, has pinned out the better pieces on velvet-covered boards: necklaces of amber, diamante, river pearls. Madeleine fingers a ring set with a green glass stone, a collection of hatpins, studded with jet, stuck into a pincushion. Victorian, explains the stallholder: very swanky, jet was in those days. Madeleine chooses a pair of flat silvery cufflinks, and some art deco clip-on earrings, shaped like wings, that curve along her ears. Egged on, Sally picks out a bracelet of jade-coloured beads. That'll be nice for my daughter. Her birthday's coming up. I'll buy a box for it and she'll pretend not to know it's not new.

They inspect the produce on the fruit stalls, choose plums and apples. Sally prods some pears. They go to the Turkish grocer's and buy almonds, sugar, vanilla pods, orange-flower water. Loaded with bags, they trudge out, past the barefoot man sitting begging, and make for home.

Approaching Orchard Street, Madeleine feels tired, her head tight, somehow scraped inside. Her brain all twisted round. She wants to fall into bed, catch up on sleep. Sally's chatting about her younger daughter, whom Madeleine has not met, who lives near Bromley. Her kids like playing celebrities, playing being on TV. I got out my wedding-dress for them, and the two bridesmaids' frocks, so they can dress up. They love wearing my shoes! The high-heeled ones that is.

In Apricot Place, in front of their black iron gates, Sally dumps her bags on the ground, opens her handbag. Madeleine pauses, stretches. Not wanting to go in.

Sally scans Madeleine with her sharp black eyes. Rose rang me again yesterday. She told me you know what's happened. I said not to be scared. Make up her mind what she wants to do, and do it. Her mum's very upset, but I said to her it's up to Rose. We'll be there for her, whatever she decides, she knows that.

Nelly wrote that to Madeleine once, years ago. Her mother, ashen and rigid: a daughter of mine going on a demonstration, going about the streets shouting about sex, you do everything you can to hurt me. Nelly wrote: your parents will love you, whatever you do, they will always forgive. Now here's Sally sounding just like Nelly.

Sally says: what worries me is where she'll live if she keeps the baby, if her squat packs up. Even if you get on the Council waiting-list you've got to take what they offer. You could be re-housed anywhere. Not necessarily round here.

Madeleine says: you'd like her to be able to stay near you, wouldn't you?

Rose's mother and stepfather have moved further out, to an estate down towards Croydon. Madeleine has met the mother in the street once or twice, when she arrives to visit Sally with her toddlers. Pale, thin, her pinched face expressionless, she lowers her eyes before Madeleine, does not speak. She wears a grey fleece over a grey tracksuit, always the same pair of trainers. No money for a coat, a pair of boots. Why should she be friendly? She's got other things on her mind.

Sally says: well, we'll just have to wait and see. It beats me how anyone can afford to buy their own flat these days. You were lucky, weren't you? One of the lucky ones!

Nothing Madeleine can say to this, so she keeps quiet. Sally nods towards the yellow Sold sign. That's for the flat above yours, did you know? I thought that flat would never go. The owner was asking too much. He moved away to live with his girlfriend, put the flat on the market, never managed to sell it.

Madeleine says: but there's a family in there! A mother and baby, anyway. I hear the baby crying the whole time. And the mother walking up and down trying to quieten it.

Sally shakes her head. No, that flat above you's been empty for months. You must've been dreaming it.

Madeleine looks towards the basement underneath Sally's sitting-room, trying to judge distances, thickness of walls. She says: sounds carry oddly, I suppose. I hear my neighbour, the chap down there under you, through my wall, banging down his stairs from the ground floor. I wish he'd lay some carpet to muffle the noise.

Sally says: what are you on about? His steps are carpeted. He told me all about having them done, when he moved in. Invited me to have a look. Nice thick carpet.

She pushes open her gate, stumps up her steps. You have the radio on a lot, don't you? I expect sometimes you forget to turn it off. You've been hearing something on the radio. Oh, Madeleine.

She closes her front door. Madeleine ducks under the overgrown lavatera, lifts aside a stem of jasmine, walks down into her basement area. Closing her own front door, she shivers. As though it's mid-winter with no prospect of sunshine or warmth, just relentless rain. She's grown used to how the flat traps chill and damp, but today it feels extra cold after the golden warmth of the day outside. Almost dank.

The baby's wail begins. A woman's voice, high and light, joins in. Sobbing. Their plaints twist together, relentless. Madeleine tries to speak out loud. All right. This time I'm ready for you. The words stick in her throat. As in a nightmare when you try to scream and can't.

Some kind of force pushes at her, thrusts her back. The baby's wail quivers, a thread of despair. A girl sobs. Oh, will you give over! The noise of the boots breaks in. Like someone kicking down a door. Breaking and entering. Coldness washes through her in waves.

Her heart thuds. Blood pounds in her throat. Her head feels dry, somehow. Airless. She swivels, faces the source of the noise: the partitioned-off space holding the boiler and fridge behind their lace veil. Bang! Bang! Bang! Someone invisible clatters down in mid-air. Dampness seizes her neck, closes round it, a cold, rough hand tightens over her mouth and she staggers, twists round, nearly falls over. She cries out, drops her shopping. She blunders through the galley kitchen, unlocks the door to the back garden, wrenches it open. She stumbles up the steps out of the area, stands in the middle of the little paved space. Cold, fresh air. She folds her arms tightly. Shivery, sick. Wanting to throw up. To cry. Stop it, stop it! Who's whispering that?

She goes back inside, turns on the central heating. Cook something. Make a late lunch. She throws tomatoes into a pan with olive oil. Consider Sally's theory about noise from the radio. She turns the radio on.

Silence for a few seconds. Then disembodied voices, eerie and pure, float in from far away, an island in the Hebrides where poets are singing, chanting, reciting, keening.

No. Radio music is radio music. Voices on the radio are not the voices she heard.

THIRTEEN

Joseph

T HEY SAT DOWN EIGHT to supper. Mrs Bonnet arrived just as everyone was settling themselves in their places and Mrs Dulcimer was standing by, ladle in hand, ready to serve out the soup. Here we are! Who's this, then? She shook Joseph's hand, peered into his face. Ah, yes, the gent from the other day. Her look said: getting your legs under my friend's table, I see.

Mrs Bonnet shed her outdoor things and hung up her bag, all the while complaining about the traffic splashing the passers-by, the darkness, the deep puddles of mud and wet you fell into as you went along. She leaned her umbrella against the back door, where it dripped onto the mat improvised by Mrs Dulcimer from old sacks. Directed to sit down next to Joseph, she moved her chair a foot away from his, declaring she needed more room for her sleeves; puffs of dark blue gauze fat as cabbages.

The five young women clustered opposite, Doll and Annie with their heads together, whispering, and the three lodgers chattering about their working day; swapping notes. A rough music; all speaking at once. Foreign languages sounded like that: an unbroken flow of syllables. On occasion Nathalie and Cara had babbled French in front of him and he hadn't understood a word. Handy for them, eh? Congratulating themselves, laughing at him up their sleeves.

Young and fresh-skinned, the girls formed a pretty enough gang; their hair knotted tidily behind their heads and their faces shining in the warmth. The lodgers were a strong-looking, lively trio, tilting back their chairs and cracking their fingers, grumbling and shoving. They'd taken off their boots, which tumbled in a pile to one side of the range. The smell of perspiring feet in felt slippers mixed with that of nutmeg and roasting apples. Now they changed the subject, from work to play: the Hallowe'en fair that was putting up on the common. They planned a visit, en masse, tomorrow afternoon. You'll come with us, they cried to Mrs Dulcimer: won't you?

Mrs Bonnet said: but how's Betsy? How's the little fellow? I ought to take another look at them both. Shall I go up?

Annie said: better not disturb them just now, missis, if you don't mind. He's been very fretful, and she may only just have got him off to sleep.

Green soup! Mrs Bonnet drank it up with relish, her spoon rising and falling in her plump grip. Clean hands, with squared-off fingertips, short nails. Female, working hands, which could gut and scale fish, wring chickens' necks, collect pigs' blood for sausages. Deliver babies. Or abort them. Mrs Bonnet's curls sprang about her kindly face. She mopped her mouth and said to her hostess: just right, with that touch of black pepper. Well done.

Mrs Dulcimer said: Mr Benson helped make that.

Mrs Bonnet said: it lacks salt, though. Not enough salt.

Joseph had arrived downstairs well before supper because he did not want to be left alone in the sitting-room beside the dying fire. Betsy's child wailed on the floor above. Its distress tore at him, particularly because he could do nothing for it; simply listen to it screaming. Poor little blighter. Colic, perhaps. Charley, Alfred and Flora had all had it, one after the other. He and Cara had stayed up, nights, taking it in turns, walking the babes to and fro. Where were they now, his little 'uns? Spooning up a bread and milk supper in Boulogne, watched by doting grand-parents. Tucked up safely in their cots, caressed and kissed. Cara recounting her troubles, his unspeakable behaviour. Milly listening, forehead puckered in a frown.

He swigged more brandy. The crying swelled in volume. Footsteps tramped to and fro. Doll, perhaps, trying to soothe the baby. The cries pierced his heart. He wanted to put his hands over his ears.

As the bawling went on, it became unbearable. Quieten it, can't you? Give it a drop of brandy, why don't you? He knocked back the last of his glassful in one fiery swallow. He wanted more. He wanted to finish the bottle, collapse insensible, make this horrible day end. Lovely drunken-ness, his true stay, his true support, brandy the golden friend who'd never desert him but accompany him every-where, never let him down. Strong drink. Dear drink, I can't do without you tonight and that's a fact. So avoid the temptation and seek company. Anything to get away from that poor child. He had gone down in the dark, knocking from stair to stair.

Mrs Dulcimer, alone in the lamp-lit kitchen, was kneading dough in a big, cream-coloured pottery bowl. Humming to herself. Her blue apron tied about her waist, a white cloth slung over one shoulder. She nodded at him. I must get this done before I start on supper. Bread for tomorrow's breakfast.

He pulled out a chair and sat down at the table. Her strong thumbs prodded the fat yeasty bundle. It seemed alive as she worked it, springing and fighting against her plunging fingers. Flour had risen up her thin wrists as far as the bangles she'd pushed back. She saw him watching her. Cheaper to make my own bread, she explained: than buying it, and this way I know what goes into it. Energetically she sprinkled on more flour, punched and fisted. That's the way, missis! That's how I hit that boy once the Hoof had taught me to box: smack on the nose.

In semi-darkness, the walls padded with shadow, the kitchen felt smaller than before. More cluttered. Piles of blue bowls and plates, wadded with straw and tied with string, filled up the dresser-top. Chairs had been pushed aside to make space for three wicker hampers in a row by the jam cupboard, their lids up, revealing rolls of blue-flowered quilts. The furniture seemed restless, ready to make off at any moment. Or to arrive, shoulder him aside. Which? His heart pounded and shook in his chest. Did nothing ever pause? A clutter of spoons and knives scattered the table. He picked them up, sorted them into two heaps. Then into lines, arranged small to large. A crock of flour stood next to an open recipe book, a jug of water, a bowl of shaved sugar. He pushed them into alignment. A still life. But things did not stay still; least of all his hands, which jumped and trembled.

Mrs Dulcimer brushed a curl of black hair from her forehead with her forearm. She said: I'm all behind. Luckily the girls are still upstairs. Betsy's not well enough to get up yet, so Doll and Annie are bathing the baby. They'll be down any moment.

Such a crowd she lived with. She had the trick of getting on with people, it seemed, could swivel confidently in the midst of chaos, direct her tenants hither and thither, goosey goosey gander, whither will you wander, upstairs and downstairs and in my lady's chamber, time to get up time to eat time to sleep. She at the centre of it all. Flourishing. In charge.

Tonight he formed part of this crowd. So abandon these worries he clutched to him tighter than any overcoat. Let the coat hold them as it waited for him upstairs, tossed onto the floor. Slip into the seethe of the household. One face amongst many. Roll up your sleeves. Join in.

He said: I've taken up a lot of your time, haven't I? Let me help you. Where do you keep your wood and coal?

He carted up a scuttleful to the sitting-room, replenished the fire, returned downstairs. He set to work cleaning the bundle of spinach that bulked on the far end of the table. The spade-shaped leaves so fresh they bounced in his hands; seemed to squeak. The muddy green waste of thick stalks he threw into a bucket, for her hens. He washed, chopped, stuffed the subdued spinach into a colander, re-rinsed it. Mrs Dulcimer jerked her chin: the butter's over there, look, with the jug of stock. Use that big pot.

Joseph moved over to the range. Heat glowed from inside it. He wilted the spinach in golden grease, poured on the stock. He found nutmeg, and a grater. He stirred, tasted. Mrs Dulcimer divided her dough into three, formed egg shapes, dolloped these into loaf tins that she covered with a cloth.

Mrs Dulcimer was treating him as part of her household; for tonight at least; so he could give vent to curiosity. Where's Betsy's husband? Or has she not got one?

Mrs Dulcimer frowned. No. She wouldn't want to marry the father of her child. He wanted her, not the other way round. That was a bad thing that happened.

She smote her hands together, flour showering off between her palms. Little white crusts, crescent-shaped, fell from her fingernails. She said: I shouldn't have answered you. Those are Betsy's private affairs.

She went outside, returned with an apronful of potatoes, which she tumbled onto the kitchen table. She sat
down and began to peel them.

Her long brown fingers moved swiftly, the ribbons of
dirty white unspooling, dropping into curls and coils. Just
so had she worked the other day, when he sat with her
here. Since then, the kitchen had changed, danced about,
embraced newness: those piles of bowls and plates on the
dresser, those hampers. Mrs Dulcimer's glance followed
his. She said: the quilts are for the girls. With winter
coming on they'll need warmer bedding. And I've begun
to collect extra crockery because I've new tenants arriving.
I'm taking on the house next door in addition to this one.
Mrs Bonnet's found me more lodgers. The ones she hasn't
got space for. She recommends me, see. So they know I'll
offer fair terms and look after them properly.

Busy Mrs Bonnet. Busy as a bee. Bee in her bonnet.
Did Mrs Dulcimer realise he knew the full extent of Mrs
Bonnet's activities? Poor Doll, poor Annie. He didn't want
them had up as criminals, nor the older woman, when it
came to it. Let sleeping dogs lie.

Joseph left the pot to simmer, came back to the table.
He took up another knife, seized a potato, began to work
the edge of the blade under the skin. A child's game: ease
it off in one long spiral without breaking it. They always
did that at Hallowe'en, with apples, he and his mother and
stepfather. They drank hot spiced beer, the Hoof fell asleep
in his chair, and Joseph's mother taught him to throw the
strip of peel over his left shoulder to land on the floor.
It forms the first letter of your sweetheart's name, see?
Hallowe'en tomorrow. Perhaps he'd teach that game to
the tenants tomorrow night, if they didn't already know it.

The potato resisted Joseph. The peel broke, and slith-
ered onto the tabletop. He went back to the range, lifted

the lid on the pot of the soup to check it wasn't boiling, burning. Green bubbles danced and burped. He was like the soup. He couldn't stay still. As though he had to keep one step ahead of everything. Catch the drop of water on the rim of the colander, before it fell. Wipe a smear of butter from the yellow horn handle of the knife, before it stained her apron. Keep an eye on the lamp; trim its wick.

Mrs Dulcimer began cutting the potatoes into dice. She said: I've a proposal to make to you. Just now I've some money put by. Sitting in the bank, earning no interest. I could lend it you, if you like, so that you can clear your debts, pay your rent that's owing.

Joseph's spoon bumped against the side of the pot. He said: I'd never take money from a woman.

She lifted her knife: no, listen. Let me finish. With the extra tenants coming in, I shall need a cook-housekeeper. My own work gets neglected when I have so many other duties to attend to. So in return, to pay me back, you could work for me here. You could cook for the household, run the kitchen. Proper wages, I mean, to set against your debt. Everything right and tight.

Work for a woman. Take orders from a black woman. Milly rose up before him in a twist of steam: a soup-wraith, finger raised. Yes, Pa. Try it. Why not? He clutched the wooden spoon in one hand, pot-cloth in the other. He blew out his cheeks. Anyone who wanted to was welcome to cart away the piano and the sideboard, but the rent had to be paid. Not least so that he could get back inside his house, find the address of Cara's parents in Boulogne, write to Cara. Saying what, exactly? Think about that later. And then pay the slavey her wages. Kathleen. Yet another female reproaching him. Just join the line! Milly dissolved in the smoke issuing from the pot and he clapped the lid back on. It clinked up and down. He slid the tin cover off again, laid it to one side.

He said: why should you want to help me?

Mrs Dulcimer gathered up her cubes of potato between her hands, walked to the stove, dropped them into the soup pot. She said: why should I not? From what I've gathered, you are in a state of great distress.

Doll and Mrs Dulcimer putting their heads together while he slumped upstairs drinking brandy, Doll recounting the tale of his misdeeds. Reciting the Cara version. The Milly version. Feckless, incompetent, failed, supposed breadwinner who couldn't keep his job, his house or his wife. Certainly not his wife. She'd slipped her leash and raced off across the Boulogne sands and he'd no idea how to whistle her home.

Cara wasn't a dog. He banged a hand to his forehead. Sorry, Cara. Sorry.

Mrs Dulcimer said: I'm offering something to tide you over. For the time being. I told you before, I'm a businesswoman. You know how to cook. I can pay you to do that. What d'you say?

I say yes, Joseph said: thank you.

The kitchen door banged open and a line of girls clattered in, exclaiming and pushing. Five minutes behind them came Mrs Bonnet, waving an umbrella like a crook, seeking a flock of sheep to herd into place, lamenting the difficult walk here, the rain, the mud. Kissing Mrs Dulcimer's cheek, calling for a tankard of beer.

Soup, a slice of cheese, bread pudding served with roasted apples. The blackened, shiny skin on each one had split: burst of fluffy whiteness around a stuffing of sultanas and honey. The sweet smells were enriched by the yeasty scent of baking bread. Annie took a tray of food up to Betsy. She reported the baby woken from his nap and crying, and Betsy rocking him, and refusing her supper. Asking for a glass of rum and water. I left the tray there for her, Mrs D., in case she changes her mind later on.

Joseph drank as much beer as he was offered. Medicine. It soothed him, as the brandy had not. The kitchen furniture stopped shifting around, and sighed, and calmed down, each piece in its rightful place. The lamp flames burned up steady and clear. The shadows thickening around the walls were comforting as blankets. Mrs Bonnet talked of the situation in the Baltic, war very likely on its way.

What kind of work did Milly want to do after training with those nuns? If war came would she want to dive into the thick of things, nurse wounded men in the stench and blood of the front line? His child watching as surgeons amputated limbs, his child holding the hand of screaming soldiers as they fell towards death. How long would she stand it? That good brave Milly, squaring up to danger. She'd manage all right. Forward the Bensons!

Joseph swallowed more beer. Mrs Bonnet went on discussing the political situation in the east. His concentration blurred. When he glanced at Mrs Dulcimer she nodded back, then returned immediately to her voluble friend. He shifted in his chair. He began calculating how much these girls made per week working as kitchen maids. Would they make better money working as tarts? What did cooks get paid? Cook-housekeepers?

The young women's chatter began to die down. Mrs Bonnet's voice trailed off. Second helpings were consumed, plates pushed away. The plentiful food made everyone quiet. Their faces reddened and slackened. Mrs Dulcimer said: now, who'll give us a song?

Annie spoke up: I will.

She pushed her hair away from her face, spread her hands, flung up her chin. Took a deep breath. In a small, clear soprano she sang a Scottish ballad. Plaintive. Mournful. A coffin in a boat shunting across a loch. Did she want them all to burst into tears? Her audience sat still. Some rapt, some merely listening politely. Hands folded in laps, faces turned to their companion. The lamplight enclosed them. Ah, that's beautiful. Ah, thanks Annie. Now something cheerful! Annie duly delivered a comic song, with appropriate gestures, which had the women beating time and joining in the chorus, finally applauding. Joseph joined in. He caught Annie's glance, raised his beer mug to her.

The tenants yawned and patted their bellies, drank up, mentioned washing out their stockings for tomorrow, didn't stir. Eventually they cleared the table, brought out a couple of packs of cards, began to play for matchsticks.

Joseph reached towards the pile of books on the yellow-painted stool, picked out a couple for reading in bed. Doll and Annie washed up. Mrs Dulcimer opened the oven door, releasing a rush of heat. She took out the loaves, tipped them onto a wire tray, tapped them underneath. Yes. Just right.

Mrs Bonnet got up. Flushed, comfortable. Bed soon for me, my lovey. I must be up very early. So much still to do. You coming up now?

Wait just a second, Hetty. Mrs Dulcimer lit a candle in a tin holder. Outside in the cramped hallway, she opened the door under the stairs, showed Joseph a cubbyhole containing a narrow bed. I've put clean sheets on it for you. The space is so small, you'll be tight as a nut in a nutshell, but I've no rooms spare. Doll's sharing Annie's bed for tonight as it is. Tomorrow Mrs Bonnet's boy is bringing over another, so we'll be all right.

Where would Mrs Bonnet sleep? In with Mrs Dulcimer? Nathalie once described to him how she and Cara shared a bed until they left home. She'd wriggle, she'd kick me sometimes, and I'd kick her back, then we found a way of sleeping like spoons, she'd put her arm over me and hold me to her. Like this, look. Nathalie's breasts pressed against his back. Her hand stroked the fur on his chest. He gripped her hand in his, nibbled her fingertips. Nathalie had vanished into the black void. He'd wanted to follow her. Now he didn't need to: the black void had got inside him. Broken and entered. A fist cracking his ribs. Internal bleeding. Nathalie was neither inside him nor outside him. She'd gone. He lowered his head, grunted. Why were there no field hospitals for men with broken hearts? He'd thought tarts were for that. Mending men. You came, bliss flooded you, your woes healed. He didn't want Milly going to the Crimea and encountering men like himself. He'd write to her. He'd find the Boulogne address. He'd borrow the money from Mrs Dulcimer and pay his rent. Get back into his house. Write to his daughter.

He hiccupped, staggered, put a hand to the wall. Mrs Dulcimer turned to face him. Now that she's back, Doll wants to stay here. Work for me as kitchen maid. Living in. Of course she knows we must consult you first.

No one consults me about anything! They make their own decisions, then scarper. In any case I've no longer a house for her to work in. Don't rub it in.

Joseph said: we hadn't got round to signing any sort of contract. She is free to do as she likes.

Mrs Dulcimer handed him her candle: you take this one and I'll fetch myself another.

Light gleamed on her full mouth. Shadows tipped and swung on the wall. It kept trying to lean on him. He put up his hand to shield the flame. How brisk she sounded. How in control.

She said: if the girls make too much of a racket, just tell them to pipe down. They should be off to bed soon, in any case.

Mrs Bonnet erupted from the kitchen. Coming, lovey?

The two women walked off upstairs. Their golden circle of light receded, vanished. Slap slap slap of Mrs Dulcimer's slippers, tap tap tap of Mrs Bonnet's boots.

Soon they'd be curling up together in that wide bed, the candle set down nearby, faces turned towards each other. How warm Mrs Bonnet would be, her soft bulk. And Mrs Dulcimer's eyes would glow black amber in the darkness.

On the other side of the wall a door banged open. The young women's voices surged out. Calling and exclaiming. Noisy as a pub at closing time. I'll carry Betsy her rum. Won't the missis mind? Dunno. Course not. No need to tell her, anyroad. They clattered out of the kitchen, past his cubbyhole, clumped up the stairs. Feet walked to and fro above him. So there must be bedrooms on the ground floor. Other feet continued up the next flight. Tall house full of women, laid in rows.

If he went upstairs now, because he ought really to fetch his coat, he could crouch at Mrs Dulcimer's bedroom door, peep through the keyhole. Just look. A long, slow, assessing look piercing the golden candle haze, glossing skin, eyelids, mouths. The charm of those books on the barrows, those books in Holywell Street: look for as long as you wanted. No one ever said stop.

He shivered. All that girl business was done with now. Over. Go to bed.

But still. Go upstairs. Fetch my coat.

He rose through the silent dwelling. He shimmered up the stairwell. He was a phantom, haunting the house, floor by floor; holding it. He could stretch, he could shrink, go anywhere, pass through walls, slide under doors. He glided through the cold, dark sitting-room. Smell of cooling ash. Glimmer of red cinders marked the fireplace. Gold light outlined Mrs Dulcimer's door, gold light knobbed the keyhole. Mrs Dulcimer's voice, murmuring. He kneeled, put his face to the gold opening, and looked in.

Darkness. One golden eye blazing. Mrs Bonnet stood behind Mrs Dulcimer, hands busy in her friend's hair. She drew out long pins, cast them down. The candle, placed on the wash-stand, shed its light on Mrs Dulcimer's black curls springing free from their tight plaits as Mrs Bonnet undid them one by one, loosened them with her fingers. She took up a square comb by its long handle, plunged its widely separated teeth into the dark mass, gently lifted it, teased it.

Both women wore dressing-gowns. Curving shapes. Mrs Dulcimer bent her head over the heap of paper in her lap. Her lips moved. She was reading aloud to her friend. Shadows surrounded them, framed them: a miniature portrait in an ebony locket.

The baby's cry throbbed from the floor above. Joseph jumped. The two women in his gold vision glanced up, looked round. Mrs Dulcimer put down her sheaf of manuscript, half rose from her chair. Joseph fled from the sitting-room, forgetting his coat in his hurry not to be seen. He stumbled down the two flights of stairs, banging from step to step, lurched into his cubbyhole and shut his door.

He pulled back the grey blanket, plumped the pillow. Less a bed than a bunk. A shelf. Just long enough. He propped himself on one elbow, tried to read. Panelled hidey-hole. A book let you escape. A ship's cabin. Run away to sea, abandon everyone and everything. Voyage through dreams this night, tempest-tossed, beach somewhere safe in the morning. Can't ask for any more than that.

The bed rocked up and down, over the steep waves. I must be pissed. Ship's cook, very well, tossing pancakes and omelettes in a tiny galley look sharp sailors arms crossed feet skipping up dancing a hornpipe singing a sea-shanty yo ho ho and a bottle of rum toss the feller overboard let the sharks have him mince him with their teeth. The mermaid clutched him with her cold arms.

Much later the green waves calmed, surely it was in the same dream that the darkness changed, a flicker of candlelight showed in the blackness, through the keyhole was it, footsteps passed by slowly and softly just outside, fingers felt along the panelling, the kitchen door opened and shut. Creak of the bolt on the garden door. Someone going outside into the dark garden, to use the privy. What's wrong with using a chamber pot? Don't wake me up. He drifted. Quite soon afterwards, it seemed, the bolt creaked again. The kitchen door opened and closed. Someone glided by, hush-hush of felt slippers towards the stairs, the treads creaked above his head as she went up, Joseph slept.

FOURTEEN

Madeleine

MADELEINE WALKS OUT OF Apricot Place, carrying the pear cake in a wide, shallow cardboard box she has tied with a red ribbon. Her finger and thumb twitch, wrapped in Elastoplast.

The Monsieur in Paris brought home the eclairs and babas for Sunday lunch in a similar flat box. His mouth pursed up like a cat's arse. She dodged him and his lips met her cheek.

Every morning Madame delivered hard strokes of the brush to Madeleine's hair. A *jeune fille* should always be *bien coiffée*. What would the elegantly coiffed, hair-brush-wielding Madame have made of these hairdressers' windows here on the Walworth Road? Her mantra: restraint in all things. The local hair salons, however, go in for gorgeous displays of wigs and bric-a-brac. Madeleine pauses in front of her favourite composition: white gladioli in pink-gleaming copper pots, magenta dahlias in purple pots, and above them an electronic sign featuring a green bracelet around an orange hand, tipped with scarlet fingernails, holding a single red rose, all encircled in blue.

Many of the local shops have begun to display these signs. Tiny bulbs in brilliant colours flashing on and off, making the pattern around the edge appear to move.

Necklaces of tiny stars that chase each other. When night falls the signs twinkle even more brightly. Like glow-worms.

In Italian, Madeleine learned on her travels as a student, one slang word for prostitutes was glow-worms. Here in London they don't twinkle on dark streets but work inside flats. When she first arrived in Walworth she would study newsagents' windows with fascination. Any piece of language in the public domain drew her, particularly the obviously home-made notices. Lost cat. Poetry group. Jesus Says Come. Tabletop sale. Virgin Brazilian Hair. One glass frontage featured ruled filing cards handwritten in uncertain blue biro capitals, amateur ads offering young women: stunning dusky voluptuous busty newcomer fresh. Overnight, it seemed, the filing cards disappeared, to be replaced by electronic noticeboards streaming photographs of local rooms to let. The ads for sexual services vanished. Away with the whores: onto the internet with them.

The little electronic signs, bright as gems, spring out, winking, in most of the shop windows Madeleine passes. The sapphire and amber sign outside Rose's office, flashing on and off, simply says Minicabs.

Today they need twinkling, brilliant signs saying Toby Loves Anthony – True. Like the heart-shaped designs lovers used to carve on tree trunks in parks. They need those badges mocking the Coca-Cola slogan: Gay Love – It's the Real Thing.

Rose has kitted herself out in a dark-blue peaked cap, a dark-blue double-breasted jacket, matching trousers. She stretches out her arms, spins round on her toes: I thought I should do the job properly.

Madeleine says: so where's the car?

Limo, please! Rose says. She lifts a thumb: it's round the back.

The metal doors to the garage courtyard stand open. Inside, a blue Mercedes has been adorned with long yellow ribbons tied to the wing mirrors, the ribbons' ends brought forward to meet at the front of the bonnet, secured here, finished with a flouncy bow. Rose says: Jerry borrowed it for me from a friend of his uncle's. He wants to stay friends – Jerry, I mean. I said OK to the car, anyway.

Madeleine says: you've split up? I'm sorry.

Conventional, inadequate words. Rose assumes her poker face, squares her shoulders. A soldier on parade. She shoots out bullet words. All for the best, according to my nan. I'll tell you about it another time.

She doffs her cap, bows. The point is, what we've got here is a cool car. What's Mercedes mean? You were a teacher. You're supposed to know things like that.

Madeleine says: it means mercy. Merciful. It's one of the attributes of the Virgin Mary. A Spanish girl at my convent school was called that. Her sister was called Dolores. Sorrow. Our Lady had seven sorrows. You see statues of Our Lady of the Seven Sorrows in churches all over Spain, with seven swords stuck through her heart. Sorrows to do with her son dying. Jesus, I mean.

Jesus was another name for Emmanuel. Emm had sorrows, didn't he? Splitting up with his wife. A sword stuck through his heart. He must have felt Madeleine stabbed him too, rejecting him. Hence his horrible, hostile gifts.

Rose cries: enough!

Just like Toby, teasing Madeleine for knowing the answer. Time she began learning new things. How to exorcise ghosts. How to complete a story. Time she completed the stories for Rose rather than writing tales for herself. She began a new one last night, basing it in the connecting spaces of a Victorian house: corridor, staircase, back entry. Trying to creep up on those poltergeist noises in her flat, decode them, turn them into a narrative.

Rose says: so you wouldn't call a car Dolores, anyway.

Madeleine says: today the car should be named Joy! Or End-of-Sorrow. End of Dolorous Dolores.

Rose opens the passenger door: hop in. Hey! What have you done to your hand?

Madeleine looks down at her plaster-wrapped thumb and forefinger. I cut myself. It looks worse than it is.

Earlier this morning, deadheading her geraniums out front, pressing back down their rumpled-up earth, she discovered the shards of glass buried upright in the big pot only when they slashed her. Blood coursed across her palm. She cried out, fled back inside, held her hand under the cold tap. Redness flowed thinly, washing out into streams of water. Emm? What could she prove? Nothing.

Flat, circular arrangements of flowers fill the back seat of the Mercedes. Glossy grey-green leaves, spikes of white gladioli, purple asters, pink lilies. The table decorations for the party in the pub. Salvaged from a drinks do Toby was working at two days ago. At the end of the night the management prepared to throw all the flowers away. Toby rang Madeleine: Anthony's out, could you give me a hand? She went over, they hailed a taxi, took the bouquets back to the Waterloo flat.

Rose says: I picked the flowers up earlier so we can take them over to the pub now. They're mad, those two. They were still in their dressing-gowns, drinking champagne. I told them to get a move on and we'd be back in half an hour's time.

Later, Madeleine remembers the day as a series of photographs. A group of Anthony's godchildren, sitting on the tombs in the grassy churchyard, weaving white daisies and mauve freesias into garlands. Toby, crowned with red and blue and purple anemones, waltzing with Anthony, crowned with marigolds. Toby and Anthony emerging from church under evergreen arches held up by the members of Anthony's drama group standing in formation on either side of the path. Francine in five-inch heels exiting a taxi, wearing a tight, narrow-skirted 1950s black satin suit, the jacket with a low neck and flaring peplum. Francine's sharp black bob, Louise Brooks-style, her scarlet mouth glossing the air. Toby and Anthony cutting the cake. Their matching red bow ties. Rose propped against her limo, peaked blue cap under one arm, tearing open a sandwich. Rose and Francine sitting together, two small figures under a big mirror in the dimly lit pub, talking. The display of white, pink and purple flowers on the mahogany tabletop.

Snatches of conversation and speeches, scraps of songs and jokes, arrange themselves like a compilation. Anthony and Toby sharing a microphone, crooning their way through *The Cole Porter Songbook*. Anthony's stepmother making a tipsy speech. A Yorkshire terrier yaps and its gold-turbaned owner picks it up, tucks it under her pink ruched-velvet arm, patting its nose: hush, sweetie, hush.

Come and sit with us! Flashing-eyed Francine pulls out a chair. This is Rose. Oh, you know each other? Francine compliments them on their outfits. They compliment her in return. She tugs at her jacket. It's the corset that does it. She wriggles her shoulders. Her décolletage sparkles, dusted with shimmery powder.

A black-clad waitress arrives, carrying a tray of lit tea-lights, slides one onto their table, shimmies away to the neighbouring seated circle of guests. Low yellow flame flutters inside a green Moroccan glass decorated with gilt arabesques. One by one the flickering tea-lights skid down into place, the gloomy pub room transformed to an underwater cave hung with emerald necklaces. Francine shakes her diamanté earrings that glitter like drops of seawater. She smoothes the lapel of her satin jacket. She smiles so buoyantly, flares and shines with such delighted satisfaction, that Madeleine has to smile back at her. So tell me about your new job.

Francine says: it's at a pop-up burlesque club in Hoxton. I'm Mistress Kitty, the welcomer. I take the money, I help with the bar, I make sure everything runs smoothly.

She fingers a crease in her satin bodice. I usually wear this outfit, but I'd rather have a Victorian one. That would be more fun. More in tune with the performers. The problem's the cost. We're on a very tight budget.

Rose folds her arms, considers. I could make you a costume, if you like. I know about the old types of clothes. I could get the material down the market, run it up on my nan's sewing-machine.

Francine leans forward, kisses Rose's cheek. You're a star.

The pub lights dim further. A golden glow pools over table edges, the wooden floor. Music swells out, people start dancing.

Madeleine tries a couple of Toby's canapés. Home-made game pâté, topped with gherkin slices, on medallions of toasted sourdough. She sips her wine, catches Rose's eye, smiles. Rose lifts her glass, nods back. Francine's on a roll, explaining the second side of her job. I'm a tour guide as well. I take people on Sex Walks. We do old Soho, Madame Jo-Jo's, the Windmill Theatre, the Naughty Nineties, we do the Bermondsey drag shows, we do Jack the Ripper in Whitechapel, the lot. Then we go back to Hoxton for the show.

The Monsieur in Paris took Madeleine for a walk down the Rue St Denis to peer at the spectacle of the tarts posing, sultry and pouting, in doorways. She dragged along at his side, ashamed, wanting to apologise to the young women for how he leered, pointed. An educational stroll, to warn her what happened to girls who went off the rails. Francine says: don't frown at me like that, Madeleine darling. It's just a job!

Madeleine slaps down her glass. Wine splashes onto varnished wood. She tries to keep her voice light. People walk all those distances? How do they manage?

In between venues we use a minibus, Francine says: fitted up with black seats and black curtains, the punters love it.

Black curtains. Like a hearse. Like the motorised confessional called a taxi. Back in the palmy days when she earned a salary, Madeleine could afford occasional taxis, would listen to the drivers' life stories, tales, running commentaries. Look at that black woman there in a fur coat! Doesn't she know it's summer? Look at that shop-front there, that was the one got burned out in the riots. Local people built it all back up. Some of these youngsters don't know they're born.

Francine jiggles in her chair, taps her foot. Dance dance dance! I need to dance! Rose, come and dance?

Rose flicks her a smile. In a minute. I'm not in the mood yet. Francine strokes her black satin tubes of gloves, throws down her cockleshell-shaped black satin clutch bag. She rises, one hand on Rose's shoulder, rights herself on her high heels, moves onto the dance floor. People hustle up, a dark mass swerving about under a sole spotlight. Anthony and Toby, flower-wreaths askew, glide around in a quick-stepping embrace. Anthony's nieces gambol on the fringes. Older people seize their hands, pull them further in.

Rose plays with her cast-off peaked cap, stroking it, spinning it on one finger poked inside its brim, throwing it in the air then catching it.

She places the cap flat on the table, folds her hands on top of it. I wanted to tell you. I've decided to keep the baby. I've told Mum and Nan. I'm going to finish my A Levels, and I'm going to apply to art school. I may have to move back in with my nan for a bit. We'll see.

Madeleine gazes at Rose's fierce young face. She opens her mouth to speak. Rose lifts her hands, palms up. Gesture meaning: don't say anything. Don't.

The music tugs Madeleine up out of her chair. Let's have that dance.

Later, Rose drives Toby, Anthony and Madeleine home. Cap tilted to one side, cheek smudged red from Francine's lipsticked goodnight kiss. The two men sit in the back of the car, upright and serious, their arms full of flowers. Rose, don't forget to come and see us very soon. Ring us up and make a date.

The car glides on from Waterloo to Apricot Place. A hasty kiss, the car door slammed, and Rose executes a neat three-point turn, accelerates away into the darkness.

Madeleine halts, hand on her gate. Disarray under the glowing street lamps. The overflowing wheelie bins have been pushed to one side, clearing pavement space. A removals van has parked at the kerb. Its open back disgorges packing-cases, boxes, what looks like a dismantled bed, pictures veiled in bubble-wrap. Three men form a human chain, passing these up the steps to the open front door of the flat above Madeleine's. Goodnight, the men call to her: goodnight.

She unlocks her front door, stands still on the mat. Perhaps, if she creeps through the hallway, she won't wake whatever, whoever, it is. Hold your breath. Tiptoe. But she shouldn't have to be doing this. This is her own flat. Is it? It was once. Not any more. Something else has taken up residence. Part of her wants to push it out. Part of her wants to run away. No. She's tipsy. She just wants to go to bed.

A cry. Someone laughing. An unaccompanied voice twists up. A golden corkscrew undoing the air, letting out liquid gold. Someone singing a ballad. A girl's voice. Plaintive, unearthly. Like those Hebridean voices on Radio 3. Have the removals men upstairs turned on a radio? A TV? Their feet pace to and fro above her head.

She stretches out her hand to the light switch. Nothing. The hallway bulb must have blown. She fumbles her way forward through the darkness into further, suffocating blackness. She swears. Where did she leave the spare bulbs, bought weeks back? Where does she keep her torch? Yes, of course, on the shelf above the fridge.

She sweeps aside the lace curtain covering the alcove. Her rummaging fingers contact something cool, curved. China. She pushes it aside. Too abruptly. It slips away, crashes onto the floor.

Her fingers close over the rubber surface of the torch. Its beam shows her smashed pieces of turquoise pot, a spilled litter of broken buttons, strips of leather, tiny shards of bone. Curses, curses.

She finds a new lightbulb, fits it. She fetches a dust-pan and brush from the kitchen, sweeps up the chinking, rustling mess. The bins outside the front gate are full. Very well. She carries the dustpan outside into the back garden, empties it into the nearest flowerbed.

FIFTEEN

Joseph

THE LIT CANDLES ON the mantelpiece scooped hollows of light from the gloom of early morning. More candles burned on the side table. The sitting-room held chilliness, the smell of coal dust. Mrs Dulcimer kneeled on the hearthrug, in front of one of the armchairs. She said: but you must tell me. Don't be afraid.

Betsy, dressed in a white nightgown, white nightcap tied under her chin, curled inside the armchair. Face turned into the gold satin cushion, arms crossed. Feet, in grubby slippers, tucked to one side. Her thin shoulders were set hard. She shook her head.

Mrs Dulcimer sank back on her haunches in a billow of blue wool, clasped her hands in her lap, and waited. Her hair, twisted into its two night-time plaits, fell onto her shoulders. One of her fur mules had come off, lay on the hearthrug. Her bare foot arched itself. Dark at the instep; like a grey breath. Mrs Bonnet sat in the other armchair, gripping its arms. Legs spread. Burly as a prizefighter. Skirts plumped out, cap pinned on, creased blue gauze sleeves. She gazed at Betsy: dearie, you don't understand. You really could be in for it now.

Mrs Dulcimer turned her head, tilted her chin, frowned. Mrs Bonnet hushed for a moment, then said: things can't be left like this.

Joseph, carting a bucket and shovel, a bundle of kindling, stepped forward, lifted one foot, pushed the door shut behind him. He'd come upstairs in his stockinged feet, having forgotten where he'd left his boots the night before. Doll hadn't wanted him blundering around the kitchen, had waved him off: look for them later, Mr Benson, d'you mind? Give me a minute, will you?

He hovered just inside the sitting-room doorway. He hadn't knocked before coming in. Was he supposed to? No one reproved him. No one took any notice of him. Two women confronted a girl in front of a dead fire, a grey-white heap of ash, blown feathery whiteness dusting the steel bars of the grate.

He hadn't cleaned out a grate before. Doll's job now, in this house, but she was dealing with the range, which had subsided overnight. When he woke, and went blearily into the shadowy kitchen, he'd found her kneeling in front of the iron monster on a piece of sacking, fiddling with a box of matches. Fingers black with coal-dust. Muddy footprints crossed the kitchen floor, a wavering line between back door and hall. Doll glanced up, sniffing, wiped her nose on the back of her hand. Her grey eyes flickered. Mouth pursed. Just leave me be, Mr Benson, and I'll get her going again in a jiffy. I know her and you don't. She has her tricks.

Feeling his way in the dimness, he headed upstairs to the sitting-room. The autumn morning surrounded the house in a crisp embrace. Ice-cold air filled the room, chafed his face. The blinds were half up, revealing frosted-over panes, the curtains pulled roughly back but not tied in place. Books piled higgledy-piggledy on the side table, Mrs Dulcimer's writing-board and inkwell balancing on top. Joseph's coat still lay on the floor, on top of the crumpled brown paper wrappings. Doll's empty teacup stood where she'd left it. The brandy-glass he'd used.

The two women were concentrating on the small figure in white. Betsy was shivering; rolled up, clenched, into herself. Mrs Dulcimer curved forward, her hand reaching out to the stricken girl. The pendulum clock ticked, its gilt weight swinging back and forth. What time did they breakfast here? All at the same time, or the tenants before the mistress? What would Mrs Bonnet devour? A nice grilled chop, a basin of blood and minced bone. No: that was in his waking dream, Mrs Bonnet on all fours, mane of wild grizzled hair, guzzling from a saucer near the back door. Growling and weeping. He choked. That novel he'd plucked from the kitchen pile, been reading before he fell asleep. Currer whatsit. Feet padding over the matting in the passage outside the bedroom. Smoke and flame. A lost creature prowling and gambolling. A nightmare. Grateful to be roused, shed it.

Darkness. Someone's feet had thudded down, kitchen opened up, crash of shutters, hall door banged, pale yellow lamplight seeped into his cubbyhole. Doll's and Annie's voices called. Feet trod rapidly down and up the stairs. He pissed into the chamber pot, hurried on yesterday's clothes. First thing: get warm. Then he'd be able to think about cooking breakfast. Let alone washing. Nobody was going to bring him a can of nice steaming water, were they?

What was up with Betsy? Poor wee girl. Had she got the toothache? He'd seen Milly curl up tight like that, pressing a washcloth, boiled then wrung out, against her cheek. Biting down on a clove. Mrs Dulcimer leaned further forward, touched Betsy's knee. The contact released something, because Betsy shuddered, and began weeping. She screwed her fists into her eyes. Tears dripped down her cheeks, around her mouth. Mrs Dulcimer said: Betsy, what happened? Where is the baby?

Betsy wailed on. A dolorous, unending cry. Just like her child yesterday evening. Into that bleat packed all the sorrow of the world. Joseph tightened his grip on the handle of the pail. The metal edge cut into his palm, steadied him. He willed Mrs Dulcimer to look round. Lord, missis, I know. Some of it.

Not a dream, then, those tentative footsteps in the middle of night. Those bolts gratingly drawn back; the clash of the latch. That hoarse breathing, as someone shuffled past the cubbyhole.

My duty to speak, I suppose. Poor little creature. Betsy or her child? Both. Joseph sighed. Wasn't pity enough? Why add to her misery? Wretched girl. His lips seemed to thicken, grow heavy. Made of iron. Wanted to stay shut. He forced them open. He said: Betsy, the soles of your slippers are thick with mud.

He put down the pail and shovel. Nobody else moved. He picked up his coat, donned it. Just concentrate. Be very businesslike. The blue china pot on the mantelpiece didn't move, either. It simply muttered: careful. Careful.

Betsy fingered away tears and snot, lifted her sleeved arm and blotted her cheeks. She addressed Mrs Dulcimer. Confidentially. A bit puzzled. She said: he wouldn't stop crying. I doubt I've slept a wink since he was born. You know that. None of us could settle him. Not me and not you either.

Betsy folded her arms and frowned. She shifted position, drew up her knees to her chin. She pulled down the hem of her nightgown to cover her slippers. Her voice pattered out like ice drops. Then I woke up, and he was next to me, he was still.

Joseph buttoned his coat. He hastened downstairs, his stockinged feet slithering over the wooden treads. Doll, her skirts pinned up, was washing the kitchen floor by lamplight, pushing suds to and fro, a cloth folded under her broom's bristles. Where are my boots my boots? Fuck sake Mr Benson how should I know? Mind my floor! He ignored her, trod into his mud-stiffened boots, wrenched open the back door, plunged up the area steps into the garden.

Cold air surrounded him, grazed his face and hands. Yellow streaks flared at the horizon. The moon showed palely in the grey-blue sky. Feathery, dew-loaded stalks reached out from the beds, brushed him with wet. Damp grit sank under his tread. He paused, to let his eyes accustom themselves to the darkness. This enclosed him, then seemed to draw back. Moment by moment the morning grew lighter.

He gazed about. Someone had gone ahead of him, and then returned. Criss-crossing footprints small as a child's showed on the sludgy path. He followed them across to the side gate, opened it, found himself in a passageway running between the side of the house and a low wall. A stile faced him. He climbed the stile, got over into a meadow.

An orange glow in the east. The new day was arriving, the colour of the sky changing to transparent indigo. They were all tilting unstoppably towards the sun.

He paused, panting. He could see clearly now. A muddy track led straight ahead, across uncultivated ground thick with thistles, to a patch of rough grass. Clumped horse-droppings, woven with straw, suggested a gypsy camp somewhere close by. They'd put out their fire in a hurry, stamped on it. The flattened mound of grey-white ash sent up a thin white plume. A heap of rags lay near him, half under a bramble bush. Time unreeled, spun out, tripped and trapped him. His mother whispered. Clots of red mess your stepfather tipped down the privy.

Joseph threw up into a bush. Pure arc of last night's supper.

Nettles stung his hands and wrists as he reached under the sprawl of thorny stems, scooped up the bundle of dirtied white. Pleats of linen stiffened with frost. He sat down on the ground, cradling the dead child in the crook of his arm.

After a while, Mrs Dulcimer arrived, a cloak dragged on over her dressing-gown, and squatted beside him.

He handed her the tiny corpse, stood up, felt for his bandana handkerchief in his coat pocket, blew his nose. Shimmer behind the mist, as the sun began to burn through. Long, low lines of gold reached out to the dug-over vegetable plots beyond them, clumps of Michaelmas daisies edging a bed of bolted cabbages. A blue haze wavering. Twisted turquoise stems and frilled fan-leaves, lavender-coloured flowers, Mrs Dulcimer's blue robe, patches of blue sky appearing.

Dogs yapped behind the far belt of trees. Figures shifted in the distance. The gypsies, perhaps, waiting to see what Joseph and Mrs Dulcimer would do. They wouldn't want to be hauled before the police as witnesses. At the first glimpse of blue uniforms they'd melt away, vanish behind the hedgerow. They'd move on, with their horses and dogs. Where did they spend winter?

Mrs Dulcimer shifted the dead child onto one arm, touched Joseph's shoulder. She said: do your weeping indoors. We shouldn't wait about here. We could be seen.

The baby's mud-smudged face. Caked eyelids shut. Curve of brown-powdered lashes. Puckered little mouth clotted with earth. Mrs Dulcimer said: we need to hurry.

Joseph took the baby, tucked him inside his overcoat, held him there. They clambered back over the stile. Joseph looked behind him at the trail of footprints in the mud. Nothing he could do about those right now. He opened the side gate, and they entered the garden's orderly enclosure. The back of the house rose up, bleak as a judge. He didn't want to go inside, face whatever trouble waited there. He loitered by a bed edged with russet chrysanthemums. Two rows of spinach. Domes of thyme and sage. Late pink roses bloomed, held by wires pinned to the brick wall. In the far corner, opposite the privy, a twig broom leaned against a heap of brown and yellow crinkled leaves, swept together and then left. In the first wind to shake up they'd whirl about, settle back all over the grass and paths. She needed a gardener. Someone who'd do the job properly, burn those leaves on the bonfire or pack them into netting, to rot down for mulch. He could do that for her. Course he could.

They stood on the brick apron flanking the back door. Mrs Dulcimer raised her hand to the latch. Joseph said: don't go in just yet. Wait a moment.

Words struggled inside him. Mrs Dulcimer folded her arms inside her shawl. Their breath hung in clouds in the frosty air. Joseph said: we must think carefully what to do.

Mrs Dulcimer stared at the front of his coat. She said: if we inform the authorities, I know what will happen.

Joseph said: yes. As I do too.

Mrs Dulcimer's brown eyelids curved down. She smelled warmly of bed, of sleep. Her skin breathed out a sour-sweet scent of apples and spice. She had not had time to wash before Doll or Annie banged on her bedroom door, reported the missing child. If the police were to be called, she'd better look sharp, get properly dressed.

She said: an inquest will be held, Betsy will be charged with infanticide and put in gaol and sent for trial. If she is found guilty, as is most likely, she will be hanged.

She studied the doorstep. White stone, fissured, with bright green weeds, tiny-leaved, in the cracks. They just needed nipping up between finger and thumb, throwing on the compost heap.

Joseph leaned closer, and murmured. Who knows about the baby? Your tenants won't inform against Betsy, surely. Or you could pack Betsy off before they come down, before anyone's the wiser. That might be safest. Tell 'em she's gone to stay with friends. Taken the baby off for a change of air. That kind of thing.

Mrs Dulcimer said: the tenants will be stirring already. On a Sunday they go out later than usual, but still. They'll be getting up. Mrs Bonnet would take Betsy home with her, I'm sure she would. Keep her there for a while. Betsy's got no family that I know of. No one to come searching for her, rat on her.

A gust of wind shook plane leaves, sycamore leaves, from the tall trees behind the wall. They sailed down, slowly twirling, rocking to and fro. Rock-a-bye-baby on the tree top when the bough breaks the cradle will drop. Stop! The cruel song snapped in two.

Joseph kept his voice low. If there is no baby, there can be no inquest.

Mrs Dulcimer's tone matched his. Let me wash him first. Let me take him into the kitchen. With luck, the tenants won't be down for breakfast just yet. Or I could take him into my room upstairs and wash him there.

Joseph said: no. Stop out here with me. Better nobody catches sight of him. Just in case questions do get asked.

From the garden shed next to the privy, Mrs Dulcimer fetched a spade. She pointed towards a space at the near end of the border under the espaliered rose trees, where clumps of asters were opening their salmon-pink buds. There. That bare patch behind the flowers.

Far from ideal. This green strip ran between the backs of two terraces. Anyone looking out of a back-facing window would spot them. Wonder what on earth they were up to. Would remember, if asked. The blinds of the houses opposite were still down. Hurry, hurry.

Spiders' webs, beaded with dew glittering in the sunlight, laced the shrubs. In the middle of each gauze veil hung a small, golden spider. They left these spinners undisturbed, their shining filaments unbroken. They took it in turns to hold the child and to dig. The damp ground yielded easily. Dug over for years it must have been, weeded, raked to a fine tilth ready for sowing seed; easy to work. The edge of the spade bit cleanly into it.

Mrs Dulcimer said: just a couple of spits deep. No time for anything more.

Joseph spat on the corner of his handkerchief, wiped the baby's face as best he could. Mrs Dulcimer hooked her little finger into the baby's mouth and nostrils, clearing them of plugs of mud. They wrapped the corpse in the bandana, which hardly covered him. Joseph took off his overcoat, folded it around the small body. He bent down and laid it in the grave. They stood still, next to each other, bowed their heads. Joseph reached for Mrs Dulcimer's hand. She breathed out something, he couldn't tell what. Then bent to the spade again. Between them they covered over the brown bundle with soil, again taking turns. They trampled it well down against foraging dogs and foxes.

Each seemed to know what to do; without speech; just a glance, a nod. Joseph gathered armfuls of leaves from the corner heap, scattered them on the flowerbed. Mrs

Dulcimer fetched a rake, and roughed over the traces of the footprints leading back and forth between the house and the garden gate. Joseph, shivering in the cold, wiped the rake and spade free from earth on a clump of grass, and Mrs Dulcimer replaced them in the shed, locked it, dropped the key into her pocket.

In the empty kitchen they unlaced their damp, muddy boots, shed them. Mrs Dulcimer stooped, slid on her house shoes. She said: come upstairs and I'll find you a pair of these slippers. There are always spare ones knocking around.

Joseph kicked the boots into a corner. I'll clean those later.

Doll rose from her knees in front of the sitting-room fire, turned to face them in a swing of check skirts. A glow of red heat. The sharp fragrance of wood and coal smoke on cold air made him want to sneeze. He'd done that, when? How many days ago, when he first arrived here? Something else burned; a darker smell, like smouldering cloth.

Doll picked up the heaped pail of grey ash, the brush and shovel. Mrs Bonnet's had to go, missis. She wouldn't wait. She had me fetch a cab for her from the stand, and off she went.

The two women surveyed one another. Mrs Dulcimer said: what else?

Doll said: she took Betsy with her.

She sounded nonchalant; concealing her feelings under a show of delivering a message correctly. Still, white face; blank expression. She said: she got her dressed, she was sure she was on the mend, just needed a bit of a rest. She would be off. She left you her best love, and she'll see you tomorrow, if she can. She'll send you a message, later, by her boy.

Two shapes like thick slices of bread curled and smoked on the fire. Doll said: oh, them. I found a muddy pair of old slippers in here, I don't know whose they were, so filthy, I chucked them away.

Joseph held the door open for her, and she tramped out, her brush clanking against her bucket. As she passed she clipped him with her gravel-grey eyes. She said: you'll need to get the breakfast on, Mr Benson, fast as can be. Come down soon, won't you?

She had cleared and tidied. Cup and saucer, brandy glass, removed. Books and writing-board straightened, inkwell placed neatly to one side. Cushions plumped, chairs pulled into alignment, crumbs of dried mud removed. Lace blinds completely up, the striped curtains tied back.

Mrs Dulcimer came from her room next door, handed Joseph a pair of grey felt slippers. Wear these for the moment. Later on, we'll find you some clean clothes. I'll come down and have breakfast with you all. That feels best.

Wouldn't the tenants remark on her change of routine? Perhaps she wanted to field any awkward questions they might ask. Didn't trust him to be able to answer. She took him for a simpleton, obviously. Had she done this before? Rows of dead babies mulching her rose trees? Sobs rose in his throat.

Mrs Dulcimer said: in a minute. You go down and I'll follow you in just a minute.

In the kitchen Doll, clad now in a clean blue pinafore, was stacking the new bowls on the dresser, lining up the new plates along the shelves. Bits of string and straw littered the floor. She nodded towards the wicker hampers of quilts. Give me a hand up with those after breakfast, would you, Mr Benson? They do get in the way so.

She'd dumped the bucket of ash and cinders by the back door. Who's going to get rid of that, my girl? Joseph scrubbed his hands, collected together oats, jugs of water and of milk. He made porridge. Tentatively stirred the gloop as it puckered, belched, sent up bubbles that burst. Doll crouched beside him at the range, jiggled the fire. You'll get to know how she works soon enough.

For some reason he counted the chairs. Two had been removed, upended, stacked with the other spares. Mrs Bonnet's, from last night. Betsy's?

Doll said: we should shift all those. Put them in the storeroom, maybe. Every time I pass I trip over them.

Something terrible had happened, and so you rearranged seats, to hide it. You moved the furniture, and wiped people out. Just as the developers put up new terraces in the neighbouring fields, turned meadows into streets. Soon you'd forget completely what those green spaces had looked like before. No one would know a dead baby had once lain there. The room was holding its breath. Wanted to collapse, bawl, strike the table. The air pushed back, held the walls up: brace yourselves. Emptiness outside him and inside him.

He fetched bowls, served the breakfast. Doll and Annie parked themselves in their places, joined by the three young women tenants, who were yawning, a bit sullen, spooning up their food without wanting to talk. They did not comment on Betsy's absence. They obviously took it for granted that so soon after giving birth she'd still be in bed. Nor did they ask for news of the baby. Perhaps their thoughts concerned the coming morning, its burden of work; they searched for courage that had to be put on like a stout baize apron. Mostly they got Sunday afternoon off, didn't they? Free time to go to church, go for a walk? Mrs Dulcimer had hinted so. Today, he remembered, they wanted to go to the fair. The provision of a half-day holiday must depend on the employer: how kindly, or otherwise, she was. Would Cara have given Doll a weekly half-day off? Probably. But first of all tackle the dirty work. Just get on with it. The refrain of Joseph's mother. Everybody's mother, perhaps.

Mrs Dulcimer arrived, took her place at the head of the table. She'd tidied her hair, got dressed, put on a blue-and-black-striped cotton gown. She'd outlined her eyes with kohl, but her red, swollen eyelids were not to be disguised. She dripped milk onto her basin of grey mealiness, dribbled black treacle on top, the solid stream carving runnels. Dipping in her spoon, she frowned at Joseph. Her expression said: you should eat. Try to look as normal as possible.

So here we are. How would they get through the morning? The day? So early still. So cold still, down here, despite the range heating up. Clamminess around his neck, his wrists. The hours stretched ahead; an unending bare corridor. How to break that up? Cook. He said: I should think about today's meals. Orders?

Mrs Dulcimer brought a loaf to the table. One of the three she'd baked last night. She picked up the bread-knife. She slashed off the crust and let it drop. She buttered the end of the loaf, sawed off a thin slice, very steadily. She repeated the gesture. One by one the wafers flopped onto the dish on the tabletop. She put a couple of sprigs of watercress on each one, rolled them up.

She said: let's see. We've a piece of bacon to boil. Cabbage. Some onions. That should do.

The tenants ate their green-stuffed bread and butter, drained their cups of tea. They pushed back their chairs, nodded at Joseph, departed upstairs. Mrs Dulcimer followed them, sweeping Doll and Annie with her. I need you two to give me a hand with something. The glance

325

she flicked him, the set of her shoulders, told him she was going to clear out Betsy's possessions, remove all traces of her and the baby.

What had Betsy got ready? For his own little ones he'd had no money to buy new things. Cara had set to, furnished napkins made from old worn towels, night-gowns and caps cut down from her own, bootees knitted from unravelled stockings past darning.

A creak and squeak upstairs. The tenants departing from their rooms on the ground floor. Rattle of chain, scrape of bolt. The front door opening. The young women stamping out, shouting goodbye. The door slammed shut again.

Cold porridge curds stiffened in the pot. Crumbs littered the table, the used plates. Clear all this up! Doll's job, Annie's also, but if he waited for their return he'd waste half the morning, never get anything done. He took down from the back of the garden door the work-apron Doll had dirtied earlier, tied it on, tried to work out what to do next. A trail of grey ash marked Doll's track across her newly cleaned floor, stopping at the overflowing bucket. The floor would have to be washed again. Did you wash up first or clean the floor? The dusty windows smirked at him. Wash us too! The range stuck out a dingy lip. Black-lead me!

Doll's broom leaned in a corner, next to some dis-carded, toppled-over footwear. His and Mrs Dulcimer's mud-caked boots. Do those straight away. A folded news-paper lay on the dresser. He plucked it up, spread it open on the table, stood the boots on it. He found brushes, polish and blacking, set to.

He heated water, scrubbed his filthy hands, washed up the breakfast things. He threw the crust of congealed porridge outside for the hens, emptied the bucket of cinders and grey dust onto the compost heap, threw the bowls of water over the bushes. The garden smelled very fresh. That earthy scent of autumn flowers. Pink points of roses opening, salmon and russet flares of asters and chrysanthemums. Golden-green leaves lifted and blew about, settled in new drifts. He turned his head aside, hurried past.

Right. Now wash the floor. First of all: clear the space. He carried the spare chairs outside, two by two, into the windowless lobby, lurched through the semi-darkness, piled them next to a door that presumably led into the storeroom. How cold it was down here. He felt stretched with tiredness; scoured out. He leaned against the doorframe, yawning. The air scraped at him like a fingernail. He rubbed his eyes, yawned again. The shadows opposite wavered. A woman stood there. Barefoot; dressed in a long robe. Loose tumble of curly hair. Yet another tenant? She'd overslept, had hurried down to forage for a late breakfast. Her eyes were red, with tiredness or tears. She was frowning at him. He backed away, excusing himself. The air seemed to blink: she vanished.

Not a tenant. He'd seen her before. The cemetery, yes. The street. A figure from one of his dreams? Dreams fled in daylight; usually you forgot them as soon as you woke. She'd got caught on one of his daylight thoughts, as you snag your coat on a bramble's thorns when you brush past. That bramble bush in the field. That bundle of white under it. He wiped his eyes on the back of his hand, returned to the kitchen.

He upended the remaining chairs onto the table. Laced with spiders' webs underneath. He found a duster, wiped off the worst swags of dirt. Yellow softness patched with grey. Now he would have to wash the duster. Curses. No. Shake it outside, later on. What was housework but a transfer of dirt from one place to another? Clouds of dust bowling into the garden, along the street, fetching up on a vast rubbish heap, to be sorted by the dustmen, then the wind picking it up and bowling it back again. So much for opening windows to air rooms; you just let in currents of London filth.

He stuffed the duster into his pocket. He carried the hampers of bedding, one by one, up to the ground floor, dumped them in the hall, stacked on top of each other. Above him the floorboards shifted and creaked as slippered feet went to and fro. Voices called indistinctly, and rang across each other, and the floors croaked their own replies.

He picked up the top hamper and lugged it upstairs to the first landing. The women's voices sounded from above, summoned him. Past Mrs Dulcimer's sitting-room, at the very end of the passage, a cupboard-like door opened. A boxed-in staircase, steep as a ladder, delivered him into the attic. Two sloping windows set into the roof let in pale light. An iron bed in disarray stood under each of these skylights. A bentwood chair next to each of them bore pillows and folded blankets. The white calico curtain dividing the attic in half had been drawn back.

Mrs Dulcimer and Doll were turning one of the mattresses, Annie bundling sheets over her arm. All three glanced at him as he entered, bumping the wicker hamper in front of him. Beyond them and behind them and above them: the grey sky, a frieze of chimney-pots, a flurry of birds' wings and scudding clouds.

Mrs Dulcimer said: that's right. Those quilts are for in here.

Rolled-up blinds topped the sloping windows. Cream-coloured wallpaper displayed a stencilled pattern of tiny scarlet flowers. Two small chests of drawers, fronted by rainbow-striped rag rugs, bore washing sets of matching white china jugs and bowls. A workbasket sat on a table, next to a heap of stockings, a couple of books. The floor had been stripped, waxed. The boards looked soaked in honey. No wonder Doll wanted to stay. Better than dossing down in his kitchen, wasn't it?

Joseph straightened his apron bib, addressed Doll. Did I take your bed last night? Sorry if so.

Mrs Dulcimer prodded the corner of the mattress, caught on the iron end of the bedframe, thumped it to make it lie flat. Was she thumping him? Don't mention last night, if you please! Doll and Annie swapped tight looks. They flapped out clean pillowcases, making a great business of shoving the pillows into them. Mrs Dulcimer laid down a woollen mattress cover, seized a sheet, spread it smooth, bent to mitre the corners, tuck them in. Doll lifted her eyebrows as she picked up her bunch of cleaning tools. Think nothing of it, Mr Benson! Annie gave him a mock bob. Glad to be of help, Mr Benson.

Mrs Dulcimer unrolled blankets, quilts. She spoke to Joseph over her shoulder. Those other two lots of bedding, leave them down in the hall for the time being, will you? I'll see to them later.

Yes, ma'am, he said.

SIXTEEN

Madeleine

MADELEINE'S NIGHT-TIME STROLL BRINGS her back across London Bridge to the Elephant. The warm October night heats the greasy pavements of Walworth Road. Litter of stained, soggy-looking paper blows along between the kerb and the black glass fronts of shops. Groups of adolescents, in hoodies and low-slung jeans, loaf along, picking at takeaways, smoking. The occasional older man shrouded in a windcheater goes by, the occasional young mother bent over a pushchair. Lit buses trundle past.

The corner before Orchard Street. Darker here: not all the street lamps on this stretch work. Some emit a sour yellow light; some have blinked off. No moon tonight to help her progress. No stars.

Shadows detach themselves from pools of gloom, shift and advance. A trio of young men in fleeces and trainers slouches towards her. Faces set to look hard, cool. They glance up when she passes them and wishes them good-night; they nod; they lope on. In winter, when they wear fur trappers' hats, such would-be toughs become trans-formed into long-eared bunny rabbits with wide-open, softly lashed eyes. In the summer, their hoodies make them sleek and dark as otters. Now, in autumn, they swim along heads down, anonymous.

Sometimes, coming back late at night, she bumps into one of her male neighbours rolling home from the pub, or making for the park with a wrapped bottle sticking out of a pocket, a dog trotting alongside. They greet each other, halt for a quick chat. One of the younger ones she recognises from afar by his silhouette: short and broad-shouldered, hair in thick braids finished with beads. He likes to seize her in a hug. Arms hold her tight then release her. One stranger asked: you married? Madeleine lied: certainly. He shook his head: and there was I, just getting ready to make my move. He went on his way, laughing.

She turns into Apricot Place, passes along under the massive plane trees. Scuffle of dry fallen leaves. Something white flashes ahead. Whiteness moves across the pavement at the far end of the cul-de-sac; towards the kerb; then floats back. A gleaming flow of whiteness that vanishes. Like a long banner trailing along the ground, then in a flurry of wind flicking out of sight.

Madeleine hurries forward through patches of wavering shadow. Reaching the black gate marking the descent to her basement area, she grips an iron finial, looks up at the flight of steps leading to the raised ground-floor entrance above her flat.

Above her, on the low balustrade inside the porch, one on either side of the door, glances cast gravely down, perch two small, still figures, clothed in shimmering spreads of white, satin robes rippling from shoulders to feet. Their hair falls in waves over their shoulders. Hands clasped in laps, heads slightly bowed, they seem impersonal as the carved angels guarding a Victorian grave.

They hold their watchful pose a few seconds more. Then turn their heads, glance at her. They open their arms: night flowers blossoming. The vision dissolves: they break into smiles. They stand up, bunch their ballooning skirts: fooled you! Madeleine sings out: yes, you did! Wonderful girls!

Sally's younger grandchildren, dressed up in her brides-maids' frocks: Madeleine claps them. They grin at her, swing their legs over the balustrade, slither down into Sally's porch. A wedge of light. Sally's voice exclaims and laughs. The front door slams shut.

A cat pads along the quiet street, disappears beneath a parked car. Madeleine swivels, checks the surrounding dimness. Just in case.

No sign of Emm. No nasty surprise on the pavement, the area steps. Good. Nonetheless she holds her breath until she's safely inside.

She yawns, stretches. She's got a bottle of Chablis in the fridge. Why not open it, have a glass? Celebrate.

For three whole weeks now the flat has felt freed of whatever presence previously haunted it. Warmth and calm flow through the space. The air seems to hum, the rooms feel welcoming again, the entrance hall seems larger, lighter. Kitchen smells: newly cut lemons, crushed cardamom.

Approaching the fridge, sweeping aside the lace curtain veiling it, she glances at the shelf above. A gap in the clut-ter of stuff. The spot where Nelly's turquoise pot formerly stood. The flat's atmosphere changed after she threw the broken pot and its hoard of garden relics into the flower-bed. The haunting simply got up and went.

Nelly's pot. I'm sad I broke it. Poltergeists break things, throw them around. Was I myself somehow the polter-geist? Did I raise the ghost, the disturbance? Why?

Think about it some other time. I'm hungry.

She takes her glass of wine, a hastily cut ham sand-wich, into the dark, fresh-smelling garden. Spiky profiles of shrubs; lax whips of climbing roses. Tomorrow, pursue autumn tasks. Rake fallen leaves, prune bushes, put in more bulbs. Second autumn task: dream up what to write next. The stories for Rose are nearly done. Rose's model of the cul-de-sac is nearly finished too. I'll show it to you very soon, Madeleine, I promise. You and Nan can come and see it together.

Brown bread, fragrant ham, cold butter, Dijon mustard. She used to make similar sandwiches in the café, before the new owner insisted on shavings of factory-farmed chicken breast, slivers of taste-free tomato, embalmed in white pap. For her next project should she do something with food? Write a food blog? Thousands of those already. Start a pop-up café? Thousands of those too.

The wine tastes coolly flinty. She lounges on an iron café chair, surveys the back of the house. Sheer brick wall, black drainpipes falling down one side. Rows of black oblong windows and window-frames, black panels of glass, one above the other.

Gold light blooms in the blackness: a lamp inside the first-floor window. The bedroom of the flat above hers. Glimpse of pale green walls, the edge of a blue picture-frame, a triangle of salmon-pink. The sash crashes up. Someone leans his elbows on the sill, looks out into the night.

Her new neighbour, presumably. She wills herself not to move in the darkness. Not wanting to be caught being a voyeur. A peeping Thomasina. Yet she is a voyeur. Coming home at night along Orchard Street, along Apricot Place, she glances at the lit, uncurtained ground-floor and basement windows of houses she passes, the framed bright images of people inside stirring saucepans, lolling on sofas, talking, watching TV. They don't know she can see in. Out in the black street she's invisible. A flash of their intimate lives. Then she's past them, stepping along in the dark.

The man tilts his head. Beaky profile. Rumpled edge of hair, as though he cuts it short to subdue it. He looks up at the grey clouds. Around them, London's garbled noises: a woman three gardens away yelling at her children to go to sleep; a plane growling across the sky; a fox barking; a motorbike revving. The garden holds the scent of stocks. Wind swishes through the branches of the ash tree.

She tips up her glass, finishes her wine. When she looks back at the house, the window is dark and the man has gone.

Inside, she slides into bed, puts out the light, waits for sleep. Images flash, like an oncoming car's headlights on a black, lonely road. Moths startle up, fizzily dash, staccato gold, onto the windscreen, across the long, slanting beams. She's a child again, sleepily enchanted in the back seat, travelling home with her parents after a party. They swing around corners into further darkness. Moths open their white wings, furred like film stars' party cloaks. Party dresses. Fancy dress. Sally's two little granddaughters dressed up in those trailing white frocks.

What would her own two children have been like, if they'd hung on inside her, been born, survived, grown up? She has never allowed herself to contemplate their possible lives. Now they arrive, running along the street with arms outstretched. Calling for her. Fighting her. Hating her. Kissing her. She can't hold on to them.

After a while she stops crying, rearranges herself, sinking in the midst of her two pillows. She puts an arm round each pillow. One is called Rose and the other Francine.

SEVENTEEN

Joseph

JOSEPH AND MRS DULCIMER ate lunch by themselves. She dismissed Doll and Annie, organised them a piece each, wrapped in paper, for carrying in their pockets. She carved leftover chunks of beef into thin squares, pressed them in between slices of bread and butter and pickle. Her two maids looked pale, she declared: they needed a dose of fresh air. Annie said: not in the countryside, though. I'm going to the Hallowe'en fair.

Mrs Bonnet's tow-headed boy arrived, despatched by his mistress with a dismantled bed on his barrow, a bunch of overblown blue and purple asters balanced on top. He said: Mrs Bonnet meant to bring you the flowers yesterday, but she forgot. She wasn't sure whether or not you'd be needing the bed, but she sent it anyway. Said to tell you Miss Betsy's settling in nicely. I'd say so too. She looked bristling with life as this gentleman's whiskers!

He bowed to Joseph, who scowled back. So what if he hadn't yet shaved? The rude child deserved a ticking-off. He wouldn't give him one, though. He didn't want to make any trouble, give the boy an excuse to go blubbing home, rouse up that righteous matron he lived with. Was she his mother or his employer? A termagant, anyway. Did she have a husband tucked away somewhere? There was a lad who needed a father, all right. Joseph could show him the ropes, if he had to. Teach him how to speak politely to his elders and betters, for one thing. Teach him to box, perhaps.

He sighed. Wives didn't hit you with their fists; just with what they said, or didn't say. Which hurt more? Fists, yes, definitely. But wives left their own sorts of scars, bruises. On the skin of your soul.

The boy announced his determination to squire the two young women to the fair. Mrs Dulcimer made a third beef and bread piece, and the threesome prepared to depart for the common. Doll tied on her bonnet, fastened her cape. She adjusted Annie's shawl, tugged her friend's skirts to bulk out in neat pleats. Just so had Mrs Bonnet tidied Mrs Dulcimer, only a few days ago. Nathalie used to do that for him, didn't she? Years back.

Doll said: we'll meet up with the others, I daresay, and we'll all come home together for supper.

The tow-haired boy squared his shoulders, straightened his skimpy jacket. He said: no need to worry about them, Mrs D., they've got me in charge. I'll take care of them! I'll see they don't misbehave! Annie clouted him on the shoulder and they all banged out, scuffling and shoving.

Mrs Dulcimer put the blooms into water, in the ebony vase she brought downstairs from the sitting-room. She patted and pulled the stalks into place, as though flower-arranging were the only thing that mattered. Joseph fetched the remainder of the leeks from where someone had carelessly left them in a heap on the windowsill. He'd been with her when she bought them, hadn't he? The leeks fell into neat ranks of slices under his knife. Leeks did not bleed when you cut them up. Just as well. Joseph didn't want to eat meat today. No thanks. A suffocated baby might not bleed but he was still dead as dead. But here came Mrs Dulcimer briskly handing him the pot of beef broth left over from the day before: see what you can do with this.

Mrs Dulcimer gathered up the litter of stray leaves. He's a smart boy, that one. He does an early shift in the market up at Covent Garden, and any damaged blooms he sees thrown down he brings back for Mrs Bonnet, and some of them she gives to me. You can hardly tell they're bruised if you arrange them right. The flowers that people throw away, or won't buy, you wouldn't believe!

Betsy the scarlet poinsettia blossom, plucked for some chap's flash buttonhole, ripped from her flowerbed, all right, Mrs Dulcimer, raped, he had her, he dropped her in the gutter.

He kept remembering Betsy's small footprints. The baby's squeals. He put the bacon into simmering water. It looked like a baby. A haunch of waif. For lunch, obediently he boiled up the broth. He disguised its meatiness, adding a minced onion, pinches of saffron and curry powder, a fistful of sultanas, a spoonful of chopped parsley. The tabletop was very clean. Somebody must scrub it every day. You could prepare vegetables on its smooth, whitened surface and feel sure no particle of dirt got into them.

The tabletop calmed him, as though it could talk. Easy, there. Easier to talk while cooking: he could put his back to Mrs Dulcimer when necessary, stop speaking while he stirred and scraped delicately with his wooden spoon, resume his flow as the broth began to reduce just as it ought. He tipped in the chopped leeks, two handfuls of rice.

Mrs Dulcimer took up a flat-edged knife, smoothed butter into neatness on its glass dish. She said: you were working for Mr Mayhew before, weren't you? That must have been interesting. Perhaps working for me here will feel like a comedown.

Joseph looked round. You've heard of him? I didn't tell you he was my employer. My former employer, I should say. I'm sure I didn't mention his name.

Mrs Dulcimer began putting the pottery jars of dry goods back onto their shelf. Lining them up exactly, patting them into place. Just so did the mistresses of households try to organise their servants. Stay still! Behave! But the servants didn't always obey. Minds of their own. They tied on their Sunday bonnets and ran out to play, barged into boys, took a twirl with them, sat on their laps on the swings at the fair, swung higher and higher. And why not? They were young. They should enjoy themselves. He'd never taken Milly to the fair, but he should have. He'd kept her cooped up too long, so now she'd broken out, flown away. Come back, Milly, please come back. He'd have to go to Boulogne and find her. If necessary, escort her to Paris, see her safely to that hospital. Did those nuns sport starched white head-dresses, like the ones Nathalie had described worn by the sisters at her convent school? White wings flapping. Seagulls hovering above the Channel, searching for food. Seizing fish in their sharp beaks. He was hungry like them. He stirred the pan of rice.

Mrs Dulcimer said: of course I've heard of him. I do read the paper, you know.

So she did. That first morning when he'd visited her here: she'd cast down her paper in order to deliver a lecture on manners. He'd been too taken aback by her cold reception of him to bother wondering about her reading-matter. He'd eyed her breakfast. Her blue dressing-gown. Drunk in the scent of warm bread, her warm skin.

She indicated the scrunched-up ball of newsprint sitting next to the shoe-cleaning box on the floor by the range. Didn't you notice that was the *Morning Chronicle*? When you told me, in the market while we were shopping,

340

about your research, I felt sure it must be Mr Mayhew you were working for.

She spotted a stray sultana on the tabletop, picked it up, ate it. Then another. She looked musingly at her fingertips, licked them, glanced at Joseph. When I first met you, that evening you first came here, I got an idea about doing some research myself.

He poked the glistening rice. Shook the pan, to make sure it didn't scorch underneath. Must be nearly ready.

Mrs Dulcimer continued. There are many predators who prowl about. Some of these gentlemen, as you may know, have precise and particular tastes. If they pay enough, they will be catered for. Talking to you, I wondered how far someone might go to buy himself a very young girl. A long way, as it turned out.

She took up a little, flat brush by its biscuit-coloured wooden top, began to sweep crumbs and green debris across the table. Careful, graceful movements, swooping in half-circles.

Joseph protested. Not under-age, at least. It was obvious to me that Doll was more than twelve years old. Fourteen if she was a day! And you seem to forget that I was only asking to talk to her!

Mrs Dulcimer continued brushing. I didn't know that then, did I? I thought you were disgusting.

She pushed her heap of mess into her cupped palm. So I decided on the spot, that evening, to experiment. String you along, if I could, then write an article about your seeking to procure a virgin of tender years. I thought I'd send it to Mr Mayhew, see if he'd publish it.

Joseph banged his wooden spoon on the side of the pot. She'd assumed he was a monster. A criminal gobbler of young girls. The white plates on the dresser stared back at him like accusing faces. The black-haired girl the Italian girl the country girl the lace-maker girl. Doll, Annie, Betsy. The tenants. Milly. Dear Lord, Milly.

Joseph blew out his breath. Concentrated on his cookery, lifting and nudging, very gently, so as not to break up the grains of rice. Rather than a spoon you needed a wooden fork for this, but he hadn't found one. He tried to sound calm. But then you changed your mind?

She bent her head, concurring. Yes. Doll intervened. That was that. Later on I realised that you and I had misunderstood each other.

She ferreted at the back of a shelf, drew out a small decanter of red wine, removed the stopper, sniffed it. She said: if we were in France eating Sunday lunch, we'd have a glass of wine with it. So I don't see why we shouldn't do the same thing in Walworth.

She'd completely misread him. A hand clutched his heart, squeezed it. Irregular beat that he could somehow taste in his throat. His blood thumped and thundered in his ears. He tipped out his rice dish onto the oval platter he had set to warm. Mrs Dulcimer arranged plates and cutlery, cut bread. She reached to the dresser, surveyed the little heap of linen squares twisted through looped raffia, tossed him the napkin he'd used the night before.

Joseph rested his fists on the tabletop. Tried to breathe deeply. Nathalie's voice whispered: *calme-toi, calme-toi*. Tears wetted his eyes. So she hadn't quite gone. He sipped his wine. Earthy and dry at the same time. He drank more. Warm redness spread through him. Nathalie murmured: *ne t'agace pas*. He sighed. His anger dried, broke loose, fell off him like a dried crust of mud.

He said: I'm still not sure what you are up to.

Mrs Dulcimer tried a mouthful of rice. You're not?

Joseph bit into a grain. It resisted, softened. Perfect. He waited for her to comment on his cookery. She said nothing, but tasted another forkful. He said: you were going to write an article?

She nodded. Certainly. Let me pour you another glass of wine. This won't keep. Let's finish it.

What did a black woman write about? A missionary had come to the church once, when he was a child, had read out a story composed by a black female, a former slave in the West Indies. So full of cruelty that Joseph had closed his ears. Could not remember. It ended in the arms of Jesus. Then they stood up and sang a hymn.

He said: you write for the newspapers?

She swirled the wine in her glass, tipped it back. She said: stories for magazines, mainly. Adventure stories, ghost stories. It's a good way to increase my income. I don't make enough from letting rooms.

Did she believe in ghosts? Or just invent stories about them? Had she ever heard the voice of a dead person, as he'd just heard Nathalie? His lost loved one had eventually found her way back to him, knocked at his soul, come to live inside him. Hardly a ghost story; interesting to him alone. What kind of adventures did Mrs Dulcimer write about? Did she compose tales of derring-do? Melodramas? Girls in peril rescued at the last minute by stern-jawed heroes, by faithful dogs, by kindly clergymen? Nathalie had enjoyed such absurdities, reading them out to Cara, laughing.

He said: perhaps you don't charge adequate rates.

Mrs Dulcimer said: but I like writing. I enjoy it. All sorts. As I told you before, some of the tenants, those who can't write, dictate their letters to me. Love letters, very often. Sometimes they ask me to spice them up a bit. Sometimes I have to tone them down!

He could feel his lip curl. Nathalie pinched his earlobe and he jumped. She whispered: you don't like her thinking about her girls, do you? You want her to think about you, only about you!

On her afternoons off, Cara would visit Nathalie, stay as late as she dared. He would come in from work, speechless with tiredness, in need of supper, find the two sisters seated beside the unlit fire, heads bent towards each other. The tinkling flow of French. Women's talk in women's time. Nathalie would jump to her feet, lift her face for his kiss, Cara pushed aside like a piece of mending you rolled up, thrust into the workbasket. Husbands came first. He'd taken that for granted, hadn't he? Now he knew Nathalie and Cara had loved each other far more than they'd loved him. Theirs was the true romance, yes. No point being bitter about that.

After lunch, he washed up. Doll's job, or Annie's, but they were out, weren't they, disporting themselves. Yet again he cleaned plates and pans. He scraped away the black grease layering the pots underneath, scoured the knife blades to make them shine. If you're going to do a job then do it properly. That was his mother talking, wasn't it?

Mrs Dulcimer reappeared in the kitchen, wearing her red walking dress, her bonnet with its curling red feather, carrying her cloak over one arm. I'm going out for an airing. I'll go as far as Mrs Bonnet's, maybe. I'll come back by the common, take a look at the fair, hope to fall in with those young ones.

He went up to her sitting-room, carrying a bucket of coal and wood, replenished the fire. The flames leaped at him, warmed him, tempted him to sit down. Finish reading that novel he'd begun last night. Or don her black eye-shade, take a doze. Wearing her velvety mask, would he dream as she did? What was it like to be Mrs Dulcimer? Just forty winks, and he'd get going again.

He stood eye to eye with the turquoise pot on the mantelpiece. He lifted its lid. Inside lay Mrs Dulcimer's gold hoop earring with its cluster of blue beads, and a small curl of black hair tied with a scrap of red thread.

His own little ring, plaited from Nathalie's hair: presumably Cara had taken it to Boulogne. He'd not considered it hers. Now, perhaps, she would wear it all the time.

Mrs Dulcimer's stack of papers perched on the side table. Foolish to leave them there, where anybody could spot them, take an idle glance. She was almost inviting someone to pick them up, riffle through them. If you didn't like what you read, her tone of voice, her turn of phrase, if you disapproved of her opinions or her plots, you could just feed the manuscript to the fire, leaf by leaf. Let the fire have it. Let the fire consume it.

The manuscript bore a title. *The Story of My Life*. Did she plan to send it to the *Morning Chronicle*? A nice serial that would make, Deptford to Walworth via Paris, rags to comparative riches. Bring her in a tidy sum too. Mayhew would seize her hand, pump it, compliment her. Bile scorched the back of Joseph's throat. Unfair, unfair.

Forefinger poised to scoop up and turn the page, he stopped. The sour taste receded as he swallowed. Her private papers. Leave them alone. Don't pry. If she wants you to read them she'll tell you.

He settled himself in front of the heaped wood and coals, which crackled and tinkled as the re-nourished flames steadied themselves. He tied on the black velvet mask, leaned back in the chair. The mask pressed his eyelids gently. Like a hand stroking him. If you couldn't open your eyes and see then you turned your gaze round and saw inside. Dreamy blackness pierced by golden stars. In just a moment he'd get up, stretch, move. He should go out, walk towards the common. See if he could spot the young ones and Mrs Dulcimer. Fall in with them, accompany them home. Protect them if need be. The police might yet turn up. Insist on searching the house, ask tricky questions. First of all, open the front door. Heavy, for some reason. Heavy as his eyelids. Out into the dark street, the dark clouds scudding overhead in the dark sky.

EIGHTEEN

Madeleine

B Y NIGHT, BOROUGH BECOMES an urban land-scape built from darkness: no lit shops, few passers-by. The railway viaduct cuts across it, carrying the trains above short rows of early Victorian houses jammed up against weed-rimmed parking lots, derelict warehouses, lock-up garages. One soot-blackened arch frames the entrance to Redcross Way, a dim tunnel running between mansion blocks. Traffic rumbles in the distance. Madeleine's footsteps tap out a percussion. Her long silk skirt flurries around her ankles as she strides along. Her shadow slinks ahead of her.

Other shadows collect, stretch out. Opposite the Boot and Flogger, on the far side of the narrow street, a small crowd, forty or so strong, has gathered, spread along the strip of pavement in front of the fence sealing off the ancient burial ground. The wind rustles the ribbons and strings of beads laced to the wire barrier, the bunches of dried flowers, the gilt streamers. People cup lit candles in their gloved hands. A few children jig from foot to foot. A musician in a striped woollen cap strums a guitar. Bells chime from an invisible church: St George the Martyr, presumably; near Borough tube.

Madeleine takes up a position to the side of the crowd, close to the kerb, with a good view of the street, the pub, the railway arch. A young man and woman nearby, muffled in coats and scarves, push up to make room for her. Thanks, Madeleine says: I may need to make a quick getaway. I don't know what this will be like. The young man says: perhaps we'll raise a couple of ghosts. There ought to be a few about on Hallowe'en.

A woman nearby shakes her head. Fur hat, a quilted brown coat with brass fastenings. Almond-shaped brown eyes in a thin face. She addresses them in a contralto Italian accent. Don't mock! This is a sacred place. Why come here if you're going to make jokes? The young man replies: but I am serious. The Italian woman frowns: I don't think so. You should respect the spirits of this place.

Marcia the estate agent. Marcia who acknowledges household gods, who salutes them as she steps over the threshold. Madeleine greets her. How's the job?

Marcia shrugs. I got the sack. I was too friendly with the clients, they said. I annoyed them. And if a place felt wrong to me, I used to say so. But I'm OK. I'm working as a teaching assistant, I like it better. See you later, maybe? Now I want to take a candle, before the ceremony begins.

Marcia wheels away, makes towards the stone Madonna on her plinth at the far end of the fence. A group of women clusters there. Bright coats and scarves, lace shawls. Friendly faces beam out smiles. One woman holds an armful of flowers, one proffers a cardboard box of candles. Tapering white sticks lifted out by their wicks. Struck matches spurt fire.

Marcia clasps her wax wand in one hand, shields its flickering flame with the other, bends her head over it. Lit from underneath, her face turns to sockets and hollows. As in that game Madeleine and her friends played in childhood, dressing up as ghouls. A sheet flung over the head, a torch gripped under the chin, its light distorting your features. Acted out in dark bedrooms, along dark corridors. You waylaid each other, sprang from cupboards, screeched. You could play ghouls all year round, not only on Hallowe'en.

The Eve of All Hallows: the day before All Saints. Sitting in the Adam and Eve with Toby and Anthony two nights ago, comparing childhood rituals and games, Madeleine recounted the rites of All Souls night, as practised by her family. Evening Confession in the chilly, incense-scented, darkened church. Latin Mass. Litanies of prayers, pleading for the release of the Holy Souls suffering in Purgatory. Invocations to the happy souls who'd made it to Heaven, performed miracles by God's grace, therefore could be hailed as saints.

Toby said: no one nowadays knows or cares what Hallowe'en originally meant. Everything's been Disneyfied. No loss for an atheist like me.

He went to the bar for another round. Madeleine said to Anthony: you're a Christian. Do you believe in life after death? He said: I'm not sure. Sometimes. What about you?

He listened while she struggled to define what she had concluded about the dead. The lost ones. Yet somehow still present, still alive in some way. In that invisible layer of the world called imagination. An army of dead people, centuries of them, marching, marching through the night. You live on earth with a host of invisible people at your back. The dead lean in on you. Some of them leave traces. The writers, for example. Mayhew, Brontë, Gaskell, Dickens, Eliot. You read the books they wrote. Relish their words. Their fought-for language brings dead authors shiningly alive. Readers make that happen; not God. All Saints: all writers, flying up out of their graves. Language is the Resurrection: holy body of imagination created by reading, nourishing reading and being nourished by it.

Anthony seemed to follow her free-associative jumps, not to mind them. He looked amused. He said: you're a heretic. You'd have been burned at the stake.

Toby returned with a second bottle of wine. They went on listing domestic religious practices. For example abstaining from meat on Fridays, the day of Christ's crucifixion. Madeleine described the fish dishes her family ate instead: the cod in cream sauce with capers, the poached mackerel. Anthony countered with his family's grilled kippers, shrimps with bread and butter. Toby said: not what I'd call abstention!

Madeleine asked: so what are you going to cook for Hallowe'en, Toby? He said: ravioli with pumpkin stuffing, served with fried sage. Pumpkin risotto, ditto. Pumpkin soup. Pumpkin pie.

Anthony explained: Rose and her pals scavenged some pumpkins recently from a supermarket skip. Rose carved Hallowe'en lanterns and gave us the insides. All the flesh. So we're going to cook supper for the people in the local church refuge.

Toby said: we're following in the footsteps of Alexis Soyer, the Victorian chef. He set up soup kitchens that could serve thousands of destitute people at a time. Rich people donated the legs of mutton or whatever. Our twist is that Rose and her revolutionary friends steal the food for us to cook and give away.

Anthony said: so we're not dishing out charity. We're recycling. Just in case you wanted to know how we see it.

She heard them saying 'we'. A couple. Lovely double act. Darting around their kitchen; a waltz of knives and chopping-boards. When you were single you had a tribe: friends and neighbours. Toby and Anthony formed part of that tribe. And 'we' could spread out to include all the people in nearby streets.

She said: can I help you? That's just the kind of thing I should like to be doing.

Toby said: help us next time. We're sorted for Hallowe'en. Too many cooks! Not that Rose will spoil our broth. She hardly knows how to cook at all.

Anthony added: you know Rose is coming to stay with us? She may not have had time to tell you yet. We only fixed it up yesterday. We're going to be great-uncles.

The fence separating off the burial ground in Redcross Way purports to divide the living and the dead. Does it? Perhaps the dark air on either side teems and flickers with spirits. Strangers stand next to Madeleine. Alive, lively. Their sleeves brushing hers. All of them pressed together. Overcoats smelling of rain, woollen shoulders damp from the drizzle earlier. Young people, older people, waiting patiently in the darkness, murmuring, chatting. Marcia stands amongst them, eyes bent to her candle. Is she praying? Madeleine tries to catch her eye; fails.

A gong resounds. Welcome! A man in a brown tweed coat steps forward from the group of women bunched near the stone Madonna. Clear-eyed; open face; his attention focussed like a beam of light on his listeners. Strong, resonant voice. Passionately he launches his words, holds the gathering's attention. Briefly he explains the history of this bleak place, invokes the outcast women who ended up here in unmarked graves. He recites a poem in their honour, reclaiming them: rebel saints dedicated to liberation, disorderly angels shunned by bourgeois wives but showing the male disciples who could appreciate them a vision of heaven on earth, of freedom, of pure sex. A shaman with golden wings he seems, beating through smoky air, wielding the sword of dissent; slashing through hypocrisy, praising prostitutes, his beautiful, misunderstood sisters. He draws the watching mass of people into his intensity. Not one of them is lifting a mobile, taking photos. They seem as rapt as he is.

Too romantic, grumbles someone jammed in behind Madeleine: prostitutes were poor slags who had to stand in freezing alleys dropping their knickers for threepence a time. Give us a break!

A voice with a slight croak and crackle to it. Madeleine turns. Tall young woman in an olive-green parka, its fur-trimmed hood tossed back over her shoulders. Black crew cut; dark, lively eyes; scarlet-painted mouth. Warmth slides over Madeleine. She whispers: I know you. D'you remember? We met before, at that play at Bart's. You're Maria.

Maria embraces Madeleine. It's you! I looked for you after the play but you'd run out on me.

Fur tickles Madeleine's nose. Maria's laughing, holding on to Madeleine's sleeve. She says: I'm here for research. Another play, same subject, but taking it all a bit further, into the present day. You?

Madeleine tries to keep her voice low, not to disturb the hushed people round about. I discovered this place by accident ages ago, but I didn't know what went on until friends told me. So I thought I'd take a look.

Toby and Anthony have been patrolling their new neighbourhood east and west of Waterloo, Bermondsey to Vauxhall, discovering it street by street. Boulders set into stone walls as markers of ancient boundaries; traces of the Marshalsea prison; classic gay pubs; the groceries and tapas bars of Portuguese and Brazilian communities; the candlelight vigils held here at the Redcross Way burial ground. Parting from her outside the Adam and Eve, they urged Madeleine to attend tonight's vigil. Just the thing for Hallowe'en, surely. We're busy early evening, taking the food down to the refuge, but we'll meet up with you afterwards, in the Boot, with Rose and Sally. They're coming over to move Rose's stuff in, and then staying to supper. Come as well, why don't you?

The dome of darkening sky shows a few faint stars. A chill wind glazes their faces. Madeleine rubs her hands together to warm them, fishes in her pocket. Her fingertips scrabble at seams. Damn: no gloves; she's forgotten them at home. Instead of gloves she's got a handkerchief, her phone, a penknife. She was tying up plants in the garden earlier, cutting string with her neat Laguiole knife, forgot to put it away. Oops. Shouldn't be carrying this on the street.

The poet-priest summons the guitar-player, who begins to sing. Maria squeezes Madeleine's arm. So great to see you again! People packed in nearby shoot them pained glances, as though they're gossiping in church. Maria whispers: talk later, OK? The young man next to her, holding his girlfriend's hand, turns, frowns. Shhh! Maria looks him over, gives him a slow smile.

Fetching, Nelly would have named that smile. But Nelly no longer speaks to Madeleine. She has gone. Nipping off, she'd call this vanishing act. Just nipping off round the corner, dear, to catch the post. A rip in the air, through which she fled. The air a screen, behind which she disappeared. Did I drive her away, getting cross with her that time? No good clutching after her. Madeleine's got her on paper: her written record of Nelly's sayings and jokes. Also the remembered, invented tales transcribed for Rose, pasted up on the front doors of Rose's model. Rose smoothed out a blister of glue with her fingertip. We're getting there. Don't think you're finished, though. One more story to go.

The plaintive ballad ends. The musician in the striped woollen cap bows over his guitar, retreats. A fair-haired girl aged ten or so, muffled in a green duffel coat, begins to recite a poem in a clear, piping voice. I wander thro' each charter'd street/ Near where the charter'd Thames does flow. Madeleine silently recites Blake's poem along with her: one she used to read with her literature students, which some of them disliked because it disturbed them. The small girl stumbles over a word, but goes stubbornly on. The youthful harlot's curse. Her audience strains forward, listening. Her voice like silvery water rippling up. A dark well of adults curving round her.

An engine pumps and roars. The screech of brakes shatters the group reverie. A minibus bangs to a halt, parks just beyond the pub, half on the pavement, half off. The metal door rattles back, disgorging a dozen or so passengers, who spill out onto the road, advance, a press of dark bodies, a wave of exclamations. Two of these newcomers are costumed as skeletons, others as witches and wizards in black cloaks with orange frills. A couple of women sport fake-fur coats open over glittery purple mini-dresses with plunging necklines, balance on lofty platform heels. All of them push and shove towards the front of the crowd, the decorated fence. Francine's voice raises itself: gently does it, Sex Walkers, gently!

Madeleine's hand flies to her mouth. Fuck. I should have expected this. She gives Maria a quick, whispered explanation. So what? shrugs Maria: I guess we're all Sex Walkers too, aren't we? I'm not a participant, that's for sure.

Madeleine hesitates. I'm intrigued. I'm an onlooker, certainly. I don't know what else I am. Half inside and half outside. In between.

Maria asks: you some kind of academic?

The poet-shaman lifts his hands. Welcome, friends, welcome. Plenty of room for us all on this pavement, if we just move along a little. He pats the shoulder of the small green-coated girl, urges her to start the poem again. She lifts her candle in one hand. Her fluting vowels rise up. The throng of people attends to her, becomes once more a single mass. Just for a moment, before tiny illuminated screens start bobbing about in the darkness.

Francine wears a tightly belted black leather coat, a rakishly tilted black fascinator, black stilettos. Black fishnet stockings. Keep the fishnet flag flying! The black sky wraps them round. Candlelight gilds the edges of the artefacts tied to the fence. The poet calls: would anyone else like to speak? To sing? No?

Face glowing, he opens his arms in farewell, in blessing. Maria mutters: surely it's all a performance. He can't really be sincere. Where's the irony?

The poet-priest drops his arms, turns back into an ordinary man, merry and sexy, full of jokes and cheek. His group of women disciples bustles up, closes around him.

Maria lights a cigarette, takes a few drags: all priests are secretly power-mad, aren't they? What makes this man any different? He's a kind of priest, isn't he?

Madeleine says: perhaps he'd call himself the master of ceremonies? He's a poet, at any rate.

She puts on her self-mocking Mrs Teacher voice: a poet in the Shelleyan tradition. You know. 'Poets are the unacknowledged legislators of mankind.' That sort of thing.

So what about womankind? continues Maria: where were the prostitutes? Why didn't we hear from any of them? I wanted to meet some of them, talk to them.

Oh, Maria, for heaven's sake. Madeleine pulls up the collar of her jacket, stamps her feet to warm them. She says: perhaps they were here, lots of them, how can we know? They're just women. Men as well, I suppose. They don't go about wearing badges!

Maria blows out smoke. OK. I guess so. I'll have to find another way of getting in touch.

Madeleine shoves her cold hands into her pockets: perhaps they're in the pub, putting their feet up. Shall we go and join them, get a drink?

There must be online support groups, Maria muses: I just haven't looked for them yet. Did I tell you that for my new play I'm doing research into online porn, online sex? Fascinating.

The gong sounds again. People blow out their candles, press forwards to tie new offerings to the fence: bows of scarlet ribbon, lengths of beads, fresh flowers. Madeleine moves off the kerb and out of their way, stands in the street, in front of the pub entrance. Light glistens on black tarmac, wet after the rain earlier. Maria drifts across to a group of Sex Walkers, starts talking to them.

Francine waits to one side. Half in shadow. Light from the nearby street lamp polishes her black leather coat, her pale, powdered face. She's posing; a parody from film noir; almost a caricature. She knows it, tilting her chin, sending cool looks flashing right and left. When Madeleine waves hello, Francine breaks her pose, darts towards her. She holds Madeleine close, kisses her on both cheeks: darling! Fabulous to see you. Another press of the soft mouth. Can we give you a lift? Is Rose here? Where is she?

Madeleine says: she's coming with Toby and Anthony. They should be along any minute.

Just as long as they don't love her more than me, Francine says: that's all!

Wind sweeps the branches of the trees on the far side of the burial ground. Silvery light behind the twisting mass of leaves: the moon beginning to rise. The crowd frays and thins, some people still hovering in groups, others dispersing along the pavement, crossing the road towards where

Madeleine and Francine stand in front of the pub's lit doorway. Further along, the minibus blocks the pavement. Maria returns to Madeleine's side, eyes Francine, nods hello. The poet-shaman and his companions remain near the fence, facing the burial ground, heads bent. They lift their hands, seeming to caress the cold air. They murmur, as though they are saying goodnight to the dead women. Maria follows Madeleine's gaze: I get it. They really love them.

A movement in the darkness further along the street. The solid shadows shift, break up. Small block of figures advancing from the black railway arch: four people, laden with bags. Their height, their gait, reveal them as Toby and Anthony, Rose and Sally. Madeleine waves and they halt, put down their bags, wave back. Francine, arms out, hurries towards them, stiff-legged in her high heels.

Madeleine says to Maria: over there, look, those are my friends I'm meeting for a drink. Come with us. Let's all have a drink together.

Maria settles her fur-edged hood around her face. Fox-lady; framed in fur. Fresh skin and sparkling eyes. Young women often don't know how beautiful they are. Madeleine didn't. No notion of it. Does Maria know? She works as an actor, has to scrutinise her face in the mirror each night as she puts on stage makeup. That doesn't mean she knows she's beautiful. Maria parts her red lips, slips Madeleine a smile: this is turning into a party. Who's the black-leather queen? Will she come too?

Francine starts collecting her Sex Walkers. She swerves about nimbly as a collie herding sheep, determined no strays shall escape. She darts to and fro, easing the group towards the minibus. Chatting, discussing, still aiming their phones and cameras, they clamber on board. Francine blows air kisses towards Madeleine. The bus door pulls shut. The engine revs.

The full moon emerges above the treetops, shines mistily in the dark-lavender sky. Moonlight silvers the metal top of the decorated fence, where stragglers are still pinning messages and offerings to the mesh, pushing loops of ribbon into wire-framed gaps. Moonlight whitens the pavement, the snuffed stubs of candle abandoned on the Madonna's plinth. Her bare, chipped toes.

Someone turns round in the shadows beyond the Madonna, at the very end of the fence, where it abuts a hoarding. He stares in Madeleine's direction. Sturdily shaped man in a black overcoat, black scarf. A white dog collar shows at his throat, in between the folds of black wool.

Emm. Madeleine's hands in her pockets touch her knife, curl to fists. He mirrors her, thrusts his hands into his own pockets, stands stiff and still. Has he recognised her? Surely she's just a black silhouette against the lit pub doorway? A black-paper cut-out folding back into shadowy night.

The small girl who recited Blake's poem stands near the statue of the Madonna, refastening a toggle of her green duffel coat, watched by a fair-haired woman she closely resembles. The musician closes his guitar-case, hoists it by its strap over his shoulder. He puts an arm round the child, addresses the woman. Let's be away.

The poet-shaman and his band of women end their meditation, turn round. A kind of collective sigh. Marcia makes part of their company, a short, slender figure amongst their taller ones. People pick up the gong, the box that held the candles. They move off in a loose group, together with the musician and his companions. Their outlines merge, become anonymous. A dark mass wandering towards the railway arch, its shadowy black vault.

The moonlit pavement in front of the decorated fence is empty. Nobody there.

Rose and Sally, bulky in fleeces, come closer, followed by Toby and Anthony. Toby wears a red scarf tucked into his overcoat, Anthony a pink one. They surround Madeleine like a friendly guard. Anthony touches her shoulder: you all right? She says: not sure. I feel very cold.

NINETEEN

Joseph

A S HE TROD DOWN the house steps into the street, thick fog met him, closed round him. Pea-souper: yellowish grittiness forcing itself against his nostrils, his mouth. Sour coal taste on his lips. He raised his scarf, wrapped it around the lower part of his face.

He felt his way along Apricot Place rather than walked. Blundered under the archway into Orchard Street, veered towards where he thought the main road must lie. He could see just a couple of inches from his nose. No sound other than his breathing. No other footfall, no dogs barking, no carriages jolting past. The fog muffled everything. No landmarks visible. No signposts.

He seemed to be the only person left in the world. In this yellow-grey dreaminess. So Mrs Dulcimer? Where was she? A bad night for a woman to be out alone. He must find her, accompany her home. He tried to quicken his step. He floundered through the billows of fog.

TWENTY

Madeleine

THE PUB OFFERS SHELTER. Heat and yellow light and soft grey shadows. Friendly tussle, buying each other drinks, pushing up around the table to make room, exclaiming, discussing. They heap the bags of Rose's belongings in a corner. Sally surveys the oak panelling, the framed engravings, the wooden tables and chairs: not bad, I suppose, as pubs go.

Rose pulls back the hood of her fleece, unzips her jacket, unwinds her long scarf. Something to tell you, Madeleine, when we've got a minute.

Maria starts questioning Toby and Anthony. Did you go cottaging when you were young? You use porn? Ever bought sex? You read Armistead Maupin? Ever been to a jerk-off party? She pulls out her iPad, looks up, waits. Toby puts on a solemn voice. We've no time for all that right now. Terrible shame. We're much too busy decorating the spare room, choosing a cot, hanging up mobiles.

Maria pouts. Rose chips in to Madeleine: Toby and Anthony are going to put me up for a while. Madeleine smiles at her. Yes, I know.

Sally says: I've met our new neighbour, Madeleine. The one moved into the flat above yours. This afternoon I was coming back with my shopping and he was sweeping up the leaves outside. We got chatting, he helped me carry all my shopping in. Seemed a nice fellow. Lovely dark-blue eyes.

She turns to Toby. I forgot to tell you before. I said to him, why not join us in the pub later on?

Sally, really, Toby says: you are a slave to your senses.

Well, he said yes, anyway, Sally counters: he should be along soon.

Maria revives. I'll wait for him to arrive. Another punter for me to interview. Excellent.

Madeleine leans towards Rose: can I come with you, next time you go collecting waste food from the supermarket skips? Scavenging, skipping, whatever you call it? I'd really like to help.

She waits for Rose to say: you're too old, you can't climb fences, carry heavy crates, can you run away fast enough, won't you feel scared?

Rose nods. Sure. But you realise you could be arrested? It involves trespass, stealing. Madeleine says: I've done trespassing before. I mean it, count me in.

Toby says: another round? Madeleine, you're coming back with us for supper, aren't you?

She says: I need to go to the supermarket first, buy a bottle of wine. Anthony exclaims. No need to bring wine, we've got plenty. Madeleine insists. I need to stretch my legs. Don't wait for me if you don't want to. I can catch you up.

Anthony says: no, we'll wait.

TWENTY ONE

Joseph

THE FOG BEGAN TO thin. It fled away in white wisps. By the time Joseph reached the low white palisade marking the edge of the common, it had dissolved completely, revealing the full moon. He pulled down the damp wool scarf masking his nose and mouth, stuffed it into his coat pocket. His legs ached from walking so tensely, balancing from one careful footstep to the next. He panted, holding on to a strut of the fence, feeling he'd run an obstacle course. The London atmosphere of soot and dung scorched his nostrils.

He plunged forwards again, just as the moon vanished behind low clouds. Darkness hung over the humped furze bushes flanking the stony path. The rain had stopped for the moment, but the cold air felt full of more to come. Somewhere ahead a bonfire sizzled and smoked, smelled of wet leaves, its plume of darkness, streaked with white, rising into the darker sky. It served as a beacon, pointing towards the common's far edge, where flaring lights and thumping hurdy-gurdy music marked the site of the fair. Nobody about on this stretch of muddy ground. The wetness in the atmosphere changed to drizzle. Net of water landing on his face. A wind got up, icy and stinging, scouring his ears.

A woman's outline appeared in the distance. Dark silhouette, buoyant movements. Mrs Dulcimer? It must be. She was making towards him, cape flapping out, hood flying behind her, the wind ballooning her skirts, she was trying to hold them down but they were tossing back over her hands, she was springing along through the wildness of the weather, trampling over gravel and mud, fighting into the gusts. He shouted her name, but the wind tossed it away.

Why was she on her own? Had she not come up with the young ones she'd walked out to meet? Perhaps they'd chosen a different route home and she'd abandoned all idea of finding them.

He hastened forward.

TWENTY TWO

Madeleine

THE FULL MOON HAS vanished behind heavy
clouds. She hurries into the dark main road. Smell
of petrol fumes, bitter on her lips. She passes the first
mini-supermarket she comes to, and the second, needing
to walk hard, to shake off something that clings to her
back, a coat of ice she wants to shed, leave as a trail of
water behind her. Was that really Emm, back at the burial
ground? What should she do? Go to the police? What
could the police do, if she did go? Probably nothing.

Just keep moving. Pools of light under the street lamps
interrupt stretches of shadow. She courses along the
deserted pavement, past shut-up offices and shuttered
coffee bars. Lines of buses swish by. Ambulance sirens
howl on-off in the distance.

The Elephant and Castle roundabout, doubled, a
figure-of-eight, looms ahead. Enormous cube of dimpled
steel at its centre, bracketed by advertisement hoardings.
Concentric rings of traffic seethe around it, spin off into the
side boulevards, as though seized and whirled by centri-
fugal force then flung out again. No jaywalking possible
here: if you tried to dart through you'd be hit, crushed flat.

To cross these torrents of traffic overground, pedestrians have to negotiate safe passage in stages, wait for long

minutes at a series of red lights. Easier to dive down into the many-tunnelled underpass mirroring the road layout above. Madeleine dislikes taking the underground route, preferring to stay in fresh air. Polluted air, she corrects herself. Hence the moon's misty shine earlier, its brilliance dimmed by exhaust fumes.

Rain starts to pelt down from the dark sky. Water soaks her shoulders, drives at her knees. She pulls up the hood of her jacket. Her long silk skirt clings to her legs, wraps them in chilliness. She splashes along, shivering. A passing bus, dashing close to the kerb, sends up a spray of filthy-looking water. She jumps aside, cursing. Stupid to wait at the pedestrian crossing for a green light. She hurries through the dark deluge to the arched entrance to the underpass.

Rain falls against her mouth. She bends her head against the driving wet, skids down the concrete slope's long curve. Slippery leaves underfoot. Cold metal handrail. Her fingers dislodge raindrops, which flurry and slide, little streams of water under her palm.

She enters a short passageway that abruptly branches in two. If she turns right, she should come to the exit leading to the top end of Walworth Road. Plenty of late-night shops there selling wine. Then she can hop on a bus, be back at the pub in the twinkling of an eye.

A long, dimly lit tunnel stretches ahead. Low concrete ceiling, puddles underfoot. Smell of tobacco, a tang of urine. She turns a corner. Again the passageway divides. She plunges into another dingy alley. Ten yards in she hesitates. Has she gone in the wrong direction? She presses on, curious to find out where she'll end up, whether or not she's lost.

Surely she has never walked along this stretch before? The green-tiled walls are patterned with clumsily painted scenes of Victorian street life, in faded, flaking colours. They run along the gloomy vaults like pages in an old-fashioned children's comic. The legend underneath, a flourish of curly black script, provides a clue: Walworth as it used to be. On the right-hand side, bonneted, ringletted women in crinolined skirts, holding up parasols, pace arm in arm with whiskered men in toppers and frock coats. Hearty and red-cheeked. A nursemaid in a frilly apron pushes a baby carriage. A small boy in a jaunty cap flourishes a twig broom. Some tiles are cracked, some missing, revealing the ridged concrete of the wall behind.

The images on the left-hand wall, the legend explains, depict Walworth Common. The Elephant and Castle roundabout has been built on top of it. Walworth Common as it used to be: furze bushes, hillocks, a stream. Grazing sheep. A windmill. A tree-shaded pond. A horse drinks, while the carter lounges alongside.

Now, the painted legend indicates, Madeleine's looking at images of the Hallowe'en fair formerly held on this site. Little pagodas of striped canvas, a trussed pig on a spit over a fire, Morris men jigging, girls in pinafores, boys in short jackets chasing and playing.

The run of illustration ceases. One grey tunnel debouches into another. She reaches the round central hall, its outer walls, gleaming with damp, pierced by openings to other passages. Long shapes on the ground, at the angle of the wall, homeless people bedded down for the night, slumped quiet and still, blankets hauled up around their ears. Here and there a coverlet twitches, a dog sighs.

Which way to go? Surely there should be signposts down here, directing pedestrians towards the exits giving onto the Old Kent Road, the Walworth Road, the tube entrances, the bus stops for Kennington or Camberwell. They seem to have been removed. Some programme of refurbishment must be taking place. None of the overhead lights seem to be working. Have they shorted, cut out? Somewhere ahead a low flame wavers. A candle, perhaps.

She'll have to go past the people sleeping on the ground. Invade their small spaces of privacy. Their night school of dreams. She mustn't disturb them, wake them. She advances as softly as she can.

Something scratches, scuttles, shoots off. Streak of black in the grey shadows. A rat? Just far away enough for her to flinch rather than screech, wake the nearby sleepers. Are they really asleep? Or are they lying awake, quaking, watching out for the scurrying vermin?

Water drips somewhere, pattering into puddles. Sour-smelling wind gusts up out of a grating. She's shivering. Sodden jacket heavy on her shoulders. No gloves. Rain inside her shoes. The hood of her jacket has fallen back-wards, her piled-up curls drip wetness down her neck.

TWENTY THREE

Joseph

S HE SEEMS SO FAR away still. A small figure beating her way towards him through the gloom, her cloak flapping like wings. Come closer, come closer. He has no golden lantern to summon her: she is no feathery-winged moth. In this darkness they may miss each other altogether, swerve away, wander all night. Both of them lost.

TWENTY FOUR

Madeleine

THE ATMOSPHERE CHANGES. VERY cold. A kind of buzzing. Her own heart pumping blood. The air fizzing, electric.

A male voice whispers behind her. Distorted; echoing in the tiled vault. A sort of sigh.

I've found you. So here you are at last.

She jerks. Freezes. Hardly dares breathe.

Emm. He's followed her from the pub. All this time he's been following her.

She dives her hand into her pocket, closes it over her penknife. She forces herself to turn round. Impeded by her wet skirt wrapping her shaking knees. Movement inside the dark mouth of the tunnel opposite. A man emerges from the shadows, advances. His boots creak and slap on the wet floor. Her skin tingles. Her scalp constricts.

Not Emm at all. Someone en route to a Hallowe'en fancy-dress party. Got up in Dickensian costume: tall hat, an overcoat with flapping skirts. Big beaky nose, in a thin, intelligent face.

He halts at a little distance from her. He says: I couldn't wait for you any longer. So I came out to look for you.

She tries to speak. Her lips shape words that won't break from silence. The air snaps and bristles with static, so full that she can't push words into it.

They stare at one another.

TWENTY FIVE

Joseph

H E   M O V E S   T O W A R D S   H E R. Even in the darkness there's no mistaking that half-swaying, half-hurrying walk, that toppling pile of curls, those curving cheekbones, that full mouth.

He calls out. I've found you. So here you are at last.

It seems to take hours before he reaches her, before she reaches him. She halts at a little distance from him. A shape in dark clothes. Her face in shadow. He says: I couldn't wait for you any longer. So I came out to look for you.

She says nothing. Has she heard him? She just gazes at him. Seems surprised, as though he were the last person in the world she expected to see. Her lips part, move. He can't hear what she's saying. He steps closer.

She's shivering. Water sheens her wool-covered shoulders. He wants to stretch out his hands, brush it away. She lifts her own hands, wipes water off her face, smooths her tumbled hair. She's lost her bonnet somewhere. She pulls up her hood.

What's happened? he asks: are you all right? Tell me.

She looks back at him. Puzzled, half-frowning.

Madeleine

S HE'S SHIVERING. SHE LIFTS her hands, wipes water off her face, smooths back her tumbled hair. She pulls up her hood.

What's happened? the man asks: are you all right? Tell me.

She looks at him. She feels her brows constrict in a frown.

Joseph

M RS DULCIMER, RAIN-SWEPT AND tousled, smelled of herself: rose-carnation pomade, a hint of vanilla sweat. She spoke jerkily. Still catching her breath. Her contralto voice sawed up and down. I was just in sight of the fair, no one about, when some fellow appeared from behind the bushes and blocked my path and accosted me. Soft-voiced. Very polite. Excuse me, madam, just a moment of your time, if you will. Let me pass, if you please, I said, but he didn't move. Held up his hands and smiled a little and shook his head. Dressed as a clergyman he was, with white bands, a black coat, a black hat, all complete. No gloves. He held what looked in the darkness like a small crucifix. White hands, soft and well-kept, with very clean fingernails. He had green eyes, which gleamed oddly, as though he'd been crying. Asked me for alms for the poor, for the homeless folks who'd be sleeping rough later on near the fairground and risked being chased away by the constables. Spun me a line about how he was going about picking up strays and trying to find them shelter and would I spare him a penny or two? I didn't like the look of him, he kept giving me sly little glances to see how I was taking his tale. He was aiming to swipe my purse, I supposed. Again I told him to let me pass. He changed his tune, declared I was one of his strayed sheep, called me a poor vagabond lady, his poor sister fallen into the muck, a fly-by-night needing rescue. Dear girl, he called me: his dear Magdalene. I told him to get away, to leave me alone. He began wheedling me then, asking how much I charged, saying he'd a nice cosy place to take me to. I cursed him. He wouldn't budge but menaced me with what I still thought was his cross. He stepped even closer, calling me a foul name. When I saw what he was actually holding I got in first, I swiped at him, I damaged his face for him I'm certain, he screamed, I pushed him aside and made off, but he came after me, swearing at me for a nigger whore, shrieking he'd fetch the police to me. So I ran. And then missed my turning in the dark and took the wrong way and got lost but now here I am.

She stepped away from Joseph. She put one hand into the pocket of her cape. She brought it out again, showed him what lay in her palm. Neat, mother-of-pearl-handled; short dagger-like blade glinting and silvery.

She said: it wasn't a cross he was holding. It was a knife. Luckily I had my own knife with me. As I always do when I'm out walking on my own.

She dropped the knife back into her pocket, shook out her wet skirts. Let's be off. If they get home before we do, the young ones will be wondering what's become of us. Doll and Annie know where I hide the spare key, but even so. They'll be wanting their supper. God knows, I could do with mine.

TWENTY EIGHT

Madeleine

TRAFFIC RUMBLES OVERHEAD. Striplights come on, bars of weak yellow. The atmosphere cracks, settles again.

You OK there?

The whisper comes from the direction of the make-shift beds laid along the tiled wall. Mattresses formed of piled layers of brown cardboard packaging. Someone has pushed back his blanket and sat up. Dark profile turned in her direction. He sounds very young. His thin hand clutches the edge of his coverings. You lost? You need some help?

Madeleine glances behind her. The man in the frock coat has vanished.

The boy peeps at her. Spiky black hair. Hollow cheeks. He wears a blue nylon sports top dull with dirt. Older than she thought at first. Seventeen, perhaps.

She says: thank you. I'm looking for the exit to Walworth Road.

Shhh! Don't talk so loud. You'll wake him. Poor old Rev.

One cardboard pallet along, a body, half-covered by a blanket, sprawls on a sleeping-bag. Head sunk in a stained pillow. Bristle of grey-brown hair. Face turned away to one side. A raw red gash crosses his cheek, blood beading its edges. An open wound like a split, emptied red pod. Her toes curl in her shoes, her stomach twists.

She forces herself to look again.

Emm.

He smells of blood and alcohol. Black overcoat glistening with wet, black scarf wound round his neck. White dog-collar, red-rimmed, half torn off. His hand, clutching a red-sodden handkerchief, has fallen to one side. An uncapped brown sherry bottle lolls nearby.

The boy murmurs: he's only just stopped bleeding, poor old bugger. I found him just now, staggering about a bit further along. I brought him back here so he could lie down.

What happened to him? Madeleine whispers: shouldn't he go to hospital, get that seen to?

The boy shrugs. I'm leaving him be. He's all done in.

Asleep, Emm looks so harmless. Harmed. The boy's wary eyes catch at Madeleine. He told me before he passed out, he was set on by some crazy woman. He goes around at night, see, telling people about the church refuge down the road in Kennington, trying to help them find shelter. Only some of them are vicious, off their heads, you mustn't go near them. This bitch had a knife.

He puts out a grimy hand, picks up the empty brown bottle, shoves it under his own pillow. He says: he didn't want the hospital and he didn't want the refuge either, he wanted a drink. Then he fell fast asleep.

He contemplates the inert body. They don't let you in the refuge if you're pissed. And I can't get in because of my dog. We're better off here, both of us.

He leans over the sleeper, puts his face close.

He's still breathing. I'll get him to the hospital in the morning. Too far for him to manage tonight. Poor old lad.

Madeleine crouches beside the sleeping Emm. His thick, sweetish breath seems tangible as felted wool. His lips open, slacken, drool collecting at one side of his mouth. He begins to snore. Bubbles of wet sound.

She glances at the red scars on her thumb, her fingertip. She studies his red wound. He's crumpled up, pierced, the air almost all gone out of him. No fight left.

I've met him before, she says: I know him.

The words tip out of her. I didn't know he was still a vicar. He told me he was about to retire. I don't know where he lives now. You have to move out once you retire, don't you?

The boy shakes his head, gives her a patient look. He says: he lives in the church refuge, or else down here. I've known him for months, ever since his wife threw him out, and I can tell you he's never been a vicar. He wears that outfit because he likes it, that's all. The people at the refuge understand. They're used to him.

Madeleine reaches out, lifts Emm's hand. Cool, limp. She tucks it under the blanket. She draws the blanket up round his neck, wraps the folds under his chin. The wound across his cheek is drying, but still seems horribly naked, exposed.

Something stirs under the boy's coverlet, wriggles. A brown snout pokes out. Brown eyes. Seeing Madeleine, the Alsatian stiffens, growls, stretches its neck towards her. The boy clasps the straining body. Hush, girl. Hush. Madeleine gets to her feet and moves back.

The boy strokes the brown head. The dog looks Madeleine over. The boy sighs, whistling spittle through his teeth. I feel safe because I've Dinah with me. She'd fly at anyone coming too near. That's what lets me go to sleep. D'you see?

The boy yawns, lies down again. He settles himself around the dog's humped shape. Madeleine says: I'll come back in the morning, shall I? I could help you get him to the hospital.

The boy flings out one arm across the body of the sleeping man. He says: don't interfere! You leave us alone. We'll be all right.

He turns his face into the dog's coat, presents Madeleine with his rigid back. The clammy-looking nylon top moulds his thin shoulder-blades.

Madeleine fishes out all the loose change from her purse, puts it on the ground next to the boy's pillow. He doesn't move. The Alsatian growls. She backs off, pads away.

Forget buying wine. Just get back to the pub, to her waiting friends. She selects a tunnel opening almost at random. Jazzy pattern of oblong wall tiles in red, green, blue. She turns a corner, finds the exit she needs. She hurries up the walkway. She plunges into the wet, windy street. She'll catch a bus, be back in Borough in no time at all.

TWENTY NINE

Joseph

THEY WALKED AWAY FROM the common. He offered Mrs Dulcimer his arm, and she took it. Her hand rested on his coat cuff. Their boots crunched over wet grit, packed rubble. For a while they went along in silence, as they had done before, just a few days back. Then Joseph said: you've never told me your Christian name. May I know it?

Mrs Dulcimer shook her head. That's not a subject for the street. We're late. We should make haste home.

She dropped his arm and strode away, towards the main road. Her cape, her skirts streamed out behind her. She turned a corner, vanished behind an angle of brick walls.

Had he offended her? He sighed. The rain had stopped but the cold wind whipped his face. He shivered in his fog-damp clothes. Perishing weather, this. Where were those girls? Would the sitting-room fire still be alight? The kitchen range? He was supposed to be cooking supper. Right, then. Look sharp. Get a move on. Catch her up.

Someone ahead of him began humming. Then singing. Mrs Dulcimer's contralto voice, dark honey, flowed back through the darkness. I know where I'm going,/ and I know who's going with me.

He picked up the tune. Joined his voice to hers. I know who I love,/ but the Lord knows who I'll marry.

THIRTY

Madeleine

S HE PRESSES FORWARD ALONG the deserted pavement, making for the bus stop. Puddles black as oil spills. Advancing cars' headlights blossom yellow-white in the darkness then vanish. Glitter of the metallic shutters of locked shops.

Footsteps sound behind her. Male footsteps, a long stride, firm and definite. She glances over her shoulder. Beaky nose; short hair; a peacoat. The man increases his speed, passes her with a nod, a slight lift of the hand. A gesture of reassurance, as Toby explained to her once: if you're walking behind a woman on a lonely street then you either cross the road or you make sure to pass her, then she knows you're OK, you're not out to attack her.

The man's glimpsed profile: very like that of her new neighbour's, his dark silhouette at his open window above her, as she sat in her garden and peeped at him. What's his name? If he does turn up at the pub, she'll find out.

He halts at the bus stop just ahead. As she comes up with him he's humming a song.

I know where I'm going,/ and I know who's going with me.

Madeleine joins in. I know who I love,/ but the Lord knows who I'll marry.

ACKNOWLEDGEMENTS

Thanks to Alexandra Pringle, Antonia Till and all at Bloomsbury. Thanks to Sarah LeFanu and Jenny Newman, my first readers, for their writerly support, close reading and helpful criticism. Thanks to all my other writer friends, too, for their affection and encouragement.

A NOTE ON THE AUTHOR

Michèle Roberts is the acclaimed author of thirteen novels, including *Daughters of the House*, which won the WHSmith Literary Award and was shortlisted for the Booker Prize. Her most recent novel *Ignorance* was longlisted for the Women's Prize for Fiction and her memoir *Paper Houses* was BBC Radio 4's Book of the Week. She has also published poetry and short stories, most recently collected in *Mud: Stories of Sex and Love*. Michèle Roberts is Emeritus Professor of Creative Writing at the University of East Anglia. She lives in south-east London.

micheleroberts.co.uk

A NOTE ON THE TYPE

The text of this book is set in Adobe Caslon, named after the English punch-cutter and type-founder William Caslon I (1692–1766). Caslon's rather old-fashioned types were modelled on seventeenth-century Dutch designs, but found wide acceptance throughout the English-speaking world for much of the eighteenth century until replaced by newer types towards the end of the century. Used in 1776 to print the Declaration of Independence, they were revived in the nineteenth century and have been popular ever since, particularly amongst fine printers. There are several digital versions, of which Carol Twombly's Adobe Caslon is one.